A LITANY OF
GOOD INTENTIONS

ANDREW HARRIS

FAITHFUL HOUND

D1347165

First published in 2017 by Faithful Hound Media

ISBN 978-1-911195-49-8

Also available as an ebook
ISBN 978-1-911195-50-4

Printed and bound in Great Britain by Clays Ltd, St Ives plc
Typeset by K.DESIGN www.k-design@virgin.net
Cover design by Charlotte Abrams-Simpson

Also by the author:

The C Clef: Volume 1 (The Human Spirit Trilogy)

To Jacqui

PART ONE

"No legacy is so rich as honesty"

–William Shakespeare

• PROLOGUE •

I'm sorry it had to end this way but I really can't go on.

There is so much misery in the world. I don't want to be part of it anymore. How can we treat people this way? They are human beings like us, yet nobody cares; it's terrible. There will never be an end to their suffering. I feel so useless.

I'm giving everything to the poor. They need it more than me. I'm one less mouth to feed.

You gave me so much but I'm not worth it. Help them now; it's too late for me.

CHAPTER 1

Niklas Blomqvist had slept badly. He'd been away too long. His body clock was out of sync with Stockholm in June. He'd forgotten what it was like. Endless daylight just made things worse.

He padded through the apartment to the kitchen area. No need to switch on the light, even with the blinds closed. 5 a.m. Prickly eyes found the tin of fresh coffee. He ran the tap, rinsed the least dirty cup and stifled a yawn.

With Ingmar away, he was left in charge. Henning Wireless Technologies pretty much ran itself. Of course, there was day-to-day pressure. A troublesome account was threatening legal action over their satellite network. And another was in the final testing phase. But things were on track. The lack of sleep derived from something far more important.

Der Sangerbund. The text message had been a warning. The call could come at any time.

He sipped a mouthful of coffee. There was a bitter aftertaste; he poured the rest away. He felt the walls watching him. Too many questions; the space in his head was getting tighter and tighter. Questions but still no answers. He'd been through it a thousand times.

He checked his watch again. There was time. He had to get out, to run, get his legs moving, blood pumping; he needed to clear his mind. The streets would be empty. He would take the device with him, just in case. No time difference with Geneva. Unlikely he would call at this hour but with the Choirmaster, you never knew. Insomnia didn't upset him. People upset him. And Niklas knew he was dangerously close to being one of those people.

Two circuits of the harbour. Three would be better. Still have time to get a shower. Rehearse what he was going to say. Must get this right. It could turn ugly. Yet this whole thing had started so well. Right place, right time. The Cantata were pleased. A commendation had been mentioned. Even a seat at the table. *You might become a Voice, Niklas.* He'd waited years to hear those words.

Now this. Despite all his enquiries, no one seemed to know. Midsummer's Day. The majestic Great Hall at Uppsala University. Just a few days away. The biggest scientific breakthrough in centuries, the media heralded. Global TV coverage. World leaders and the rock stars of the scientific world all coming to town, yet Niklas remained ignorant, and had no idea what this breakthrough could be. Codename Project Amrita. The only people who knew for sure were in India. And they weren't talking.

He closed the front door quietly and zipped the device into his inside pocket. He would feel the vibration if the call came in. The street air was cool and fresh. There had been no rain for weeks. Rubber soles squeaked on dusty cobbles as he set off at a brisk pace towards the harbour bridge. He didn't need to set the monitor. His heart rate was already off the charts. If anything, the adrenalin surging through him would help bring it under some kind of control.

Without thinking, his feet took the familiar route. From Gamla Stan he would cross to the main shopping centre, then follow the waterfront down to the Strombron Bridge, back over to the old town, sharp right along Slottskajen, then round again.

He quickened the pace down Stora Nygatan. No need to wait for the lights at this hour. He skipped across Riddarhustorget and on towards the main Vasabron Bridge. He wiped the first beads of sweat from his face, shielding his eyes from fingers of sunlight that poked out between the far buildings across the harbour.

Did Ingmar know? If he did, why didn't he say? They trusted each other, no secrets between them. But maybe Ingmar had signed a personal guarantee, something Niklas wasn't even aware of? It was plausible but didn't make any sense. *Why keep this a secret?*

He had nearly completed the first circuit and was powering down Slottskajen towards Myntgatan. He had only seen a couple of taxis in the old town. A few tourists were standing around admiring the ornate buildings of the Royal Palace. He would veer off right onto Riddarhustorget, then right again at the lights and back across the Vasabron. Three circuits, he decided. It would need three circuits.

He sidestepped a middle-aged tourist taking a selfie and nearly tripped over a high kerbstone. Suddenly he felt his chest vibrating. It could only be one caller. No other member of the Cantata would be using the secure line at this hour.

He slowed to a jog and saw a quiet alcove set back from the main street. He took deep breaths, tried to find some composure, flicked away the sweat, came to a halt and unzipped the pocket.

"You've been running, Niklas." The voice was clipped, quietly spoken. A familiar face filled the tiny screen. Dark lines were etched under eyes hidden in shadow. He was not the only one lacking sleep, Niklas thought.

"It helps me think." He noticed the tourist had moved away and crossed the deserted street.

"We are past thinking." Irritation in the voice. "I want this stopped. Uppsala must not happen. Do you understand me, Niklas?"

"I understand, Choirmaster, but it won't be easy. The whole world will be watching." Niklas saw the shadows deepen on the screen.

In the silence that followed, Niklas could hear gulls shrieking high above him. He looked up to see ghostly white figures circling in the pale-blue sky. The noise level was too great. He followed a passageway under a sign saying "Brantingtorget", and found himself in a courtyard where a fountain was playing around the statue of a water nymph. The plaque said "Morgen". This was a morning he wouldn't forget.

"Easy is not a word we recognise in Der Sangerbund." Burning dark eyes emerged from the shadows, set in a face of pure rage. "I want you in my office at eight tonight. Clear?"

The screen had already gone dead before Niklas could mouth a reply.

CHAPTER 2

"So you're saying slavery was a good thing? Jeeze."

"You're twisting my words again." Lawrence passed her the suntan lotion for a liberal dousing over raspberry-ripple skin. A faint hint of coconut oil mixed with the fading charcoal aromas from the hotel kitchens nearby.

The morning mist had burned off long before the conference had finished. They had the pool to themselves. Hannah soon realised why; thirty-eight degrees was proving too much even for her olive-toned skin. A fierce sun was beating down from a sky more grey than blue. They'd retreated to sunbeds under a poolside parasol.

"Excuse me. You just said – and I quote – 'the economic argument for slavery is a sound one'. Or did I just dream that?" Hannah retorted.

"No, you didn't dream it. That's exactly what I said. I think you're mixing up economics and ethics – two very different things. The economic argument for free labour is unquestionable. It was ethics, not economics, that brought down slavery," Lawrence explained.

She peered at him over the top of her sunglasses. "Your British Empire was built on slavery. Even here in India, that's why they kicked you out."

"Every empire's built on slavery. Indians were slaves for centuries before we arrived. Anyway, they didn't kick us out; we decided to leave. But not before we educated them in speaking English and playing cricket, which reminds me . . ." Lawrence tried to rise elegantly from the sunbed, but still managed to stumble out onto the burning hot tiles.

"Don't change the subject. There's no excuse for slavery." Hannah folded her sunglasses, got up and squinted as she emerged from the shade. She skipped over to the pool and dived gracefully into its inviting depths. She luxuriated in the nothingness, her mind drifting in the cool water as she kicked out with mermaid strokes.

She surfaced, treading water, pulling handfuls of long, dark hair out of her eyes and plastering them behind her ears. She watched in comical fascination as the new man in her life attempted a triple salchow with tucked pike. His corpulent silver-haired figure and total lack of technique proved a deadly combination.

"Only a four point eight from the Russian judge." she spluttered as he struggled to the surface next to her.

"There's still time before the next Olympics." he replied.

"Not for you, lover boy."

She could feel his hands exploring the one-piece swimsuit. They kissed again, slower this time, the chlorine water pooling around them. Just for that moment, that very moment, time stopped. She hadn't been this happy in years. Maybe she'd never been this happy.

The last twelve months had flown by and yet, like a tiled mosaic or a page of fine newsprint, it seemed to be a collection of moments, little fragments pieced together, blurring into each other, a collage of awkward adjustments that needed to be made. She realised the glue holding it all together was the joy of sharing, the joy of laughter. Hannah was falling in love. She wanted to fall in love.

Before Lawrence and his faithful friend Trigger had moved in, she hadn't realised how inert her life had become. She'd created a sterile apartment, overlooking the Brooklyn Bridge, a place bereft of warmth or emotion; a place where she ate and slept and displayed meaningless objects that someone else classified as art; a place to be alone and to be lonely. Her world had become so dry, so brittle. Dull routines filled the space outside work.

After the initial shock, she'd surprisingly enjoyed the disruption of living with another human being again. Little things created pressure points, yet it was those pressure points, she could see now, that had brought about the much-needed change. Sleeping on the other side of the bed; indeed not occupying the whole bed. The distinctive smell of his Earl Grey tea over breakfast; finding dirty socks on the bathroom floor; the toilet seat being up; not to mention sharing dinner with the mournful eyes of Trigger, a golden retriever in a permanent state of gnawing starvation.

And Lawrence himself? He wasn't the best lover she'd ever known, but at least he was caring and so wanted to please her. He was work in progress, she decided. This long weekend conference could only help. She'd always wanted to visit India. He'd only been once before on a business trip, many years ago, before his divorce. He couldn't remember if it had been to Delhi or Mumbai.

The New Delhi Nirvana International Hotel & Conference Centre was enormous and the perfect setting for the 3-day Global Diabetes Conference, accommodating nearly three thousand delegates. Hannah hadn't appreciated the extent of the diabetes epidemic across India, the numbers having swollen to over 70 million sufferers in recent years. The conference had jarred her into wanting to do more.

By appointing Lawrence as her new Head of Diabetes Research at the Klinkenhammer Institute, she had attracted much criticism. He did lack the medical training. He hadn't won the hearts and minds of his team. Eyebrows had even been raised about them living together. *Sleeping with a subordinate, Hannah, it never works, you know that.*

Sleep, she pondered, sleep, the greatest healer. A gentle snoring drifted across from the sunbed beside her. He had slept all the way from JFK. They both needed a break but she could see now how difficult the last year must have been for him. The complete change in lifestyle from his monochrome existence in London had been stressful enough. But the knives had been well and truly out for him at work. Getting him away for a few days was the right thing to do. They should plan a proper holiday soon.

Lawrence stirred, turning towards her. "I'm hearing the words *gin and tonic.*"

Shadows had crawled across the pool from a row of impossibly tall palm trees. A swarm of brightly coloured kites was playing in a light breeze high above them, the strings leading down like fishing lines into a slum area at the back of the hotel. Hannah could hear the laughter of children coming from the crowded streets nearby.

"Churchill once said," he continued, "that gin and tonic saved more Englishmen than all the doctors in the Empire. It was their way of taking quinine to prevent malaria. We've just time for a swift one before the Gala Dinner. But no ice, remember." Lawrence wagged a finger.

Raspberry ripple was softening into rich mocha with hints of peach and chocolate. Hannah applied more suntan lotion to her face and arms just in case, before slipping on a T-shirt with New York Yankees emblazoned across it. She tucked her hair up into a baseball cap and gathered her things.

"The guidebook says there's an old gin distillery on the

way to the cricket ground." Lawrence slipped on his hotel Havaianas. "If we leave early, we could call in, pay homage to my British ancestors. Maybe take a bottle home?"

"We need to talk about this cricket thing over dinner." Hannah pulled open the heavy door leading back into air-conditioned splendour.

"Well, you can blame Paul Revere for that. We gave you guys a chance – and look what happened? Now Americans have to play sport all on your own. It must be the only World Series that doesn't involve anyone else." He smiled as he avoided a jab to his shoulder.

"Not true. The Japanese play baseball," Hannah retorted, following him towards the lifts.

"My dear girl, I'm talking about Sir Garfield Sobers, Don Bradman, Sachin Tendulkar, Jack Hobbs, Brian Lara and Dr W G Grace," he corrected. "You can't talk about baseball in the same breath. It's sacrilege."

Hannah relented; the argument would keep. Right now something else was on her mind: the inner glow she used to get on holidays, coming off the beach . . . a delicious tingle deep inside. Minibar, not lounge bar, she decided. Lawrence got the hint, smiled and offered no resistance. She took his hand as they waited for the lift. The appearance of a hotel waiter prevented her taking hold of anything else, for now at least.

As they stepped into the corridor on the 22nd floor, Hannah noticed a beautiful young girl walking towards them with flaming auburn hair and a beach bag slung over her right shoulder. She was soon joined by an older man wearing a colourful T-shirt, carrying hotel towels.

They'd only taken a few strides when Lawrence stopped abruptly. Hannah could see puzzlement playing across his face.

"I know him."

Hannah carried on walking. The corridor wasn't wide enough for all four of them to pass. She could tell Lawrence was struggling to remember the man's name; the urge for devilment was too strong for her to ignore.

"That can't be his wife. She's just a bit of fluff," he whispered, his pace slowing.

"You're always jumping to conclusions. It may be perfectly innocent," she surmised.

"A man his age, he should know better. Why can't men grow old gracefully?"

"You should know. Well, who is he then?" She could almost taste the gin now, each step taking her closer.

"Not sure. Must be a long time ago. Funny how he's gone all wrinkly while I'm just as handsome as ever."

"Remind me to put Trigger in for guide dog training." She went to punch his shoulder but missed.

"My God, Lawrence, is that you?" the T-shirt bellowed out in a rich Geordie accent. "What are you doing here?"

"I might ask you the same question, you old devil. And who is this charming young lady?"

Hannah watched Lawrence as he squirmed, the name still eluding him. It was an impressive display of playing for time.

"Lawrence, this is my beautiful daughter, Octavia."

"Oh Pops, you're making me blush. Please call me Okki; everyone does."

"Okki," her father said, "this is my good friend and fellow Rotarian, Lawrence McGlynn. We go back a long way. Weybridge East, in fact."

Hannah saw Lawrence's eyes light up; he'd remembered.

"Toby, may I introduce the love of my life, Dr Hannah Siekierkowski, the pride of New York City. Hannah, meet Toby

Stanton, one of Rotary's finest, and his beautiful daughter Okki." Lawrence beamed.

"Toby, it's great to meet you at last. Lawrence has told me so much about you." She couldn't resist.

After the handshakes, Hannah toyed momentarily with the idea of joining them after their swim for a drink in the bar. Toby could fill in some blanks in Lawrence's earlier life. Okki seemed charming and was certainly worth getting to know. Thankfully the idea was short-lived; she discovered Toby was also a delegate at the conference. They agreed to meet up at the Gala Dinner.

When they got to the room, Lawrence poured the drinks and went to make the call to change the table booking. Hannah had other ideas.

He never got to the phone.

• CHAPTER 3 •

"And for the main course, the tandoori fish for me as well, please ... medium rare." Lawrence laughed as he finished ordering, then put the menu down.

The immaculately dressed waiter noted his order and handed him a wine list. Lawrence looked at the lonely bottle of house wine in the middle of the table and passed the list across.

"Toby, I think you should do the honours. This calls for a celebration."

"Indeed it does. Moet & Chandon, the 2004. This is certainly a most welcome surprise."

Most of the delegates had gone home but the Gala Dinner still attracted over 800 guests. The atmosphere was fizzing with alcohol and expectation. A long table on the stage displayed various trophies and awards. A small group of sitar players sat cross-legged to one side, their music lost in a sea of deafening conversations. Around the room, large screens were running a loop of sponsored videos, which, to Hannah, all looked the same. A kaleidoscope of coloured lights flashed over the walls and ceiling.

"Hannah, did you say you are a doctor?" Okki sipped champagne and fiddled with her blanket-sized napkin.

"Yes, but nowadays I work in medical research." Hannah could feel her face flushed and glowing in the candlelight. "I manage a research institute in New York called The Klinkenhammer Foundation."

"My father here thinks I should study medicine but I keep telling him it's too late for me now." Okki twisted an errant lock of hair, then brushed it away.

"It's never too late. How old are you, if you don't mind me asking?" Hannah probed.

"I'll be twenty-three this year."

"Sounds like a perfect age to me. You should start right away. The world needs more beautiful, bright, young doctors." Hannah leaned across and squeezed her arm.

"I've been thinking about finance. My last boyfriend's studying accountancy."

"Probably why he's not here tonight." Hannah smiled. "Sorry, Toby; if you're an accountant, I apologise."

"Me? An accountant? God invented accountancy to give work to all those people who'd never get a job doing anything else." Toby drained his glass and reached for the ice bucket. Hannah noticed Lawrence was keeping pace with him – no doubt part of the ritual of being a Rotarian.

"So what are you doing now, Okki?" Hannah hadn't expected her starter to be gazing up at her. The Sukha Jhinga prawns still had their eyes.

"Actually I'm taking a gap year before doing a Masters in Palaeoanthropology. I'd like to get some real-world experience first. I think it will help with my studies."

For his starter, Lawrence had taken the soft option, as ever. His chicken tikka looked perfectly cooked and was beautifully garnished with fresh coriander and tamarind chutney. He chewed on a piece of the delicate, fragrant meat.

"I always fancied a gap year but life got in the way," he said. "Don't rush into the marriage, kids and mortgage routine. That's my advice, for what it's worth. Is the gap year why you're here?"

Okki's eyes lit up. "Yes, I'm working as a volunteer for a charity called SINAC – Sanitation in Action. Of course the lads in my group call it Shit in Action."

He wished he hadn't asked: suddenly the chicken tikka wasn't quite so fragrant.

"Over two point six billion people," Okki explained, the fire burning in her eyes, "a third of the world's population, have no access to a toilet. They live in filth, they drink polluted water and they die in their millions. In India alone there are over seven hundred and ninety million people living in dire poverty without proper sanitation."

Hannah could sense how deeply she felt about their suffering. Clearly Okki had taken this cause to heart. It was more than just a gap year. She actually wanted to make a difference, to right the wrong. For someone so young, so inexperienced, Okki was a breath of fresh air. It was good to see.

"Teenage girls drop out of school because there are no toilets," she continued. "I can't imagine starting my period and having nowhere to go. If just ten per cent more girls continued with their education, the effect on world poverty would be massive. They would understand how poverty can be eradicated. SINAC is doing something about it. We dig toilets in schools and poor communities. It saves people crapping in the fields . . . or worse, on the streets."

"I think you'd make an excellent doctor, Okki." Hannah's eyes were sparkling in the candlelight; a mother's admiration for her daughter, the daughter she never had.

"Thank you, Hannah, I appreciate your encouragement. Can I ask you something?"

"Anything you like, Okki." Hannah was relieved when the main course arrived. At least the tandoori fish wasn't giving her the evil eye.

"SINAC's organising a big event on Midsummer's Day. It's in a place called Uppsala."

"Sweden's one of my favourite countries," Hannah replied, spooning rice onto her plate. "I've been there many times. In fact, I chaired a lecture series at the university only a couple of years ago. It snowed solidly for two days. We couldn't even reach Stockholm airport."

"Well, Jock said our medical expert has had to pull out. He's looking for someone to present on the link between poor sanitation and the spread of disease."

"Who's Jock?" Hannah loved the girl's energy. It was infectious. And the subject matter was close to her own heart. It might be fun getting up to speed on the latest medical thinking. Sweden in June? She was running through the diary in her head. Maybe this could be the break she was thinking about. Could Lawrence get away? Maybe they could extend the trip, make a Scandinavian vacation out of it.

"He owns SINAC. He's based in Singapore but he's over here for a few days. We've got a toilet project going live next week. He's come to cut the ribbon. I could introduce you, if you'd like to meet him."

"It would have to be tomorrow; we go back to New York on Tuesday morning." Hannah looked across at Lawrence. She could see he'd worked it out. He was about to protest but she silenced him with a smile. Her immersion into the world of test cricket would have to wait.

"Are you sure your diary is clear for the twenty-first, my love?" Lawrence prompted, clearly thinking about his last chance to see England hanging on for a draw in front of a fanatical Indian crowd baying for British blood.

"Yes, Lawrence, if you remember I was supposed to be speaking at a world cancer-research conference in Paris on the twenty-first but obviously that's been cancelled." Her smile had turned into a beam of satisfaction.

Lawrence explained to their puzzled dinner companions that Hannah had managed to put thousands of her fellow cancer researchers out of work with her medical discoveries last year. Toby nodded, remembering the news headlines, and congratulated her. Another celebration was required. Lawrence got the waiter's attention and ordered more champagne. It was an art he'd perfected in restaurants all over the world.

"Thanks, Hannah, that would be great. Jock'll be at the field centre first thing. Nisha should be there as well. She's awesome. They got engaged last year. She's doing the science behind all this. She's really clever, you'll love her." Okki checked her phone, then scribbled Jock's mobile number and the field centre address on the back of a menu. Hannah slipped it into her purse and gave Okki a business card in return.

The room fell into momentary silence with the ringing of a bell. The lights dimmed as a procession of waiters paraded in from the kitchens, their white jackets reflecting the candles on a huge birthday cake, which was presented to the Conference Chairman. The waiters formed a makeshift choir and burst into "Happy Birthday".

When the lights came back on, the formal proceedings took place with trophies being awarded and speeches made. The official ceremony over, the lights dimmed again and a seven-piece band appeared on stage. The screens became a riot of Bollywood dancing and the room pulsated with a heavy desi beat. A dance floor was cleared in no time and the party was on.

Hannah stood up, looked across at Lawrence and started swaying to the music. She held out her hand, shimmied her bare shoulders, leaned over and kissed him full on the lips "Wanna dance?"

He didn't move. "Why don't you show us how to do it? Time, I think, for the old colonials here to enjoy our brandy and cigars."

Hannah understood. "Okki, I guess that means us."

They high-fived, linked arms and danced over to where a crowd was now pressed together by the stage. Arms shot up to greet a medley of *Slumdog* favourites and the girls disappeared.

* * *

"She's a cracker Lawrence, congratulations." Toby topped up their glasses. "Where did you find her?"

"She just appeared in my life, like she was sent to me. I needed it, mind you. The last few years have been pretty tough, what with losing my job and the divorce."

"I'm sorry to hear that," Toby said. "Was it Gayle? She came with you a few times to Rotary. Can't say I ever warmed to her."

"Well, she warmed to someone else in the end. Left me high and dry. Somehow she managed to get me kicked out of the house. Manipulation was her blood-sport of choice."

"So what did you do? The bachelor pad?"

"Yes, with the family dog Trigger. It's true what they say about man's best friend. The most faithful hound you could ever want."

"Where are your kids now? Wasn't it a boy and a girl?"

"Grown up and fled the nest. Grace is married and living in North London. She keeps in touch by email and the occasional Skype call. Simon finished at Cardiff last year. He's considering his future or something like that."

"I take it you're not close then."

"If we were close, I'd strangle him, so best to leave things the way they are. I sort of know he'll turn up one day."

"And Hannah?"

"Hannah is the best thing that ever happened to me. She always wanted kids but was married to her job, never found the right guy."

"Until you came along?"

"We've only known each other for a year but it feels like we've always known each other. I didn't believe in ghosts or life-after-death until we met. Now it feels like we were partners before, in an earlier time."

"How did you meet?"

"I was temping at a pharmaceutical company . . . it's a long story." Lawrence smiled. "We met by chance and sort of clicked."

"And the children thing?" Toby folded his napkin and placed it on the table.

"I've offered her my kids but she just laughed. We might be able to repair that one day, who knows. Or maybe we could adopt. For now, we're just enjoying finding out about each other. She'll just love dancing with Okki." Arms waved towards them in the distance before the girls were swallowed up again by the writhing mass of sweaty bodies.

"Okki's a great kid, we love her to bits. Only-child-spoilt-rotten syndrome, I guess. It's a real shame about her mother and the way things have worked out." Toby went to reach for the bottle. He paused and took a mouthful of water instead.

"Wasn't she in hotel management? Good-looking Dutch girl, blonde. Wendy?"

"Wanda . . . yes, she was a real stunner. I've been so lucky, in many ways. It's such a pity. We met when I joined IBM in London. She worked at the hotel we used in town. Late-night meetings, conference calls to the States; I was eating alone all the time or crashing out late. She must've taken pity on me.

"Our early years were fantastic. Okki was a real blessing.

I thought life couldn't get any better. IBM promoted me to the Amsterdam office. We did worry about Okki. She was quite a serious kid and had settled into the primary school in Weybridge. She was six when we moved. But how wrong could we be? She learned Dutch in no time. I think she's more grounded because of the dual nationality, language thing. She's been a big help to me."

"And how is Wanda?" Lawrence sensed the pain; the question was clearly invited.

"Well, that's just it. We've been living in Amstelveen for nearly eighteen years. It's very close to her parents." Toby paused, sipped more water and put the glass down carefully. "Wanda contracted Parkinson's Disease about three years ago. It's been a steady downhill slide. She can't travel anymore, has lost her confidence ... it's tragic really. There's nothing her doctors can do for her."

"I'm so sorry . . . one day we'll find a cure," Lawrence offered, and instinctively squeezed his shoulder. "So how are you both coping? Is Okki back at home now?"

"We're just taking it one day at a time. Okki stayed in London after graduating. She'd returned to live in Weybridge for her university studies. She was commuting to UCW every day. I let her have the apartment. I hardly use it now and don't get over to London much these days. The odd meeting in town, I suppose. Mostly it's a base when I come to check up on the old folks."

Lawrence managed a smile. "Did you say UCW? Okki went to UCW?"

"Social Anthropology; she got a 2:1. Why?"

For a moment Lawrence was back in the UCW office where he met Hannah for the first time. He'd been working as a contractor for a few weeks and had been involved in setting

27

up a meeting for her with one of his colleagues. Hannah had just flown in from New York and wasn't in good shape. Not the best of starts for their relationship, he reflected. It all seemed a lifetime ago.

As he got older, Lawrence had started to believe more and more in the power of coincidences. The job at UCW, the meeting with Hannah and the adventure that brought them together, felt like some kind of coincidental destiny they both shared. Now Lawrence found himself sitting in a hotel in India with a man he hadn't seen in nearly twenty years. Bizarrely, the coincidence this time was a conference on diabetes, a subject on which he was still very much a novice in his understanding.

Toby ordered two large snifters of Remy Martin XO. "I'm a board member of the UK Diabetes Action Group. When I found out the conference this year was in Delhi, it was too good a chance to miss. It's been great spending time with her this weekend. Okki reminds me so much of Wanda. Sadly I'm off early tomorrow morning."

"So are you still with IBM?" Lawrence was trying not to be rude but he could feel his eyelids getting heavier. After all, it had been a long day, what with the plenary session and closing speeches in the morning, then doing virtually nothing except read, swim and conjugate his undying love all afternoon. Three times on the same day was a new PB.

"No, I bought a company called Kampion. I'm the chairman but work part-time these days. I hired a very capable guy called Max Hartley as my CEO. He's ex RAF; you should meet him, quite a character. Our offices are in Blackfriars. I sort of flit about, I suppose. We've got sales offices all over the world. Just opened one on Sixth Avenue in New York, as it happens, overlooking Central Park. Max and I are there next Friday interviewing. You must come over for lunch."

"We'd be delighted to, thanks. So what does Kampion do exactly?" Lawrence noticed two very happy women meandering back through a forest of tables and chairs. Time for bed, he thought. I hope she's as tired as I feel.

"Systems integration."

"Glad I asked." He smiled. "What does that mean?"

"Kampion Integrated Software Solutions – our marketing genius calls us KISS-IT. We work with large corporates to help them integrate different systems or install software or migrate data from one system to another. It gives me a chance to see the world and get drunk in exotic locations." Toby sighed. "It pays well but it's still just a job."

"You sound disappointed." Lawrence was given a sweaty hug before Hannah collapsed into the chair.

"Not really disappointed ... the thing is, Lawrence, I keep asking myself: what is my legacy? Businessmen used to be philanthropists: they put something back; they created jobs; they left their mark; they gave to charity to help the poor. That's how Rotary got started. Paul Harris, a Chicago businessman, wanting to put something back. Then there were the Lever Brothers, Charles Rolls, Henry Royce, John Cadbury."

He gazed at the amber liquid as it swilled around the balloon glass. "I'll be fifty-four this year; wealthy, successful, life-long Rotarian, self-made man. But I haven't got any true friends to speak of. Most people have no idea how I've made my money. So what will be my legacy? What am I leaving for the benefit of future generations?"

He downed the dregs. "I'm no different to any other modern-day business leader – it's all about me, me, me, and stuff everyone else."

Lawrence was about to reply when Okki intervened. "Oh,

not this again, Pops . . . I know our friends here will not agree with you; I certainly don't. You have created jobs; you *have* put something back. This will keep for another day. It's late."

Toby smiled at her in quiet resignation, Lawrence thought, the alcohol pushing him back gently with the tide into calmer waters.

After the goodnight hugs and kisses, Lawrence and Hannah strolled out onto the terrace under a starless sky. The moon backwashed a benign cloud cover. The heat was still oppressive. Cicadas fought against relentless traffic noise. The air was infused with a heady mixture of night-flowering jasmine, incense and petrol fumes.

"Do you think he's right?" Lawrence whispered as he emerged from a long, airless kiss.

"Kiss me again and I'll tell you."

"You're a hard woman to please." He duly obliged.

"Now, do you mean, is Toby right about the legacy of our generation?" Hannah came back for another taste. "Yes, he probably is. We are more selfish, more detached somehow. We tend to think of legacy as financial inheritance; wealth transferred between family members rather than doing something good to help or inspire future generations."

"I *think* I agree." Lawrence shrugged. "Surely we must give everyone a crack at a good life, even the poorest people? Thing is, though, the gap between rich and poor is just getting wider."

"I don't think he's talking wealth. A chance for a good life must include electricity, clean drinking water and a toilet, for God's sake?" Hannah took his arm.

"Talking of toilets . . ." Lawrence did a little dance as they quickened the pace towards the lifts.

As he fumbled with the room key, he turned to her and smiled. "Are you sure about tomorrow? We could delay the flights and meet Jock and Nisha on Tuesday. The game's poised for a big finish."

Hannah pushed him into the room and stood watching from the bathroom doorway, "They've played for four days and you're hoping to shoot for a draw? Jeeze, what kind of a game is this?"

Lawrence was about to reply when the simple act of flushing the toilet stopped him. One easy press of a button. *A little water clears us of this deed.* He wouldn't normally have thought anything of it.

But tonight, standing there in a luxury hotel suite in Delhi, that simple act took on a whole new meaning.

CHAPTER 4

The afternoon flight out of Stockholm Arlanda was uneventful, until the descent into Geneva. "A light shower passing the runway" turned out to be pilot-speak for a raging thunderstorm. The A320 was buffeted like a toy plane by towering cumulonimbus, which swirled high above the lake and surrounding hills.

The storm didn't help his mood. Niklas felt uneasy. He searched outside Arrivals for the usual driver. The muscular hulk they had sent would not have looked out of place in a cage fight, despite his peaked cap, ill-fitting jacket and a message board with the correct code word etched across it.

They drove in silence, Niklas lost in the click-clack rhythm of the windscreen wipers. Torrents of rain had made waterfalls from the downpipes and guttering. It had washed all the tourists off the cobbled streets of the old town. A shroud of darkness had settled in early.

The Mercedes swung into the side street away from the main entrance and pulled up outside an unmarked door, set heavily into a tall, stone building. The keypad was the only light. The driver made no attempt to get out, instead drumming his fingers impatiently on the steering wheel.

Niklas dashed over, entered the eight-digit pin and found himself confronted by a new security guard who immediately demanded his passport and locked it in a drawer. The guard, taller even than the driver, made him complete the full entry procedures, which now included a thumb print and retinal scan. He was told to wait until another guard came to take over the front desk.

After a few minutes, he was escorted in the lift to the sixth floor and shown into a small, airless room. He had never been beyond the fifth floor before. The strip lights hadn't been cleaned in years, judging by the collection of moths and other dead insects. A pall of dried sweat and stale coffee seeped from dull, brown curtains.

He waited, ignoring his latest batch of emails. When this meeting started, he knew it would need his undivided attention. It was nearly nine o'clock when the door finally opened and a short, balding man in a dinner suit entered.

The man sat down heavily at the head of the table and didn't speak for what to Niklas seemed like hours. He could feel the man's eyes scanning him, looking for the cracks to prise open, reading his expressions, his body language, peering into his very soul. Niklas sat up straighter, resisting the urge to clear his throat. He would be told when he could make a noise. Noise was not tolerated when the Choirmaster was thinking.

"Why Uppsala?" The voice was soft and low. It came from pencil-thin lips that barely parted.

Niklas had to choose his reply with great care. One wrong word could spark a firestorm. There was no escape. Had his ambition brought him here? This was not the time for reflection.

"They wanted the most prestigious seat of learning in Europe with strong connections to the scientific world." Niklas saw impatience wreathing across a face of stone. "Oxford, Cambridge, the Sorbonne, Humboldt, Padua . . . they all said no. Even Stockholm refused, but Uppsala stepped in. It was not their first choice, Choirmaster."

The man had risen to his feet and was pacing slowly behind him. As he brushed against the curtains, flashes of streetlight from a distant world entered momentarily.

"How could they attract so much media attention? Some Voices in the Cantata have been invited. *I've* been invited, Niklas. I'm told that fourteen TV stations will be covering this. How have you allowed this to happen?" The whispered voice was directly behind him now, as if coming from beyond the curtains.

"I don't know, Choirmaster. Curiosity? Intrigue? They claim it will 'light up the world for the good of humanity'. Maybe the TV channels want to witness another scientific failure, ridicule the claims." Niklas turned his head as far as it would go. It wasn't far enough.

"But what if it isn't a failure? What if this breakthrough proves to be the start of a new science? What if the next announcement is being made in Beijing or Mumbai or fucking Kuala Lumpur?"

Niklas jumped as a fist slammed on the table next to him. He sat perfectly still. Body heat poured over him. Moist lips pressed into his right ear. The tip of a snake-like tongue darted into the space, then withdrew.

The voice returned even quieter than before. "There is a reason why I brought you here tonight. Come with me."

Niklas followed in silence, out of the room, back to the lift. When the steel doors closed, the Choirmaster swiped a card and pressed B2. He loosened the bow tie, unclipped the stud and released his bulging neck from the grip of a starched, white collar.

They stepped out into total darkness. Niklas heard a click as an endless corridor appeared in front of him, suddenly bathed in neon light. They walked past a row of closed doors until they reached one edged in red light. The Choirmaster didn't knock, instead striding into an anteroom where they donned protective clothing, masks and glasses.

In the room beyond, Niklas witnessed a sight that made him want to retch.

CHAPTER 5

Next morning, the taxi ride out to the field centre proved an education in itself for Hannah. Until now they'd only seen the inside of the hotel. Suddenly India was all around them. It was permanent rush hour, she thought, as they weaved between vehicles of various sizes, not to mention cows, dogs, mules and a bewildering range of other animals that treated the highway as a place to live, sleep and generally get in the way.

They were due to meet Jock and Nisha at 9 a.m. The plan was to catch up with Okki at the village later in the morning. The toilet project was at a critical stage and she needed to be there early, she'd said.

Hannah thought they'd left enough time but she was beginning to wonder. When the road widened into an expressway of sorts, Hannah felt they'd finally broken free from the clawing hands of the city. The taxi picked up speed and blared its horn, scattering mopeds, tuk-tuks and assorted lesser vehicles back into the roadside or the central median.

Hannah did a double take as they passed a truck with a fully-grown elephant standing on the back. She could see it was chained up, but was less than reassured when she saw the driver gesticulating on his mobile phone as they slipped by.

"Did you see that?"

"See what?" Lawrence was staring out of the opposite window.

"An elephant. You didn't see the elephant?"

"I've seen dozens of elephants. They live here, Hannah, get over it. This is India: 'expect the unexpected.'"

They came off the expressway and turned into a wide, busy street, lined with shops and animated traders plying hungry customers with piles of colourful rice dishes ARE food. They came to a grinding halt at the tail of a queue for a distant red light. Within seconds horns were blaring, cars and trucks poured in from unseen side roads and the whole chaotic scene reminded Hannah of downtown Manhattan on a bad day.

Two traffic policemen appeared from the crowd, sauntered towards the heart of the congestion and started waving their arms. Hannah quickly understood the pecking order – the bigger the vehicle, the more right of way it had. Then priority was based on who made the most noise and who pushed themselves the furthest forward.

She was amazed when the road suddenly cleared in front of them, only to realise that the taxi driver had slipped a bundle of notes to one of the policemen, who nodded to his mate before blowing his whistle frantically. Clearly it was half each. Honour amongst cops, she thought.

Even though they were making progress again, Hannah thought they might be late. She called Jock's mobile number and left a voicemail message. *In India you are always late,* Okki had explained. Her prophecy proved correct. It was ten past when they walked into the reception area. The receptionist was chatting to an older gentleman in traditional Indian dress who was leaning on a stick. He introduced himself as Dr Yadu Bhattacharya, the field centre manager. Hannah was about to explain the reason for their visit when a tall, breathless young man jogged in.

"Hi, you must be Hannah? And Lawrence? I'm Jock. Pleased to meet you both." The young man apologised to

Dr Bhattacharya for interrupting and they all exchanged handshakes. Hannah was intrigued by the calmness exuded by the older man but the introductions were short-lived.

"Come on, we must go, there's a Land Rover leaving in five minutes. I'll explain everything on the way." Jock was already halfway out of the door.

Hannah had thought the taxi was uncomfortable but at least it had air conditioning and proper seats, albeit covered in old cushion covers. Now she found herself struggling to sit tight on a hard, wooden bench. The flaps were pulled back, allowing dust and hot dry air to fill the cabin. At least it can't be for long, she reasoned. She was wrong.

They were sat opposite two young men who could hardly have been more different in appearance. Jock was Asiatic with a tanned complexion, meticulously well groomed, tidy, straight, black hair, and there was a sense of playfulness about him. He had the soft hands of a businessman. There was genuine warmth in his dark, chocolate eyes.

On the bench next to him was a Scandinavian, a blond boy, shorter and thicker set. He was introduced as Bjorn Slagle, a project leader and SINAC volunteer. Hannah guessed he was also in his mid-twenties. He appeared quite intense and cautious. His pink yet ghostly pallor was not helped by layers of suntan lotion. Large, calloused hands were fiddling uncomfortably with the straps of a heavy rucksack, nestled between his feet. His eyes of cobalt blue were as sharp as a bird of prey, hungrily watching for any movement or an opportunity to strike.

"Nisha? She's picking up two new volunteers and meeting us there," Jock explained. "We should be another thirty minutes. Sorry, it will get a bit bumpy when we leave the metalled road."

Hannah braced herself and took a firmer grip of Lawrence's leg, the only secure hold she could find. Suddenly the vehicle swerved round a tree and plunged off the road into a ditch. The driver engaged four-wheel drive, causing the gears to groan like an old horse on its way to the glue factory.

They started to plough through a rock-strewn moonscape until they found the grooves of a dirt track leading up a short incline.

"Okki's very excited about this project. She wanted us to see it while we're over here. I hope we're not getting in your way," Hannah offered.

"Not at all, we're delighted you could come." The light shone in Jock's eyes. "Your timing couldn't be better, isn't that right, Bjorn?" The synaptic pause made Hannah feel uncomfortable. Bjorn eventually replied. "Well, next week would have been better. New volunteers will bring our timeline forward, assuming they work hard. By then the toilet project should be finished."

Hannah was relieved when Lawrence picked up the conversation. She could sense Bjorn didn't want to talk. In fact, she thought Bjorn saw them as a nuisance and didn't want them there at all. It clearly wasn't in his project plan.

"So is SINAC all about toilets?" Lawrence shouted over another crunch of the gears.

"Yes and no, really," Jock replied, "it depends what level you're looking at?"

"Level?" Hannah was curious. Are there levels of toilet, she wondered.

"Yes," he continued, "I like to think we're making a difference to all kinds of people caught in the poverty trap. I prefer the term 'Cycle of Misery'."

The Land Rover jolted to a halt.

When Hannah looked through the dusty windscreen, she could see a large brown and white cow stood squarely across the track. It was chewing what she assumed was imaginary grass because the surrounding area was bleached dry. Nonchalantly, it plodded over to the shade of some trees and the vehicle lurched back into motion.

Jock continued with puppyish enthusiasm. He explained that people in the villages were caught in a deadly cycle. Without toilets or mechanical means to access underground springs, they ended up drinking filthy water.

This lowered their immunity levels to disease, he continued. Their weakened state reduced their capacity to feed themselves properly, only adding to the problem. Without adequate proteins and minerals, mortality rates increased, especially amongst the vulnerable, the children and the aged. With high infant-mortality rates, they needed the girls to marry young and produce more children to keep production in the fields going. So education levels fell away.

"I'd be honoured to make your medical presentation in Uppsala on this subject," Hannah interjected. "I studied waterborne pathogenesis as part of my Masters. It's a fascinating subject."

Jock nodded enthusiastically, accepting the offer. He stretched out his long legs and continued, "Overall life's a bitch and things never get better. That's how we grew up in a village in China. Somehow my father managed to get us out and break the cycle."

"So you set up SINAC to help villagers have access to toilets and clean water?" Lawrence added. "I see that now, but you mentioned about different levels?"

"Toilets and clean water are only part of SINAC's mission," Jock continued. "You see, my father was an entrepreneur.

He was capable of building a large profitable company that created wealth and employed thousands of people. I call this 'generative economics'."

Jock explained that entrepreneurialism was the key. There were potentially millions of entrepreneurs across India and China who could do the same as his father, creating wealth and employment.

"Once they escape the Cycle of Misery, I suppose," Hannah suggested.

"Well, sort of." Jock grabbed the back of the driver's seat as they swung into a dried-up riverbed. "It depends on having the infrastructure around them to improve the quality of life. Until now, people like my father had to leave the village to find a new life. Perhaps we could reverse that trend."

"How do you mean 'infrastructure'?" Lawrence probed.

"Toilets, pumps for clean drinking water, solar panels, waste water treatment plants, electricity, hospitals and medical supplies, decent roads and transport connections, telecommunications, access to the Internet, computers ... all the things that we take for granted which help generate economic sustainability." Jock opened his hands as if waiting for applause.

"Hey presto," Hannah replied "*generative economics*. So digging the toilets is just the first part of your vision. You want to bring these people and their village into the 21st century?"

"Exactly. If we can kick-start the entrepreneurs amongst them, then we won't have to keep digging toilets or feeding them in times of famine or drought. They can look after themselves, create wealth, pay their taxes; and play a full part in the wider community." Jock continued, "Not only that but we can reduce the population explosion in cities like Mumbai, Kolkata, Chennai, even up the road here in Delhi. If we can help create successful villages, then the young people wouldn't have to move to the city slums to find work."

Jock argued that family units could remain intact; the slums would empty and the cities' infrastructure could cope again, as Indian cities had done in previous times.

Hannah noticed that they were slowing as they entered the village. But one thing was puzzling her. It all sounded plausible but infrastructure was expensive. And as she'd discovered at the Diabetes Conference only the day before, there were millions of people in India living well below the poverty line.

As they jumped down onto the baking earth, Jock caught her eye and smiled. "I know what you're thinking, Hannah. How could we afford to do this? Even if all the SINACs in the world pooled their resources, we couldn't create enough funding to deliver a vision on this scale."

Hannah gazed at the mud-brick buildings with thatched roofs that were scattered around a patch of smooth ground. Closer inspection revealed the smoothness was the result of layers of cattle dung, which acted like a sealant. The top-most layer was sticky in the sweltering heat and was caked in flies.

They were less than a thousand feet above sea level yet Hannah was struggling to breathe. The heat seemed to have burned off all the oxygen and there was no breeze. Her wide-brimmed hat provided some shade but her sunglasses kept slipping down her nose in a steady stream of sweat. She was amazed anyone could live in these conditions let alone do manual labour. The SINAC volunteers must be truly committed, she decided.

She noticed Okki coming towards them from between two of the mud buildings. Her flaming red hair was pulled back into a knot. She was covered in dust with muddy streaks of sweat running across her face.

Hannah waved to her before turning back to Jock. "I

suppose the chances of getting the G20 nations to pay for this infrastructure are even less likely. Sanitation, drinking water and electricity don't come for free, let alone roads, hospitals and Internet access. So how are you going to do it?"

"The answer's very simple. It's called Project Amrita. We'll use an exciting new scientific breakthrough to help us." Jock pointed to a cloud of dust on the near horizon. The Jeep underneath it was bouncing towards them.

"My beautiful fiancée Nisha will explain."

CHAPTER 6

"The Cesspool of Human Misery: Fighting the Diseases Linked to Poor Sanitation. Catchy title." Hannah took the briefing note from Jock after he'd fished it out of his bag. She was happy to work with that title, especially taking the slot before lunch in Uppsala. It gave her scope to make a real impact, she decided.

Jock and Bjorn headed off towards the centre of the village to get the meeting started with the other project leaders. The first generators were scheduled for later in the week, the solar panels arriving the day after. Hannah noticed Bjorn didn't share Jock's enthusiasm. *Did he have another agenda or was he just naturally quiet?*

Okki was chatting to Lawrence when the Jeep thundered in, heavy tyres crunching in the gravelly earth. They covered their eyes until the cinder-hot dust had cleared, by which time a young, tall, Indian girl with shoulder-length, straight, blue-black hair had climbed out, quickly joined by her two passengers.

"You must be Nisha." Lawrence stepped forward. "Jock's been telling us all about you. It's a real pleasure to meet you. I'm Lawrence, and this is Hannah, my better half."

As they chatted, Hannah noticed the village was deserted. The only people she could see were SINAC volunteers. She assumed the villagers must be sheltering from the heat somewhere, which is what they should be doing. It was late morning. It was hot – seriously hot – and, with a cloudless sky, it was going to get even hotter.

Okki explained that most of the villagers were already out in the fields, tending to the meagre crops of rice, castor oil and mustard seed. The proceeds barely bought enough essentials to support one family, let alone the dozens that clung to life in the village. Hannah could see the distress in her eyes just talking about it. The only people remaining were the elderly, the sick and the children, left to huddle together in any patches of shade they could find.

Hannah pointed to an electricity cable, only to learn that the power had long since been cut off when the unpaid bills mounted up. Attempts at reconnection had been frustrated at every turn. Loose piles of cable were left to rot in the trees behind the school.

The only noise Hannah could hear above their conversation was the constant buzzing of flies. There were flies matting the ground around them, pricking every piece of exposed skin; squadrons of flies hovering over mounds of fresh and dried dung near the school building; flies diving in and out of crevices in the mud walls; flies swarming over any scraps of food left by the stray dogs.

Hannah hadn't appreciated how tanned Okki was until she saw her next to the two new girls. Their shiny blonde hair and translucent, white skin made them look completely out of place, like they'd stepped out of a TV shampoo commercial.

"Okki, meet our latest volunteers: Annemiek and Angelique Wiss. They've just arrived from Holland." Nisha was smiling as the two girls reached over and shook the calloused hand Okki had just wiped on her shorts. Okki slipped into Dutch to greet them, which was quickly followed by warm embraces.

"Please, call us Annie One and Annie Two. That's what our friends do."

"I'm Annie Two – I am taller than my twin sister. It's the best way to tell us apart. I try to wear darker colours and Annemiek wears white."

"Not sure white's a terribly good idea in India, especially when you're digging out toilets." Okki laughed.

"Okki, I thought you could show them the ropes. And we thought you could use a little help. Three diggers must be better than one." Nisha smiled. "They'll be staying next door to you so I thought you could welcome them to the neighbourhood."

Hannah and Lawrence said goodbye to Nisha as she went off to join Jock at the meeting. It was agreed that Okki would show everyone around, then Nisha and Jock would take Hannah and Lawrence back to the hotel. Nisha would explain more about Project Amrita on the way.

"So welcome to SINAC India – I hope you're ready for some hard work." Okki was explaining the layout for the new school toilets and what needed to be done.

"And you dug all this out on your own?" Annie One had deep, blue eyes, set into heavy mascara. Straight, blonde hair framed a sharp, angular face with a protruding jawbone and narrow lips. Hannah thought it gave her a cold, stubborn look.

"Yes, we've all got a job to do and this is my little home. I could see it as weeks of backbreaking work or as a way to help needy children. And you'll love the children, guys; they're so beautiful."

"That's a great attitude, Okki, we must remember that," said Annie Two this time. She had a softer face with a high fringe, and thicker blonde hair with more of a strawberry tint. Her paler-blue eyes were just as sharp, her fuller lips glistened with sweat and she had the prominent chin of a serious competitor who expected to win, Hannah decided. True to her word, she was wearing a dark-brown T-shirt with 'Don't Shoot the Messenger' scrawled across her chest.

After the grand tour, as Okki called it, Hannah and Lawrence were taken over to where Nisha and Jock were finishing off. They let the girls get on with the digging and all four of them climbed into the Jeep, which was much more to Hannah's liking. On the way back to the city, they called in at the field centre to drop off some boxes.

Hannah had been impressed by the enthusiasm of all the SINAC volunteers they'd met, with the exception of Bjorn who remained stoically passive. He'd managed a feeble goodbye but there was no offer of a handshake. It was late afternoon by the time they'd crawled back to the hotel.

"The Nirvana. We're here with Okki for a presentation on Wednesday evening," Nisha announced as they went through the security check and pulled up in front of the main entrance. "I'm hoping Jock finally gets at least some of the science behind Project Amrita, before we go ahead and change the world."

Jock looked at Nisha nonplussed. Hannah admired her for trying. She knew what it was like being the scientist in a relationship where the other half positively celebrated their ignorance. She kissed her on the cheek as they said their goodbyes. Over a quick drink in the bar, they both agreed that Jock and Nisha seemed a genuinely happy couple. Hannah had probed about possible wedding plans, but Nisha said everything was on hold until after Project Amrita went live. Maybe later in the year, she'd said.

"I'm thinking swim, then G&Ts with nibbles on the balcony?" Lawrence proposed as he pressed the button.

They had the lift to themselves. Hannah was pleased it wasn't one of the glass bubbles. She put her arms around him and pulled him close. "Nibbles first, big boy."

* * *

47

By mid-afternoon the flies, heat and heavy digging had exhausted the three young girls. Annie One produced bottles of water and passed them around. Okki returned the favour, pulling out a bag of shiny, red apples.

"So what brings you to India?" Okki crunched into the sweet flesh.

"We needed a gap year." Her lips hardly moved as Annie One replied between sips.

"Yes, we'd had it with the whole 'when are you going to settle down' bit. We wanted to see the world and do something to help others. India is the first place we thought of. SINAC came up on Google and here we are."

Annie Two seemed calmer and more level-headed, Okki decided; the one who could be relied upon to pay the bill, to get them home safely.

"How long do you plan to stay?" Okki put the cores into a plastic bag to take back. She knew they would rot if she left them but tossing them away was sending out the wrong message, in a country where tossing away rubbish had become an Olympic sport.

"We've no plans really. Annemiek wants to do Thailand; I fancy Australia. We'll just take it as it comes. This looks a good place to be right now." Annie Two picked up the shovel and jumped back into the hole.

Darkness had set in when tired bodies were hunched over plates of stew dotted along refectory tables back at the field centre. Electric wall fans swung like metronomes, stirring up warm air and droning in the large characterless room.

"Bread? Well, it's more like roti actually." Okki held out a plastic box to the two girls but there were no takers. The best attempts to wash the dust and grime off their hands and faces had not worked. Annie Two's T-shirt had lost the word

'Messenger' and had become a dusty-sand colour.

"Okki, where does Nisha fit into all this?" Annie One asked, getting straight to the point.

"Nisha's Jock's fiancée. He's the chairman of SINAC. They met in Singapore a couple of years ago, I think. She's quite spiritual, a devout Hindu. She says it helps her balance her scientific understanding with the nature of things. Also she helps out with the digging when she can but most of her time is spent in the lab at the university. She's awesome."

"And what does she do in the lab? Is she a chemist?" asked Annie Two this time. It was a casual question, a softer approach, but Okki could sense more than idle curiosity behind her eyes.

"No, she's a physicist. She has told me what she does but I didn't really understand it, to be honest. I'm going to a lecture with them later this week, which might help." She finished poking around with the stew. If it contained mutton, she certainly couldn't find any. She put down her fork. "Hey guys, I don't want to be rude but I need to catch up with my emails. The Wi-Fi is slow but it does work. You just have to be patient. If you need anything, I'm right next door. Sleep well and I'll see you both at breakfast. Six a.m. sharp."

The room was almost empty when Okki left. The last few volunteers were finishing off their meals. The dishwashing rota had moved into action and the two Dutch girls added their names to the list.

"When does he arrive?" Annie One whispered the question in Dutch as they stacked the plates, then headed back to the hut.

"Wednesday."

"Then we've got some work to do."

• CHAPTER 7 •

Niklas felt queasy. He couldn't quite believe what he was seeing.

The room had no windows. It was hot and cramped. The red lighting – better for keeping the patient sedated, he was told – made him disorientated, a feeling intensified by the surgical mask and Perspex glasses, which kept steaming up. It smelled like a hospital yet it was carpeted and looked more like a converted office.

The solitary attendant in the corner was also wearing protective clothing. They communicated with him through earpieces. Some kind of table or trolley was set in the middle of the room. Did it have small wheels? Niklas couldn't be sure. It did have thick leather restraints, which seemed unnecessary. They were strapped to the wrists and ankles of the patient. It was a young child. The skeletal figure was clearly unconscious.

Niklas moved closer. Despite the lighting, he surmised it was a young girl, dark skinned, most likely Indian or Pakistani. Eyes closed, her breathing was shallow and occasionally she let out a sharp, rasping cough that cut straight through him. She was naked.

There were old scars, small cuts and nasty, fresh wounds on her shoulders, upper body and neck. Dozens of small pinpricks dotted the insides of both her arms. Bruising on her stomach and thighs left deep shadows on her smooth skin. Her legs were painfully thin and her small feet were blistered, as if she'd been walking for days.

He guessed she was no more than eleven or twelve years old.

She was just reaching puberty, with small buds on her chest and patches of black downy hair under her arms and between her legs.

"Who is she?" Niklas looked closer. He noticed a rash down her throat. There was what he presumed was dried blood around her lips and nostrils.

"She is Nobody," the voice in his ears replied, a voice strangely detached from the squat figure standing nearby. "She has no name. She does not exist."

The voice, matter-of-fact, devoid of all emotion, continued its clinical explanation. "She was probably given or sold to a drug dealer in Rajasthan. It happens every day. The dealer will have made her an addict – probably cocaine or perhaps something cheaper – then sold her to a pimp for sex. Unfortunately for her, she contracted AIDS. Then she was of no use to him. She will have been beaten, then left for dead. Before she crawled her way to a refuge, she picked up tuberculosis and several other diseases. In the West, she would have been vaccinated against them. But in India, nobody cares, not even her own parents."

Niklas turned his head away when another bout of coughing left the child gasping for breath. Still her eyes remained closed.

"What is she doing here?"

"That does not concern you," he snapped back. "I want you to understand what kind of people we're dealing with. Indian, Chinese, Korean, Pakistani . . . they're all the same. They have no honour, no respect. They do not value life. They sneer at our values, our western culture. They lie, cheat and steal from us. They want our science, our land, our wealth, our designs, our heritage, our genius. They are jealous of us. So now they want to own us, to destroy us. But we will stop them. Der Sangerbund will stop them."

The attendant was given instructions, took out his earpiece and left the room.

"All your partners in this Project Amrita are Asian," the Choirmaster continued. "Jock Lim is Chinese. His fiancée is Indian. Gupta Geothermal is Indian. Sangbu Electronics is Korean. SINAC is run out of Singapore. They are only using you to fix a problem, and then you will be replaced with their own wireless technology company. I know how they work."

"But Choirmaster, we don't know yet what the Project is going to deliver? Whatever they may claim, the science is not proven," Niklas countered. He saw a flicker of movement in the young girl's eyelids. She coughed again.

"And when it is proven, it will be too late. You say they plan to release it across the Internet, 'for the good of humanity'. There will be no control, no intellectual property, no ownership. This announcement must not happen. Uppsala must not go ahead." The voice pierced deep inside his head.

Niklas knew not to react. He had heard these arguments before. Although the Choirmaster spoke with ultimate authority within Der Sangerbund, Niklas had recently detected some lack of unity amongst the Cantata. Not all the Voices seemed to be singing in harmony, he suspected. But he had no way of knowing for sure. And his own position was precarious. The Choirmaster was powerful and had to be respected.

"Even if I'm successful, Choirmaster, and get the Uppsala event cancelled, they could just go ahead and announce the scientific breakthrough from India," Niklas suggested.

"We will handle the situation in India. I have already made arrangements. The scientist behind all this, his fiancée—"

"Dr Nisha Patel," Niklas added.

"She was funded by SINAC to work here in Geneva last year. Her research at CERN tested The Large Hadron Collider to its limits, so I'm told. She is clearly a brilliant physicist. The results were extraordinary, but we cannot interpret their usefulness. Even to our experts it is just meaningless data. Her demands for extra capacity have driven a major upgrade." The voice had returned to a whisper. "I understand the Chinese are now building a collider that will be five times more powerful. It will replace CERN. The global centre for nuclear research will move to China."

Niklas knew from the partnership agreement between Henning Technologies and SINAC that the work of this young scientist was protected. Jock Lim, for all his apparent carefree approach, had made sure the interpretation of Nisha's research findings was kept secure.

Jock Lim. Niklas had yet to meet him. They had corresponded by email. He knew he would find out from his CEO what the erudite Chinese philanthropist was really like when Ingmar Persson returned from Delhi. For now, what he did know was that his real name was Yuan Lee Lim, 26 years old, born in the Hebei Province of China. The nickname Jock came from his mother's side. He understood she was from Glasgow originally and had married the local blacksmith while doing voluntary work during her gap year. Jock was their only child.

"Do you think this new Chinese hadron collider is a result of her work?" Niklas looked round for a glass of water to give the child. The coughing continued; small drops of spittle and blood foamed around her lips. The dryness in the room was even making him feel thirsty.

"I don't know." The voice remained calm. "Jock Lim may have connections within the Chinese government. I am making those enquiries through the Cantata."

He may well have, Niklas thought, but that was not what his inquiries had discovered. Jock's parents may have had help from the Communist State when getting started, but there was no doubt about their entrepreneurial skills and determination.

They successfully created one of the largest industrial fastener manufacturers in Asia. At its peak, the company had seventeen factories employing over sixty thousand people across mainland China, Korea, Vietnam and Taiwan, making nuts, bolts, hinges, nails, screws and rivets.

Niklas learned that both parents died when their private jet crashed in a thunderstorm landing in Hong Kong. Jock inherited everything and decided to sell out to an American corporate. Allegedly worth over US$100m, he established SINAC to provide sanitation in developing countries and ultimately to eradicate world poverty. To Niklas, it didn't sound like the profile of a man hell-bent on destroying western civilisation.

"Tell me what you're making for them." The Choirmaster was peering over at the little girl. Niklas could sense the door opening. The attendant returned, carrying a small kidney-shaped enamel bowl.

"It is a new microwave technology that can carry secure transmissions via satellite broadcast. We have christened it EMX-Band. SINAC have patented it for now. That's all I've been allowed to know."

Niklas could sense the frustration.

"Secure transmissions of what? Voice, data, what? We must know, Niklas." The Choirmaster took something from the bowl. He turned away towards the brightest red light.

"I don't know. Ingmar doesn't know. No one in Henning knows." Niklas was being consumed. He felt his lungs burning. All the oxygen in the room had suddenly evaporated. Like the helpless child before him, he was gasping for breath.

"The only person who knows is Dr Nisha Patel, Choirmaster."

"Then we need to send her a message."

• CHAPTER 8 •

India had a split personality, Okki decided, gazing out of the window as the super-clean, air-conditioned Metro train rumbled into the newly built station. It was the richest country in the world and the poorest country in the world, at the same time. The two countries occupied the same space. Both were on full display; all you had to do was look.

A few minutes later, she dived into a tuk-tuk and headed off towards the University. The driver decided, for a few extra rupees, he would sing to her all the way but she wasn't listening. Her mind was back in the village, a village only a few miles down the road yet light years away.

She'd heard that three of the villagers had died yesterday, including a young child. Nobody seemed interested. The bodies had been taken away, she didn't know where. They could have been cremated or buried or left in a ditch by the roadside somewhere, for all she knew. It didn't even make the local news headlines.

As the tuk-tuk driver chirruped on, they weaved in and out of teeming traffic. Many of the European cars looked like they had just left the showroom. Above and around them, modern high-rise office blocks and brightly lit government buildings displayed the trappings of wealth and success. For a moment, she thought she was back in London or Amsterdam.

When they stopped at a red light, they were suddenly surrounded by beggars and the seething underbelly of Delhi's street life. Tiny, weak hands knocked for mercy on tinted windows. Okki found a few rupees in her purse and handed them over, despite the protestation of the driver.

Before we build Metros and office blocks and mansions for the rich, surely we need to provide everybody with clean water and toilets, medicines and fresh food, shelter and security? How can so many Indians live in luxury while people, their own people, their own flesh and blood, are suffering, begging on street corners and dying needlessly?

The singing had stopped. She was facing a barrier. The university guard explained entrance must be on foot after the bag search. She paid the driver and made her way to Nisha's office. Daylight had gone but the crushing, airless heat remained. The campus was quiet. The main door to the Science Block was open.

Upstairs she watched her friend transform from cocoon to butterfly, from research scientist into party animal. Nisha took off her white coat, revealing a peacock-blue silk skirt and tight-fitting creamy white blouse. Her flawless coffee skin brought out the richness in the gold jewellery and an oversized watch perched neatly on her thin wrist. Around her neck she draped a fine-spun pashmina in gold and sunrise orange.

Okki felt underdressed by comparison and hoped the lecture wouldn't be too posh. She reached into her bag. "Have I got time to do my make-up?"

"Yes, it doesn't start till seven. Jock should be here soon."

"Thanks again for inviting me. I'm not sure I'll follow it; I gave up with physics at school. Still, you got me out for the evening. Any excuse for champagne and canapés."

Nisha was touching up her nails. "I heard this guy in Jaipur last year. He's so passionate, he even brings electromagnetism alive . . . and he avoids jargon, so you should be all right."

"Electromagnetism? Sounds heavy." Okki went to touch up

her nail polish too, but decided to get the soil out from under her fingernails first.

"To a scientist, the title is quite provocative. 'Come to the Light: Waves, Particles or Something Else?' This has perplexed us for hundreds of years. We used to believe light travelled in waves, a disturbance in the air that moves like ripples on a pond." Nisha's eyes were on fire. Okki could make out flecks of amber highlighting the rich motes of ochre brown.

"James Clerk Maxwell was the first to calculate the speed of light through mathematical equations. Ultraviolet, infrared and visible light are all variations of electromagnetic waves with different frequencies, he argued. Only forty per cent of sunlight is actually visible. We know the other rays are there, which is why all of us must use sunscreen."

Okki was combing her hair using the reflection in the office window. She noticed a solitary figure on the footpath heading towards the entrance. "The wave idea makes sense. So what's with the particles?"

"A wave is a pulse of energy moving through a medium like air or water. But space is a vacuum. We can see stars, planets, comets, suns and moons that can be millions of miles away across a vast frozen desert of nothingness. Light has no medium through which to travel." Nisha stretched out her fingers and examined her handiwork.

"I may need a drink *before* this lecture." Okki smiled as she turned and got the nod of approval for her hair.

"So when we discovered the electron, the whole idea of light being a wave came into question. And not just light. We used to believe electricity was a fluid until we found it was made up of electron particles."

"So sunlight is a stream of particles that fly across the universe? I'm getting it now."

"Well, yes and no. Einstein talked about light having a *wave-particle duality*. For him it didn't really matter which was right, it was all about how we used the knowledge. He referred to a unit of light as a photon; an elementary particle, a quantum of light that has no mass and can fly across the vast nothingness of space unhindered."

"But it couldn't exceed the speed of light, is that right?" Okki's face lit up. "That's all I know about Einstein, apart from him being a Jewish scientist who fled the Nazis, worked on the atomic bomb and was friends with Marilyn Monroe . . . and he is still the perfect image of a mad scientist or everyone's favourite uncle."

"Yes, that was his theory . . . well, that's what the history books say." Nisha turned away but not before Okki noticed a strange look fall across her face, like a veil being drawn across the entrance to a temple. The uneasy silence that fell between them was soon broken by the sound of footsteps on the stairs.

"In Hinduism, sunlight is celebrated each year during the festival of Diwali, our New Year." Nisha spun round; the veil had lifted and the room was filled with her radiance once more. "It symbolises the triumph of light over darkness, knowledge over ignorance and hope over despair. It begins with the darkest new moon of Kartik, the seventh month of the Hindu lunar year. It's my favourite time of year. In Diwali, we celebrate the Goddess Lakshmi. She is the consort of Lord Vishnu and goddess of wealth and good fortune. People light candles to welcome her into their homes. She brings riches and happiness to our families. Houses are cleaned and freshly painted to make the goddess feel at home. The whole city becomes a fairyland with thousands of lamps lighting up the trees, shops and streets. You must come to a Diwali festival in Delhi, Okki."

"Can I wear a sari? I've always fancied that."

"I will personally dress you." They both started laughing as Nisha struck a pose.

The door swung open. Jock surveyed the scene, dropped his bag and grabbed Nisha. They submerged into a long, deep kiss, eventually coming up for air. "Well, you two have scrubbed up mighty pretty."

"Sorry, Jock, you'll have to kiss the gooseberry as well." Okki offered her cheek but Jock took her by the waist and kissed her full on the lips.

"This is my lucky day – a ménage à trios. And here at Delhi University, not usually a hotbed for erotic dreams." Jock laughed.

"Don't even think about it. Okki can't cope with particle physics *and* your groping paws." Nisha pushed him away as a broad grin lit up her face.

"So that's what this is all about?"

"I told you weeks ago, if only you'd listen." Nisha continued. "For Project Amrita to succeed, you need a basic understanding of particle theory. This seemed the quickest way of getting it into your thick skull."

"You're not the only one with a postgraduate qualification, Dr Smarty-Pants," Jock retorted.

"I'm sorry; sociology doesn't count as a serious subject, even at Princeton. I still think your parents bought you the degree as a Christmas present."

"Oh, scratch my eyes out, why don't you?"

"Come along, children, play nicely . . . or Okki will make you sit through the lecture afterwards. What was it called again, Nisha?"

"'Exploring the suppression of symmetry violation in advanced gauge theory modelling.'"

"Exactly . . . so behave."

"Jesus. I hope we'll be well into the buffet before that one starts." Jock picked up his bag, "OK, let's do it, guys."

Nisha flicked the switch and locked the door behind them. Okki felt the humid air outside hit her like a hot towel being slapped across her face. They found their way over to the staff car park.

"Beauty or Beast?" Nisha delved in her bag for the keys.

"This calls for Beauty," Jock replied as he walked past the dusty Jeep and waited by the rear of a sports car. He buried his bag in its cavernous glass mouth and joined the two women in the creamy leather interior.

Okki had crawled into the back. "Not a bad little run-around, Nisha. Where did you find it?"

"Jock told me classic cars are like true love – you don't find them, they find you."

"Jock, you're a real smoothie." Okki flicked the back of his neck through the hand-stitched headrest.

"Ouch!" Jock yelped. "The car belonged to my Scottish grandfather. It's been in the family for years: just needed a lick of paint. I wanted nothing but the best for the future Mrs Lim. I just knew there was a gorgeous little petrol head sitting on those beautiful shoulders."

"What is it?" Okki clipped the rear seat belt.

He stroked the walnut dashboard. "It's a seventy-two Mark III Jensen Interceptor, the finest sports coupe ever produced . . . or so my mother told me. The Pride of the British Midlands, she called it. Anyway, it did the trick. How could any girl refuse this as an engagement present?"

The powerful V8 growled into life. Nisha let the engine purr while she pulled a CD from the tray. She pushed it slowly into the slit that had been added to the dashboard during an elaborate restoration project. She leaned across, mouthing the words to him. Jim Morrison's sultry tones turned the car into a cathedral of sound.

Jock smiled. "I'd no idea you liked The Doors."

"I'd never heard of them until I started researching the car. They had some great music back then . . . you can light my fire any time you want, baby."

"Get a room." The voice from the back seat was just audible over the intricate Ray Manzarek keyboard solo.

"You sure about the threesome idea?" Jock settled comfortably in the buttery leather seat, pushing it back.

"Quite sure, now let me concentrate." Nisha nosed across the stream of traffic filing out of the city. She turned towards the neon glow in the sky beyond the tangle of jacaranda trees and ignored the petulant complaints from an engine thirsting for the open road.

"How did it go with the Henning guy?" Nisha touched a button, lowering the music into the gentle hum of the air-conditioning system.

"Ingmar? He was great. All signed and sealed. The last bit of paperwork for Project Amrita. We're having dinner with him tomorrow night, a celebration before he goes back. Want to join us, Okki?" Jock twisted towards the rear seats.

"I like celebrations; count me in. Who is he?"

"He's running the satellite technology bit. He reckons they'll be ready to go live after Uppsala."

"What satellite technology bit?" Okki felt as if she'd come in halfway through their conversation again. She must get herself to Uppsala. Maybe then it would all make sense. Her dad had offered to pay the airfare.

Within a few minutes, Nisha swung off the main highway and pulled up at a barrier. After the routine security check, the barrier lifted and she continued down into the underground car park of the New Delhi Nirvana International Hotel & Conference Centre.

"We need to reach the whole of India for this project to be a success. Henning can help us access the existing telecoms network." Jock unclipped his belt as the Jensen pulled into their allocated space. "The technology is amazing. I've no idea how it works. Must be particle physics; is that what you called it, Nisha?"

Nisha locked the car as they made towards the lifts. She pressed for the seventh floor. "Jock, just pay attention in the lecture, will you? If you behave, you might get a drink afterwards."

The lift eased to a halt and the doors slid open directly into a large room dotted with clusters of well-dressed people sipping champagne and chatting. The futuristic one-way glass walls allowed the colourful lights of the nearby buildings to penetrate the space and sparkle off the high ceiling.

Okki thought the subdued up-lighting created the atmosphere of a jungle at dusk. It was the time when all the forest creatures put aside the hostilities of the day and drank together at the waterhole, in a welcome, if unnatural, truce.

"Thank God; drinks *before* the lecture." Jock grabbed glasses from a tray as it whisked past, remembering a sparkling water for his fiancée.

"So what are you broadcasting?" Okki persisted. She was struggling to see the connection between digging toilets in a remote Indian village and a Swedish satellite communications company.

"You'll be the first to know, Okki. We'll be starting in your village. From there Ingmar reckons we can roll it out all over India," Jock added triumphantly.

"But roll out what?" Okki pushed again. Maybe the lecture would give her a clue.

"To understand that, you need to meet the handsome gentleman standing behind you," Nisha interrupted.

Okki turned to face a tall, middle-aged, thickset Indian businessman resplendent in a knee-length green silk Banyan jacket and matching turban. He was bathed in an aura of scented charm and old-fashioned chivalry. She could feel a deep blush burning itself into her smooth, freckled skin as she was drawn into his broad, playful smile and sparkling, brown eyes.

Taking a slow, deep bow, he lightly kissed the back of her outstretched hand, his finely groomed moustache caressing her with the softness of a badger-hair shaving brush.

"Okki, may I present Mr Ranjit Guraman Mahindra Singh," Nisha announced.

"Delighted to be at your service, Miss Okki," the man said, with a smile.

"The pleasure is . . ." She blushed even deeper as the words caught in her throat.

"Ranjit has been a good friend of my family since I was a little girl," Nisha explained. "For me, he will always be Uncle Ranji."

Jock switched his empty glass for a full one as a waiter danced by. He explained that Ranjit was to play a vital role in the success of Project Amrita.

"So what . . . do you do?" Okki said, finding her voice, the colour easing.

"To help me answer you, please let me ask you a question. What do you know about radioactive decay?"

CHAPTER 9

"I thought you said no jargon." Jock shook his head and grabbed a corner table, pleading with the waiter to leave the bottle and bring over some cold water.

"That's a bit harsh, Jock; even I could follow it." Okki topped up the four glasses. Jock gulped down a large mouthful and invited her to continue.

Okki stared at the ceiling to see if the words were written up there. She dived in. Maxwell believed light needed a medium to travel across. He assumed space was full of a gas called "the ether". And Maxwell was no dummy, she continued. He produced the first ever colour photographs, won a prize for his theory about Saturn's rings and used mathematics to prove that electricity travels at the same speed as visible light.

"I'm impressed, Okki; you really were listening." Nisha hugged her, almost knocking over the champagne bottle.

Okki took another mouthful before continuing. "We now know that space is a vacuum, so waves cannot travel across it. Light must be made up of particles like electricity that travel in straight lines, radiating out from the source. But unlike electricity, light particles don't need a conductor to travel along. Electricity can only traverse a vacuum for a very short distance, whereas light can travel across the entire universe."

Okki eyed up the plate of canapés that had appeared but wanted to amaze her friends first. Einstein, she said, argued that gravity was the key. Even though light particles had no mass and space was indeed a vacuum, gravity still worked on both as it caused space itself to curve around large objects. And once he proved space could bend, then why not time, as space and time were linked.

"I didn't get that mass-can-turn-into-energy-and-back-again ... the $E = mc^2$ bit. But I thought the lecturer was great. Maybe I should have tried a bit harder in physics. Thanks again for inviting me."

As Okki reached for the plate, Nisha added, "Einstein certainly had a way of getting people to believe him."

Okki stopped mid-chew, studying Nisha's face for any crack of humour. Instead the distant look had wreathed itself over her again. "You make it sound like you knew him?"

And, just as quickly as it had darkened, Nisha's face brightened again, and the moment had passed. But Okki wasn't convinced her question had been answered.

Ranjit took the plate and finished off a bite-sized vegetable pakora before turning to Okki. "Bravo. You've gone from layman to quantum physicist in one easy lesson. Never mind digging toilets for the Dalits, you should be working in the lab with Nisha."

"Dalits?" Okki spluttered.

"The Untouchables," Ranjit explained. "The great unwashed, the people in the villages. If we can help them integrate, we'll become the most prosperous nation on earth. Poverty will be eradicated from India."

"Jock's dream, yes, I see that. But light particles? Electricity? Einstein? Radioactive decay? By the way, I'm happy to declare complete ignorance on that one." Okki topped up her glass and snaffled a pakora in the same swift movement.

Jock apologised for not introducing their guest properly. He explained that Ranjit was the general manager and major shareholder of Gupta Geothermal PVT Ltd, India's newest power generation company.

"Okki, can I tell you a little about what we're doing?" Ranjit's whispered voice and mysterious gaze captivated like a snake charmer. His young red-haired cobra sat in spellbound amazement.

He explained that traditional methods for generating geothermal electricity used the heat in the earth's crust to turn water into steam, which drove the turbines. The process was expensive to run and capital-intensive, despite being more environmentally friendly than fossil fuels. They planned to support Project Amrita initially using one of these methods, Hot Dry Rock technology.

On cue the cobra bit. "And radioactive decay?"

Ranjit smiled. "Extremely high temperatures are created in the earth's crust by mass being converted into energy when atoms decay. Solid rock becomes molten lava or magma. As Einstein and others have proven, a huge amount of energy can be released from a relatively small amount of mass. Okki, we'll be able to produce limitless electricity for virtually no cost using the earth's own natural resources."

"The Greens will love you."

"With the help of Nisha and her team, we'll drill down into the earth's crust and commission the world's first magma power station next year. Once established, the generators will pretty much run themselves."

The cobra wanted more. "But I'm still hearing drilling, start-up costs, high-voltage cabling, step-down transformers and power-hungry electrical devices. The people in my village can't afford a litre of diesel to run a generator even if they had one, let alone pay for mains cabling or buy water pumps."

"Okki," Jock interrupted, "sometimes you just have to believe."

Nisha glowered at him. "What he's trying to say in his rather tactless way is that . . . we've got that covered too. But this is where it gets heavy. If you're really interested, I'll explain in the car on the way home."

"I was going to take the Metro," Okki protested.

"No, I won't hear of it. We'll drop him off first. It won't take long at this time of night." Nisha smiled into her fiancé's half-closed eyes.

As Ranjit squeezed into the crowded lift ahead of them, he waved goodbye, then disappeared behind the sliding steel doors.

"We'll take the next one." Jock waited, and then pressed the button again.

"Ranjit was charming and so well informed." Okki clung to Nisha's arm. "Thank you for introducing me. So where does he fit into your master plan, Jock?"

"Come to Uppsala and find out."

Nisha edged the Jensen out into the evening traffic and headed towards her apartment in the affluent Hauz Khas district of the Green City. Okki was amazed that security was even tighter here than at the hotel. Despite the noise made by the security guards slamming the bonnet and dragging a mirror underneath the lowered suspension, the front seat passenger continued to snore gently.

Jock's eyes rolled open when the engine was turned off. He climbed out and turned his sleepy head back into the car to kiss Okki goodnight. He grabbed his bag from the boot and set off up the two flights of stairs, fumbling for his keys.

Nisha powered back up the drive and headed towards the outskirts of the urban sprawl. The traffic was light and they made good speed. "Project Amrita will be a major breakthrough for humanity. Jock's right – we can create a sustainable quality of life for everyone on earth."

"This magma project of Ranjit's, you mean?" Okki winced as the bright lights of an oncoming truck flashed across the windscreen. She ducked below the dashboard when she realised the truck was on their side of the road. At the very last second, it swerved back across the median.

"No, something far more exciting. The technology's already there for Ranjit and his team. We just need to make the applications far more robust and commercially viable." Nisha found a recently repaired stretch of road and let the V8 rip, pinning them both to the seats amid whoops of delight.

"What then? C'mon, Nisha, you know you can trust me, I won't tell anyone."

"All right, let me explain . . ."

An hour later Okki had said goodnight to Nisha and was gazing up at the starlight filtering through a tangle of ashoka trees on the edge of the field centre. A pale moon was hiding behind distant clouds and the humid air was heavy with the chirruping sounds of India at night.

As she put the key in her door, she heard movement in the bushes away to her right. She was about to call out but strangled the cry. The late hour would only disturb the much-needed sleep of the other volunteers. Tomorrow was another important day in the project and they would need all their strength.

Once inside she locked the door and put on the bedside light. She decided against taking a shower and started to undress for bed. She had just lifted up the mosquito netting when she heard a noise. Someone was tapping on the window.

*   *   *

It was well after midnight when Nisha slipped into her apartment. She could hear snoring coming from the bedroom.

Jock's bag had been dumped in the lounge and clothes were strewn over the bedroom floor.

After a short prayer giving gratitude to her two favourite deities, she climbed in and buried her head beneath the duvet onto his smooth chest. As her eyes closed, out of the darkness, she could make out a familiar face smiling back at her. It was a youthful, innocent face she hadn't seen in a long, long time.

As the darkness faded into the dream, she became aware of her surroundings. The scented blossom on the trees. The fresh spring flowers. She remembered the place, knew exactly where they were. The overhanging willow; their favourite little park by the river.

He was kneeling down, the twinkle in his eye a reflection of the small cluster of diamonds in the ring. The early morning light was behind him, casting a halo around his tangle of unmanageable brown hair.

She held out her hand and he slipped the ring onto her finger. He stood and wrapped his arms around her. They drifted slowly out of the park gate and up the hill, onto the cobbled streets of the old town.

Nisha felt the warmth of the sun's rays on her face. She squeezed the hand of the man she trusted and believed in. He was her soul mate, her first true love.

She closed her eyes as they strolled, the only sound coming from the chiming of the bells in the 16th-century clock tower that seemed to be blessing their union from on high.

CHAPTER 10

The movement was deliberate, almost rehearsed.

The Choirmaster was not a graceful man but the way he leaned over and took the girl's arm was just like the action of an experienced doctor. He pressed in the needle, pushing the clear liquid directly into the vein. The attendant wiped off the pinprick of blood and covered the spot with a small plaster.

No sooner had they stepped away than her eyes opened. Large and almond-shaped, they appeared black in the dull, red lighting. They fixed on the Choirmaster, holding him in a steady gaze.

Niklas assumed he had given her a sedative or, worse, something much stronger. But was this what he was supposed to think? He needed to get out of the room. He felt the bile rising in his hot, dry throat. Did he say AIDS? Tuberculosis? How had she got here, to Switzerland, through the most rigorous airport security systems in the world?

As he looked down at the pathetic creature, she slowly turned her head towards him. Her look burned itself through the protective goggles into his very soul. The child's face was expressionless, calm, resigned. But it was the look in her eyes he knew he would always remember. She was accusing him, blaming him for what had happened. He bore witness and did nothing to stop it.

Her eyes remained fixed until the eyelids slowly closed. Her breathing stopped. There was no more coughing, no more movement. The child was dead.

The attendant unclipped a brake and pushed the trolley over to the door. Niklas could sense that the Choirmaster saw the child as no more than a piece of meat, a carcass, uncovered, stripped of any human trace. The body had almost dissolved before his eyes, melting into the thin mattress, becoming part of it.

He felt outrage, disgust, and he wanted to shout out. This is not Der Sangerbund. The Cantata would never agree to this. This is not what we believe in. This is murder – cold-blooded murder. This has nothing to do with western civilisation, or our values, or our way of life. This is wrong.

But he remained silent. The pressure to throw up was becoming too great. He was relieved when the Choirmaster led the way back to the lift. By comparison, the air in the corridor was tepid and stale but it was at least breathable. The feelings of nausea were soon gone. Niklas looked back to see the attendant pushing the trolley towards a door labelled Boiler Room. He felt a sudden blast of heat before the trolley was pushed through and the door closed behind it.

Niklas could feel his head spinning. They were back in the room on the sixth floor, to the familiar brown curtains; nothing had moved. It was like nothing had happened. He knew by now the flames would have devoured her pathetic little body, leaving no trace that she ever existed. Had he imagined the whole terrible scene?

But her eyes kept burning into him. He was a silent witness. He did nothing to stop it. He could have protested. He could have saved her. There are drugs, treatments, medical care. She could have recovered, gone on to lead a healthy life. How many more victims were there like her?

"You murdered her," Niklas blurted out, almost in disbelief.

"How could I? She didn't exist." He poured himself some water.

Niklas wanted a glass, to quench the thirst, but the shame prevented him. Would it even be water? Nothing was certain now about the Choirmaster, about Der Sangerbund. But was this the work of Der Sangerbund or the vile sadistic cruelty of a deranged madman?

"Niklas, she was dead the minute she was abandoned. She had no value to anybody. I merely released her from the burden."

"You killed her, for Christ's sake!!" His outburst met with no reaction.

"Choose your words carefully." The reply was cold, measured. "Please remember, it was you who brought Project Amrita to the Cantata. It was you that told us about Henning's involvement and SINAC and the work of Dr Nisha Patel. It is you that wants to become a *Voice*, Niklas."

Niklas was cursing his ambition, his loyalty to Der Sangerbund and the Choirmaster. But it was too late now to go back. How would this play out? He was too revolted and too scared to think about it.

He must have taken a taxi back to the airport. He didn't remember boarding the plane or the safety video. The flight attendant had to help him buckle up when the seat belt sign illuminated.

As they began their descent into Stockholm, he looked out of the tiny window for reassurance that he was nearly home. In the reflection, all he could see were her eyes. He knew then she would never let him go until her death – and the deaths of millions like her – was finally avenged.

• CHAPTER 11 •

"Is that seat taken?"

"It will be when you get in, Bjorn." Okki raised a ripple of laughter from the half-awake volunteers scrunched into the overcrowded Land Rover. He bent over as he climbed in, awkwardly pulling the door closed behind him.

In a cloud of diesel fumes the vehicle trudged out of the compound and headed off on its familiar journey into the wilderness, bringing up the rear of a small convoy.

"You missed the meeting last night so I thought I'd update you." He was rummaging through his rucksack and eventually found a chewed scrap of paper.

Okki was tempted to tell him all about her experiences with Einstein and radioactive decay but decided to stay quiet. Instead she studied him closely.

Bjorn Slagle could only have originated from one country in the world. His singing accent brought a lilting drama to each handpicked word. He was no doubt attractive to most women, but Okki found him cold and standoffish. The rumour that he was bisexual seemed groundless but it did create an air of uncertainty about him. Proceed with caution was her intuitive position.

He told her that more funding had been released for the school project, which would now have a septic tank in the block with twin flushing toilets directly above it. There would be girls' and boys' cubicles with an airtight valve to keep out the smell. He was trying to explain the drainage system using the paper diagram.

"We're bringing in a generator to pump more water from the well at the far end of the village. There'll be a header tank on the roof, which will be strengthened to take the weight, and kitted out with solar panels. This should provide enough electricity for lighting and basic classroom equipment," Bjorn continued.

Okki raised an eyebrow.

"And before you ask," Bjorn said, getting his retaliation in first, "the funding won't stretch to mains cabling or access to telecom networks or the Internet, but it's a start. SINAC will pick up the running costs for the generator and any maintenance bills."

"You know the real question though, don't you?" Okki asked; she was flexing her shoulder muscles in anticipation.

"Yes, I'm ahead of you. We don't expect you to dig out the space for a tank by hand, line it with water-resistant concrete and sort out the plumbing." Bjorn flipped the paper over. "We're putting Steve and Will into your team next week once they've finished the header tank installation."

"So there'll be five of us on the school project?"

"Yes, and we'd like you to be team leader, if that's OK?"

"Perfectly OK. It will give me a chance to practise my delegation skills and get the boys to do all the heavy work."

Bjorn didn't rise to the bait. "There's another meeting tonight for team leaders. We'll sign off the project so far and map out the next three months' work. It's in the canteen after dinner." Bjorn tweaked his left stud earring, which Okki decided was a tell of some kind.

"Sorry, I'm making up a foursome for dinner tonight with Nisha, Jock and an important guest ... well, they told me he was important. Can you take some notes and I'll catch up with you over breakfast tomorrow?"

The vehicle slowed as it pulled off the metal road onto the dirt track. Okki knew it would be hopeless trying to continue the conversation as they bounced around through the bush. She watched a "mission accomplished" look sweep across his face as he leaned back in his seat.

By the time Okki got to the school, the two Dutch girls were already hard at work. Annie One downed tools and came over. "Okki, we're so sorry about last night. We didn't mean to frighten you."

"It's OK, I was fine. In fact, it's reassuring to know I have such good neighbours." Okki put down her bag and reached for the shovel.

Annie Two wiped the sweat off her brow. "We'd heard noises and wanted to check you were OK. The compound can be quite spooky at night. That perimeter fence is not very secure. We've had people following us sometimes."

"Thank you, I do appreciate it. Did you go to the meeting last night?"

The girls smiled at each other.

"Oh yes," Annie One replied, "best meeting so far. About time we had some boys to play with."

"She's only joking, team leader. We think it's great that we'll now be building something we can all be proud of." Annie Two poured a soothing dose of political correctness over the situation, as ever.

"By the way, Okki, how was your lecture? It sounded fascinating – light waves, wasn't it?" Annie One probed.

"Yes, it was a real eye opener. I wish I'd taken science more seriously at school. Anyway, I'll tell you all about it later. We've got toilets to dig."

CHAPTER 12

Jock complained about the traffic all the way out to the field centre. He'd nearly written off the Jensen twice. Nisha wished she'd driven. "How do you live with this chaos?"

"It's my home," she replied. They'd covered this ground before. This particular conversation had started over plans for the wedding. Delhi or Singapore? Jock had to admit no one organised a wedding quite like Indian families.

Nisha checked her watch. This was most out of character. The timing today was critical. She flicked on her phone; still no signal. There was nothing else for it, she announced, as she set off at a brisk jog.

Salmon pink was washing the grey out of the timid clouds overhead. The heat was building already. As she ran, her mane of black hair rippled in waves over her shoulders. She passed a small group of volunteers huddled together in the half-light. They were standing over piles of equipment and enough rations to see them through another long day at the village.

Jock added their rucksacks to the pile as he jogged after her, long, spindly legs pumping clumsily. The ground had churned up in places with the overnight rain. He skipped his way around glistening puddles of sticky mud.

"You youngsters, it's hard to keep up," he wheezed.

"Not even two years' difference, that doesn't count. Anyway, it's not about age; it's about alcohol. I saw you finish the bottle last night." She stopped as they reached the corner. Single-storey buildings stretched off to the right along an unmade track.

"I couldn't let a good claret go to waste."

"Feeble excuse. If you were a Hindu you would eschew strong drink ... then maybe you wouldn't be talking when you should be listening." She fired him a playful glance as she set off again.

"But I'm not a Hindu," he parried, trying to keep pace, "and, besides, claret is not mere alcohol. It is the elixir of life, as my mother used to say. God rest her soul."

"I wish I'd met her. Both of us could've knocked some sense into you."

"OK, rewind. What do you mean by 'should be listening'?" Jock caught her arm.

Nisha pulled up. "Project Amrita is on track. It will improve the lives of millions of people who will rely on your generosity and savvy commercial skills for their very survival. I'm not sure 'nice one, Ingmar, now let's get a proper drink' was quite the right sound bite for such an historic occasion."

She turned towards him, hands firmly planted on hips. "He must have been shattered. He'd only flown in the day before."

"I was happy. Is that such a crime? It was a big day for all of us. Just like today only different. That was about business success. Today is about ... is about ... well, it's about shit really."

"So eloquent. *It's about shit*. Our next Gandhi speaks to his people." She looked up in time to trace the arc of two green parrots as they squawked across into a nearby tree. Daylight was fast approaching.

"OK, I promise, I'll never be happy again. Let's move on. So which one are we looking for?" He was studying the flimsy signage dotted at random along the track.

"Brown door, number thirty-one ... over there." She pointed towards a miniature doll's house, a uniform bungalow block second from the end of the increasingly uneven track, near where it was swallowed up by a clump of trees. "The curtains are still closed. I don't get it. She didn't have that much to drink. She must have been back well before eleven o'clock."

Nisha banged on the door. No movement. She peered through the glass. A thin break in the old moth-eaten curtains gave a glimpse of a darkened room beyond. No signs of life. She tried the handle. Locked.

Jock checked his watch. The vehicles would be arriving soon. They couldn't be late, not today. There was nothing else for it, he decided. He would take any consequences. He moved Nisha to one side and squared up his right shoulder. She thought about stopping him but quickly changed her mind. Okki might need them. It seemed the right thing to do.

The brown door offered no resistance, the frame shattering into thousands of splinters and detaching itself from the crumbling plasterboard walls. Inside the darkness was cloying and sticky sweet. The room was airless and heavy with the pungent smells of leaf mould and rotting vegetation.

A thermal of mosquitoes danced around a virginal white shroud draped over a made-up bed. Their high-pitched whine was barely audible over the distant rumble of diesel engines.

"The Land Rovers. We must go," he whispered. "Looks like she didn't sleep here last night."

"Let me check round first," Nisha insisted.

Jock pulled hard at the curtains, which almost brought the ceiling pole down. Caramel light oozed in through grimy windows. The rattan furniture had seen better days and threadbare rugs were thrown loosely over rough wooden flooring. He stood quite still, took a slow, deep breath and looked carefully around the room. Then he noticed it. Or rather, he didn't notice it.

Luggage. Personal possessions. Photographs. Clothes. In fact, anything at all. The room was bare. Completely bare.

Silence.

"You OK in there?" He turned towards the bathroom door, a yawning void that had pulled Nisha inside.

Silence became a murmur; the murmur a low sobbing noise and eventually an earthquake of emotion powered out through the emptiness.

He ran across the room, almost tripping over a rug, and flicked the switch, flooding the cramped bathroom with tired, yellow light. The nightmare before him etched itself with hard serrated slashes into the backs of his eyes.

The forlorn figure before him was swaying with uncontrolled convulsions while she tried in vain to steady the body swinging from the roof beam. Great sobs rang out as she wrapped herself around the pale, white legs. Nisha was pushing upwards, trying to take the weight, trying to free some slack into the short thick cord protruding above the lifeless head.

He rushed to help her but it was too late; too late by many hours. The ice-cold skin now belonged to a mannequin already cast deep into rigor mortis. Her flaming red hair was limp and had lost all its sheen. Her body was still wrapped in the dress from last night but there were no shoes and no watch on the left wrist, which hung frozen in space. Okki had showed it off over dinner, a 21st-birthday present from her proud parents. Ingmar had read the inscription on the back.

At last Nisha let go and threw her arms around him. She buried her head into his chest and wept. He looked at the rim of the bath. Too narrow. He went back into the bedroom and looked for a strong chair. There was one next to the bed. As he grabbed it, a sealed white envelope fluttered innocuously onto the rug beside him. He picked it up.

He took the chair back into the bathroom and set it down next to her. Nisha was perched awkwardly on the edge of the bath. A shadow gently passed over her like a loose sail on a calm sea.

"I found this," he announced almost to himself. "It's typewritten and signed but not addressed."

She looked up, mascara streaked across her face. She was searching for some clue, some explanation, some release from the nightmare. "What does it say?"

He managed to croak a response. "It's a suicide note."

• CHAPTER 13 •

3–1.

The ball was tossed to the other side of the court.

Dr Katherine Shosanya – known to all inside The Klinkenhammer Foundation as Kitty – made sure she had one foot in the service box as she thwacked another winner. The ball kissed the side wall at just the wrong height for her struggling opponent, before dying gracefully into the back corner.

4–1.

"Kitty, you could at least take off your track suit."

The pounding was relentless. Hannah managed to return the next serve but Kitty was dominant on the T and cracked another forehand off the front wall, an inch above the tin. It shot away like a tracer bullet.

5–1.

When Hannah finally reached the sanctuary of the oak-panelled locker room, it was with a combination of relief, exhaustion and some celebration. To have taken the last game off her younger opponent was worth all the pain that she knew was yet to come limping back to the office.

As Kitty stripped off before slipping into the showers, Hannah could only admire the perfection of muscular power and elegant beauty encapsulated within her diminutive frame. The scar from a bullet wound on her right thigh was barely visible.

Kitty's black skin glistened in the torrent of steaming hot water. As she rubbed honey and oatmeal conditioner into her short frizzy hair, she filled the echoing chamber of the Lexington Racquets Club with the gospel voice of an angel.

The rooftop cafe looked out over the Upper East Side through a curved glass canopy. Some of the windows had been opened to let a summer breeze cool the members as they gathered round the juice bar.

"Thanks for looking after Trigger last weekend, Kitty. We do appreciate it." Hannah slurped her fresh orange and paw paw smoothie.

"Oh, he's a big softy. I enjoyed it, any time. It's a great pad you have there. I love the bed in your spare room, so comfy."

"So how are you finding life in New York?" Hannah sucked up the juicy bits at the bottom.

Kitty returned the smiles from two fit young men as they took their drinks over to a corner table. She took off her large black-framed Dolce & Gabbana glasses and placed them deliberately on the marble top.

"We came here on holiday years ago. I just fell in love with the place. It's so sassy and in your face. When you asked me to move here, I couldn't believe I was so lucky."

Hannah waved the glass for another. "You're doing a fantastic job, Kitty. You make it look easy."

"I never did thank you for saving my life." Kitty smiled. "Without you, the police would've locked me up and thrown away the key."

"And I never thanked you for Ally. She'd lost all hope. I can't believe how quickly she recovered."

Kitty finished her drink. "That procedure was so difficult. This intravenous therapy is much quicker."

"When'll you be through?"

"Where are we now, June? I reckon by September. I'm getting great support from the medical profession. Whatever you said to them certainly did the trick." Kitty added.

They took the lift down and made their way out onto the quiet Manhattan streets. As they waited for the lights on Park Avenue, Hannah noticed the stunning array of flowers in the central median. All along the boulevard the trees were in full leaf and birdsong was layered over the burble of the light morning traffic.

"Any chance you could get wrapped up by August? I've got another job for you." Hannah felt a jabbing reminder from her aching calf muscles as she skipped onto the pavement.

"For you, boss, anything. Where's the action?" Kitty led the way towards Fifth Avenue. The Klinkenhammer Foundation's concrete and glass entrance was just across the road from the park gates. "Hannah, do you know that guy?"

"What guy?" Hannah looked across the street to where Kitty was pointing.

"A tall guy in a smart, grey suit. He's been following us from the club." Kitty shrugged. "He was right over there."

"Following you more like it," Hannah suggested. "When you get to my age, men don't follow you anymore."

"I think you're wrong. He was looking right at you. Anyway, what's this job you got for me?"

"My Head of Diabetes Research could use some help. It was a gamble appointing Lawrence. I know he'll work out in time."

Kitty smiled. "The office grapevine's been busy. I heard he was struggling."

Hannah let out a sigh. "I've worked with some of his team for years. I can't believe how negative they've been towards him."

"They say love is blind."

"Who says?" Hannah snapped back at the mischievous grin.

"They do. Everyone does. Shakespeare, wasn't it? 'Love

looks not with the eyes, but with the mind. And therefore is winged Cupid painted blind', or something like that."

"They just won't listen to him. Unless something gives, heads will have to roll. I need you on the case," Hannah continued. "He's a good guy with some great ideas."

"It's office gossip, Hannah, that's all. Don't let it get to you. I'd be delighted to help. You two make a great couple. Lawrence is a good man." Kitty swiped her card and pulled open the door leading off the lobby. "Much kinder than my ex, anyway."

As they breezed down a long corridor, Kitty confided that her husband had taken his chance with her New York move to end their marriage. "I hope he's happy with his new woman."

"Was it four children?"

"Five, aged fourteen down to eight months. He blamed me for not giving him a son. Now he's got three of them and two daughters."

"You don't miss him?"

"Nope. Nor any guys, come to that. I've put men on hold for now. In a city like this, I'm not short of offers."

"I bet."

"The look on their faces when they try it on and I answer them back in Afrikaans."

Hannah pushed the button. "Did you say you were moving from Brownsville?"

"Yeah, the apartment's great but it's too far out. I'm moving to Hell's Kitchen, just off West Forty-third Street. It's smaller but I can cycle here."

They took the lift to the third floor. Kitty opened the meeting room door and flicked on the light. "How was your trip, by the way?"

"India was a real eye opener. We'd need longer next time. And the conference was an inspiration. We must make some real progress in diabetes research. That's why I want you behind Lawrence."

Kitty was reaching for the water jug when the door burst open. Lawrence flustered in and threw himself into a swivel chair. He dumped an armful of files onto the clean glass surface of the table.

"Tough day, huh?" Hannah tried to lighten his mood.

Lawrence looked exasperated. "We had a brainstorm session yesterday. I want ideas on what causes Type 1 diabetes. I prompted, encouraged, rewarded ... I did everything right by the fucking book ... sorry, Kitty, pardon my French."

"No apology needed." She had to hold it in; this was not the time for uncontrolled laughter.

"There are three hundred and forty-seven million diabetics in the world. The disease has maimed and killed millions." His anger was pumping. "I asked them to get back to me *in plain English*."

He pinched his eyes in disbelief and read out one of the replies. "We know that the release of insulin is strongly inhibited by norepinephrine which leads to increased blood glucose levels during stress. The release of catecholamine by the sympathetic nervous system has conflicting influences on insulin release by beta cells. More research is needed into this area."

The two women sat in silence as Lawrence ripped the page into little pieces. "If that's plain English, then I'm Lady Gaga."

After handing him a glass of cold water, Hannah put on her best Mother Teresa smile. "They're testing you out. This is a marathon, not a hundred-metre sprint. Be more patient, you're loosening them up."

"I'll settle for five thousand metres but no further. Diabetes is a killer and it's getting worse. You heard the numbers last weekend. We must beat it."

"And we will. But it's a team game, Lawrence. Kitty has agreed to ride shotgun for you. She can cover your back and help you bring in some fresh blood."

Lawrence looked pleasantly surprised. "Kitty, welcome on board. Working with a friendly face will certainly make a change."

Kitty hesitated over the high fives and went for the hug instead. "I've got to go now, guys, but, Lawrence, flick me a diary date for your next meeting. At least I can help you dish out some laxatives."

Hannah waited for the door to close before kissing him. "I'm so glad she's here. She's a real dynamo round this place."

Later that morning, Hannah took Lawrence's hand as they left the building. She was going to call a cab but he insisted they should walk, cutting through Central Park. Hannah stretched her leg muscles and agreed the walk was a good idea.

"Why didn't Toby say he was a Type 1 diabetic?" Hannah prompted.

"In his email he said he thought I knew. Maybe he was embarrassed or didn't know how to tell me. Anyway this could work in our favour."

Lawrence checked the GPS as they passed a playground full of mums with toddlers playing in the sunshine. He pointed towards a tall building rising high above the lush green canopy and took the left-hand fork. "How do you mean, work in our favour?" Hannah took his hand again, squeezed it.

Lawrence explained that, with a newly opened sales office in New York, Toby was looking to strengthen ties this side of the pond. A partnership with The Klinkenhammer Foundation could get him into the American Diabetes Society and open up a new customer base.

"I get it: he donates to us, we help him sell software; everyone wins, I guess. Tell him we take card or cheque." She smiled.

As they passed through the park gates, Lawrence spotted the building across the street. They just made it as the light began to flash. Lawrence checked the floor number. "He'd had an email from Okki. Apparently she's now thinking about medicine after her gap year, thanks to you. She'd enjoyed that physics lecture with Jock and Nisha and decided science wasn't so tough after all."

"She'd be great as a doctor." Hannah moved aside as the lift passengers streamed out. "Compassion for patients is half the battle. What floor?"

As the lift doors closed, Hannah thought she recognised a tall, distinguished man in a pale-grey suit entering the lobby.

• CHAPTER 14 •

After Toby had shown them round, Hannah concluded the dreary office looked like so many others, with one major exception.

The view looking down on Central Park from the boardroom was truly spectacular. She'd grown up in New York, yet never failed to be amazed by the foresight of the planners who had created an oasis of calm in the heart of such a frantic city. From the fourteenth floor she could pick every detail. Sunlight was reflecting off The Klinkenhammer Foundation Building away to her right, beyond the carpet of green.

Toby could see the delight in her eyes and suggested they sit facing the windows. The restaurant on Seventh Avenue was booked for 1 p.m. The morning interviews had been a waste of time so a good lunch was called for, Toby announced. Max was saying goodbye to the last candidate before joining them.

The first thing Hannah noticed about the man entering the boardroom was his moustache. She couldn't tell if the ends had been waxed but, if they were, it would be entirely in keeping. He was comfortably over six feet tall, judging by the way he subconsciously stooped as he walked in. His plain, charcoal-grey suit fitted his slender frame too well for an off-the-peg brand. The perfectly creased trousers had been hung by an artist and were only allowed to brush the very top of his laces.

The two-button jacket was finished with hand-stitched edging and displayed just the right amount of Emile Borghese silk shirt in silver white. Gleaming black shoes were designed to walk on gold leaf or cashmere carpeting. Down his front a slash of red tie with highlights of yellow. Hannah noticed Cambridge blue stars came out as he got closer.

"Max Hartley, my CEO," Toby enthused. He'd prepared them well for this introduction.

"Pleased to meet you, Max." Lawrence stood for the occasion, his hand wilting from the iron grip. Woven gold cufflinks flashed briefly during the ritual handshakes, then retreated into their woollen cave.

Hannah's legs nearly buckled as she stood up, reminding her of the morning's squash. The handshake finished her off. She noticed the room had filled with the scent of freshly squeezed bergamot oranges laced with undertones of sandalwood and cloves.

It was one of Max's own creations, Toby had explained. Wing Commander Hartley's passion for aftershave developed during the first Gulf War. His nose had been educated by an old Bedouin trader he met in Al Qatif, a Jeep ride away from his base in Dhahran. Max had subsequently persuaded Toby himself to sample the delights of Jeavons in Jermyn Street, arguably the last London emporium to encourage their clientele to create their own infusions, or so Hannah was told.

"Sorry to delay our lunch appointment, Toby, bit of a crisis, I'm afraid. Can I take a few minutes?" Max was clutching a handful of paperwork.

Hannah and Lawrence remained standing. Lawrence suggested they should leave, which Toby waved away, citing his trustworthiness under the Rotary Four Way Test, the fundamental creed that all Rotarians obeyed.

Rotary founder, Paul Harris, required Rotarians to be honest, law-abiding citizens who believed in telling the truth. Hannah acknowledged Toby's nod of acceptance and lowered herself back into the boardroom chair. She was momentarily dazzled by the flash of silver lining from Max's jacket.

"It's our friends in Geneva again. I get the feeling we are being used as a stalking horse." Max had taken the next chair and was laying out pieces of paper for Toby's informed gaze.

"Looks like the CRM system has been hijacked by persons unknown on the sixth floor. We've just received this email from the Director of Security and Compliance, a Herr Doktor Klaus Buchwald."

"Buchwald? I thought Herr Schwartz was the compliance guy? How many directors do they have, for God's sake?" Toby held up his hands, inviting a divine response.

"If you're the pride of the Swiss banking community, you can have as many directors as you like, I suppose." Max produced his *pièce de résistance*, a single page of creamy white parchment, complete with gold, embossed letterhead.

"Buchwald is saying access to client information can only be granted by the relevant section head –" Max wafted the scented air with his paper "– and in case we didn't quite understand his wishes, this communication arrived by courier here, this morning."

"But this is ridiculous." Toby caught the puzzled look on Lawrence's face. "Sorry, Lawrence, our best-paying client but always a handful. Our contacts want all client information held in one database for marketing and account management purposes, but the bank operates a patchwork of ramshackle old systems."

"A bit like Switzerland itself," Max added. "Petty fiefdoms, independent cantons, worlds within worlds, all vying for power and control. The Borgias had nothing on this lot."

"Some bank clients can hold a private investment account," Toby explained, "a corporate business account, a family trust, an offshore portfolio, equities in obscure legal entities or pension schemes . . . the list goes on. We're trying to tidy it up and give them a full picture of their clients' business interests."

"But knowledge is power," Max said, continuing with their education, "and clearly Buchwald has had his cage rattled by someone fearful of the new database. The bank itself owns a large number of European companies, offshore assets, gold and oil reserves, which are managed by their Corporate Affairs Division. Having an electronic record of which clients sit on which boards and who owns what could be very damaging information in the wrong hands. I'm sure a few government tax agencies would pay folding money for a quick peek below the duvet."

"Well, they'll have to sort it out between themselves – calculators at dawn or something." Toby made a note of the signatory and handed the letter back.

Max delivered his *coup de grâce*. "But until this issue is resolved, Buchwald is putting our CRM project on hold . . . and sitting on our invoices."

"He can't do that! It will screw us up for the year-end. Fuck!"

"Toby, I'll need to reply to this. Is that OK?"

Toby got the nod of assent from Lawrence and Hannah. Max checked his watch and asked for fifteen to twenty minutes, confirming he'd let the restaurant know. "Perhaps Herr Buchwald can be persuaded to loosen the reins. I'll book for Galileo's, overlooking the lake."

"Good thinking, Max. If he's in compliance, chances are he thinks the rules apply to everyone else." Toby raised an ironic smile.

"One more thing, the next candidate has withdrawn so we're clear now until four p.m. It will help our digestion."

As the door closed, a calming silence filled the room.

"You're right, Toby, very impressive. Where did you find him?" Lawrence ventured.

"Max is another example of the commercial world's abuse of our distinguished servicemen. These guys lead action-packed lives in the armed forces, then sniff the money washing along Civvy Street only to find they hit a wall of discrimination."

Lawrence raised an eyebrow.

"Max flew Tornados over Baghdad before trying his hand as a test pilot with British Airways. When they stopped investing in new planes and his job settled back into the long-haul routine, he moved into software sales with an avionics developer. He just hated it."

Toby poured some water. "I suppose he still had romantic dreams of making a difference but soon discovered it was all about key performance indicators, sales targets and schmoozing overpaid purchasing managers in the airline industry. I met him at a trade fair and gave him a chance to impress me. He'd been in command of sixty air and ground crew in wartime with the RAF, for God's sake, yet his employer wouldn't let him sign off his own expenses." Toby leaned back in the chair. "He's been the best CEO Kampion has ever had. I'd be lost without him."

Lawrence suggested Max was a good man to have on the team. With the company working smoothly under his control, Toby could be released for high level sales targeting and to pursue other business interests.

"Talking of which –" Hannah picked her moment, handing Toby a signed contract "– The Klinkenhammer Foundation would be delighted to welcome you to our Sponsorship Programme. Just sign here, please. The timing of your offer couldn't have been better. We are about to launch major new research into the causes of Type 1 diabetes. Your funding will help towards the trial costs."

"Sounds exciting; count us in. So what's the angle? Diabetes research in the UK seems to have stalled, the agencies going back over old ground." Toby countersigned the contract and handed it back.

As he did so, the boardroom door flew open. The man standing before them was not the same man who had danced out of the room a few minutes earlier. Hannah thought his salt and pepper hair looked dishevelled. His moustache was drooping somehow and the rosy colour had drained from his handsome features.

"What is it, Max? You look awful." Toby stated.

"Toby, I'm so sorry. I don't know how to tell you . . ."

• CHAPTER 15 •

Dad

I'm sorry it had to end this way but I really can't go on.

There is so much misery in the world. I don't want to be part of it anymore. How can we treat people this way? They are human beings like us, yet nobody cares. It's terrible. There will never be an end to their suffering. I feel so useless.

I'm giving everything to the poor. They need it more than me. I'm one less mouth to feed.

You gave me so much but I'm not worth it. Help them now; it's too late for me.

Give my love to Mum.

Octavia

The note had been scanned, attached to an email and printed out. Hannah re-read it. It was signed but the signature wasn't clear. Nothing was clear.

They tried to console him. Toby had buried his head. After a few moments, he looked up and grabbed the paper, forcing himself to look at it again through bloodshot eyes. Hannah could see the shock turning to anger across his face, a volcanic eruption powering to the surface, ready to explode.

"She did *not* write this," he blurted out and screwed up the paper, slamming his hand down, making the room shake. "That's not her signature."

"Toby, you need some time. I'm so sorry." Max retrieved the crumpled paper from the floor. Hannah could see Toby wasn't listening.

"I want to know exactly what he said. I want to talk to him. Now. Call him back," Toby insisted.

"We mustn't call him; it will only make things worse." Max lowered the pitch of his voice, slowed his words. Hannah could sense it was the Wing Commander talking, no doubt his RAF training to relieve tension, to deflect emotion into a more controlled response.

"How the fuck could it *be* any worse? She's gone, my baby's gone." Toby went to stand but his legs buckled and he crashed back into the chair.

Lawrence spoke quietly. "Toby, you've got to give yourself some time. Dealing with the police is never straightforward, especially the Indian police from what I've seen first-hand. You can't go making allegations without knowing the facts, it could obstruct any investigation. You need to rest . . . we're here for you."

A fresh tray of glasses and iced water was brought in. They drank in silence before Toby took a slow, deep breath and looked up. "From the beginning please, Max. I am listening . . . oh God."

Max had taken a call from Senior Constable Chaudray in the New Delhi police. He'd asked for Toby but his English was very poor. Max tried to explain that he wasn't available and to send an email or leave a message.

Chaudray told him that his daughter had been found hanging in her room at a university field centre on the outskirts of the city. They presumed suicide because of the note, which he then emailed over. They will conduct an investigation but it may take some time because of a backlog. They get five suicides every day in New Delhi, Chaudray had told him.

"It was such a bad line . . . his English was . . ." Max choked. "She was a gorgeous kid."

"I don't believe this . . . she was so happy when I left her . . . she was talking about Uppsala . . . she'd decided on doing medicine." Toby grabbed the paper back. "Hannah, Lawrence, you were with her on Monday. Did she look so unhappy to you?"

"Toby, we don't know the facts or what she was thinking. People who commit suicide aren't thinking straight . . . it may be that . . ." Lawrence's words dried in his mouth.

"Look . . . here." The fire was blazing again in Toby's eyes. "She always called me Pops, since she was a little girl . . . never Dad. *Hi Pops*, that's how she started every email."

Hannah looked across at Max for a lead but he was lost in his own thoughts.

"And Mum?" Toby continued. "Wanda was always Mummy, never Mum. And Octavia? She's Okki, always Okki, for Christ's sake."

Toby gulped down a mouthful of air and looked Max full in the face. "She's been killed . . . murdered. I just know it."

"Toby, it's too early to think that." Max was shaking his head.

"Max, did this policeman, Chaudray, say anything about releasing her body? Where is she now?" Hannah glanced across at Lawrence as she spoke. He seemed to understand.

"There'll have to be an autopsy. Suicide is illegal in India, he said, so various authorities need to be involved," Max explained. "I had some dealings with Indian officialdom during my Air Force days. They can be infuriatingly slow at paperwork."

Max needed to excuse himself and make some calls. Soon after he had left the room, Toby struggled to sit upright. "I must go to her, bring her home. I want to know what happened. I want the truth. And I want to catch the bastard that did this."

"You can't go alone, Toby. Lawrence will go with you." Hannah's mind was swirling.

Lawrence was expecting her offer, supported her intention. "Yes, Toby, we'll go together. We'll get to the truth. Together."

"No, it's very kind of you but . . . I'll take Max. I can't impose on you like this."

"Toby, we're your friends, you wouldn't be imposing. We want to find out what's really happened." Hannah was picking her words. "You need Max here, to keep things running. You and Lawrence should go." Toby had drifted into a trance-like state. Hannah stayed with him as Lawrence went to find Max, who was fumbling with the printer in the main office. He explained to Max what they had agreed. Max immediately jumped online and booked their flights. He emailed Chaudray to let him know what was happening.

They managed to get the last two rooms at the Nirvana International Hotel in Delhi; it was almost fully booked out with the Indian Cement Manufacturers Annual Conference. Lawrence was happy they'd have at least some familiarity to start their enquiries.

On the way back through Central Park, Hannah could hear her stomach growling. She'd lost most of her appetite but needed to eat something. It had been a long day. She made a detour to her favourite hot dog stand and treated them both to a chilli dog. They found a bench in the shade, and Lawrence took off his jacket.

"Straight question: do you think she topped herself?" Lawrence mumbled through the chilli sauce. They shared a bottle of cold water.

"I've been thinking about that. She was certainly

passionate, quite intense, I suppose. Red heads can be volatile, but with Okki . . . . I don't know. It's possible, I guess. We don't know what it's like living with such misery. Maybe something flipped her over the edge . . . who knows." Hannah wiped her hands, but only after licking the spicy sauce off her fingers.

Lawrence handed her the water. "I'm not sure either. She seemed a bit frustrated when we left her at the village. It must be tough turning up, day after day, seeing all the suffering, especially for the children. Then next minute, you're chauffeur-driven back to a cool shower, tasty meal and a comfortable bed. I could see how hopeless it could look."

They finished up and carried on walking past a colourful bed of gerberas in full bloom. Hannah stopped and pulled him to her. "I want you to look after yourself, you hear? I want you back in one piece. It's taken me all this time to find you. I don't want to lose you now."

The embrace brought derision from a passing skateboarder. Hannah didn't care. She kissed him again. "Toby'll be a handful. Don't let him lead you astray, promise?"

"I promise. You'll really miss me that much?"

They had reached the park gates. She hugged him. Traffic was streaming past, oblivious to their embrace.

"Han, you got any free time when you're in London next week?" Lawrence pushed for the flashing man to appear.

"Sure. The Alzheimer's MRI thing won't take all day . . . and Ally wouldn't mind a late dinner. Why do you ask?" The light changed and Lawrence led the charge, much to the annoyance of a yellow cab that thought he could just make it.

"I'm thinking about the Indian policemen we saw, the ones who took the back-handers? What if Chaudray and his team are well . . . you know . . ."

"Spit it out, lover boy. What do you want me to do?"

"Remember that British policeman we met last year, in Vienna. Can't think of his name."

Hannah scratched back through the memory of that crazy evening. It was cold, freezing cold. She'd never seen anyone look so pale. Like he'd seen a ghost. "Steven . . . Mole. Detective Sergeant Steven Mole. Yes, I remember him. He was kinda cute. Why?"

"Wasn't he based near London?" Lawrence held open the door.

"Guildford . . . for Christ's sake, Lawrence, tell me." She punched him on the shoulder.

As they slipped into the concrete and glass entrance of The Klinkenhammer Foundation building, Hannah failed to notice the tall man in a pale-grey suit sitting in a corner booth off the lobby, talking animatedly into his mobile phone.

CHAPTER 16

The Choirmaster sensed something was wrong as soon as he made the call. The drawling ring-tone meant he must be overseas. He'd only wanted answers to a few simple client queries. The twist in their conversation had taken him by surprise. He didn't like surprises.

"It's personal, OK? You got a problem with that? Want me to fill in a form or something?" The American's sarcasm grated. For sure, they'd had their differences over the years but the Choirmaster had never needed to question his loyalty. Never. Up until now, he'd had absolute trust in him. But trust must always be a virgin as the membrane can never be repaired.

To the Choirmaster, the voice sounded distant, worryingly distant. He was obviously in a cafe or a lobby somewhere judging by the background noise. *Could they be overheard? Was this confidential?* The call kept cutting out, adding to the frustration.

Loose ends that needed tidying up, he'd said. *But what loose ends? From when he lived in New York? Or was it something else? Or someone else?* It was a flying visit, just a long weekend; good to see Central Park again; he'd return to Switzerland on Monday.

But this wasn't like him. Just to disappear without saying anything. True, he'd always been a devious bastard but that's what made him the best investment banker in the business. That's why he'd hired him.

The Choirmaster disconnected and threw the mobile across his desk. A slow mouthful of single malt suddenly tasted sour. He was going to spit it out but swallowed it instead. Sometimes swallowing was what he had to do. Humiliation was a welcome relief. It carried no pressures of duty or responsibility. At that moment he begged for relief.

He put the glass down. The headache had been niggling all day. Now it was pressing into his eyes, making the strip lights overhead much too bright. He sidled across the office, unsteady on his feet, knocking a chair out of the way. He flicked the switch, staggered back, put on the green desk lamp.

Voices were whispering in his head. He tried to settle, gazing at a mosaic of figures on his screen. They were meaningless columns of numbers. The cursor blinked expectantly at him from the command box. But he had no commands left. His eyelids grew heavy. The edge of his vision was getting hazy, with a steady flutter of interference. *New York? Why New York? When did he leave?*

He was drawn over to the window by the softer evening light. A face he recognised was staring at him, etched into the glass. He tried to look straight through it. It was getting harder to do.

Silent shadows smothered Lake Geneva in darkness. Pealights from a flotilla of pleasure boats were dancing on calm waters. The last few yachts had furled their sails and were motoring back to the marina, making long, rippling vees in their wake, pinpricks of red and green puncturing the gloom.

What was he up to? The Choirmaster had no contingency for this. The man knew everything. Der Sangerbund must never be compromised. After all, he'd introduced this man into the ranks.

And what would his father think? As the previous Choirmaster, his father would never have tolerated any disloyalty. He'd fought the Russians to uphold the true German values that were the very foundation of Der Sangerbund and formed a bedrock of discipline within the Wehrmacht. *Tapfer und Treu.* Courageous and Loyal. He was a proud soldier, loyal to the flag. He'd be ashamed to think his own son had brought a traitor into their midst.

Was there anyone left who could be trusted? Niklas was loyal but he was weak. There was nothing else to be done. The Choirmaster himself would have to see this through. He had come too far to see things fail. If Uppsala went ahead, the consequences could be disastrous. There would be a new world order. It was unthinkable. The world must never be run by Orientals. He had to act now.

The face in the glass continued to stare at him. For a moment, it became his father, accusing him of dropping his guard, allowing his weakness to get the better of him. *You trusted this man? Now see what you've done. The Cantata will remove you. How could you let this happen?*

He must be strong. If the media wanted a circus, he would give them one. But it would be a circus of his choosing. Uppsala will be a media circus, he decided, but not the one everyone expects. The announcements must never happen. This must be stopped. And it must stop in that filthy hellhole called India.

The mobile rang several times before he answered it. He recognised the number. About time. What had taken so long?

"Did you get my message?"

"Yes."

"And?" The Choirmaster grew impatient.

"Suicide."

Although it was what he expected to hear, he knew how fickle the Indian police could be. A decision one day would change the next. He considered using local influence but didn't want to arouse too much attention. Any investigation might uncover coincidences and coincidences always created suspicion. Things were on track. He needed to be patient.

"Good. Then proceed."

CHAPTER 17

"Good evening sir and welcome back."

"Good evening." Lawrence recognised the barman. He panned around the empty room and saw what he was looking for.

"Can I get you something to drink?" The waiter was polishing a tall glass.

"Tomato juice, please."

"Lea & Perrins, sir? Ice?"

"No, thank you, just straight from the bottle is fine." He had remembered the warning about the ice. "That gentleman in the corner. Can I ask what he's drinking?"

"A most discerning and welcome guest at our hotel, sir; he was at the same conference as your good self only last weekend. He is enjoying our special twenty-five-year-old Glenmorangie single malt. He is a man that knows his whiskies."

"And how many whiskies has he known so far?" Lawrence slipped across a bank note.

The note disappeared into a pocket of the starched white jacket "Four, sir."

"He may well appreciate his whiskies but I'd rather he didn't broaden his knowledge any further tonight please; we have a busy day tomorrow."

"I understand, sir."

"Can you arrange a quiet table for two in the restaurant and bring over a couple of menus?"

"With pleasure, sir. Can I take your name and room number please?"

"McGlynn, Lawrence McGlynn, room one-seven-two-one."

"I shall be right over, sir."

Lawrence weaved his way between clusters of empty tables across a desert of sand-coloured carpet. He stopped by Toby's right shoulder, put his tomato juice down on a solid brass coaster and admired an enormous floor-to-ceiling aquarium. Magnified fresh-water fish drifted past with unblinking eyes, slowly wheeling around a central rock display featuring an incongruous lighthouse and the wreck of a Spanish galleon.

"Impressive isn't it? I don't recognise any of them apart from that lazy catfish." Toby put down his phone and pointed into the clear water at the far side of the tank.

"Toby, I need to get a couple of things off my chest." Lawrence was now sitting bolt upright across the small marble-topped table, blocking the view.

"I could sense you weren't happy at the police station earlier," Toby replied. "Let's have it then."

"Firstly I'd like to agree that we don't go near alcohol until we sort this." Lawrence fixed his eyes on Toby's. "I like a drink just as much as you but we are in a tight situation here. Are we agreed?"

"I'm not sure I follow. What tight situation?" Toby took another mouthful, no doubt fearing Lawrence might snatch the glass away.

The barman brought the menus and confirmed the table was reserved in the restaurant over to their left; there was no rush tonight so they could take their time. After he'd gone, Lawrence continued. "The barman? What religion is he?"

"He's a really nice young guy; I was chatting to him before. He worked in software development before he came here, I was wondering about offering him a job." Toby refocused. "Sorry, I've no idea what religion he is. Why?"

"Exactly. He could be Hindu, Muslim, Sikh, Christian, Buddhist or Jehovah's Witness, for all we know."

Toby's hand stopped in mid-air well before reaching his glass. "So what's your point?"

"Okki may well have committed suicide. She was a serious young lady who cared deeply for the people she was trying to help. It does happen." Lawrence had rehearsed this speech in his head but the words still didn't come out right. "One way or the other, we will get to the truth. Personally, I still believe Okki was caught up in something. She mixed with the wrong people, she knew too much, she said the wrong thing, she got too close to someone or something, she asked the wrong question . . . if that was the case, she paid the ultimate price for it."

He saw Toby's eyes drift onto the rhythmic tail fin of a passing sturgeon.

Lawrence pushed on. "If Okki was brutally murdered, the murderer could be in this room, watching us right now. It may be that *you* are really his target and he killed Okki to get you here. He could be a policeman in Chaudray's office or a charity worker at the field centre . . . or even the barman, for Christ's sake."

He watched the colour draining from Toby's face, a fading rainbow of hope melting into the cloud of self-pity swirling around him. Lawrence accepted a slight nod of acquiescence. He pushed home his advantage. "Toby, we're in a strange place. It may look familiar with so many British-style buildings but . . ."

"I get it, Lawrence . . . thank you."

"I'm only trying to help. They see things differently here. People die for their religion. People kill for what they believe in. We need to get inside their heads if we're going to understand what really happened."

Lawrence rubbed the stubble on his chin. "Now, we've had a long tiring day. I think we should get some dinner and a good night's sleep."

"You go ahead, I'm not hungry."

"That's the other thing," Lawrence snapped back, "I know enough about Type 1 diabetics to know that they have to eat regularly. We're both going to the restaurant and having dinner . . . dinner without wine."

A feeble smile creased the corners of Toby's mouth. "Lawrence, you must be the first teetotal Rotarian I've ever met."

"Not teetotal, Toby, just aware of our situation. Let's go through."

The main restaurant at the Nirvana International Hotel & Conference Centre was as quiet as the bar area, with only three other tables occupied. The maître d' proudly announced that the hotel was hosting a banquet downstairs as part of the Indian Cement Manufacturers Annual Conference and that cricketing legend Sachin Tendulkar was their guest of honour.

For Lawrence, that explained the even tighter security at the main entrance when he came back from stretching his legs around the grounds. He found the mobile signal was stronger outdoors and the garden areas were actually quieter. He could at least hear what Hannah was saying even if he didn't want to hear the actual words. At least she was missing him just as much.

The starters were cleared away. Lawrence ordered another bottle of San Pellegrino, "Jock was going to meet us here tonight but Nisha isn't feeling too good. He sends their apologies. We're meeting them at the field centre tomorrow morning. Okki was a close friend to both of them, but especially close to Nisha."

Lawrence could see Toby was like a passenger on a ship in heavy seas. He was desperately hanging onto the railings. Each mention of her name caused him to pitch and roll into the dark waves breaking over him. He started fidgeting with his spoon.

"It's going to be OK." Lawrence reached over and put his hand on Toby's arm. "I understand, we'll get through this . . . together."

"Seeing her lying there today . . . I just wanted to pick her up. She looked so little, so helpless . . . I kept thinking she was going to open her eyes and look at me . . . *Hi Pops, what are you doing here?* She's so beautiful."

Lawrence was struggling for the words. "She is a very special young lady . . . we must do our best for her."

"Can you remember what they said about taking her home? I wasn't really listening." Toby put the spoon down but kept running his fingers over the curvature.

"They delayed the autopsy because we were coming. Chaudray said it could be ten days before we get the final report . . . and they had eleven other cases waiting. The police will be hard work."

Toby flipped over the spoon, started caressing the other side. "There were bruises under her arms . . . and a swelling on her right knee . . . oh Lawrence, every time I close my eyes, I can see those marks around her neck. I feel so fucking helpless."

Lawrence thanked the waiters as the main course arrived. "Chaudray said he might give us the names of the three SINAC volunteers they have yet to interview. I think he could sense we'd find them long before they did."

"Do you think he was telling us the truth?" Toby was chewing a mouthful of grilled chicken with a complete lack of enthusiasm.

"Difficult to say, but I think so. He looked like a genuine guy beaten into submission by sheer volume of work. With a city of twenty-five million people and growing, it's no wonder they don't know where to start."

Toby sighed. "I know the feeling . . . so where do *we* start?"

"We need to talk to her friends, the other volunteers and the manager at the field centre. He seemed a decent guy." Lawrence was enjoying his lamb bhuna just a little too much. "We need to know who she spent time with and what this Project Amrita is actually all about."

"You mean Uppsala?"

"Not really . . . well, it could be that. I mean her voluntary work in the village. Uppsala is a much bigger deal, I think, but I don't really know."

Toby's jaw continued to chew but Lawrence could see his eyelids flickering just before his head suddenly dropped. "Sorry, you were right about getting a good night's sleep. I never sleep on planes. It must be catching up on me."

Lawrence signed the bill and wished the barman goodnight as they passed through the lobby on their way to the lifts. Toby was looking up inside a huge covered atrium as four glass bubble lifts darted between floors like hummingbirds looking for nectar. Eventually one plummeted down towards them.

"Do you really think I could be the target?" Toby's words were lost in a yawn.

"Unlikely but anything's possible here. We've got to keep all options open at this stage."

Lawrence waited for the lift doors to open. "According to the guidebook, we were just two of the thirty-four million people passing through Indira Gandhi International Airport this year. It was the cleanest and most impressive terminal building I've ever been in. We drove past unbelievable Victorian buildings, tree-lined boulevards and magnificent temples . . . all mixed in with tons of rubbish on the streets, hundreds of people milling about in dirt and even crapping on the pavement. I may never understand India."

Lawrence sighed. *Expect the unexpected.* He confirmed the taxi was booked for 7.30 a.m. and wished him goodnight. They peeled off in different directions around the outside of the 17th floor.

Far below, hotel guests moved about like sedated ants. The faint tinkling of piano music filtered up through the void, the tune barely recognisable as a Lennon and McCartney classic. Lawrence was humming along as he opened the door and put the plastic key card into the power switch. He did believe in yesterday – but he believed even more in tomorrow.

The room filled with subdued lighting. After a few seconds the familiar hush of the air-conditioning kicked in. He locked and bolted the door, putting on the chain for good measure. He was going to check his emails but the numbing combination of jet lag and mental exhaustion won the argument. He set the alarm for 5.30 a.m. and turned in.

Goodnight Hannah, I love you.

*   *   *

The figure in the armchair sat next to the piano, and watched the lift descend back to the ground floor before folding up the business section of *The Times of India*. "*Moon River*" had washed away all the troubles of "Yesterday", at least for now. The tall, well-dressed man paid cash for the mineral water, checked the time and moved towards a different set of lifts for the underground car park.

With the touch of a button the indicator lights flashed orange in synchronised obedience. Making sure not to be seen by any hotel guests or CCTV cameras, he carefully took the handgun from his inside pocket, wrapped it in a soft cotton cloth before stowing it with the tools under the shelf by the spare wheel.

He had just closed the boot of the hatchback when his mobile phone sprang into life.

"Yes?"

"Are they at the hotel now?"

"Yes."

"Good – keep me informed."

• CHAPTER 18 •

The journey out to Guildford had been a staccato affair that stretched even Max's endless patience. They stop-started through miles of roadworks on the M3, yet still managed to arrive a few minutes early.

Hannah was convinced that her previous dealings with the Surrey police would carry forward into a positive dialogue. As Lawrence had said, they needed wise counsel and this seemed a good place to start. The arduous journey and overcast grey skies didn't fill her with much enthusiasm. She was beginning to feel tired as they climbed the stairs to the first floor.

She recognised one of the two police officers as soon as they entered the rather drab meeting room. Steve Mole looked genuinely pleased to see her again. His boss, Detective Inspector Lonsdale, was more circumspect, his sharp eyes flicking backwards and forwards between them, searching for clues.

The meeting commenced with a slow cocktail of polite formalities and agreed parameters, in which Max was happy to lead. Hannah, on the other hand, could feel her eyelids closing, the voices growing fainter. A kaleidoscope of faces merged into each other, eventually forming a floor-to-ceiling curtain of rich purple velvet.

She knew she was dreaming but curiosity drew her into the unfolding drama as the curtain slowly parted. It revealed an ornate stage with banked rows of seating at the rear and a lectern standing proudly in its own spotlight. Around the vast room, towers of black loudspeakers crackled into life.

Your Royal Highness . . .

Hannah found herself in the middle of a huge audience. Well-dressed people of all ages sat expectantly, their eyes glued to the stage.

. . . distinguished guests, ladies and gentlemen, it is my special privilege to advise you of an additional prize being awarded by the university today.

Around Hannah the glitterati were rustling through their programmes. A buzz of excitement sparked like an electric charge across the room.

To make this special award, please welcome the Vice-Chancellor of the university, Emeritus Professor Magnus Sorensen who will be accompanied in the presentation party by Dr Charles Wolfenden, Dean of Applied Sciences at Princeton University.

A huge round of applause greeted the two distinguished guests. Hannah could see the American professor was carrying an impressive trophy made from what looked like glass and burnished bronze.

The Vice-Chancellor stepped up to the lectern, brushed aside a lock of silver-grey hair and took out a single piece of paper from deep inside his flowing, crimson robes.

He cleared his throat. "Since their introduction in 1901, Nobel Prizes have been awarded on the tenth of December each year in honour of Alfred Nobel, on the anniversary of his death. Physics is one of the six categories recognised by a Nobel Prize. Each laureate has made a legendary contribution to their field. They have helped us achieve an ever-greater understanding of the world around us and our place in the universe."

Outside, Hannah could see the snowflakes piling up on the granite sills beyond the lead-lighted windows. Inside, the archaic heating system was pumping oceans of warm air into the space, turning cold faces to rosy pink.

"Of the one hundred and ninety-nine prize-winners in Physics, only two laureates have been female." The Vice-Chancellor paused while a collective hubbub of disbelief and guarded anticipation pulsed across the room. "I mention this purely to put in context the remarkable achievement we are witnessing and celebrating here today."

He paused again to acknowledge a spontaneous outburst of applause.

"We have just been notified this morning that the Nobel Prize for Physics has been awarded this year to the youngest ever recipient. Her work in radiation theory is causing a revolution in our understanding of the universe. A new Faculty of Radiation is to be established at Princeton University in her name."

It was all too much. Hannah was slipping underwater, the words becoming muffled and the colourful images on the stage blurring as the waves lapped over her head.

"The Nobel Prize itself will, of course, be awarded in December. Today we wish to recognise her outstanding achievement. Please welcome our most worthy Nobel prize-winner, Dr Octavia Siekierkowski."

Along with two thousand other people, Hannah found herself on her feet, cheering and applauding wildly. She watched her daughter stride out onto the stage in slow motion. Tresses of auburn hair were cascading over her green robes edged in gold. She caught glimpses of a dress in blue and green silk shimmering underneath.

Okki graciously received the trophy and seemed to whisper something into the ear of the Vice-Chancellor, who immediately started gesticulating for quiet. He returned to the microphone. "Dr Siekierkowski has just informed me that she is not the only Dr Siekierkowski we have in the room today."

Hannah felt the warm waters gently pulling her down into the clear blue depths.

"Can I ask Octavia's mother, Dr Hannah Siekierkowski, to come up onto the stage please?"

The audience burst into rapturous applause again, people looking round to see if they could spot her first.

"I understand Octavia's mother has travelled from the USA to be with us here today. Dr Hannah Siekierkowski must be the proudest person in the room." Loud cheering echoed off the old sandstone pillars, pushing up the vaulted roof and making the windows rattle. A male voice at the back yelled out, "*Go the USA!*"

"Dr Siekierkowski Senior is a doctor of medicine and Head of Research at The Klinkenhammer Foundation in New York City," the Vice-Chancellor announced as he scanned the room.

Hannah was floating now, deep in the blue ether, a thousand colours reflecting off the coral reefs around her, small fish gliding by amid waving banks of kelp and sea grasses. She could see a distant light shimmering down from the surface above her, showering crystals of diamond, ruby and sapphire into the clear waters.

"Can I ask again for Dr Hannah Siekierkowski to come forward to the stage ... Dr Siekierkowski ... Hannah Siekierkowski ... Hannah ...?"

Hannah was rising now, up from the depths, slowly at first but the pace quickening as she reached towards the surface. The light grew stronger and she could just make out the muffled voices again. Figures started to emerge as her peripheral vision cleared.

"Hannah . . . are you there? Hannah . . . are you all right?"

She blinked her eyes open and gazed at a figure that strangely resembled Buddha, sitting proudly at the head of the small table.

"Hannah, would you like some water?" The voice came from a well-dressed man with a moustache sat to her left who had started fussing around with glasses and a charmless Pyrex jug.

She looked back up the table. Buddha had taken the form of Detective Inspector Lonsdale. He opened his palms and spoke only to her with his twinkling blue eyes, a gesture of "welcome back" or perhaps "I understand how hard this is for you".

"I think water is a good idea. I'll get some fresh . . ." The young man to her right made a play for the jug, wrestling it away from the moustache as he stood and moved towards the door.

". . . and perhaps some tea and biscuits?" Lonsdale kept his eyes on her, the hands now resting on neat piles of paper before him.

After a few minutes, Detective Sergeant Mole returned with the water jug full to the brim, and was soon followed by an unsmiling policewoman in a shapeless uniform, making a drama out of carrying an old tin tray.

"Shall I be mother?" Lonsdale pronounced, causing the moustache to smile. As he picked up the teapot, he nodded towards the young officer. "Perhaps you could update us on your recent conversation with Senior Constable Chaudray?"

Steve Mole picked up on cue. He reported that the Indian police had interviewed seven of the SINAC volunteers who had been on site when the body was found and were hoping to talk to three others who had not been available.

"Not available, Detective Sergeant?" Lonsdale enquired, offering the biscuits to Hannah, who politely refused.

"He wasn't sure when those interviews would take place, sir, as the volunteers had gone to other sites ... I'll stay on that, sir."

"So what have they learned from the interviews that have taken place?" he asked, then, once he had completed the tea ceremony, helped himself to a biscuit.

"He said it was all fairly routine. No one heard any noises or sounds of a struggle; the campus had been quiet the night it happened. He said each person they interviewed expressed surprise because Miss Stanton ... sorry, Octavia ... was a happy, outgoing individual who hadn't shown any signs of being depressed or threatening to take her own life."

"Did Chaudray tell us anything else, Detective Sergeant?"

"Yes, sir, he said they'd taken statements from the two individuals who'd found her. They'd both been ruled out of any involvement in her death. Their names –" he checked his notes "– Dr Nisha Patel and Jock Lim."

"They were Miss Stanton's friends, the ones who dined with her the night before, as I recall." Lonsdale leafed through his Manila file, the information at his fingertips where he liked it.

Detective Sergeant Mole completed his report. Chaudray expected the autopsy report to show the cause of death being commensurate with hanging. The case was being filed as suicide and they would be scaling back their investigation. Subject to a straightforward autopsy report, they would release the body to her father, now that he was in Delhi.

"So pretty much an open and shut case, Detective Sergeant?" the superior officer suggested. He symbolically closed the thin file.

"So is that it?" Hannah was on her feet, hands braced on the table, eyes flashing at the emotionless Buddha. A scarlet rash was searing up from her neck and bursting out across her cheeks and forehead. "An innocent girl is brutally murdered. And all the British police can say is case closed? Is that what I'm hearing?"

Max was on his feet. "Calm down, Hannah, this is not going to help. What do you expect them to do?"

"I expect them to . . . I expect . . . Okki was just trying to . . ." Hannah slumped down into the chair. Max tried in vain to comfort her but the anger and tears just kept coming.

Detective Inspector Lonsdale was the first to speak. "Mr Hartley, I need to talk to my colleague in private. We will return in a few minutes. Please excuse us."

Eventually Hannah came up for air. Max persuaded her to take a mouthful of sweet tea.

"What is it about the British and tea?" The words sharpened on the cutting edge of a pure Brooklyn accent. She accepted his handkerchief and started to mop up the carnage of smeared mascara and hot tears.

"We built an empire on tea. You might say it's in our DNA. It's our way of taking time out to reflect and come up with a better idea," Max explained, once the storm had passed.

"You asked a good question. I don't know what I expect them to do. I don't know why Lawrence suggested we do this." Hannah was somewhere between trying to find composure and screaming out for justice. Justice for the daughter she never had; justice for an innocent life lost. It may have been a dream but it felt so real.

Max managed a weak smile. "*Per Ardua Ad Astra*. It's the mantra of the RAF, which I always took to mean, 'Push through adversity and you will reach the stars'. Justice will overcome adversity. The truth will come out. We just have to believe and a way forward will appear."

A quiet knock on the door announced the return of the

two policemen who resumed their places, the senior officer carrying a thick buff folder. Detective Lonsdale waved away Hannah's attempt at an apology, the Buddha's smile once more blessing the scene with beatific calmness.

"In answer to your question, Dr Siekierkowski, the British police has no jurisdiction in this case as the alleged crime took place in a foreign land over which we do not have sovereignty . . . well, have not had sovereignty since we gave them independence in nineteen forty-seven. Having said that, Octavia Stanton is a British citizen. She travels on a UK passport, grew up in Weybridge and returned to Surrey during her university studies. I also understand she was a Neighbourhood Watch volunteer and a very helpful witness with a nasty rape inquiry we were conducting some years ago. She even appeared for us on *Crimewatch*, appealing for witnesses to come forward. With her help, we nabbed the bastard and put him away. In short, she is a friend to the Surrey police . . . and we like to look after our friends."

Hannah's alert eyes flashed up the table, then across to Max. She wondered where this was leading.

Lonsdale paused and looked across at his junior officer. "I believe there are two possible circumstances in which I could let my capable Detective Sergeant here jump on a plane and get to work finding out what really happened."

Hannah's eyes reflected just a glimmer of hope. Maybe Lawrence was right; they might be able to help. Max looked equally engaged, yet bemused.

"If – and I stress the word *if* – we were invited to help by the New Delhi police, then we could allocate resources accordingly. Alternatively, if our Foreign Office agreed with the Indian High Commission that our involvement would be mutually beneficial for justice to be served, then I'm sure my colleague here would be readily knocking back the anti-malaria tablets in the departure lounge in no time."

Hannah was about to launch in when Max intervened, "Hannah, I have some connections with the Indian Air Force. Junior ranks I trained with then may be commanding officers today."

Lonsdale expressed a smile of understanding. "I'm guessing, Mr Hartley, that you still keep a little black book?"

"I never go anywhere without it, Detective Inspector."

"And of course, you will have signed the Official Secrets Act?"

"Of course."

"Then permit me to show you some highly confidential information that I will strenuously deny was ever in this room." Lonsdale opened the buff folder.

Hannah could only sit back and admire the graceful wheels of British Fair Play begin to turn. As she chewed one of the soggy biscuits, she pondered what the Latin translation might be for 'you scratch my back and I'll scratch yours'.

"Mr Hartley," Lonsdale announced, "have you ever met the Maharajah of Jalore?"

CHAPTER 19

Jock breathed in the familiar smell of incense coming from the spare room, her *temple*, as he called it. He could hear the quiet murmur of the prayers although he'd no idea what it all meant. She'd slipped out of bed and padded through just after 4 a.m. as usual. He'd pretended to be asleep but he knew neither of them had slept much last night.

She would give blessings to the miniatures of her deities; loosen her body and her mind with yoga, then spend at least an hour in silent meditation. The murmurings and candlelight flickering under the door indicated she had now begun her arti ritual and was expressing her gratitude for being granted another day. She'd told him once that she also prayed for him and those close to her. No doubt today she was asking for some divine guidance to make sense out of what had happened.

They had gone to bed late. He'd spent most of the evening trying to reassure her. He continued most of the night in the forlorn and sultry darkness of her bedroom. He still felt numb inside. Had they brought about the death of their friend? Suicide? Murder? She was dead either way. It felt unreal.

He looked around the room. Clothes were strewn on the chair. Sunlight was pouring in through the bedroom window. The enigmatic photograph of Albert Einstein with his tongue sticking out was laughing at him from the far wall. There was the bag of used clothes in the corner that Nisha would give to the poor on Saturday morning. It was all so normal, just another start to another day. Like nothing had happened.

He wrapped himself in a bathrobe and went through to the lounge. He pressed the button for voicemail messages. There was one from Ingmar Persson offering his deepest sympathy and numerous condolences from SINAC volunteers in India and the head office in Singapore.

There was a heart-felt message from Ranjit expressing his disbelief at what had happened and vowing her death would not be in vain. Jock was reassured that he had pledged the full support of Gupta Geothermal, including the use of his connections with senior police officials, even if he wasn't sure what that meant.

He went through to the kitchen and fixed scrambled eggs with toast, freshly squeezed mango juice and filter coffee.

Nisha emerged after a quick shower. She seemed restless, complaining that she couldn't meditate properly and felt remote from her spiritual self. She managed a piece of the toast but couldn't face the eggs. He'd made them the way she liked with black pepper and coconut milk. The coffee went cold. The waste disposal celebrated his failure with grinding derision.

"Ingmar said they'd had a really good conference call with Sangbu yesterday. They've agreed on how to create the connectivity interfaces." Jock sipped a mouthful of juice. He saw the disapproval in her eyes. "It's just my way of coping. If I keep focused on the work, it takes my mind off it . . . stops me getting angry."

"I'm sorry . . . please go on, tell me what he said." She tidied up the breakfast things and loaded the dishwasher.

"He believes the receptors can be simplified if we put more transmission capability into the satellite dishes. That way the unit cost can be reduced and bring the project back to budget." Jock was looking for the car keys.

"Sounds like Sangbu and Henning are on the same page. Now we need to get our act together and sort out a time with Ranjit for some lab testing. Maybe we both need to take our minds off this." Her voice was quieter than normal.

She grabbed her things. "Have you got the keys to the Beast?"

"I thought you had them. They'll be in a coat pocket somewhere. No problem, let's go."

Nisha powered the Jensen into the outside lane. They made good progress before turning off to pick up the country road out to the field centre. Jock checked the clock. Lawrence and Toby would be meeting Dr Bhattacharya in a few minutes so they needed to keep moving.

The chaotic scene coming down the off-ramp changed everything. It reminded Jock of a travelling circus. There were trucks and cars and animals everywhere. Their route ahead was completely blocked. He tried not to look at the time again. Should he call Lawrence and apologise for being late?

Suddenly the road ahead cleared for no apparent reason, like a parting of the waves. As Nisha accelerated away, a clump of other cars and motorbikes followed in hot pursuit, taking advantage of the unexpected intervention by the gods.

The Jensen led a procession through the crowded back streets out into the open countryside, as the sound of horns and shouting voices became a distant echo. At the back of the procession, a dirty off-road vehicle swerved and danced through the clouds of dust.

"Did Lawrence say how Toby was holding up?" She checked the mirror. The procession behind was thinning out as she pushed hard on the accelerator.

"Only that he was taking it one day at a time. The meeting with the police sounded quite painful."

"The poor guy. It must be difficult losing a child at any time but especially like this. Suicide must be the hardest." Nisha could see only dust behind now.

"Come on." Jock shook his head. "There's no way it was suicide."

They stopped at another busy junction. Cars and trucks were streaming both ways. Jock could see the road beyond was clear as it wound off into fields of mustard seed, the colours already shimmering in the early morning heat. A translucent yellow haze was overlaid against a cloudless grey sky. It was the nearest it ever got to blue in Delhi, he reflected.

In the near distance, Jock was fascinated by a forest of silent chimneys, rising up high above sprawling brickworks on both sides of the single track road. The countless erect stalagmites of white plaster and red sandstone were dotted all around, each tapering bizarrely up into nothingness. At their feet, worker ants busied themselves with cartloads of bricks – stacking and drying, moving and piling.

As he attuned his eyes to the landscape, he could see more and more people; people sitting under trees, people drinking chai by the side of the road, people carrying enormous bundles of what looked like rags and sticks and boxes full of fruit.

There were people dressed in colourful, flowing robes, laughing and smiling to each other; some men were just sat staring into space; some girls were pumping up water from a well, and filling enormous earthenware jars. All of them were seemingly just happy to be blessed with one more day in the sunshine.

"You sound very sure it wasn't suicide." Nisha saw the gap, and plunged her right foot down. The Jensen responded and lurched across the junction, the heavy tyres scrunching through some loose gravel as she swerved round one of the deeper potholes. "I knew her better than you. Okki did worry about things. She was deeply moved by SINAC and what we are trying to do. Maybe we didn't appreciate how she was feeling. We're just more used to living with poverty. It hurt her seeing the misery every day. She really cared for the children. Well, she cared for everyone in the village."

For a moment, Jock remembered the joy on Okki's face at her triumph in explaining what the lecture had all been about. And the fit of giggles after she knocked back the champagne too quickly, which made her sneeze. "But I thought suicide victims suffered from depression? No way was Okki depressed. She could see how we could help create a better life. It just doesn't make sense. What do you think our resident Brahmin knows? Did Okki ever open up to him?"

"Dr Bhattacharya? He wouldn't tell us even if she did. He's a lovely, gentle man and highly confidential. He's a great mentor for the students, but I can't think he ever studied depressive behaviour or mental health. It doesn't feature much in the *Mahabharata.*"

Jock noticed the flicker of a smile melt across her face. Talking about Okki and what had happened was clearly helping. Whatever the truth, one thing was certain: things would not be the same again. Time would heal the wound. For now, keeping them both busy with Project Amrita was the best treatment he could administer.

The Jensen continued to swallow up big mouthfuls of open road. Through the haze, the ragged outline of distant buildings came slowly into view, breaking up the horizon and drawing them on. Not far now, he thought.

The single file road had narrowed even further. The blacktop had been patched up in places, which tested the Jensen's suspension. They sped past numerous passing places. With little traffic moving up ahead and the sun driving the local villagers towards whatever shade they could find, Nisha was able to accelerate amid throaty growls from the twin exhausts.

Jock was going to suggest some music to lift the mood but the sudden look on Nisha's face made him freeze. "What's wrong?"

She paused, looked again hard into the rear-view mirror, seeming to shake her head in disbelief. "I know why you couldn't find the other keys."

"What . . . the keys to the Beast? Why?"

"Because the Beast is right behind us."

• CHAPTER 20 •

"We can be there in an hour, Viren. Does that work for you?" Max was slowing as they approached a red light.

"Perfectly, Wing Commander."

Hannah placed the voice as polished, professional and confident, perhaps straying into arrogance at times. She concluded high-caste Indian with just a hint of West London yah, perhaps centred on Sloane Square.

"I have a delightful young lady with me I'd like you to meet," Max continued. "The Saints Lounge, I think."

"Good choice, I fully understand. I'm looking forward to meeting her. Just in time for tiffin. See you there, over and out." The voice melted back into the unseen speakers.

"The Saints Lounge?" Hannah had given up trying to scribble notes on her pad. The constant stop-start of the London traffic, combined with the circuitous route Max had chosen from Guildford back into the City, had provided enough of a challenge just to avoid being carsick.

"The Mach II Club is one of London's most exclusive watering holes. It's a sort of officer's mess for retired fighter pilots. All nationalities are welcome provided they have the right sort of military credentials . . . and can pay the exorbitant fees."

"So pilots who've been on opposing sides can join?" Hannah enquired, taking a sideways glance at her driver, sensing the emergence of yet another facet within his intriguing personality.

"Absolutely. We are pilots first, and loyal citizens second. There aren't many jobs that provide you with a sixty-million-dollar company car and a licence to kill. We're something of a rare breed, I suppose. And the club is one of the few places where we can relax and preen our feathers."

"Go on then, I'll take the bait . . . the Saints Lounge?"

". . . is on the ground floor. There are other lounges upstairs." A broad smile swept over his chiselled face, making the ends of his moustache twitch.

"I think I can guess . . ." She put the pad in her handbag and fished out her compact case. Instead of her own familiar reflection, Hannah could suddenly see the happy-go-lucky girl with the freckles and gorgeous auburn hair dancing to the heavy desi beat. Her mood switched back, the steel returning to her eyes.

"You'll see when we get there." Max had turned off the expressway and was heading towards St James's.

"Tell me about Viren. He sounded very polite. Where does he fit in?" Make-up complete, lips restored to pimento red, hair combed out, Hannah was ready for action. She had a job to do and time was pressing.

"I knew him as Flight Officer Viren Cherieth. He was seconded to my squadron back in the nineties. I'd say more than capable pilot, quick on the uptake, good technical knowledge of avionics and a reliable wingman. And believe me, Hannah, reliability in a wingman is a precious commodity."

The drizzle had turned to heavy rain, windscreen wipers metering out Max's words in two-tone rhythm. Hannah noticed the dashboard temperature had dropped to an unpleasant twelve degrees outside. Beyond the tinted windows, colourful lights from extravagant shop windows called out into the gloom. With a surgeon's precision, Max threaded his way expertly through the narrowing streets of London's West End.

"The RAF's always worked closely with the Indian Air Force. I suppose it's a Commonwealth thing. There've been strategic partnerships in place for decades. We provide training and weapons expertise in exchange for using their airbases, mid-air refuelling services . . . that sort of thing."

He swung the car into a tight, cobblestoned back street and pulled up in front of an unmarked, garage-style door cut into an old brick wall. He pressed a small button on the dashboard, causing the red light above the door to flash green. The door lifted gracefully into the roof space, revealing a mysterious cavern beyond.

They crept forward down a ramp into the basement, halogen headlights casting long shadows into the darkness. Hannah heard the door close behind them as Max manoeuvred around solid brick pillars and the gracious curves of expensive vehicles jutting out from every nook and cranny. She was no expert on Italian sports cars but this poorly lit netherworld seemed to be a breeding ground for Ferraris and Maseratis.

He pulled into his allotted space, grabbed a plain black credit card from the glove and killed the engine. "I lost track of Viren when I moved on from the RAF. He got back in touch when he was posted to London some years ago."

Subtle floor-level lighting led them to the lift, which was summoned by a button bearing the symbol of a jet fighter, illuminated in green. Above Hangar, the car-park floor, the ascending choices were Saints, Sinners and Stars. Max swiped his card and pressed Saints, causing the lift doors to close with the silken movement of a pole-dancer's legs.

"There's another floor above Stars . . . not even I have access to that. The old boys refer to it as Heaven."

The lift whispered to a stop. Hannah shook her head in

mild amusement, stepping out onto what she presumed was the ground floor. With no windows or seemingly any access to the real world, it was difficult to tell which floor they were on.

They were standing in a small, brightly lit, white-walled room devoid of all signage. At a simple, white-marble reception desk sat an incredibly beautiful coffee-skinned young girl, Iranian in origin, Hannah guessed, dressed in a smart, white, military flying suit.

There were no badges or insignia to decree which air force she represented, just some attractive gold braid and decorative striped epaulets to continue the military branding. A cascade of blue-black softness poured down over her neck and shoulders. The single front zip was discreetly pulled up but the skintight outfit was less than demanding for any male visitor's imagination.

She looked up through almond-shaped pools of pure amber and scanned the two new arrivals with obvious approval. Hannah could see her slender fingers caressing a silent keyboard beneath the desktop.

Honey-sugared words slipped from her kiss-kiss lips. "Wing Commander Hartley, how good to see you again. Your guest has already arrived. He's waiting for you in the Saints Lounge."

"Thank you, Faria. We'll go straight through." Max showed Hannah the way as the sliding glass doors behind the reception desk slowly parted.

The snow-white carpet changed in the corridor beyond, split down the middle into green and red. The red carpet led to the bottom of a wide metallic staircase that spiralled its way up into the hidden floors above.

Hannah pointed. "Sinners that way, right?"

Max smiled. "Any sharper and you'd cut yourself. We'll take the green carpet today."

"I bet you say that to all the girls."

He smiled. "And by the way, I don't come here that often. She picked up my name from the swipe card."

"Who? Faria? She'll go far, that girl . . . no doubt to Heaven one day."

Max led the way as the green carpet took them along another corridor, past numerous closed mahogany doors. They turned a final corner to where a pair of impressive double doors proudly announced their arrival at the Saints Lounge.

The doors opened into a large, oak-panelled room with a high, Victorian, sculpted ceiling, from which dangled numerous crystal chandeliers like a display of expensive diamond earrings. There were alcoves around the walls where windows should have been, each containing a marble bust of an unknown military leader or famous pilot, Hannah surmised.

Waiters dressed like clergy fussed around the twenty or so tables where smart-suited businessmen pored over seemingly important matters. Not businesswomen, Hannah noted, and immediately felt conspicuous. Heads quietly turned to the typewriter clicks of her heels on the lacquered parquet flooring.

Occasional leather chesterfields sat proudly on colourful Persian rugs around the outside of the room. Hannah breathed in their warming body odours of beeswax, horse blankets and sweet liquorice mixed with undertones of old tobacco and polished walnut burr.

Sitting strangely upright in the middle of one sofa was a bald-headed, smartly dressed Indian businessman, flicking through a well-thumbed copy of a military magazine. He stood to attention as they approached, carefully replacing the magazine on the bottom shelf of the coffee table in front of him.

"Max, how good to see you again," he said, taking the

outstretched hand in both of his, as if blessing him with a prayer. "You're looking so well."

"Viren, may I introduce a very good friend of mine, Dr Hannah Siekierkowski."

"Hannah," he announced as he threw his arms around her, ignoring her hand, "I never liked such formality with beautiful women. I'm so pleased to meet you."

"I forgot to mention, Viren is a compulsive ladies' man. Watch him like a hawk." Max was laughing as they made themselves comfortable.

"If you're a ladies' man, Viren, you are clearly in the wrong place," she said, looking around the room.

"Quite so, Hannah, we rarely enjoy the pleasure of female company in the Saints Lounge." His dreamy brown eyes held her gaze, before glancing away.

She was struggling to imagine his ample frame squeezing into the cockpit of a jet fighter. He looked much more at home in the opulence of these well-upholstered surroundings. A few minutes later they ordered high tea from a tall, slim waiter dressed as a Roman Catholic Cardinal. Hannah quickly acclimatised to her new environment, the steely resolve keeping her focused on the matter in hand.

"Viren, I really appreciate your time this afternoon," the soft voice of the Wing Commander returned to signify an end to the pleasantries.

Hannah noticed both men sit up a little straighter. The briefing had begun.

"We need your help, Viren. I'm afraid there's no easy way of explaining this so please forgive me if it sounds very blunt and direct."

He looked across at her, more for reassurance than approval, Hannah concluded.

"My boss Toby's daughter allegedly took her own life a few days ago while working as a volunteer for a charity in India. She was on a gap year. As yet we don't fully understand the circumstances. My boss has flown to New Delhi along with Hannah's partner, Lawrence, to investigate further. They have confirmed the identity of the body and an autopsy will now be conducted."

"Sorry, Max – her name is Octavia. She is still Octavia." Hannah coloured up.

Max paused, then briefly cast his eyes down to the coffee table. "Of course . . . Octavia. The local police are following up a number of lines of enquiry that, to say the least, seem very suspicious."

Viren sat in stony silence, drinking in the information, impassive.

"We believe the police officer in charge is very competent but he has his hands full with other investigations," Max continued, "and, as a result, they are likely to file it as just another suicide and close the case."

"I understand," Viren eventually replied, "I'm so sorry to hear this, Max. It is a growing problem in India, especially amongst young people. I can appreciate where the local police officer is coming from."

"Viren, we believe Octavia was murdered but we don't know why. We've discussed the situation with the British police. They sympathised and would like to help because Octavia is a British citizen, amongst other reasons, but explained they could not get involved unless they were invited to by the local force."

"I see . . . and did *they* believe that a crime had been committed?" Viren had formed a pyramid with his hands, the index fingers lightly touching the end of a bulbous nose, thumbs pressed firmly into a small dimple at the point of his chin, partly masking the outline of his cherubic face.

"In short, yes, they agree with us."

"This is very sad news indeed but . . . but where do I fit in, Max?" Viren sat back and loosened his shoulders. "I don't have any connections with the New Delhi police."

"Could you help us through the Indian High Commission here in London? Perhaps they could facilitate an invitation through diplomatic channels?" Max suggested.

"That's an invitation from the Indian High Commission to the British Foreign Office, requesting the assistance of the British police," Hannah clarified, her patience fraying at the edges, fingers holding on tight to the handbrake.

"Ah . . . I understand now. You think, because I'm attached to the Indian Ministry of Defence, I might be able to put in a good word with the High Commissioner?"

"Do you know him?" Hannah ignored the flash in Max's eyes.

"Yes, I know him very well. We meet up for monthly briefings. He is a most charming and agreeable individual with a lifetime of diplomatic service."

"Then can you help us? Sorry, I'm from Brooklyn; we don't do diplomacy." Hannah fixed him with the warmest glare she could muster.

Viren looked across at Max, who offered no comfort. He was clearly waiting for the answer as well.

"I'd really love to help you but there is a problem." Viren's head wobbled ever so slightly. "You see, the current High Commissioner is soon to be replaced. Officially he is taking up a new post in Fiji in a couple of months' time. Unofficially, he is being put out to grass and replaced by one of the new breed of diplomats."

"New breed?" Max picked up the lead.

"Yes, a commercially minded entrepreneur; someone who will push business opportunity for India. Our new government wants us to be more like an IBM sales office and less like a Hindu temple."

"Well, he sounds like an interesting character but we can't wait several months. The case will be buried by then, along with our hopes for justice," Max continued. "Is there anything you could do with the existing Commissioner?"

"I possibly could, Max." Viren was squirming into the chocolate-brown leather. "I'm not due to see him again for a couple of weeks."

"Would you like to use my phone, Viren?" Hannah thrust the small plastic object into his face.

He backed away. "It's not that ... from what you've said ... well, it's all a bit up in the air, isn't it? The local police are still investigating. As yet, there's no autopsy report." Viren regained some ground, took a deep breath and continued. "I can understand how you are both feeling. I stress again my deepest sympathies. I'm sure she was a delightful young lady ... but don't you think you are ... well, being a bit premature?"

This time Max restrained Hannah with his eyes before she found another use for her phone.

Viren continued before Max could respond. "Apart from which – and I didn't really explain this properly, so my apologies – the old boy, well, he's going a bit gaga to be brutally honest." He recoiled in horror. "Oh Max, please don't ever repeat what I just ..."

"Don't worry, Viren, you are amongst friends. And I do remember the club rules."

"Of course, yes, I was forgetting. What's said in the Saints Lounge stays in the Saints Lounge."

Hannah casually moved from the armchair to the sofa and put her hand gently on Viren's thigh, leaning into his ear. "We just need someone to make a phone call or send an email. It can't be that hard?"

Hannah watched as Viren slid as far away from her as he could. He was running a finger around the inside of his collar, which was suddenly three times too small for his rolling neckline. Prickly heat bumps appeared on his temple, colouring his skin deep reddish-brown.

Max put on his best voice of quiet conciliation, trying to reach an honourable agreement. "Viren, I agree with you. In other circumstances, we would all be best advised to wait until things are clearer. But we don't have that luxury. The case will be closed and the killer long gone. We need to act now."

"Max, we've known each other a long time. You know you can trust me." Viren paused and glanced across at the woman fidgeting next to him. "It would be too difficult for me – I mean politically difficult for me at the present time – to get involved."

Viren moved as if about to stand up. "I'm afraid I have another meeting across town and must be going."

"Viren, I need to share another piece of information with you; some highly confidential information. It will only take a moment." Max gave him the look reserved for old time's sake. Viren slumped back into the sofa, still hunched as far away from Hannah as he could get.

"The last official Maharajah of Jalore was Jahangir Suleiman Singh who sadly died last year at the age of seventy-four. His only son Shakir inherited the title and a considerable fortune, although, of course, nowadays the title is more symbolic as the position carries no real political power."

Viren had piled restless hands onto his lap and appeared to be waiting.

"Shakir is studying for an MBA at Henley, which should be completed by the end of next year." Max had his full attention. "Sadly, I understand that the young man has been released on bail following a police raid on a property in Cobham. Although the house is owned by the Indian government, it does not come under the protection of the laws concerning diplomatic immunity."

Hannah could see that Viren had turned a shade paler, his skin taking on an oily texture like greaseproof paper. She nodded to Max. He needed to keep pushing.

"Apparently the police had received complaints from the neighbours and turned up en masse expecting trouble. What had started as a party had spiralled into a full-blown rave. Quite a number of people were interviewed for possession of illegal substances. Ongoing investigations have also indicated irregularities concerning immigration conditions for some of the partygoers."

"You bastard . . . how do you know all this?"

Max ignored the question. "Now, of course, this has got nothing to do with me. If you wanted my advice, I would say it is too early to get involved. The police need to complete their investigations and present a file with recommendations to the Crown Prosecution Service. The only problem is that by waiting, it would be too late to change the outcome. Justice would have to be seen to be done. The pity is that the careers of Shakir and some of his friends will be ruined . . . and, dare I say, the reputations of some quite high-ranking officials attached to the Indian High Commission may also be in jeopardy."

Max twisted the knife. "The police dragnet trawled in quite a surprising catch. I'm sure it will come out in the wash that things have got a bit sloppy. The Commissioner has taken his eyes off the ball and will find himself in Fiji sooner than he thinks."

He jerked the knife sharply upwards. "This will give the new guy an excellent mandate to clean house, make a name for himself and, no doubt, bring in some fresh blood for his future London team."

Hannah saw Viren's shoulders slump in silent resignation. She added a softer touch. "Max, I take it this situation doesn't have to end so badly?"

"Indeed not, Hannah. The time to change official decisions is before they are made. Afterwards is too late as loss of face and honour are then at stake if a grovelling reversal is needed."

Hannah was satisfied the final blow struck home. The heart was punctured.

"Max ... what guarantees can you give me?" Viren was lurching for safer ground, reeling from the blows.

"No guarantees, Viren. You help us, we help you. It's that simple. The time to act is right now ... today." Max was on his feet; he brushed cake crumbs from his pinstripe suit trousers and offered his hand.

After a pause the handshake was accepted, a conclusive act in the political chess game raging across the table, Hannah decided. Viren would have to take the risk if he was to find a more solid defensive position.

They left him as they found him, sitting upright on a leather sofa in a corner of the Saints Lounge. The lift descended back to the Hangar floor.

As the headlights picked out a miserable rainy evening, Max turned up the heater and put the wipers on automatic.

Hannah smiled across at him. "How did you know he was connected with that police raid? I don't remember Lonsdale saying anything about other people they had interviewed?"

"I didn't. In fact, I still don't. Maybe he has a friend who was caught in the net. I'm not sure we'll ever know. As long as it does the trick."

"And how quickly do you think we'll find out?"

"Can't you hear the jungle drums beating?"

"And if it doesn't work? What then?"

"Then it will be time for Plan B."

"We have a Plan B? What happens in Plan B?"

"We talk to my old friend Pete Kostopoulos."

CHAPTER 21

In all his years, and in all his travels, Lawrence could honestly say he had never met anyone quite like Dr Yadu Bhattacharya. The mystical figure stood before them seemed somehow to have appeared from another world. Of course, they had met briefly last time Lawrence visited the centre but he hadn't fully appreciated the intensity or charisma of the man.

"Please accept my deepest condolences."

Short and rotund in stature, the man seemed to glow in a pool of his own light, an aura of wisdom emanating from his neatly tied white robes. He stood slightly angled to his left side and needed the support of a long, gnarled walking stick to keep his balance. Thin leather-strapped sandals had seemingly grown up from the ground around his old dusty feet. The sandals shared the sun-washed colours of his skin and creaked gently as he swayed.

A pair of elliptical, gold-rimmed pince-nez glasses were tucked neatly onto the bridge of his nose and gave him the appearance of a learned professor from a bygone age. Passive, calm eyes acted like a filter, drinking in and making sense of the world around him before sending out coded messages from his innermost thoughts.

Riding atop his deeply wrinkled forehead was a white turban, which rolled at anchor with each fluid movement. Lawrence found himself in awe of the man, even though he had only responded to Toby's machine-gun volley of questions with a few chosen words. Lawrence sensed the man was waiting for the next verbal assault. He felt the need to intervene.

"Dr Bhattacharya, perhaps you could explain a little more about your role here at the field centre and how well you knew Octavia." Lawrence fixed Toby with a glare that he could see was reluctantly understood.

"Before I answer, perhaps we should consider retiring to my office." He opened the palm of his hand to show the way. "The sun can be quite unforgiving at this time of the morning, if you're not used to it,"

They followed him in solemn procession towards the main administration block.

"We haven't got time for this," Toby hissed under his breath. "This old codger knows nothing. I bet he never even met her."

"We don't know yet what he does know. Remember, they do things differently over here. We need to respect their customs if we're going to learn anything. And, until Jock and Nisha get here, we need this man's co-operation even to set foot in the place. So chill out and let me do the talking."

Eventually they entered a room that could have been a time capsule from the days of the Raj. Despite the additions of a computer and other modern-day technology, the office bore the resemblence of an unkempt library with piles of books teetering on every available flat surface. Fading watercolours of Hindu gods peered out from bare plaster walls, giving Lawrence the distinct feeling that they were being watched, with some disapproval.

Dr Bhattacharya dragged an extra rattan cane chair over to the side of his heavily cluttered desk. The offer of some iced water was kindly declined. The great man settled easily onto his throne, resting his walking stick against the edge of a darkened computer screen and indicated that he was ready to respond.

"Now, to answer your question, Mr McGlynn. I am honoured to be the field centre manager. As you know, we are part of the Agricultural Sciences Faculty within the university. Most of the work carried out here is research by undergraduates into farming methods, animal husbandry and arable crop production. They are able to see the rural communities of Northern India first-hand and often stay with us for several days at a time."

"Yes, so we understand. But where do the SINAC volunteers fit in? Why would Toby's daughter be based out here?" Lawrence looked across at his friend in the forlorn hope that he would sit quietly.

"For a number of years now, we have supported the excellent work of SINAC. Their volunteers come here to help those less fortunate than ourselves." He carefully lifted the glasses from the top of his nose and wiped them on a small piece of muslin cloth. "They are indeed a blessing to us in many ways."

"A blessing?" Lawrence was starting to see how things fitted together. Unfortunately he could sense Toby's growing impatience, which was threatening to break the spell. He just needed a few more minutes.

"SINAC has given to the poor in our villages. They have funded research projects and provided much-needed resources for our campus – new dormitories, access roads and off-road vehicles. They have established a joint venture science incubator within the university that promises to change the world around us. Most importantly, they have brought bright, caring young people to our community who have mixed well with our students. We are happy to accommodate them."

"And my daughter was one of those bright, caring young people. Now she is dead. She was in your care. What have you done to her?!" Toby was on his feet, fists pounding on the desk. A pile of forms fluttered to the floor like sycamore seeds spinning at random in the breeze.

The old man hardly flinched, his head slowly moving in Toby's general direction with the steadfast purpose of an owl detecting a disturbance in the woods. Deep brown eyes absorbed his fury, sympathised in silence, then waited for the response to come back from within. Lawrence was about to restrain his friend when he realised it was unnecessary. The minimalist movement of the owl had done that for him.

"Mr Stanton, I share your grief but you need to understand our ways. Are you ready to listen? Until you are, my words will just add to your anger, which will not be helpful."

Lawrence saw the colour draining away from Toby's face. He deflated like a punctured balloon and folded slowly back into the rattan chair. A heavy silence filled the space. Toby nodded in resignation.

"Your daughter did not take her own life, of that I am quite sure. She was such a spirited young lady with everything to live for. She would sit just where you are now and talk to me about her hopes and dreams, about you and her mother, about SINAC and the wonderful work they were doing." The words were delivered with warmth but there was no outward show of emotion.

"How can you just say that? My daughter has been murdered and you . . . you just . . ." Toby cracked his knuckles, twisting the joints in grinding frustration.

"Mr Stanton, we believe that everything happens for a reason. We are born, we live our lives according to our karma, our destiny, we die when it is our time to die, and then we are born again. It is the Circle of Life and it is written to be so. My emotions or inner feelings are of no consequence. You must find out why she has been taken from you. Once you truly understand then you will be able to celebrate her life. I can help you with that understanding."

Lawrence checked his watch. Jock and Nisha should be here at any time. He leaned forward. "Dr Bhattacharya, who do you think killed her and why?"

He sat quite still while the question was assimilated and considered. Eventually he replied, his voice even slower in delivery, even quieter than before.

"From what she said to me, I believe the answer will be found in the work she was doing with SINAC. For that, you should ask the two people who will be here shortly. Nisha, in particular, was a close friend. They confided in each other. As well as being a brilliant, young scientist, Nisha is a devout Hindu and understands the meaning behind samsara, the Circle of Life."

Lawrence looked at Toby and again at his watch. A sudden thought flashed across his mind; he pushed it away, back into its dark corner. This was not the time. He just needed to be patient. Stay focused, press on. What about the question of who, he prompted.

Again Dr Bhattacharya went into deep thought. "Three volunteers have disappeared since the tragic event took place. The finger of suspicion points towards Bjorn Slagle, who worked very closely with her. I am told he returned to Sweden when he heard his mother was seriously ill. I have no proof that is where he is now."

"You must have a contact number. He can't just disappear." Toby again, colour back in his cheeks, sparks igniting in his eyes.

"Toby, we can't just call him up and ask him if he murdered your daughter. Think about it, for God's sake," Lawrence jumped in, then wished he hadn't. He breathed out heavily and shook his head, turning towards the Brahmin for forgiveness . . . or was it divine inspiration?

The owl looked on impassively. "I am happy to provide you with his contact details. Sometimes it is best to do that which is the most obvious. Would you like to call him?"

Lawrence gulped down a mouthful of composure. "You said three volunteers have disappeared. Who are the other two?"

"I don't care who they are – I want to talk to this Slagle guy . . . right now." Toby went to pick up the phone before realising he didn't have the number.

The owl looked towards an old-fashioned card index buried under a pile of journals on his desk. He made no movement towards it. Instead he turned back to Lawrence. "The other two only arrived recently from the Netherlands. They were twin sisters taking a gap year. They were working in her project team."

"So where are they now?" Lawrence tried to remain calm.

"We do not know. They said they were too shocked by what had happened and wanted to get away. I believe they were heading to Australia."

"Did you say Dutch girls?" Toby interjected "Where are they from? They must have a home address?"

Dr Bhattacharya flicked through the well-worn cards and pulled out two. "The address I have for them is in . . . Utrecht. It is their parents' house, I think."

"Utrecht? Let me see that . . ." Toby grabbed the cards. "I know this address. It's not that far from where I live. I can check this out . . ."

"Wait, Toby, you're doing it again. We need to know more about all three of these volunteers before we go charging in with accusations. We need to talk to the other SINAC volunteers first."

Lawrence tried not to look at his watch again; maybe they had been held up in traffic. He could try Jock's number. "And we still need to know why. We're not ready to make those calls yet."

"I've got to do something. Let me get Wanda checking out the Utrecht address at least . . . and we can find out if Slagle is really in Sweden." Toby stood up, drumming his fingers on the edge of the desk.

Dr Bhattacharya leaned back in his chair, gently lifted his walking stick and slowly pointed it towards a faded watercolour on the far wall above a groaning bookshelf. The semi-naked figure was sky-blue in colour, had four arms and was holding a collection of things Lawrence could not quite make out.

"Gentlemen, may I introduce you to Lord Vishnu. He is one of our three principal gods, known as Vishnu the Pervader. He is the cohesive force that binds the universe together; he pervades everywhere and is in everything. He is the source of all knowledge and of life itself; he is our salvation and will protect us from evil by defeating the powers of darkness, the powers of destruction."

Lawrence noticed a soothing calmness had spread over the old man's face. His eyes were fixed on the painting yet seemed to be looking into a distant world.

"Lord Vishnu comes to us in different guises when we most need him. You don't have to be Hindu to benefit from his wisdom, Mr Stanton. You just need to open your mind to his presence and accept the help that he can offer to you."

Toby eased further back, making the chair creak.

Dr Bhattacharya made himself comfortable. "Many years ago, a wise king was bathing in clean water brought to him by his servants. When he looked closely into the water, he saw a tiny fish, which he scooped up into his gentle hands. The fish spoke to him and asked the king for protection from all the larger fish that were trying to eat him. The king granted his wish and created a special pond where the little fish could live in peace."

Lawrence looked across at Toby who had slipped almost into a hypnotic state, listening to the old man's words. He was going to look at his watch again but somehow time had lost all meaning.

"The fish grew and grew until the pond was no longer big enough to hold him. As the wise king released him into the wilderness of the oceans, the fish told him to prepare for a great flood, which would soon wash away the land and everything on it. The king was to build a boat and save the plants and animals from the deluge. The fish would guide the boat to safety when the waters receded. It was then that the king recognised that the fish was in fact Lord Vishnu, come down to earth to save and protect him, just as he in turn had protected the tiny fish."

Toby's mouth opened slightly but no words came out. Lawrence could see he was in a deep trance. He felt the same hypnotic pull on his own senses. They were floating in a mystical world of men and gods and cosmic oceans . . .

"During the flood," the old man continued, "all the land disappeared and the boat was rocked by great waves in a most violent storm. The giant fish protected them from a sea monster, which had eaten the Vedas, the books containing all the knowledge and wisdom in the world. The fish recovered the great books and presented them to the king, showing him how to use them for the future good of humanity.

"Then the giant fish guided the boat to the safety of the first land that emerged from the waters – the high mountains we now call the Himalayas. The king was the only human survivor. He gave thanks to the gods, and was then blessed with a female companion who became his wife. Together they created the new human race from which we are all descended; we are all one big family, despite our differences, Mr Stanton."

"Who was this king?" Toby found his voice.

"He was called Manu, the progenitor of humanity; this is why we are known as mankind. Lord Vishnu had taken the form of an avatar called Matsya." The old man pointed his stick at another smaller painting on the far wall, this time depicting the top half of the blue god with the body of a fish. "He comes to us in many forms so we must be aware. The cow is sacred in our religion as it is seen as the giver of life and nutrition. It was the companion of the god Krishna, another and much later incarnation of our Lord Vishnu."

"Pardon our ignorance, but why is Lord Vishnu blue in colour?" Lawrence forced the words out of a seemingly parched throat.

"He is the Pervader, as I said before. He is blue like the formless pervasive substance of the universe that you call outer space but which we call the ether, a symbol of the cosmic oceans, out of which we were born and into which we will die, only to be reborn again in samsara, the Circle of Life."

"So what is the meaning to this story of the great fish?" Lawrence probed. Suddenly his mobile phone chimed into life. He looked down at the screen and went to press the button. "Please excuse me, I must take this call."

The old man directed his answer towards Toby. "In India, nothing is as it first seems. You should never assume you know the full meaning until you understand the will of the gods. Our suffering stems from ignorance. To avoid our pain, we must find the meaning within ourselves. It is what the gods ask us to do."

"Hello, Lawrence McGlynn. Hello . . .?"

"And the tiny fish becoming a big fish?" Toby shook out the words slowly.

"We recognise the law of dharma, which you would call justice. A wise king will practise dharma and protect the poor and the weak from the mighty who wish to devour them. By protecting the tiny fish, the king pleased Lord Vishnu, who saved him from the flood and helped him to create a humane world. We all must do the same."

"Hello? I can't hear you . . . what did you say had happened?"

• CHAPTER 22 •

"Kitty, that's great. Just let them know I'll be at the next meeting and will push for approval. Can you email me the capex?" Hannah smiled across at Max, gesturing one minute. "Did you say two-point-eight million US dollars?"

Max had allowed for the mid-morning traffic. They still had plenty of time.

"OK, better make that two-point-nine. Let me have the minutes and I'll front up to Chuck when I'm back." She waved her hand in a circular motion. "One last thing. Did you get any joy with Lawrence's team? They were doing a presentation for the Diabetes Conference. I thought Lawrence had . . ."

A bright scarlet bus suddenly pulled up just short of the hotel entrance, causing the traffic behind to billow into the congested outside lane amid much squealing of brakes and blowing of horns. The noise made Hannah push her passive finger deeper into her ear.

"What? That's not what we agreed. You can tell Gene from me it must be ready to go by next Friday . . . yep, the board will need to sign it off . . . we're playing for big bucks here. It could be our next . . . I don't want excuses . . . what did you say to me once in Vienna? You'll bring me solutions, not problems? Explain it to those jerks, will ya?"

The bus moved on, pulling up at a set of pedestrian lights further down Piccadilly. Both lanes back-filled with subservient streams of traffic, a typical rush-hour scene now bathed in shadow as an apologetic sun slipped behind yet more threatening cloud.

"Oh, and Kitty? Thanks for the heads-up; I really do appreciate it. I'll call you tonight my time. Give Trigger a hug from both of us. And don't push it too hard in the gym, right?"

A few minutes later Hannah was clipping herself in and checking her make-up in the vanity mirror. Max set the satnav for Guildford and took the exit towards Richmond-upon-Thames and the M3.

"What time are we on?" She pushed the visor back into place.

"Lonsdale said eleven-thirty a.m. He sounded quite excited."

"Did he say anything?"

"Just that he was impressed at our progress."

"That British stiff upper lip again, huh?"

"I'm guessing our friend Viren has come good for us." Max swung a right and took the dual carriageway, picking up speed as they approached the Thames river crossing.

"Well, I hope so or we're back to Plan B. Was that the Demis Roussos option?"

Max laughed. "I hope not, he's dead, the poor man ... great voice though, in his prime. I think you mean Pete Kostopoulos."

"All Greek to me." Hannah checked her phone; still no word from Lawrence.

"Pete was with me at British Airways. Best test pilot I ever flew with, quite fearless. He got banged up in the Nevada desert; both engines failed just after take-off, software glitch, so they said. He was flying a desk after that, which didn't work out."

"So what's he doing now?"

"Freelance journalist. He still dips his fingers in the glycol;

geeky aviation magazines, in-house journals, airline stuff. But recently he landed a sort of upmarket gossip column in *The Times*; not under his own name, you understand. All that *who left which hotel bedroom in the early hours....*but tastefully done, of course, it being *The Times*. Politicians at play and TV personalities mostly; none of your old slappers or footballers' wives."

"And I guess you thought he could run a feature on the hapless young Maharajah of Jalore to see what we could squeeze out?"

"Right on the money. A blunt instrument but the media packs some punch over here and can certainly loosen a few tongues . . . I still prefer Plan A."

Within the hour they were pulling up in front of the main Surrey Police Force Headquarters building, the flags waving in unison from their neat row of pristine white poles. The steady drizzle that had smeared the windscreen as they cleared the roadworks on the M3 had smudged into heavy rain, sucking all the light from the leaden grey skies overhead. The headlights blinked off as Max killed the engine.

They completed the security screening and returned to the upstairs meeting room. Unlike the day before, they found freshly brewed tea waiting for them. The two police officers were poring over documents strewn across the table, as if planning some kind of secret military incursion.

"Ah, come in, come in." Lonsdale cleared some space. "Tea?"

Hannah noticed a street map of Delhi casually draped across a pile of folders. "No thanks . . . my, this looks intense."

"Indeed so, quite the little mission-control centre." Lonsdale resumed his seat at the head of the table and welcomed the entourage to his court. "But then it appears you've been just as busy. My congratulations."

"You're ahead of us." Max smiled "What's happened?"

"Detective Sergeant?" Lonsdale savoured a mouthful of tea.

"First thing this morning, we received a request from Senior Constable Chaudray to assist them with a murder inquiry. A preliminary autopsy report has indicated that Octavia Stanton must have been unconscious or, at the very least, heavily sedated at the time she died from asphyxiation due to hanging. They had still to formally identify the substance found in her bloodstream but he suggested a powerful derivative of ketamine."

"Ketamine?" Hannah exclaimed. "That's the date rapist drug of choice in the Big Apple."

"Well, this must be its daddy from what Chaudray said. He's sending us the lab reports but the dosage would have been strong enough to knock out a horse. Intravenous injection, they think," Steve explained and handed her a copy of an email.

She skimmed the words, pushing back the nightmare scene flooding into her imagination. "Intravenous? Well, there must've been some kind of struggle. Okki wouldn't just sit there and let someone stick a needle into her."

"They did find bruises on her body but—" the young policeman stopped in mid-sentence "– but we'll know more when we get the full report. The autopsy has now become a priority."

Hannah brushed away a tear and handed the email back. She looked across at Max to pick up the lead.

"I take it there's been some movement in the diplomatic channels overnight?" Max helped himself to a digestive biscuit.

"Apparently so. As well as the change of heart from our erstwhile colleagues in New Delhi, I've been asked for a full report on the Maharajah case by our own beloved Chief Constable. I'm invited to join him at the FCO in King Charles

Street next week. We're reviewing criminal charges for officials within the Indian High Commission. It's all high-octane stuff for a humble plod in Guildford."

"You mean dropping any criminal charges?" Max enquired.

"Quite." Lonsdale allowed himself a wry smile.

The power of afternoon tea, Hannah concurred. *You just gotta love the way these guys do business.*

Max put down his cup. "So what happens next?"

"That is what we wanted to discuss with you. Detective Sergeant Mole is leaving for New Delhi tonight and will tie up with the local police. I will co-ordinate the investigation at this end and get our forensic teams involved as we need them. Have you had any word from your colleagues over there yet?"

"They're meeting up with Jock and Nisha at the field centre this morning and will interview the SINAC volunteers who worked with Okki. I should hear from Lawrence at any time." Hannah checked the screen again. As she did so, she reached into her laptop case and fished out a slim plastic wallet.

"Toby wanted you to have this," she explained. "He left it with me for when you guys finally came on board. It contains copies of her passport, birth certificate, driving licence, engagement letter from SINAC, even university degree certificates, girl-guide badges . . . everything he could find that he thought might help."

Lonsdale nodded to himself as he flicked through the documents. He passed the wallet over to his Detective Sergeant. "Then he is either psychic or an optimist."

"He is both," Max interrupted, "and I should know; I've seen the whites of his eyes in battle. He's a very determined man. He will not give up until he finds out who did this. Can I warn you now? He is extremely stubborn, not very diplomatic, tends to shoot first and take aim second and he can start an argument in a room on his own. Despite all that, his heart is true. He'll be delighted to know you're now involved."

"I'll go through this file with him tomorrow." Steve tucked the wallet into a sturdy black document case. "The more background information we have, the better. Whoever killed her knew what they were doing. The odds of us catching him just tipped in our favour."

After the handshakes, Lonsdale held the door and looked at Hannah. "Without your persistence this case would have been kicked into the long grass as just another suicide. Please let Toby know we'll do everything we can to bring this person to justice, whoever they are. My own daughter is not much older than Octavia and also did voluntary work during her gap year. She chose Africa. I worried about her every day, although I never told her. For me, this case is personal. Rest assured, we will get this bastard."

With the windscreen wipers on full, Max pulled out into a stream of traffic and headed towards the motorway junction. "I think I need to make the call. We clearly have someone to thank."

No sooner had he clipped the phone into its cradle than it sparked into life. He checked the screen and smiled across to Hannah. "Talk of the devil."

"Max, is that you? I meant to call you earlier but . . . well, I wasn't sure if . . . anyway, can you talk? Are you alone?"

"Good afternoon, Viren. I'm in the car with that scary American woman. She's just had a plate of raw liver so she's ready for action."

"Raw liver? I don't . . . anyway; I just wanted you to know that I spoke to the High Commissioner last night. He was most understanding. "

"And he has used his influence wisely, so we've just been informed," Max interrupted.

"Oh, right . . . then I take it the wheels are turning?"

"More like spinning. So we'd like to thank you for reacting so quickly."

There was a long pause on the line, during which time Max took a left turn, then indicated before taking the slip road up onto the M3.

"Max, I was wondering—"

"Viren, we can't offer any promises. You've made a very sensible decision. We'll do our best to help with the police inquiries. Just one question: who are you trying to protect?"

"What?" the voice spluttered. "You mean you don't know?"

"No idea."

"My son, of course. He was at the party. He said the police planted drugs on him."

"Viren, that's not the kind of thing the British police get up to and you know it. But whatever, you made the right call. Please let me know how things work out. We should catch up for a beer when I'm back from Switzerland."

"The Sinners Lounge?"

"Perfect."

They accelerated back onto the M3 heading towards Central London. Hannah heard a ping, fished the phone from her bag. The text wasn't from Lawrence. She didn't recognise the number. An American cell phone.

Han ur looking better than ever. Squash keeping u fit? Followed u 2 r old hot-dog stand in CP. Xtra hot chilli sauce, right? Bin 2 long. Can we talk? Curtis.

• CHAPTER 23 •

"The Beast? Behind us? It can't be?"

Jock strained his neck. Despite the sunglasses he had to shield his eyes from the glare shimmering off the Jensen's curved rear window. He could just make out the shape of a Jeep weaving through a mirage of heat and dust, accelerating hard towards them.

"They must've been following us. I didn't notice." Nisha swerved to avoid a deep gash in the road surface.

"Not *they*. There's only a driver. Pull over. I want to talk to him."

"But I can't, I can't stop here," Nisha protested. A short but steep drop fell away on both sides of the narrow road, now elevated as it dissected a large rice paddy. She pointed to a passing place up ahead.

"Nisha, just stop the fucking car!!" Jock kept his eyes on the Jeep and slammed his left hand on the dashboard. As she hit the brakes, the Jensen's tyres bit sharply into some loose dirt. It sent the car fishtailing across the road, Nisha fighting for control. The front driver's wheel spun close to the edge, flicking a shower of gravel out over the fields below.

Before the car came to a halt, there was an almighty explosion. A thousand crystals of glass filled the air, a starburst of light catching each shard before it bounced against the inside of the windscreen, peppering the back of the headrests and showering over the front and rear seats.

"What the . . .?" Jock instinctively ducked as a second bullet flashed between them, this time through the void where the back window used to be. It smashed into the windscreen, which turned to a sheet of ice before disgorging itself out over the bonnet.

"Get us the hell out of here! Go!!"

Nisha rammed the car into manual drive, flicked the sports button and floored the accelerator. The V8 engine let out a deep roar and the car leapt forward, careering back into the centre of the road, wheels spinning on the blacktop.

Jock wrestled with the seat belt as he pushed the remaining pieces of windscreen out of Nisha's line of sight. They were both covered in diamonds, which he swept down onto the floor as carefully as he could, using a cloth from a pocket in the passenger door.

"Jock, he's gaining on us. Whadda we do?"

"We get the fuck out of here. I'll call the police. Just get as far ahead as you can. The Jensen's much faster." Jock fumbled in his pocket, trying not to cut himself, leaning into the curves as they swung and bounced through the potholes.

"Much faster on a proper road but not out here. I hope there's no traffic coming the other way. He must have chosen this stretch." Nisha was wincing through the open windscreen. Flies and grit pebble-dashed her face in searing heat. Her eyes were streaming behind her sunglasses. She checked the mirror again. "There are two of them. The other guy must've been in the back. They're both wearing ski masks."

Another burst of gunfire like a demented drummer on speed. Jock saw the tracer lines shooting ahead into the blacktop. "They're aiming at the tyres. Keep weaving. Faster."

He found Chaudray's number and went to press the button, but the car lurched out onto an unmade road surface, sending the phone spinning out of his hands, down between the central column and the front passenger seat, deep into a pile of glass diamonds.

Nisha looked across at him. She had a cut on her left cheek. And panic in her eyes.

"Concentrate. How much further?" He could just reach the phone with his fingertips, but couldn't grip it.

"About ten minutes. We rejoin the main road just up ahead . . . oh no, look!"

Jock peered out at a large sign slung across the road, surrounded by piles of traffic cones. ROAD CLOSED – DETOUR. An arrow, pointing down to their right, picked out a dirt track skirting round an unmanned construction site ahead. Digging equipment, rollers, abandoned resurfacing trucks and wheelbarrows were strewn across a lunar landscape where the blacktop used to be.

In the middle distance, Jock could see traffic cruising along the main highway. Toy cars and trucks were heading serenely towards the clear outline of the field centre buildings and the small village beyond.

Another burst of gunfire zipped past them, shattering the arrow sign into thousands of tiny splinters. Jock could see old brickworks off to their left across a field of yellow mustard seed. A metalled roadway ran between the crumbling white chimney stacks and the kilns.

He pointed. "It must lead to the main road." The Road Closed barrier was powering towards them as the Jensen picked up speed again.

"You crazy? There could be rocks in that field. We don't have enough clearance."

"We've no chance the other way. Go for it."

Nisha rammed into third gear, used the handbrake to swing the rear end round and shot down the bank into the mustard seed. The Jeep was only seconds behind, powering through clouds of dust. It swung a right, clipping off the corner. Jock looked back to see the brake lights blurred by the dust, the vehicle sliding helplessly down the wrong slope.

"Head for that chimney."

The Jensen seemed to be hovering at high speed over a calm sea of surreal yellow waves, the wheels riding above the baked brown earth that held the lush crop. Nisha sneezed against the pollen and wiped away clouds of insects as she accelerated back up into top. She checked the mirror.

"They're back."

Within seconds, the Jensen burst out through a wooden gate, onto a sealed metal track that weaved between two old kilns. There were piles of unfinished bricks lining the route. The Jensen's tyres gripped firmly into the road surface as they accelerated away. Jock was straining to reach his phone. Blood dripped onto the soft leather from small cuts on his hand.

Nisha changed down and swung a hard left round the rubble of a chimney stack. At last they were putting some daylight between them and the Jeep. "Who are they? What do they want from us?"

Jock gave up. He felt a jolt of pain searing through his bleeding hand. The phone was just too far out of reach. The call would have to wait until they reached the safety of the main road.

He could see it clearly now. Just a couple more minutes. "We've been careless. They would've known where to find the keys. Your calendar will be in Outlook. I bet they've followed us from the apartment, waiting for the right moment. The roadworks are a perfect trap."

The surface was getting smoother as they powered on. The remnants of the brickworks were thinning out, with fewer piles on either side. Ahead Jock could see the road dissected what looked like the old entrance to the site. Small, square, brick buildings like sentry-boxes were guarding two solid-looking posts, one of which still held a rusty old gate hanging open and mostly off its hinges. The other gate was propped up nearby, clumps of stray mustard seed pushing up through the rusty iron latticework.

"But why try and kill us? What are they hoping to—" Nisha's words hung in the air between them, no time to finish the sentence. No time to finish anything. The space where the windscreen had been just minutes before was suddenly filled with a sight as old as India itself. It was an image that reached into the car and touched the very soul of the driver and her terrified passenger.

Nisha screamed and spun the wheel, sending the Jensen crashing into the side of a brick building. The twin retro-fitted airbags exploded into action, the noise deafening inside the car, pellets of glass tinkling like icicles.

Jock hit his head on something. He thought he heard the words *I love you* and *I'm sorry* before he blacked out. The side of the building collapsed onto the car. The roof surrendered to the weight of masonry, plasterwork and timber from the interior joists. Clouds of steam hissed out between the bricks from the shattered radiator, jets of hot oil ejaculated across the dusty track, the engine noise screaming momentarily then falling silent.

A solitary cow was standing in the middle of the road. It had wandered out from the side of the building. The animal was totally oblivious to the carnage it had caused. Instead, its long eyelashes flicked nonchalantly at a swarm of irritating flies. A long, thin, scraggy tail swung listlessly in the still morning heat. A couple of other cows looked on from the shadows, then returned to chewing the withered grasses nearby. They were joined by yet more cows from the adjacent field. One stuck its head through the open windscreen and sniffed cautiously at the two unconscious passengers still strapped into their luxury leather seats.

It soon lost interest and moved away, just before the Jeep came screeching to a halt.

CHAPTER 24

Jock could vaguely remember a sharp, painful impact quickly followed by a loud explosion before a large, white marshmallow appeared to cushion his face. It smelled of chemicals and stale air. He panicked at first, unable to breathe, the plastic surface folding in around his nose and mouth.

After a few seconds, he discovered the surface was pricked in tiny holes. As the marshmallow deflated, he began to relax and deflated with it. Taking slower, deeper breaths, his mind drifted back to a calmer, safer time when he was a child. Finally his eyes closed. Out of the grey void swirling around him, Jock could see the image of his father emerge, crouching over as he arranged home-made fireworks into small piles on the cold ground before them. "You ask so many questions, Noodle." The lips moved but it was obvious that his father wasn't really listening. He tried again to get his attention.

"What is lotus-seed paste, Papa?"

This time the man looked across and smiled. He leaned back on his haunches before raising himself to his full height. He stood next to the boy, resting large, rough hands on his willowy shoulders. "It's the sweet filling your mother uses for the mooncakes. Only she knows the recipe. She's been blessed with the secret by our ancestors."

He explained to the boy that they celebrated good fortune when the harvest was gathered in. The Moon Goddess was thanked for bringing rebirth after the winter snows when the fields became fertile once again.

"But my teacher said the harvest this year has failed us, Papa. He said the dry weather and summer heat had parched the fields leaving us barely enough to live on."

"Stop this nonsense! I will not hear of such talk in my family! It is the language of defeat, of ingratitude . . . of poverty. There will be enough to eat if we plan carefully and work hard." He gathered up the fireworks. "Hurry up or we'll be late for the festival."

The boy struggled to keep up. They followed other villagers down to the clearing by the bridge over the river. The light was fading fast, cold fingers of night rustling the solitary leaves now tinged with gold on their stick-thin branches. Brightly coloured lanterns were being hung in the willow trees near the water's edge and from the thatched rooftops of the mud-brick houses.

A small crowd had gathered by a towering bonfire, which was throwing out sparks and crackling spits of heat. Nearby, the village elders were standing by an old wooden table groaning under the weight of fireworks. As more villagers appeared, so the pile of fireworks grew. Jock could see that important decisions were being made about which fireworks would be lit in which order.

The women of the village were setting up trestle tables. Clouds of steam filled the night air from cauldrons of hot soup and wontons. Bowls were filled with fresh baozi and mooncakes. Large flagons of cassia wine and local honey ale were being unloaded from a wagon. The boy waved back to his mother as she stirred the soup. Despite the floating lanterns and the crackling bonfire, the village had been bathed in the coal-pitch of darkness. Suddenly the ground beneath their running feet was alight as the clouds parted and the full moon smiled down on their festivities. The first rocket pierced the night sky. Jock was excited. The thanksgiving party had begun.

"Papa, what is poverty?"

"So many questions." He shook his head after adding his fireworks to the pile. "Poverty is our greatest failure. In past times, there was no poverty. Each villager helped each other. We would share our good fortune and help others suffering hard times. In that way, people would help us when our harvest failed or the village was plagued with sickness or disease."

"So are we poor, Papa?"

"No, son, we will never be poor. We are privileged to be alive. We share our food, our laughter, our gratitude, our respect. We will always find a way to help others, to help ourselves. We will never be lonely or afraid, never feel unloved or forgotten, so long as we keep the love for all humanity burning in our hearts."

The boy cocked his head towards the bridge, caught the faint sounds of music coming from the dark woods beyond the river. As he listened, the music grew louder: drums, whistles, reed pipes, lutes, crashing symbols, zithers and a riot of other sounds. His eyes traced the moonlit line of the dirt track over the wooden bridge, across the open fields before it plunged into a V-shaped clearing in the far trees.

A troupe of players danced their way out of the darkness, lanterns swinging as they came, coloured lights and playful shadows bringing the trees back to life. Behind them followed a caravan of wagons that swayed to the rhythm of the oxen, as they plodded towards the bridge. Running alongside the wagons, the boy could see jugglers and fire-eaters, magicians and dancers in brightly coloured costumes. Weird exotic animals, the likes of which he'd never seen before, skipped along in time to the music.

The boy scampered to join a horde of other excited children

racing across the bridge. Within minutes the players and their caravan had arrived. They pitched their tents in the middle of the clearing; puppet shows, animal rides, games of pitch and toss, stalls selling trinkets and lucky charms, magical people with bells on their fingers, mysterious painted faces that could see into the future. The music grew louder. A space was cleared for the dancers to perform; costumes of orange, pink, red and a thousand other colours caught in the golden light from the bonfire.

The boy sat mesmerised by the shadow puppets as they enacted great feats of bravery and honour, life and death, love and treachery. The music and dancing seemed to fade into the background as he watched the heroic figures weave the thread of their timeless stories before a silent and enthralled crowd of adults and children alike, seated patiently on the cold ground.

The words of his father seemed to be coming from the mouths of the puppets in the play. He must learn their truth, must see how light will always overcome darkness, must never be afraid of the unknown and must believe in the richness of spring that drives away the desolation of winter.

Suddenly the boy felt a strong hand grip his shoulder, shaking him. Jock looked up at an unfamiliar face wearing a green mask, reaching into the car, mumbling to him.

The cows had gone. The Jeep had gone.

Nisha had gone.

CHAPTER 25

"Just a second, Wanda, I can't talk in here." Toby was pressing the phone deeper into his ear. He nodded towards Lawrence and slipped out of the ward.

Jock was sitting up. The sour-faced nurse had straightened his pillows. His bandaged hands lay listless on the clean, white sheets. A monitor on the wall behind him was tracing out a steady heartbeat.

"No, Jock, it wasn't Bjorn Slagle in the Jeep." Lawrence offered him a sip of water. "We called him in Stockholm. He was very upset about Okki. We reckon he was already in Sweden when you found her. Incidentally, his mother passed away; the funeral is on Friday. We sent our condolences."

"Poor guy . . . I can't believe we even suspected him. I will arrange some flowers."

"Jock, you're not arranging anything for a few days. The paramedic said you were severely concussed and lucky to be alive. You're under observation until they're sure there is no lasting damage. How much can you remember?"

Jock paused for a minute. His glazed eyes seemed to be searching through a thousand nightmare images. "I was angry; I lost my temper . . . I shouldn't have . . . but how dare they try to kill us. We're here to help these people . . . I'm sorry, I'm not making much sense."

"You're doing fine." Lawrence could see the nurse scowling at him. She attended to the monitor, and then left the room. Lawrence knew they didn't have much time.

"There was a cow in the middle of the road . . . then it all went blank. I hadn't appreciated . . . Nisha said . . . her religion . . . where is she?" Jock closed his eyes.

"We don't know. She'd gone before the police arrived. You must have called Chaudray before he called me. They searched the whole area. They found the Jeep a few miles away. Forensics are running tests on both cars. The Jensen is a write-off. I'm so sorry."

"Nisha gone? Oh my God, no . . . I must find her . . . she has to be OK. They must've taken her. But why just her and not me?" The monitor skipped a beat and then pulsed erratically, a buzzer bringing the nurse scurrying back into the room.

"The patient must rest. You're stressing him too much. I must ask you to leave." She extracted a thermometer, wiped it and noted the reading on his chart.

"No, Nurse, I need a few more minutes please, it's very important we talk. It won't take long." Jock's bruised eyes peered out beneath the bandages swathed around his head.

She paused, then jabbed at her watch. "Very well, five minutes, no longer. I will come back. Five minutes."

As she reached for the door, it swung open, Toby holding it for her, the faintest of smiles on his lips. He waited for her to scowl through, then closed it quietly.

"I think we may have a lead." Toby pulled up a chair, lowering his voice. "Wanda went to the address in Utrecht. It's a retail outlet selling shoes with an apartment upstairs. The owner has lived there for thirty years. He'd never heard of the two girls."

"Chaudray also drew a blank with them. He's checking with Immigration," Lawrence added.

"What, the two Dutch girls? You think they're involved?" Jock pinched the top of his nose before he tilted his head back to stop a trickle of blood. Lawrence helped him with a tissue.

"Dr Bhattacharya said they'd left before breakfast. The receptionist overheard them talking about a charity project in Sydney. The taxi was taking them to the airport," Lawrence explained.

"Did she catch the name of the taxi firm?" Jock asked the ceiling fan.

"Yes, we're on to it." Lawrence looked across at Toby and got the nod of approval. "Jock, we need to know more about Project Amrita. It looks like someone doesn't want this to happen."

Lawrence saw Jock's head relax into the pillows. He could sense the turmoil going on behind the young man's eyes; a swirling brew of anger, fear and confusion. "My father had a dream. He died before it came true. I vowed to make it happen. Now it is my dream. With Nisha's help, we can end this suffering."

Jock's eyes drifted to the door behind Toby as it slowly creaked open. Lawrence and Toby looked round. A small Indian boy was standing in the doorway, perhaps seven or eight years old, Lawrence guessed. His painfully thin body was draped in rags. Spindly brown legs showed the early signs of rickets, bowing out from skeletal hips down to his deformed bare feet. His black eyes were fathomless pools, drinking in the bright lights of the hospital ward. An outstretched arm was trembling, bony fingers clutching a small, white envelope.

In a flash the boy shot into the room, dropped the envelope on the bed and ran out. Lawrence spun out of his chair and chased after him. Despite his infirmity, the boy was lightning fast and had reached the top of the stairs by the lifts long before Lawrence was halfway down the corridor. He saw the boy stop, look back, almost for reassurance, then scamper off down the two flights of stairs towards the main hospital entrance.

Lawrence slowed to a stop, put his hands on his knees and slumped over gasping for breath. The exertion, relentless heat and humidity had sucked all the air out of the corridor. He was sheathed in sweat, his thin, cotton shirt painted onto his back and chest. He was about to turn away when he saw a man's head appear above the top step.

Lawrence straightened himself up and watched as the head became a chest, an outstretched right arm holding something not yet in view. The man was immaculately dressed in a brilliant white shirt and red silk tie beneath a dark-blue blazer with round gold buttons. Steel-rimmed sunglasses rested carefully on top of his short, neat haircut.

The man had a firm grip on the back of the boy's neck. The two figures were rising like a phoenix to the top of the stairs. Lawrence could see the man was tall, very tall. Expensive grey slacks were creased to a sharp edge and brushed the top of his highly polished black brogues. The boy gave up the struggle and walked alongside the man towards him, taking two paces for every one of his. Lawrence admired the way the man walked – ramrod straight, shoulders back, easy strides, uniform steps, confident without any arrogant swagger, the rhythm evenly paced. He was a man who made a statement with every move, a gunslinger striding to the final showdown. Lawrence had the distinct feeling he had seen him somewhere before.

"His name is Ravi. He is from the slums. He would like to apologise for being so rude." The man was towering over Lawrence, perhaps 6'4" or even taller. He had unbuttoned his blazer. The fit was perfect for his lean muscular body. Lawrence noticed a slight bulge under his left armpit.

"Thank you for your assistance. We need to ask this boy some questions." Lawrence noticed the man was showing no signs of exertion or that he was even warm. He looked like he had stepped off the front cover of a men's fashion magazine.

"I may be able to help you. Ravi doesn't speak much English." The man nodded along the corridor. "Down here?"

"Again thank you." Lawrence was struggling to regain some composure. *Expect the unexpected.* "Can I ask, have we met before?"

"Sort of," the man replied as he marched the boy off towards the ward, catching Lawrence in the slipstream. As they drew near, Lawrence could hear Toby's voice protesting. He knocked and pushed the door open.

"If you do not leave right now, I will call security and have you thrown out!" The nurse had taken up a protective position between an agitated Toby and her dazed patient. With hands firmly planted on her ample hips, she presented a fearsome sight. Lawrence realised he was just in time.

"Toby, this gentleman kindly apprehended the boy for us and has offered to translate while we ask him some questions. Can you bring the letter? I think we should get some cold drinks downstairs and leave the nurse to tend to her patient." He smiled towards her but there was no flicker of response.

"Visiting tonight is from six until eight –" she spelt the words out slowly "– with no more than two per bed. Do I make myself clear?"

The cafe on the ground floor lay just off the main entrance and was mercifully quiet. Lawrence chose a table under an electric fan, which, he soon realised, was just moving the hot air around. The man positioned the boy in the corner seat, blocked in by Toby on the other side. Lawrence arranged for a tray of cold bottled water and some fizzy drinks. He was tempted by the smell of fresh samosas but decided they could eat later.

The man introduced himself as Lal.

"You must forgive us, is Lal your first name or your family name?" Lawrence kept his eyes fixed on the man. *Where have I seen him?*

"Just call me Lal." He had let go of the boy's neck. He placed his sunglasses in the middle of the scarred Formica table. "Are you Mr Lawrence or Mr Toby?"

"I'm sorry?" Lawrence glanced quizzically at him.

"Gentlemen, I know who you are and why you are here. I shall explain but first we have a more pressing matter." He turned to the boy and spoke to him in Hindi.

The boy became animated, speaking faster and faster, his eyes pleading to be released, bone-thin fingers pointing towards the door where more and more people had started pushing through, the noise level rising.

The man straightened his tie. "He says he was promised another fifty rupees when he delivered the letter. He must go outside to collect it."

"Promised? Promised by who, for God's sake?" Toby leaned forward, about to grab Lal by his lapels.

"Ah, you must be Mr Toby," Lal replied calmly. "Mr Hartley told me about you."

"Max? Max Hartley? How do you know Max Hartley?" Toby was on his feet, sweaty hands sliding across the tabletop. The boy stood up and was quickly pushed back down by a strong, blazered arm.

Lal explained the boy must return to the street outside in the next few minutes. He asked him another question in Hindi, which seemed to relax him. "I shall go with him. If the man doesn't appear, I will give him the other fifty rupees he

172

was promised. If he does appear, I will bring the man back with me. You wait here. If something should go wrong, meet me in my office."

"What the fuck is going on? Who are you?" Toby had moved round the table. Lawrence intervened. He grabbed hold of Toby's arm and twisted it gently until he stopped. A security guard in a military style uniform sitting by the main entrance looked across. He stood up, slapped his truncheon into his empty hand for effect, assessed the situation, decided his involvement was not required and sat down again.

"Lal, we can come with you," Lawrence suggested in a quieter voice. The idea seemed to meet with Toby's approval.

"No, it will scare him off. No disrespect, but you both stand out like – how do you say – sore fingers?" He had hold of the boy by the neck again. His left hand was fishing in the pocket of his blazer.

"Sore thumbs," Lawrence corrected. "And you're right. So how do we find your office?"

"Wait here. If I'm not back in say, thirty minutes, meet me at this address at two p.m." He handed Lawrence a gold-embossed business card. "Any tuk-tuk driver will take you there."

Lawrence fingered the card and looked up at Toby, by which time the man and his captive had vanished into the crowd. Lawrence managed a smile. "I think I was wrong about not drinking on this trip. I could use a very large Glenlivet right now."

"I'm sorry; I shouldn't have lost it like that. It's just that ever since we got here nothing seems to have gone right. Who the hell is this guy? Where did he come from?" Toby poured the rest of the bottled water into their glasses and took a mouthful. "Not quite a single malt, is it?"

Lawrence inspected the card. It was written in Hindi with English on the reverse in italics. "No name or website; just a mobile number and an address in the Paharganj district. BKR Security."

"Did Lal say the boy had been hired by a man to deliver the letter? I thought the two Dutch girls were behind all this?" Toby pulled the letter out and handed it over.

"We don't know anything for sure. We thought the Swedish guy was a murderer until an hour ago. Maybe the girls are innocent as well. They could be in Sydney by now." Lawrence read to the bottom of the page, then checked the other side – blank. The envelope was equally unhelpful. *Jock Lim, Ward 23, 2nd Floor* neatly typed, centred, 18-point Times New Roman, Lawrence guessed. "Have we accessed this drop box address yet?"

"You kidding me?" Toby held up his mobile "I don't know why the signs bother saying No Mobiles in here; there's no signal anyway. We need to get back to the hotel . . . assuming Lal is a no-show."

Lawrence read the words out loud in case he'd missed something. "If you want to see Nisha again make the instructions to the online drop box and enter using password Amrita. She will be killed if you talk with the police. We are watching you."

Toby took it back and folded it into the envelope. "Jock buzzed for the nurse to get a Wi-Fi access code and that led to the argument. He was pretty much out of it anyway. We'll talk to him later. I hope to God Nisha's OK."

Lawrence looked concerned. "I'm worried about leaving Jock here. They know where he is. They might come back."

"Lawrence, they could have kidnapped him from the wreckage this morning or finished him off before the police got there," Toby explained, "apart from which we don't know who we're looking for. It could be Lal for all we know or one of the doctors or maybe even the nurse. God knows she's scary enough."

"You're right." He checked his watch. "OK, that's it, thirty minutes. Let's get back to the hotel and get online. By the way, can your tech boys find out who set up the drop box?"

Toby offered a half smile. "I think you already know the answer to that."

CHAPTER 26

Curtis Opperman.

He's got a bloody cheek, after all these years, Hannah thought. But then, it's typical of him. No consideration for anyone else. Curtis only does what Curtis wants to do. To hell with the consequences. So what does he want this time? It's not like him to hide behind a text message. Curtis is a balls-out-front kinda guy. He's not known for his diplomacy, even less for his sensitivity.

Maybe he's changed? It must be twenty years after all, she reasoned. Hadn't he run away to Europe? Isn't that what Davina said? And she should know. She'd kept his bed warm all that time. Davina? Davina Kowalski. Whatever happened to her? Some friend she turned out to be. Funny how memories were never intact: like a scratch-card, you had to scrape away the crap to get to the truth.

Over dinner last night, Hannah had tried to push his name out of her mind. Ally and Tom had been perfect hosts, as usual. She could hear herself asking how Stella was getting on at school and what her new boyfriend was like. She tried to console them that nowadays facial tattoos and a nose piercing were perfectly normal.

But it was no good. Ally could see straight through her. If you can't fool yourself you've no chance with your own sister. In the end, she confessed about the text. No, she didn't know how he'd got her number. The bigger worry was why? Why did he want to talk to her? Had he been following her? Curtis always had an ulterior motive. It wouldn't be a social call.

Her day had started off OK. Max had dropped her at Terminal 4. He was flying British Airways to Geneva from Terminal 5. He wasn't looking forward to dinner with their troublesome banking client. They were still sitting on the invoices. At least they'd heard Toby and Lawrence were making progress and that Steve Mole had arrived in New Delhi and was meeting up with Chaudray. Max had kissed her on the cheek and wished her a safe flight home.

After he'd gone, Hannah started to feel strangely light-headed. She knew Lawrence was OK if a little frustrated with Toby but that was to be expected. Everything was under control back in the office, according to Kitty. She was in good time and knew what she was doing, as she'd caught this flight to JFK many times before.

Yet she felt uneasy, somehow distracted. She managed to leave her passport in the plastic tray at security. They had to call her name twice before she realised. She bought a thank-you present for Kitty at duty-free and tried to pay with her squash club membership card.

Curtis Opperman, you bastard. Even now, he could just show up and disrupt her life. She wanted to tell Lawrence. But how could she? It might be something and nothing. Besides, Lawrence had his hands full. Worse, he might think she was being disloyal. She loved him, loved their new life together, the past was the past. But was she being disloyal? Why was she allowing this man back in? As they called her gate number, she made the decision. It was only a conversation. She would take the short Skype call and that would be it.

She found a quiet corner of the gate lounge and logged on. Even before she'd fixed her earpiece, he was there, filling her tiny screen. He must be in an office somewhere, she decided.

His head was framed against a sunlit window, the light casting a halo around his distinguished features. He was wearing different glasses from the last time she saw him. They suited him; more modern, less formal somehow, showcasing the boyish twinkle in his blue-grey eyes.

His dark hair was distinctively styled as ever and combed through in places with silver. The years had been kind to his smooth, olive complexion. For a moment, Hannah hoped he thought the same was true of her. But it was only for a moment. She tried to stay focused.

"Hello, Hannah."

She wanted to reply but instead found herself listening to the gate announcement. They were boarding by row numbers. She didn't hear which. Besides, she was in business class so the row numbers didn't matter. She could board at any time. Damn him, damn him to hell!

"I was in New York last Friday morning. I had a meeting on Lexington Avenue," Curtis explained; matter-of-fact, almost apologetic. "You came out of the Racquets Club with someone. You looked terrific. I like your hair like that. Sorry, I guess I just followed you, like a regular stalker."

He hadn't lost his sense of humour. That's what she'd first noticed about him. A Wall Street banker who thought life was a game. He wasn't like the others. They were so serious, so up themselves. Curtis was rich, handsome and just didn't care what people thought of him. He must have been good at his job or else they'd have fired him. Most importantly, he made her laugh. She hadn't even tried to resist.

"Your office gave me your number. I lied and said I was your long-lost cousin in town for a few days. They were very helpful."

The light in the window behind him had faded just enough

for her to make out a range of snow-capped mountains. *Where was he?*

"OK, I can see this is a bad time. You'd better catch your plane. There's just one question I wanted to ask."

She tried to remain impassive, forcing herself to block out the feelings stirring deep inside; frustration, confusion, attraction, revulsion, pain, deceit. This man could bring out the best and the worst in her without even trying. For her own sanity, she had to go. *What question?*

"Will you have dinner with me in Uppsala?" Curtis fluttered his long eyelashes and tilted his head to one side as he spoke. The full charm offensive had begun. "I've been invited to hear your presentation. 'The Cesspool of Human Misery.' I'm looking forward to it."

"What do you want, Curtis?"

Hannah was angry with herself. Why didn't she just disconnect? No, she didn't want dinner with him in Uppsala or anywhere else. For the first time in years, she'd actually found a man she wanted to be with. He was loving and kind and considerate. He cherished her and had filled her life with passion and fun. Now, as soon as his back was turned, while he was overseas helping a friend through a horrendous tragedy, here she was being propositioned by Curtis bloody Opperman. "There's something important I want to discuss with you. You're the only person who can help me. I think you'll be very excited when I tell you. Now's not the time to talk, I know. If you join me for dinner, I'll put my cards on the table. Whatever you decide, I'll go with it. No pressure, I just need a chance to explain. Please say yes."

A few minutes later, Hannah was sipping a Bloody Mary as the American Airlines Dreamliner taxied to its take-off position. The captain announced a flying time of seven hours and ten minutes, given the strong head wind. He would update them on weather conditions at JFK when they began their descent. Sit back and relax, he said.

How the hell could she relax?

CHAPTER 27

Lal had become quite demonstrative as he pointed to a dot on the map spread across his desk. "The boy stood on this corner and I observed from here."

Lawrence had wasted no time when they got back to the hotel. He'd updated Hannah while Toby had spoken at length to Max. Lawrence could hear Toby's initial anger at not being told about Lal. It quickly turned to praise. Over lunch they had formulated a plan; or so Lawrence had believed.

"The boy took the money and disappeared back towards the slum area here. I took some photographs and followed the man along Chelmsford Road towards Rajiv Chowk or Connaught Place, as you would call it, just . . . here."

"So were you on foot?" Lawrence interjected, wondering if he should believe this story.

"At first yes, but the man jumped into a tuk-tuk so I did the same. He was dropped off here on Babar Road near the Bengali Market. It's an area famous for fresh vegetables and street food stalls. There were lunchtime crowds. I lost him about here. I tried asking some people if they recognised him but nobody did."

"And what about the boy?" It was Toby interjecting this time. "Did he say anything about the man? How did they meet?"

Lal hesitated and then explained that the boy said he was begging at the gates to the hospital as usual. He said people had more compassion when they came out than when they went in so late morning was a good time. He had sold all his box of lighters. The man just asked if he'd like to earn a hundred rupees. That was more than he'd taken all morning. The boy had never seen him before and said that the man spoke with an unusual accent like he wasn't a local.

"Do you think he meant from another part of Delhi or another part of India?" Toby prodded.

"Another part of India, I'm quite sure of it." Lal turned the camera round. "Here is the man. From his clothes, I'd say he must live south of the city, Uttar Pradesh maybe. See here, there is some jewellery. I might be able to enlarge these pictures."

Toby peered at the screen. "Did you think of apprehending the man? Inviting him here to meet us?"

Lal sat back abruptly in his chair, the question stinging him, or so Lawrence thought. The flash of anger soon passed, his calm demeanour restored. "Yes, Mr Toby, I did consider bringing him here but I thought it best to see where he was leading. I might have found the girl. Did Mr Hartley say her name was Nisha? Do you have a photograph of her, by the way?"

Lawrence caught the nod; it was time for them to make sure. If Lal was to be part of their team, they needed to know if he could be trusted. Instinct alone was not sufficient. There was too much at stake. And they didn't have the time to learn the hard way. It was now or never.

Toby stood up and strolled over to the bookcase leaning against the far wall. It had seen better days; the wood veneer was chipped in places and there was a long crack in the glass panel on one of the doors. Inside Lawrence could see a ramshackle collection of books, mostly in Hindi but one or two in English. Most prominent was an out-of-date copy of *Jane's Military Aircraft*.

Toby picked up one of the model planes gathering dust and

twirled it through its paces. He spun round in mid manoeuvre. "This is one of the new ones. Do they call it a Tejas?"

Lal looked confused for a moment. Lawrence could see him searching their faces for an explanation but none was offered. Eventually he spluttered a reply, "Yes, the HAL Tejas Mk2; single-seater multi-role fighter. It is replacing the old MIGs."

Toby resumed his manoeuvre, brought it safely in to land and taxied it back into its allotted place on top of the bookcase. "Hindustan Aeronautics Limited is one of my clients. We've done some work on the radar and avionics systems for this plane and its big brother, the Mark 3 Stealth Fighter."

Lal was fidgeting uncomfortably. Lawrence saw a bead of sweat on his forehead for the first time, despite the efficient air-con system whispering away in the corner of his surprisingly modern office.

Toby pulled himself to his full height and took up an attack position. "Flight Lieutenant Chakrapani Lal, aged thirty-two, single, no dependents, formerly based in Jodhpur with 15 Squadron, trained on MIG 27s before upgrading to MIG 29s; successfully completed a joint IAF / RAF tactical air supremacy course at RAF Cranwell last year; awarded a commendation during a tour of duty over Kashmir; recommended for promotion to Squadron Leader and completed initial training on the HAL Tejas Mk 1 before ... well, before something happened."

The room went silent. Lawrence could pick out the drone of traffic noise filtering up from the street below. It was punctured by a siren, perhaps a police car or an ambulance in the distance. Uneven wafts of cool air breezed across the open space as the swing filters played back and forth. A door opened and closed somewhere down the corridor; maybe the accountants' office next door or the travel agency next door to them. Lawrence was undecided, uninterested, the unfolding drama just too absorbing.

After an eternity, Lal was on his feet, held their gaze, thought better of what he was going to say, Lawrence surmised, then spun away to look out of the dusty window. In that moment, Lawrence knew what they would hear next would be the truth. It would be the truth they needed to understand and believe in before any further progress could be made with the young private detective.

When it came, his voice was much softer. The words reflected off the window and filled the room with their apology. "There was a girl ... she was an actress, a rising star in Bollywood ... she was beautiful ... and I mean stunningly beautiful. I was flattered, it happened so quickly ... she was Muslim. I later discovered she had family in Pakistan, some of them connected to the military ... I didn't know; she never said. I was foolish."

His head slumped onto his chest, supported by uncertain arms clutching hold of the windowsill. When he eventually turned back into the room, Lawrence could see the hurt etched across his handsome features. "I did nothing wrong, I only breached procedure. I'd forgotten it was a restricted-access area. She wasn't a spy but they didn't believe me. They forced me to resign my commission. It was the biggest mistake of my life."

"And the girl?" Toby kept up the pressure.

"Gone, of course, gone back to the movie screen where she belonged. She was not real; she was never real. She fell in love with my uniform ... she will break many hearts, just because she can." He unclipped his top button, loosened his tie. He fell back into his chair, awaiting his fate.

"So why security?" Toby again, searching for answers.

"I couldn't get a job doing anything else. The Air Force was my life. It's all I've ever known. My parents were so proud . . . now they're ashamed." He blinked, drew breath. "I got my security licence and NPB firearms certificate in only a few weeks. You must understand, I want them to be proud of me again."

"And what kind of security work do you do?" Toby was unrelenting.

"Mostly protection and bodyguard work for wealthy businessmen. I can provide testimonials. I said this to Mr Hartley," he spluttered. "Security is big business in India. There were over three thousand children kidnapped in Delhi alone last year. The ransom demands can be lucrative."

Lawrence saw Toby look across at the certificates on the wall by the door. The story seemed to make sense. They exchanged a glance. They'd heard enough.

"Thank you," Lawrence replied. "I'm sorry we had to put you through that. When Max told us what he knew, we had to fill in the blanks, get the rest of the story. Your face was so familiar. Then I remembered. You were sat by the lifts at our hotel last night."

"Gentlemen, I've been following you since you arrived. India is not a safe place to be asking the sort of questions you must ask. It is not what it seems. I'm so sorry for what happened to your daughter, Mr Toby. If only I could have been there to protect her. Please . . . perhaps I can offer you some tea and we can start again, at the beginning. My name is Lal and I'm at your service."

After drinks had been served, it was Toby who broke the silence. "Lal, I've provisionally agreed with Max to double the amount we're paying you. Now that you've answered our questions, I will confirm this arrangement. I don't want money to get in the way of this investigation. I need your undivided attention. Please cancel any other work and invoice me accordingly."

Toby's blue eyes were piercing. Lawrence could feel the energy coursing through him. "I want to find the man you were following. I want Nisha returned unharmed. I want the event in Uppsala to go ahead as planned."

He paused.

"I want to find the bastard who killed my daughter."

CHAPTER 28

"Intellectual property? For fuck's sake!!" Jock was livid.

The rest had clearly done him good. Lawrence could see the head wound was not as serious as they feared. A row of tidy stitches was clearly visible under the new dressing. Jock's empty plate confirmed his appetite had returned. Anyone who could have eaten that greasy concoction must have been hungry. Another good sign, he concluded.

"The drop box is asking you to transfer all the intellectual property rights connected with Project Amrita to them . . . well, to a legal entity to be nominated by them when you indicate acceptance of their terms. Once the transfer is complete to their satisfaction, Nisha will be returned unharmed." Lawrence was pleased they had privacy on the ward. Sadly the bunch of flowers he bought for the nurse had proven to be a poor investment. He had to put them in some water himself.

"And who is *them*?" Jock had freshened up and put on the clean pyjamas, dressing gown and slippers Toby had brought. He was sitting in a sturdy armchair next to the bed. The machine had been disconnected. The dressings on his hands and arms had been changed. The ward had been sprayed with disinfectant and now smelled to Lawrence like a proper hospital.

"We don't yet know," Toby explained. "I've asked my tech team to contact the drop box people and see if we can squeeze out a name. It's unlikely and, even if they do, it probably won't help. Whoever is behind this knows what they're doing. It will be a labyrinth of user names and server addresses, but we will follow it up."

"I still can't believe this is happening. How do they know? Each of our business partners is sworn to secrecy." Jock ran long fingers through his short, black hair, flicking the ends up into a forest of spikes.

Lawrence opened a notepad. "Jock, tell us, how does Project Amrita tie in with your dream . . . your father's dream?"

Jock hesitated, scanned both their faces as if for the first time and took a slow, deep breath. "Please don't think me rude or ungrateful, but I hardly know you. I'm not sure who . . ."

"You can trust?" Toby finished the sentence for him. "I fully understand your caution. Jock, I am convinced my daughter is dead because of this project of yours. Your own fiancée is being held hostage somewhere. God forbid but she may already be dead or being tortured as we sit here. Whatever you both know is clearly worth killing for. The sooner you tell us, the sooner we can help you . . . and help ourselves. I need to get my hands on these people."

Jock gripped the arms of the chair and made as if to stand up. Lawrence could feel the anger running through him; sensing the need to move around, piece things together. The effort proved too much and he collapsed back, relaxing his grip. Jock looked helplessly at them.

"We love Okki; she is our friend. We never thought getting her involved would lead to this . . . I'm so sorry for what I've done. I should never have introduced her to Ingmar."

"Ingmar?" Lawrence scribbled his first note.

"Ingmar Persson is the CEO of Henning Technologies, one of our business partners. He had flown over to sign the heads of agreement contract . . . we had dinner to celebrate . . . Okki was so excited to meet him."

"She never mentioned his name," Toby retorted. "And yet she emailed me after that dinner."

"Toby, I asked her to keep everything she heard confidential."

"Even from her own father?" Toby coloured slightly, his voice stronger. Lawrence raised an open palm to restrain him. It caught his eye.

"Toby, I've been trying to keep a tight hold of this project. I feared our scientific breakthrough would get out. It's all down to Nisha and her team. It's her genius that's behind it. I see now my actions have actually created suspicion. I cannot release the IP rights if my dream is to be fulfilled."

"But why not? What's so important?" Toby pushed.

"Because it is the key we've been looking for. I want to announce it in such a way that there is no going back. I want everyone's attention; for all the right reasons." Jock pressed his fingertips lightly onto his temples, massaging the soft skin around the dressing. He narrowed his eyes against the glare from the lights.

Lawrence wanted more answers. "Jock, what role does Henning play in Project Amrita?"

The words seemed to bring him back. He lowered his hands onto his lap, opened his eyes wider. "We've developed a new transmission frequency called EMX-Band. Ingmar and his team will enable us to transmit to all territories across India currently reachable by voice and data communications. They're adapting existing transmission technology to handle it, working closely with the engineers at Sangbu, another of our business partners."

"The Korean company? But they make TVs and hi-fi equipment. How can this eradicate world poverty?" Toby shrugged his shoulders.

"Toby, you don't understand, I'm trying to—"

189

"Please go on, Jock, we will stop interrupting." Lawrence made more notes.

"Sangbu equipment is being adapted to receive the EMX signals and transform the frequency to the required setting. Nisha understands this better than I do; you'll have to forgive me."

Lawrence could hear footsteps coming down the corridor. "So how many other business partners are involved in this project?"

"As well as Henning and Sangbu, we are working closely with the University of Delhi, using their research facilities for our incubator company. They also provide accommodation for SINAC volunteers. Dr Bhattacharya has been a tower of strength for us."

The knock on the door was firm but gentle, causing a ripple around the room, breaking the intensity. For Lawrence, it was an unwelcome interruption but somehow he felt the timing would be opportune, giving Jock a chance to gather himself for what must be difficult questions.

"Come in," Toby responded, his impatience barely contained.

Through the doorway stepped a well-dressed, solidly built man carrying a huge wicker basket of fresh fruit tied with an elaborate blue and silver bow. He put the basket on a low table by the door. "Jock, I'm so sorry, I didn't realise you had guests."

"Ranjit, your timing as ever is impeccable." Jock managed a weak smile.

"My dear friend, how are you? How are you feeling? Are they looking after you? I have some influence in this hospital, I can . . ." Ranjit had moved to his side and was inspecting the bandages.

"Don't fret, Ranjit, they are treating me well. The doctor has said he will release me tomorrow if the test results are clear." Jock pointed to a chair nearby.

"And have you heard from Nisha? I've been worried sick."

"All we know is that Nisha has been kidnapped. Whoever has done it has promised to keep her safe until a ransom demand is met. These gentlemen are here to help us." He turned awkwardly. "Gentlemen, may I introduce Mr Ranjit Singh, CEO of our most important business partner, Gupta Geothermal."

After the introductions and handshakes, Lawrence accepted the business card and slipped it into his pocket. He explained about their connection to Jock, the meeting they'd had with the police yesterday and the events of today. Lawrence noted the genuine look of surprise and dismay on Ranjit's face.

"I know Chakrapani Lal very well. In fact, he recently joined my Rotary club," Ranjit announced. "Gentlemen, although there are many people living in Delhi, it is a close-knit business community. Rotary is more like a family circle for the elite."

"We are both long-standing Rotarians," Toby explained, producing a Paul Harris pin from his pocket and flashing it with pride.

"Then I am amongst friends." Ranjit smiled. "I still haven't given up hope of persuading Jock to join us. I've tried to explain he will realise his dreams much quicker within Rotary but he is not yet convinced."

Lawrence didn't hear the footsteps this time, the door suddenly bursting open as an angry figure powered into the room. The nurse anchored herself resolutely and glowered at them. "No more than two per bed. I've had enough today, you have tested my patience. Now all of you, get out!!"

Ranjit stood up, turned slowly towards her, bowed his head slightly, and then spoke in his native tongue. His voice was calm, measured and hardly raised above the steady whirring of the ceiling fan. When he'd finished speaking, he bowed his head again and sat down. To Lawrence's surprise the nurse let her eyes fall to the floor and backed out of the room without saying another word, slowly closing the door behind her.

Ranjit resumed as if nothing had happened. "Rotary is a most influential network across all of India . . . Jock, I really think you should reconsider, once, of course, we have Nisha back and Project Amrita is the success we all know it will be."

Toby smiled at him. "What did you say to her? That woman's been a pain in the butt all day."

"It's not important. She just needed reminding about one or two things. No disrespect, but you have much to learn about India. That's why you will need the help of people like Chakrapani Lal and my good self to guide you through," Ranjit explained.

"Thank you, we're happy to accept the help of a fellow Rotarian." Lawrence opened up a clean page. "So please, can I ask again? Project Amrita, EMX-Band, Gupta Geothermal and Nisha. What's the connection?"

It was Jock who responded. "After studying this for many years, I am convinced poverty can be eradicated when four factors are present at the same time. I have created the acronym PHEW."

"PHEW?" Lawrence wrote it down, tried to guess what each letter stood for, gave up and listened instead.

Jock sat up straighter in the chair.

"*Peace*; people must feel safe and secure, with the freedom to practise their religion or express their opinions without the threat of repression, violence, war, injustice or criminal activity."

He paused, took a sip from the glass by his bedside.

"*Health*; having access to clean water and proper sanitation, vaccines and medical facilities and relief from famine with proper nutrition and a healthy diet."

Lawrence scribbled away frantically as Jock continued.

"*Education*; people need to be literate and numerate with an understanding of how modern society works. We need citizens with marketable skills and self-confidence, having the intellectual ability to help themselves."

Lawrence was struggling to keep up.

Jock completed his acronym: "*Wealth*; people must develop entrepreneurial skills within a free market economy; financially independent with the ambition to better themselves and provide for their family and their community. These are the building blocks to eradicating poverty," he concluded.

"So where does Project Amrita fit in?" Lawrence caught the smile on Ranjit's face, a smile of acknowledgement for an argument well made, an argument he had no doubt heard from Jock many times before.

Jock was quick to respond. "For me, it's all about health. Unless you have clean water and proper sanitation, you'll never escape misery and disease. As Ranjit knows, so many Rotary projects fail because of the costs involved in buying diesel oil for generators to power water pumps or waste water treatment plants. These costs seem so small to us, yet are beyond the reach of most poor villagers. Project Amrita will overcome this obstacle using the ingenuity of science."

The door opened again. This time the nurse was joined by a colleague who held it open. The nurse entered bearing a tray of hot tea and biscuits. Her colleague pulled up a small table next to the bed. Mugs of tea were served with benevolent smiles before the two nurses left the room. Lawrence basked in the look of total astonishment on Toby's face.

Jock bit into a biscuit. "Amrita is to be the first of many projects that will utilise our scientific breakthrough for the good of humanity. Science will once again be owned by the people, for the benefit of the people. As Nisha would say, we're at the very beginning of a whole new era of scientific discovery. The early results have been astounding. Some of the other work she's involved with will eclipse even this breakthrough, in years to come. Uppsala will be our showcase."

"I'm sorry; I'm not following, Jock. Go back to my question. – what's the connection?" Lawrence thought a smile might sweeten his insistence.

This time Ranjit replied. "Gupta Geothermal will shortly be producing electricity that will be free to our customers in the villages for at least the first five years after they come online. We will do this using advanced magma geothermal power generation. The secret is protected under the Project Amrita IP. Does that make any sense?"

"Sort of . . . but power generation is only a part of the cost factor, surely? What about getting the electricity to the villages? There are huge costs involved for cabling to remote areas, power transmission poles, etc." Toby drew breath. "I know from my Rotary experience, buying and installing water pumps and waste water treatment plants just drinks funding . . . and the bloody things silt up and get forgotten. Where's all the money coming from?"

Lawrence saw a look pass between them. He knew that a silent agreement had been made between Jock and Ranjit, allowing them access to confidential information. Jock explained. "Nisha's been able to modify the molecular composition of electricity to enable us to transmit an A/C current anywhere that the signal can be received, just like voice and data communications."

Silence. Lawrence looked at Toby, his mouth partly open like a fish longing to return to the sea.

"But . . ." half-formed words slipped from his tongue. "That's impossible. Electricity can't be transmitted."

Ranjit smiled. "Oh, believe us, Toby, yes it can. Please don't ask us how it works. Nisha's our expert on this. She's developed a piece of equipment we're calling an EPT – Electron Particle Transformer – based on work she completed at CERN last year. It connects to our power-output equipment, allowing us to transmit electricity directly to the customer's appliances. Jolly clever if you ask me."

Lawrence's mind was racing. "So you wouldn't need all the cabling and sub-stations. Electricity could be generated and transmitted directly to the villages . . . or anywhere else covered by a telecom mast. EMX is the frequency that would be picked up by . . ."

"That's right, Lawrence, by Sangbu water pumps or water treatment plants on site, avoiding the need for mains connections." Jock's tired eyes had regained some of their sparkle. "Their product development teams are working with Henning to implant receivers in the equipment that can step-down the signal to the required voltage, making them portable and effective anywhere."

Lawrence interjected. "But there's still the cost of buying the water pumps in the first place . . . and the maintenance costs of keeping them working, as Toby said."

"Sangbu will retain the rights for the new receiver technology and Henning will own the rights to the new satellite dish designs. This will earn them both millions. The water pumps will be loaned to the villages who will have tax exemption from the Indian government for five years to get them started. After that, they will pay a reduced rental rate only when they are in a position to do so. This will make them financially independent citizens." Jock sat back and winced as he put a hand up to his forehead.

Lawrence checked his watch. It was well past visiting time and he could see that Jock needed to rest.

They accepted the offer of a lift from Ranjit back to their hotel and wished Jock a good night's sleep.

In the car, as they pulled up in front of the hotel, Ranjit suggested that he give them a demonstration of the EPT equipment in the lab tomorrow morning. He would pick them up at 9 a.m.

As they waved goodbye to the speeding BMW, Lawrence noticed a sliver of new moon creeping out from behind a row of palm trees along the hotel's driveway. "I still can't believe what we just heard. Maybe the demonstration will help. Wouldn't we all get electric shocks if the current went through the atmosphere?"

"Lawrence, there are forces or waves passing through us all the time. Infrared, ultra-violet, telecommunications, gravity, X-rays, electromagnetic waves, gamma rays; the list is endless. I guess one more wouldn't make any difference." Toby looked up. "Even the moon affects us, but don't ask me how. Are you sure about this night-cap rule?"

"Quite sure. We'll need to be even sharper now. If anything, tonight has made our search more difficult. With so much at stake, I can see why someone wants to own this technology. Fortunes will be made . . ."

". . . and fortunes will be lost. Who will need oil, gas, coal or nuclear power when free geothermal electricity can be generated and transmitted anywhere? Motor cars could receive electric power on tap anywhere with no need to fill up. We wouldn't need the power transmission sector or cable manufacturers or national grids? The implications are ..." Toby paused. "Well, quite frankly, revolutionary ... and extremely dangerous."

Lawrence thanked the doorman as they stepped into the cool air of the hotel. He nodded to the shadow of Lal, who had ghosted past them and was now reading a newspaper in the lobby.

"Yes, but only if this technology sees the light of day. It all seems to hinge on Nisha."

"Wherever she is tonight."

• CHAPTER 29 •

Where am I? Where's Jock? Is he OK?

Nisha tried to stand but found her legs had been tied to a rough wooden chair. It was the only chair in a large depressing room that smelled of cat's pee and stale beer. The room was poorly lit with long shadows stretching away like dark corridors between loose piles of boxes that had grown at random out of a dirty, concrete floor. Hooded bulbs hanging limply from the ceiling spewed out conical pools of yellow light that captured dancing motes of dust and tiny flies. Nisha could feel insects biting into her soft skin.

She realised the aching muscles in her shoulders were the result of having both hands tied behind her back. Whatever rope or plastic tie they had used must have been woven through the chair-back as any lateral body movement just added to the jolts of pain. Her attempt to call out choked into an oily cloth that had been pushed deeply into her dry mouth. She almost gagged on the sickly fumes and coarse material rasping the back of her throat. She tried to push it out with her tongue, only to end up with the material knotting itself around her front teeth. She started convulsing on the bile and spittle that must have pooled in her cheeks while she was unconscious.

How long have I been here? With no windows it was difficult to know if it was day or night outside. Her growling stomach told her it must have been some hours. The throbbing pain in her head and dried blood she could see around the cuts across her thighs were proof enough that the accident really had happened. She was fighting back the tears, determined to stay strong and get the hell out of there.

As she watched, the solitary metal door in the far wall opened in slow motion and the figure of a man shuffled in. He looked like a labourer, aged in his late twenties, she guessed, heavy build, dirty clothes, local dress and what looked like oversized industrial boots on his large feet. Without even looking across at her, he walked slowly over to the first pile of boxes, picked up three with a deep grunt and carried them out.

She kept her eyes fixed on the doorway expecting the man to return. To her surprise, a young woman breezed into the room. The walk, the blonde fringe, the white T-shirt and shorts all looked familiar. She caught glimpses of her face passing from shadow through the cones of light, getting closer with each confident stride. Nisha's eyes opened wide when she stopped in front of her and yanked the cloth out of her mouth.

"Don't even think about it." The woman held up the cloth, waving it in front of her startled eyes. "No one can hear you anyway and I'd rather not have to put this back. It spoils the shape of your pretty little mouth."

"Annemiek? Is that you ...? What did you just say?" Nisha heard her own ridiculous words but disowned them immediately. *Did she really say pretty little mouth?*

"Oh, come on, all those degrees and doctorates, you can't tell me you didn't work it out?" She struck a pose, her left hand resting on her hip. With her right hand, she gently stroked away a loose lock of Nisha's wavy, black hair, tucking it carefully behind her ear.

"Don't touch me." Nisha shook her head and the strands of hair resumed their rightful place, draped across her face.

The reaction was swift and painful. The slap jolted her

cheek, causing it to redden and swell, a ring mark bruising the skin, drawing a thin line of blood. Nisha saw the flash of anger disappear and melt back into the warmth of a pouting smile.

"Well, not as bright as we thought obviously. Sadly, princess, my name is Lotte, not Annemiek. My beautiful sister is Lieke, and not Angelique. And yes, we are Dutch and yes; we are twins, to save you working it out. She is still seven centimetres taller and much more sensible than me. The rest, I'm afraid, was just horseshit. It's funny how students can become almost invisible. People see what they want to see."

Nisha caught the figure of the man over her shoulder carrying out more boxes. She thought about screaming out but decided against it. He almost certainly worked for them. She had to be patient.

"Where am I? Where's Jock?" She spat the words out this time, trying to control her feelings, not really knowing if she would believe the answer.

"You're with us, darling. And will be staying with us for a little while, I'm delighted to say. Well, until your other half gets his act together and then we can all get on with our complicated little lives. Mind you, he didn't look so good when we saw him last. It was a nasty head injury despite the airbags. He was well out of it when we pulled you from the wreckage. Barely alive, I'd say."

"You bitch, you fucking bitch!!" Nisha knew what was coming, didn't care, almost welcoming the slap, harder this time, the ring catching her upper lip, tearing the skin. As before, the lightning storm raged and was gone just as quickly.

"Now you must excuse me, we've got rather a lot to do. Just ignore the boys, they don't speak much and they're, well, a bit rough and ready to be honest. Like all men, they have their uses, sometimes."

"Where are we? Where are you taking me?"

Lotte had already turned and was pacing towards the doorway. She stopped and looked back over her shoulder, a thin smile creasing the corners of her mouth. "We're going where it will be very quiet and we can all get to know each other much, much better."

Nisha watched her stride out of the room, dodging round the box carrier. A few minutes later a second man appeared. He used a trolley to pick up several large bottles of spring water. He was taller, not as strongly built with much shorter hair, probably a bit older. She could just about overhear them. They spoke in Hindi but she didn't recognise their accents.

The older man was in charge, kept taking the lead, giving the instructions. She caught the urgency in his voice. They needed to leave as soon as possible. He laughed, looked across at her and reminded his friend that, unlike the Dutch girls, Nisha could understand every word they said.

The piles of boxes kept slowly disappearing. Nisha heard a woman's voice suddenly barking instructions in English. The woman swept into the room and pointed to a pile of what looked like tea chests and blankets. The two men nodded but she grabbed the older man by the arm as he went to pick them up.

"What took you so long?" she snapped. "Has it been delivered?"

He nodded, mumbled something, keeping his head bowed.

"Did anyone see you? Did anyone follow you here?" she gesticulated, her blonde hair flicking out as she fired the questions at him. Nisha could see the man shake his head but she knew that didn't necessarily mean no. The woman pushed him away in frustration.

"Get that stuff in the truck."

She marched over. It was a different walk – less swagger, more purpose; each step controlled with an economy of movement. Angelique? Lieke? She was dressed in dark-brown khaki shorts with a loose blue and green cotton shirt. A small black leather bag was slung over her shoulder. "We're running late because of you."

"Me?" Nisha tried again to wriggle a hand free behind her back. The tie just sliced deeper into her wrist.

"You're a much better driver than we anticipated. We'd planned to intercept you long before we got to the roadworks. Lotte was convinced Jock would be driving and would stop the Jensen as soon as he saw the Jeep."

"Then what would you have done?"

"Well, we could have delivered the letter there and then, once we'd tied him up and brought you here . . . at gunpoint, of course." She smiled. "Also it might have saved that beautiful car. We'd spun a coin to see who would get to drive it back. I won."

"And where is here? Where am I? Why are you doing this?"

"Here's not important as we'll be leaving in a few minutes. As for why . . . well, we can discuss that. You see, we've done this before. Our clients pay us well. This client wants to know all about Project Amrita. And please, spare us the surprised-little-girl looks. You've been very foolish."

Nisha's mind was back in the village, the day she dropped them off. Two young Dutch volunteers, the perfect fit for SINAC. They walked in off the street. Happy to dig toilets, keen and strong, students on a gap year, wanting to help the poor. Okki needed some help with the school toilets. She'd been brought up near them in Amsterdam, she spoke fluent Dutch, and they'd all be friends together.

They were in the dorm next to her, in her project team,

bleeding her for information, the dinner with Ingmar, the introduction to Ranjit, the conversations about SINAC, the launch in Uppsala, the chat in the car going back to the field centre that night. Why hadn't she realised?

"This is how it plays out. You continue to be difficult, tell us nothing and make things hard for us. Jock ignores our demands, involves the police, comes looking for you." Lieke paused. "Which will be very sad as we will end up killing both of you."

Nisha could see the ice crystallising in her eyes, her pupils dilating at the thought. But was it ice or the lick of a sadistic pleasure?

"Or you can both co-operate. After all, it's only money or science or some other great thing that will be forgotten in a few years' time; it usually is. Things can be replaced but people like you are very special. It would be such a pity. Be nice to us. We get paid and our client gets what they want. You can save the planet and both still live happily ever after." She checked the time.

"We should have been long gone from this shit-hole by now." She leaned forward and inspected the swelling and cuts to Nisha's cheek and lips, her voice softening. "You must excuse my sister; she never could control her temper."

Lieke took a soft, clean tissue from her pocket, gently dabbed the blood from Nisha's face, hesitated when she met her eyes, and then kissed her full on the lips, briefly exploring her with the tip of her darting tongue before pulling away. She smiled and wiped the back of her hand across her mouth, inspected it carefully.

"How dare you! You disgust me!"

Lieke made a wide circle around her, admiring from every angle like a trainer relishing the joy of breaking a wild mustang. On the second pass, she stopped directly behind her, touched the fresh blood oozing from her wrists, used the same tissue to dab the wounds.

"They look nasty. As I said, the harder you make this for us, the more painful it will be. You really should try to relax and enjoy the ride. We intend to." She fished into her bag. "Now let me give you something for the pain."

Nisha could see the needle out of the corner of her eye, called out into the empty void, jerked away from it, tried to stand or roll over, something, anything. A firm hand gripped her shoulder, a sudden prick in her arm, the sensation of fluid leaking into her veins. Then it was over, the needle sliding out, the grip relaxed and a tiny spot of blood on her smooth brown skin the only telltale sign.

Lieke paced round to stand in front of her "Now get some sleep. We will look after you. Please, you must trust us . . ."

Nisha was listening despite the cotton wool in her ears. Her tongue was a slippery eel no longer at her command, writhing against her teeth, swimming into her cheeks and oozing slime out of the corners of her mouth. She tried to speak but the words just played in the warm waters, no longer words but a school of colourful fish.

She watched Lieke walk into the dark shadows beyond a pyramid of boxes bathed in one of the conical pools. She traced the line of a shadow back up to the top where she could see a girl in a pretty blue dress standing on a box. The girl had flame-red hair draped over bare shoulders. A single piece of cord was wrapped around her neck. Nisha could see it was tied to the same crossbeam as the light. The girl slipped the noose from her neck, shaking her hair free from its coils. She turned and smiled before carefully climbing down the pyramid, box after box, positioning her red stiletto shoes to bite into the cardboard, inching her way towards the cold, concrete floor.

Okki walked over and kissed her lightly on the cheek. "Lieke is right; you must get some sleep now. Don't worry, things will be just fine, you know that. Lakshmi will look after us, she always does. I will stay with you, just close your eyes . . . I love you, Nisha."

CHAPTER 30

Go left. Jock pointed to a road sign barely visible above the crowds of people milling around the market stalls.

"We're not taking you to the apartment, it's too dangerous. You're staying with us at the hotel," Lawrence replied from the front passenger seat, leaning into a right-hand bend as Lal took the side road. The doors were locked and a loaded semi-automatic was tucked neatly under the driver's left arm.

Lal dropped them off at the hotel and arranged to meet up again at 7 p.m. They helped Jock to unpack, then met up in one of the meeting rooms off reception. Toby poured three glasses of mineral water. "I've got to say, Jock, the EPT demonstration was mind-blowing. The signal strength was so strong."

"Well, it has to be. We can't have water pumps stopping every time a cloud goes over. Did Ranjit mention the power storage link?"

"Yes, and he asked us to tell you that they'd achieved eighty-five per cent reliability at five hundred megawatts in the tests yesterday, if that makes any sense," Toby added.

"Eighty-five per cent! That's fantastic news! The best we've had so far has been seventy-two per cent. Nisha will be thrilled . . ." Jock's beaming face fell at the mention of her name. He gulped a mouthful of water. "Sangbu have developed a capacitor that can store electricity when it's not needed. It will act like a holding tank in the village. Of course, technically, it can sit anywhere but we want the villagers to take ownership, so monitoring usage levels and storage capacity is very important."

"Jock, we were talking to Ranjit about how many people are now engaged in Project Amrita. The list of suspects is just too long," Lawrence explained. "We almost don't know where to start."

Jock protested that the five people in Nisha's team at the university had been hand-picked and were completely loyal.

"Jock, we're talking about technology that could be worth billions on the open market," Toby insisted. "And you say this is just the start?"

"Only Nisha has the full picture. Our business partners can only see their part of the project."

Toby put his hands on the young man's shoulders. "Jock, I mean no disrespect, so please forgive my bluntness. You've been very naive. Few people share your dream. Most couldn't care less if the villagers live or die. They care about themselves, their own lives and making money. And your breakthrough is a money-spinner. How do they know about it? Come on, it's time to get real."

Lawrence saw the young man deflate. From his exuberance at hearing the test results just a few moments before, he watched the clouds of self-doubt drift in. What would Jock's father have said? It might have averted this tragedy.

"Jock, we're having dinner tonight with the British policeman sent over to investigate Okki's death. He was meeting Chaudray this morning. You're welcome to join us but we think room service and another good night's sleep is a better option for you," Lawrence suggested.

Jock went quiet. Lawrence could see that Toby's words had struck home, making the clouds finally burst. It took several minutes for enough composure to return. "I . . . I think you're right. There's not much more I can say. You know everything I know."

The last of his resistance washed away. He buried his head in his hands, tears draining through clenched fingers. Both Lawrence and Toby put their arms around him, squeezed his shoulders.

"We need you to do something for us." Lawrence spoke softly.

Jock looked up, wiped his eyes, tried to hold a glass of water in shaking hands.

"We need you to say you'll accept their terms and get Nisha released. We can send the email for you but we need you to understand why we must do it," Lawrence suggested.

"I can't. I won't. We must find Nisha before she gets hurt. I need her back, I can't go on without her. She is everything to me. I love her . . . but I must fulfil my father's dream, my dream."

Lawrence was too slow to stop Toby interjecting. "Jock, Nisha's life's in danger because of you. We're only trying to help."

"I'm sorry, Jock, what Toby is trying to say is that we need to act quickly if we're going to get Nisha back unharmed." Lawrence held him by the shoulder again. "The longer they have her, the more likely the trail will go cold. Until we know who *they* are, we'll be clutching at straws. The police can help but it may be too late."

"I will not sign over the IP rights to anyone. Nisha would support me in that. The project will fail; my dream will fail. We've come such a long way. We're so close now."

"Jock, you may not have to," Lawrence continued. "Toby and I think whoever's doing this must be connected somehow to the project. They may be one of your business partners or a supplier. Transferring IP rights is a complex legal procedure. They might slip up and reveal themselves. It's the best chance we have."

"So –" he lightly touched the stitches underneath the dressing "– you want me to say I will agree to their terms to see what they want me to do next?"

"Exactly." Lawrence smiled. "And that's all for now. Let's see what they come back with. In the meantime, we'll do everything we can to find her."

Jock moved his other hand towards the glass. It had stopped shaking. He took a slow mouthful of water and nodded his agreement. Lawrence helped him upstairs, back to his room.

When Lawrence returned, he found Toby aimlessly pacing round the table. He called room service, ordered fresh tea and sandwiches and positioned himself in one of the six empty chairs.

Lawrence watched his friend spiralling in ever slower and decreasing circles before dropping, exhausted, into a chair opposite. Room service arrived in double quick time. Toby seemed distracted as he slowly pushed the needle into his arm and released the insulin dosage. Lawrence's nod prompted Toby to explain.

"I've been thinking about this poverty thing. I can't make sense of it. I can see what he's trying to do. And I suppose some good has already come from it with this electricity idea."

Lawrence passed him a side plate and offered out the sandwiches. "Slowly please, I'm not with you."

"OK, let's say this all works. Jock can provide clean water and sanitation. Can help poor villagers get on their feet; keep the young people at home, staying longer in school, better educated girls no longer needing to marry so young and have such big families to work in the fields. It keeps people away from the slum areas of the big cities. They find employment locally so start paying taxes, get proper medical facilities. They even pay for local police to reduce rural crime figures so people feel safe."

Lawrence took a big mouthful of tea. "But?"

"But . . . all that will have happened is that we've turned them into us. Like the British in India. We introduced them to our way of life but as second-class citizens. We gave them our diseases; we inflicted our rules upon them, our language; our ways of doing things. Cricket, for Christ's sake! We made them foreigners in their own country. We raped, we pillaged and we squandered. In the end, they kicked us out."

"So what's that got to do with Project Amrita?" Lawrence went for another sandwich.

"It's the same thing happening all over again. Jock delivers them from poverty so that they can become second-class citizens. Pay taxes like us; suffer the stress of modern life; become greedy for more, get into life-long debt, increased suicide rates. They will become alcohol dependent once they start getting the stuff poured down their throats by a drinks industry looking to make a quick buck. We will force-feed them fast food. They can become statistics in the fight against diabetes, new customers for your yet-to-be-devised wonder drugs."

Lawrence went to take a bite. He thought about his own blood-sugar levels; about the calories, saturated fat and the processed sugar content of the white bread. "Toby, do you think it's right that two point six billion people don't have a toilet to crap in? And would you like to explain to a mother whose child is dying that we won't help because we want to save her from our way of life?"

Toby was silent. He rubbed his face, leaned back in the chair and swallowed some cold tea. "Of course not . . . I don't know what I mean anymore. I can still see my beautiful little girl lying on that cold slab because . . . because of what? Intellectual Property rights? Someone's greed? A scientific breakthrough?

A new technology that could do more harm than good . . . it's all just so crazy."

Lawrence felt the need for some old-fashioned consolation. "Toby, you know I agree with you. But can I suggest we split this into two distinct issues? I believe it is our duty to alleviate suffering for all humanity. The eradication of poverty is a noble cause, one we both support; otherwise we wouldn't be in Rotary. Jock's heart is in the right place. We must help him fulfil his dream."

Lawrence could see the tears welling up in Toby's eyes; they were tears of grief, he decided; tears of bewilderment at his own confusion; tears of a friendship rediscovered after so many years; tears of relief that someone else understood what his heart was telling him.

"The second issue here is the sickness in our own society. It's right that we should share what we've achieved. The advances in medical science, improvements in our quality of life, reducing infant mortality rates; the things we do so well. But we shouldn't inflict on them the worst aspects of our so-called modern society. We must put our own house in order. We've lost the human spirit of gratitude, fellowship, community, family, caring for each other. Fixing that is the real issue."

Lawrence was surprised by the strength of the hug Toby gave him. He wanted to tell him how much he understood, that he felt his loss as if it was his own daughter. There were no words; they were beyond words now. The silence between them was all that was needed.

The knock on the door came from another world. Lawrence found himself instinctively drying errant moisture from his own eyes, pulling himself back together. "Toby, I think we need to continue this conversation another time. We've got things to do." He checked before opening the door. "Dr

Bhattacharya? What a pleasant surprise. Please come in."

"Gentlemen, I hope I'm not disturbing you."

"Not at all," Lawrence replied, a thousand thoughts crowding into his mind as he gazed at the face of benign peace, love and spiritual tranquillity. "How can we help you?"

The old man sat down slowly, leaned his walking stick against the table and took a long look around the room. Lawrence had the distinct feeling that the Brahmin had been sent to them. Almost as if the very dilemma they had just touched on about poverty and the malaise of modern society had somehow conjured him up to help guide them. Eventually the old man spoke.

"I need to explain to you about moksha."

• CHAPTER 31 •

"Jock, where have you been?"

Nisha piled up the cushions around her. She tried leaning on her elbow but her flowing satin robes became tangled so she let herself slide back into the rich furnishings. The room was filled with strangely scented air. She could see an earthenware censer slowly roasting small crystals of frankincense near the entrance. The whole scene felt unreal somehow, like a waking dream.

"I've been to the bazaar. I've brought you a surprise. Now turn around." The voice was soft but insistent. It didn't sound like his voice. She turned away, kneeling at first until she felt a weight across her back, pushing her gently forward. She allowed her hands to be wrapped around the wooden stanchions rising up in front of her.

She took hold of them obediently, balancing herself in the swaying mattress of cushions, feeling hot breath on her neck. A silk scarf was stretched across her eyes and knotted comfortably behind her head. Her other senses were now awakened.

She could feel the air leaking out, her chest contracting. She could not breathe, did not want to breathe. They were as one, drawing in the same air. Her heartbeat was echoing inside her ears, a drum measuring out her uncertainty, her excitement and a tingling expectation.

She felt her wrists being tied to the stanchions. She let go, fingers uncurling from the wood, her body now floating, supported only by her outstretched arms, her knees burying themselves deeper and deeper into the cushions. She moved them further apart for balance as the cushions seemed to give beneath her.

Just as she was about to speak, the words ebbed back into her mouth, the space being filled with a soft sweet ball of what she imagined was Turkish delight. She tried to taste it, chew it but more and more of the sticky sweetness kept coming, filling her mouth, her tongue confined to running itself over the jellied surface, licking the inside of its gelatine cell.

Then nothing. Nothing moved, nothing happened. Every nerve was alive, waiting for his touch. She could feel the heat flushing up her neck, flooding out over her cheeks. The heady smell of incense mixed with a sweaty musk.

Then a sound, a new sound; she heard it before she felt the tug. The rasp of satin on satin, the knot holding her belt in place slowly pulling free, her robes falling open, hanging loosely now over her arched back, exposing her nakedness. The slight change in temperature made her skin react; small goose bumps like a rash over her chest, belly and upper thighs.

Soft hands slipped over her hips and down her legs before prying fingers found the hem. The material was being folded over and over. With each fold another inch of her bare thighs was exposed. More and more until the satin folds were lifted clear then neatly placed like a tablecloth onto the small of her back. An artist's eyes assessing her, drinking her in, admiring every curve, ready to capture her essence.

The hands withdrew, leaving pendulous breasts pushing down into an aching void. Then the weight was on her again. She flexed her body, bracing for the joy of their union. To her surprise, she felt an arm snaking up between her legs, smooth skin brushing aside the wetness now matting her as it found its way to her navel.

She gasped at the lightness of touch as a finger explored the indentation before slowly, deliciously tracing the curve of her belly, down and down into her femininity.

Her breathing had stopped as waves of energy took over, pulsating through every vein, her body alive as never before. Then another finger, or was it a tongue, she wasn't sure. Drawing circles on the cheek of her buttock, wider circles to start with, inching ever closer. She gasped when it found her, bathing her with a fragrant gel, lining the rim, pushing into the muscles, gently at first but then firmer. One finger, two fingers, she could feel herself stretching to receive them.

The pressure was filling her, stretching her, pushing for more but there was no more she could give. The glow became an ache, the tingle of uncertainty hardening into fear as she contracted. She tried to scream but her tongue was swimming in jelly. She went to free her wrists but the ropes were too tight. She shook her head but could not release the knotted scarf holding her eyes prisoner, helpless captives in the darkness of her startled imagination.

When the next push came it was unbearable. Shards of pain cut like glass deep inside her. She gripped the stanchions, sensing there was more to come, its lust yet to be sated, bracing herself as she felt the brief withdrawal. When it came, the powerful thrust pushed her out over the edge, her muscles forced into surrender, the dam wall breached, collapsing under the relentless pressure, swallowing the full length.

She had lost all her senses, pinioned by a confusion that filled her every thought. There were hands, more hands, hands everywhere, cupping her, stroking her belly, teasing her nipples, playing with her long hair, draining the hotness from her face. She could feel lips and tongues and fingers. Her robes were being pulled back over her shoulders, replaced with a blanket of warm soft skin. *Jock, why are you . . . how are you . . . Jock, you're hurting me.*

When Nisha awoke, she found herself lying in a padded cell of cushions. She was swaying to the movement of the truck, jolting as it crashed into potholes, stopping, starting, turning off the smooth road onto dirt tracks, then back again. Her arms were tied to the metal struts that formed the ribcage of the vehicle, supporting a membrane of tarpaulin. A single bulb barely lit the dry, dusty space filled with the boxes she had seen in the warehouse.

Pain was stabbing deep inside her. The presence had gone but her aching muscles and the blood stain on the towel beneath her confirmed the nightmare she had endured. She was naked, completely naked. Her clothes had been strewn over a pile of dirty blankets covering the hard, metal floor.

The sickly sweet smells filling the room were unfamiliar. A soft barrage of bursting shells filled her peripheral vision like the prelude to a migraine. She seemed to be alone yet could hear whispered voices somewhere. She tried to call out only to find her mouth was already wedged open. Her tongue was gagging on what felt like a ball pressed tightly against the inside of her teeth. It tasted of rubber and vomit.

The truck stopped, jerking her forward, almost wrenching her arms from their sockets. The ropes burned deeper into the cuts on her wrists, the braided horsehair inflaming her wounds. She struggled to slide back on the towel. She tried leaning against the canvas wall, only to feel the rough cloth scratching at her skin, or was it hungry fleas looking for their next meal?

The pain was too much. Her head slumped, sending greasy

black hair all over her face. She could feel the tears welling up again. She could not let them go, would not let them go. She had to gain control. The truck began to move, crunching up through the gears, its engine whining under the strain, vibrations making a tower of boxes sway in the half-light.

Her eyes were drawn towards the whispers. She became aware of a young girl, her face in shadow; a slim body leaning against the boxes. She was quickly joined by another girl, taller this time, yet just as slim. The second girl reached out and took her hand. They giggled as they stepped forward into the light, their faces covered in a pall of blue-grey smoke from hand-rolled cigarettes.

"Welcome back, princess," Lieke whispered as she bent down, took another drag and then stubbed out the cigarette in a bowl on the floor. Next to it, Nisha could make out the folds of a crumpled scarf half covering an object the size of a cucumber.

Nisha watched as Lieke stayed folded over, reached for the object and handed it to her sister. Lotte kissed her lightly on her naked back, moved slowly round behind her and teased it into her amid yelps of pain and pleasure. They collapsed into a giggling heap on the blankets, kissing and fondling each other, fingers probing into writhing bodies, sucking and licking, heaving breasts, then deep moans and quivering spasms as they each came.

It was Lotte who fell back first, flushed cheeks behind strands of blonde hair and a chest stained with a scarlet glow. She looked across at Nisha. "You are one great fuck, did you know that?"

Lieke stood up and strolled over to her, smiling as she put her foot up onto a box and pushed herself forward. "Want some?"

Nisha protested and kicked out with all her strength. As she did so, she noticed a tattoo on Lieke's lower abdomen. It wasn't so much the shape of the scarecrow's face that caught her attention; it was the mouth, a long, thin, angular scar, creasing awkwardly at one end. There were other marks on her ribcage and left breast. There was a second tattoo, much smaller this time, a delicate butterfly on her inner thigh.

Lieke was able to sidestep the flailing legs with ease. She leaned over and ran the tip of her right index finger over her, into her, teased out a tiny drop of moisture and sucked it clean. "We are really going to enjoy you. I do hope Jock takes his time over this ransom thing."

Nisha was looking into huge black pupils. She could smell some kind of substance in her hair and on her smooth fair skin. She shook her head and gave the look that promised to be good if they removed the gag. Lieke understood, got the nod of approval from her sister and eased the ball out of her mouth.

"Do we disgust you? Did you know that sisters can do this sort of thing?" Lieke stretched out her arm behind her, beckoning Lotte to her side. "Well, we're not like other girls. We know each other so well. We know what we want and how we want it. We don't really like boys. But we do like girls, especially beautiful Indian girls who taste so good."

When Lotte moved into the light, Nisha could see marks and small tattoos on her body as well, including a large phoenix rising from the flames over her lower belly. It was a riot of colours, a unique etching, truly a fine-art creation. Even so, the left wing was not quite symmetrical, misshapen lines making irregular patterns despite the artist's best intentions.

Nisha drew a slow, deep breath, remembered her meditation breathing patterns, looked for the calmness that lay within, channelling the anger inside herself, trying to find a place to regroup. But the anger was seething. "You can stick needles into me. You can dope me up. You can fuck me if you like, but I will never be yours. And when I get my chance – and I will get my chance – I will kill both of you."

Lieke threw back her head as gales of laughter rang out. Lotte joined in, embracing her sister, falling back with her into the pile of cushions once more as the truck came to a halt.

Rich yellow sunlight suddenly filled the space from a small window cut into the cab. The drivers were leering at them through dusty glass.

Lieke was on her feet. She struck a pose, cupped her breasts and shouted out, "Haven't you seen three women fucking each other before? Well, you'd better get used to it, boys. Now drive the fucking van, will ya!"

The curtains snapped shut, plunging them back into twilight. Lotte took a swig from a bottle of mineral water, offered it to her sister. Nisha could feel the dryness lining the back of her teeth, the taste of rubber still thick on her tongue. Lieke took a big mouthful, then held it out to her, and poured some of it over her thighs. "Two ways we can play this, remember?"

"I remember. Now untie me."

CHAPTER 32

Lawrence was pleased when the two Korean businessmen exited the sauna. They were a distraction. Today there was no time for distractions. "How many lengths?"

Thirty was Toby's reply, as he ladled tepid water onto the hot coals. Tired arms stretched out his wet towel. Toby slapped himself down on the upper level of pine slats and gingerly leaned back into the heat.

Lawrence could see a patchwork of shadows under bloodshot eyes. The cold sore that had irritated him during dinner had taken hold overnight and was sitting angrily on his upper lip. Toby seemed more agitated than usual. The exertion in the pool had failed to soak up his frustration. Or was it something else?

"Is thirty good?"

"Not in a show pony pool like this one." Toby lay down, resting his head on a wooden block, bare legs stretching out, hands fidgety by his sides, eyes staring beyond the heated pine ceiling.

"So have you decided?" Lawrence probed. Toby's response would help him break the news about the drop box.

"The short answer is no. It's so confusing. I keep thinking over his words . . ." He paused. "I can never pronounce the man's name. Dr Batty?"

"Dr Bhattacharya. You mean about 'moksha'?" Lawrence sensed progress. Or rather, sensed his friend might at last be prepared to confront some of the demons that had been robbing him of precious sleep.

"I didn't follow all of it. Moksha is the final state of bliss Hindus seek all their lives. It releases them from the circle of birth, death and rebirth. What did he call it?"

"Samsara," Lawrence replied.

"So they believe in life after death, being reborn as someone else?"

"Someone or something else," Lawrence explained, "Human being or another living creature. The quality of your life, how you behaved, what actions you took and what you did will determine your destiny in the next life. He called it karma."

"So the only way out was to break the cycle, to reach moksha. But how?"

Lawrence could sense the question behind the question. Maybe it was time? "He said it was the ultimate goal; the fourth goal in all human life. First we must attain 'dharma': the need to be dutiful, virtuous and live a moral life. Then we must strive for 'Kama' and seek emotional fulfilment, sensuality, pleasure."

"Kama? As in Kama Sutra?" Toby offered.

"Correct. He described Sutra as the thread that holds all of life together. Must be the origin of the word suture."

"It lost something in translation." Toby managed half a smile.

"They believe the need to fulfil our innate sexual desires is a duty bestowed on us by the gods for procreation and to protect the future of our species."

"Fair enough excuse for having a good time, I suppose. So what was the third one?" Toby sat up, wiped the sweat from his face.

"'Artha'. We must strive for Artha and create wealth, financial security and material prosperity."

"And once we've attained those three we reach moksha? Was that it?" Toby rotated his head, twisting and loosening his neck muscles..

"Not really. Moksha seemed to be on a different scale. To attain moksha, we have to overcome ignorance and all forms of desire. Very few people achieve it. But you're well on the way, I reckon, Toby," Lawrence suggested.

"Me?"

"Well, from where I'm sitting, you have fulfilled three of the four. You lead a dutiful life: supporting Rotary, paying your taxes, helping others, employing people. You don't have to go to church every week to live a virtuous life. Many Christians I know are the least Christian in their attitude towards others," Lawrence continued. "And you've been hugely successful in your business life, for the benefit of your family and society. And what a beautiful family you created. You've achieved Kama and Artha by the bucketful."

Toby could hold it back no longer. "Well, that's just it. Despite everything, it's all gone wrong. What did I do? What've I done to deserve this?"

Tears mingled with the sweat, his eyes holding Lawrence's gaze, hands now tightly gripped around the edge of the towelled pine bench. Lawrence knew it was time. Time to help him release it, drain the poison, cauterise the wound. "Tell me what you're thinking."

Toby let his shoulders drop, his head slumped back onto the wall; he closed his eyes. "I've run out of dreams. I just can't see the point in carrying on. I tried so hard. And it's come to this."

Lawrence didn't need to reply. The threshold had been crossed. Now he just had to listen.

"Batty was right," Toby said. "Life is a burden we are made to carry for all time, no escape. Even death doesn't release us from it. I will be haunted forever. I did nothing to save her or to help her when she needed me most. We brought her up to feel special, cherished, happy in a loving home. I can't believe we gave her a life just to be ended so needlessly. I can't bear it, it's so pointless."

The heat was becoming too much. Lawrence led him gently out past the hotel pool into the changing rooms. They showered, changed and went through for breakfast. The cooler air in the dining room was most welcome. They ordered from the *à la carte* menu.

"Toby, if I understood him, moksha means different things to different people. It could be truth or freedom or self-awareness." Lawrence took a big mouthful of freshly squeezed orange and papaya juice. "My take on it was self-love or self-worth. You can't blame yourself for what has happened with Okki . . . or with Wanda, for that matter. You're a good man, just doing his best. That's all any of us can do. We have to make the best decisions when life throws them at us."

Toby sat in silence, lost in thought. He poked at the food on his plate. Lawrence tried the diabetes argument again to get some food inside him.

"Let me ask you a question," Lawrence resumed. "Do you think Jock is a good man? Do you believe in his dream? Do you think Project Amrita will work?"

Toby chewed on a slice of pineapple and digested it slowly. "Yes, I do. And I think you're right. We need to fix our own society so we don't infect them with our diseases. But that shouldn't stop us trying to help them enjoy a better quality of life. Jock's dream must become a reality. It's what Okki would have wanted, what she worked so hard to achieve. For her sake . . . for our sake, we must help him. But . . ."

"But?" Lawrence knew what was coming.

"But Project Amrita will fail without Nisha at his side."

"Then what could *your* dream now become?" Lawrence saw the words strike deep into his heart. It had become a cold, barren place, devoid of life, of love, of hope. Yet that was where the answer lay. This was painful but necessary.

Waiters delivered fresh pots of Earl Grey tea and a jug of cold water. They cleared away the debris. The question continued to hang silently over the table.

Toby seemed to find some solid ground. "I must help him. This will be my legacy. For Okki. For Wanda."

"And who else? Remember moksha?"

"For me."

Lawrence could not restrain the smile sweeping across his face. He saw his own hand reaching out. The handshake sealed the matter. The decision was made.

Thirty minutes later they were waiting for Lal in reception. Lawrence ran through the diary with Toby. Chaudray at ten, then back to pick up Jock at noon to take him over to the university. Steve Mole was conducting interviews with the volunteers. *Good old-fashioned police work.* They were catching up with him around five.

They sat in silence watching the security guards searching everyone who came in through the revolving glass doors. "So why did he come?" Toby asked. "Dr Bhattacharya?" Lawrence knew they had only scratched the surface. "Ostensibly to tell us that more information had come to light about Okki's death. He said he also wanted to see Jock and it was on his way home."

Toby remained silent.

"All right, I think he cares deeply about all his students. He feels he has let you down. He wants to help you. Okki's death has just added to your misery. He sees you as a soul in torment. Now he wants to show you the path towards moksha, true eternal happiness."

Lal appeared through the swing doors, held out his arms

to be searched. Lawrence continued. "He cares. I care. You're worth saving, Toby."

"Good morning, gentlemen. Are you both well?" Lal breezed over, bringing them back.

"Sorry, I've got to ask. How do you get through security with your revolver?" Toby nodded towards the door.

"I don't. Even with a certificate they would detain me. It is safely in the car. When I park downstairs they search it as well but they haven't found it yet. Shall we go?"

Lawrence waited until they were strapped in and sitting quietly in the rush-hour traffic. "Lal, we've agreed over breakfast to see this thing through. We will arrange with Chaudray this morning to have Okki flown back home. Toby's spoken to Wanda. She's very upset but has agreed to meet the plane. The funeral will take place in the Netherlands when this is over."

"I'm so pleased to hear this news," Lal replied, "Mr Toby, I couldn't imagine you sitting on a plane going home while her killers are still on the loose. Talking of which, I spoke to the taxi driver who dropped off the two girls. He took them to Connaught Place. They said airport initially but changed the route after they had set off from the field centre. They didn't give him an address. He dropped them off on the main road with all their bags. They paid cash, with a big tip. That's all he could remember."

"Did he overhear any conversation in the car?" Lawrence prompted.

"I'm afraid not. He didn't speak much English but he said they talked to each other in a language he didn't recognise."

"Dutch," Toby surmised.

"Maybe Chaudray can get access to CCTV coverage for the area," Lawrence suggested. "It's pretty central, we might get lucky."

"That's a good idea," Lal replied, "but it may not be necessary. I went back to the Bengali Market. From my photographs, one of the traders recognised the man I followed. His name is Mukka, or something like that. He's not from Delhi. He's a truck driver from the south. He delivers produce from the countryside – vegetables and fruit mainly – but he has a mate with him so they can lift heavy things like furniture. He'd seen him around many times."

"A truck driver? So do you think they've moved Nisha out of the city?" Lawrence was cursing his lack of local knowledge. *The south?*

"Maybe not. The trader thinks they use a lock-up round the corner from the main market stalls. It is not the nicest part of Delhi. From what he said I think I know where it is. We can go there after the police station."

Lawrence checked the time. "Can we go there now? We might get lucky. I'm sure we can push back the meeting with Chaudray."

Lal fiddled with his satnav, then accelerated into the outside lane.

"You mentioned the man's clothing and jewellery," Toby prompted from the back seat. "Did the photos come out any better?"

"Oh yes, most certainly." He pointed to a bag next to Toby on the back seat. "The gold medallion is quite distinctive. Someone will recognise it."

As Toby leafed through the photos, Lawrence took out a single piece of paper from his inside pocket. He re-read the words, unable to believe the coincidence. The girls hadn't written this; the English was too good, too cautious, too cleverly worded. The instructions were too precise. Whatever they had stumbled into had already cost one life and possibly another. He could feel an icy hand gripping him by the neck. The implications for getting this wrong were too great. Their next move had to be planned with meticulous care.

"Toby, did you say over breakfast that Max was in Switzerland?" Lawrence folded the paper.

Toby pulled out the two clearest photos. " Yes, Geneva. Remember the banking clients playing politics with our invoices? Dinner at Galileo's, I was supposed to be there? Max said it could get messy. Why do you ask?"

Lawrence struggled for the words. "We had a reply in the drop box this morning. They've identified the legal entity where they want Jock to transfer the IP rights."

"You mean. . .?"

"Yes. It's a company in Geneva, Switzerland."

PART TWO

"Poverty is the worst form of violence"

–Mahatma Gandhi

• CHAPTER 33 •

Winter/Spring 1943 – Stalingrad, Russia

"Was he your friend?"

They had been under fire all morning. Since leaving the engine room at first light, they had been continually picked off by snipers. One at a time. Nothing to shoot at. Killed by ghosts. Three dead, a further three seriously wounded, worse than dead in this cauldron of death.

Better make that four. There was barely a pulse. The head wound was deep; blood and burnt flesh where his inquisitive left eye used to be. The eye of a thoughtful boy caught up in someone else's war. He would never be an engineer now.

"He's still my friend. I've got to get him out of here." He tried to move the boy, a squeal of pain ringing out across the eerie silence. The truce wouldn't last. Too many fingers on too many triggers. No time for the wounded. No time for the dead. And here was another young life draining into a concrete floor. Maybe they could save him. They still had morphine. It was his only chance.

"Let me help you." The Russian orderly slung the kit bag over a shoulder and grabbed an arm. They had him up on his feet, turned their backs away from the machine-gun nest. Another pointless target in a ruined city of pointless targets. They were struggling with each painful step through a menagerie of grotesque bodies and broken machinery. Shouts came from the pockmarked wall in front of them, fleeting glimpses of dirty faces cheering through a patchwork of shell holes. It was just a few more steps.

"You speak German?"

"Obviously."

He could see a large pressing machine between them and the wall. It would give some cover if the shooting started again. They could crawl from there. The weight between them was getting heavier as he passed in and out of consciousness. A whispered voice. Asking his mother for help. Would this war ever end?

"You must go back. You're not safe here. I can take him . . . and thank you."

"My job is to save lives. Russian. German. They're all lives."

Progress was slow. The ceasefire was holding. Just another few paces. He saw something moving in the shadows. Sniper? Ours or theirs? A shot rang out, a single shot from a high-powered rifle. Then another. From a different direction. A spark flew off the top of the press, metallic ricochet. He didn't hear the bullet; you never hear it.

They dived behind the machine as all hell broke loose. Machine gunfire, rifle fire, a smoke grenade landed only feet away. They had to move, use the cover. They went to pick him up. It was too late. A single shot through the back had blown out a grisly hole in his chest. He wouldn't have felt a thing. Lucky bastard.

"You can't come with me."

He had seen what they did to Russian prisoners. *Tapfer und Treu.* Courageous and Loyal. *My arse.* This was not the Wehrmacht he joined. Or the Wehrmacht his father was so proud of. Men hardened by war, bonded by pride. Their voices as one voice. For the honour of the Fatherland. But where was the Fatherland now, in this godforsaken place? This was not war. This was butchery. He was ashamed. Deeply ashamed. But shame was just a coward hiding in his fears. For now, he had no choice.

"I will take my chances." The voice quieter, softer, yet more confident somehow, a beam of light piercing the darkness. They slithered and squirmed together across the floor, a constant stream of bullets fizzing over their helmets. Hot shrapnel biting into frozen hands. Lumps of concrete and twisted metal grabbing at them. Their boots pulled into a spider's web of cables. Blood oozed from fresh cuts. Paper-thin uniforms were no match for old nails and rusty bolts.

He was first to round the corner, a bullet ripping through his uniform trousers, grazing his buttocks. Pulled up onto his feet, helping hands everywhere now they were not needed. He turned to see the Russian scamper behind the wall, then flip over, empty hands held out more in resignation than surrender. Heard the click of rifle bolts. The brown uniform lost in a forest of gunmetal branches.

"Put them down. He's with me. Help him up," he ordered, brushing away the rifles, agitated that good people were always the object of suspicion.

"But he's . . . yes, Lieutenant." The private knew this was not the time.

The battle continued to rage across the smoke-filled factory floor. Light arms fire was underscored by the woodpecker drill of a 7.62mm heavy machine gun. He'd met the Maxim before, the faithful warhorse of the Red Army. New holes appeared in the wall. Chunks of plasterwork and masonry were smashed out and strewn across the uneven floor.

Part of the roof had collapsed from stray mortar fire outside. Theirs or ours? It didn't matter; just as deadly either way. His men had been too busy defending the wall when it hit the floor behind them.

He looked up. It must be late afternoon. His watch was still set on German time. Unhelpful orders followed unhelpful orders. He could see the light fading from the bleached yellow sky above. Angelic flakes of fresh snow. They froze where they fell, the temperature sliding still further down.

In an instant the guns went silent again. He gave the order. Two to remain on watch. Tired soldiers put down their rifles and gathered around a bucket of ice-cold water. They took turns with the ladle, trying to slake a thirst that went well beyond their meagre ration. Like everything else, water had become a precious commodity. The bucket kept from freezing by a dwindling fire. Flames but no heat. The wood-smoke pungent, sucking all the clean air out of the room.

"And who do we have here? Looks like a Russian spy to me. We still shoot spies?" It could have been one of a dozen voices. But he knew who it was. Kruger.

"Listen to me. This man tried to save Grossmann. He's a medic. He'll help us with our wounded until we can get . . ." The words dried up. He knew they had no chance. They all knew. The field hospital was near the river. It could have been on the moon.

"I take full responsibility. This prisoner is under my command."

The Russian was squatting near the fire, bare hands rubbing life back into a shaven scalp; a thin stubble of reddish hair, the helmet on the floor nearby.

"Lieutenant?" The voice of the youngest platoon member. "While you were ... I mean, when you went to rescue Grossmann . . ."

"Spit it out."

"We lost Gruber and Muller, sir. I went to give them some water and . . ."

The others had gathered round the Russian. Bloodstained fingers probing; feeling the uniform, checking pockets for weapons or cigarettes or rations. Hands on shoulders; hands on the waistband, taking off the belt, testing the leather, emptying the pouches. Other tired faces inspecting the boots, untying the laces, measuring them for size.

"I see." But he didn't see. He wanted to check. He didn't trust what he was being told. They were just boys like him. He was in command; it was his fault.

"And Fassbinder?" he asked.

"Oh, he's still alive, sir; well, for now. He's in a bad way. He said he was hungry. I told him we're all hungry."

The Russian stood up and looked across at him. Enough was enough. There needed to be ground rules. POWs had to be turned in. That would take several days. And the way things were going, it may never happen. *The Russian must stay with us.* But how was this going to work? His mind was full of conflicting thoughts.

Most importantly they had to get back to the engine room before dark. It was the only place they could make secure. Food and water would be delivered there. Bread and hot soup. Something. Anything. They'd eaten nothing all day. And maybe they would get more ammunition and medical supplies. But could they get back? Were they surrounded? The radio was lying smashed under the collapsed roof, the few visible fragments now buried under a virginal white blanket.

"Lieutenant, can I ask you a personal question?" Kruger was wearing his mischievous smile, and didn't wait for the reply. "How long since you got laid, sir?"

Raucous laughter echoed around the battle-scarred room,

filtering up into the darkening sky. Some of the men had gathered behind him, a phalanx of German muscle, a brief show of unity, smiling faces reflecting the dying embers from the fire.

He reached for his revolver, knew it was fully loaded. He would use it if he had to. They were good men, in the main. He didn't want to be in this situation any more than they did. But here was where they were. *Courageous and loyal.* We are Wehrmacht, not SS thugs. This will not be tolerated.

"It's just that it must be quite a long time, sir. Our Russian friend here is a woman. And you didn't notice?!"

More laughter, the group pushing in around her, hands on her chest, between her thighs, a slap on the backside. Her eyes flashed with anger. She stood her ground. He knew then it had happened to her before. But it would not happen again. Not while he was in command. He aimed at the clouds and fired. Three shots. Three was enough. He needed the ammunition. He lowered the angle and pointed the gun straight at Kruger.

"She is my responsibility. You will not go near her. Any of you. That is an order. I am in command. Do you want to disobey my command, Kruger?"

Heads went down. Hands withdrew and reached deep into pockets. Jackets were buttoned up against the cold. The group of soldiers moved back, leaving Kruger standing alone. He looked up and apologised.

Their eyes locked, for not the first time since he had taken command just a few short weeks ago. He had been a private in the ranks. One of them, yet not one of them. Certainly not one like Kruger.

The previous lieutenant was arrogant, became sloppy. He referred to the enemy as hairy-arsed Bolsheviks not worth a shit. He never made it. A sniper on the roof of the railway station. A single bullet. A clean shot. The look more of surprise than anguish or pain on his face as he hit the tracks. Promotion followed within hours.

Before the war, he had longed for military service. He waited to be old enough, a career in the Wehrmacht. He was encouraged by a father who had fought at Passchendaele Ridge. Rewarded by a medical discharge with honours. *Could it have been worse than this?*

He told them to be ready to leave in fifteen minutes. He scanned their eyes for any lingering dissent. He picked two volunteers to carry Fassbinder. Kruger was to lead the way.

He led the Russian over to where Fassbinder lay unconscious, slumped against the outer wall.

"What is your name?" His words crystallised, frozen between them.

She looked at him with cold, grey eyes. "Svetlana Zaytseva. If I had any friends left alive, they would call me Lana."

There were too many questions, all pushing to be asked first. He saw a hint of warmth as if she knew what he was thinking. "Lieutenant Hermann Blindt, 79th Infantry Division. At your service."

"I owe you my honour, Lieutenant." She held out her hand. He noticed how small it was. "And my life."

"Why didn't you go back?"

She turned to the patient, peeling away a dirty rag, calmly assessing the gaping wound, his intestines writhing like a mass of eels feeding on a bloody carcass. She picked up the first aid bag beside him, fingered through it in disbelief. "Is this all you have? An elite army on a mission from God to defeat us? It looks like your God has abandoned you."

She reached into her own kit bag and produced a clean dressing and some bandages, and did her best to make him comfortable. Administered an ampoule of morphine. His eyes shot open at her touch. Trembling hands went towards his stomach, a strangled scream catching in his throat. She gently pushed his hands away, soothed his brow, whispered to him and gave him a sip of water. He lay back, breathing heavily, drifted back to sleep.

"It was in your eyes," she finally replied. "You risked your life for your friend."

He looked across the room and could see that the men had fallen in. They were ready to leave. Order had been restored. Kruger was at the head. He had buttoned up his tunic, bayonet fixed, ready to lead them back.

Two men were running towards them carrying a makeshift stretcher.

CHAPTER 34

"This is disgusting. Tastes like rat stew."

She tossed the tin bowl onto the pile, a trickle of foul-smelling liquid slopping onto the floor.

"Welcome to the Wehrmacht." He offered a cold smile, slurped his bowl clean and picked hers up, finishing off the dregs.

They had made it back safely. The old engine room was quiet at last. Guards had been posted. The glass in the solitary window miraculously still intact and now etched in snow like a Christmas card. Heads were kept well away from the temptation of snipers in the building opposite.

In the distance, the pounding of heavy artillery was incessant. It's amazing there is anything left to fight over, he wondered. His men were exhausted, frozen, hungry, frightened. But they were alive. And they had a roof over their heads tonight.

The orderlies who brought the soup had disappeared back into the night. No more orders. No more supplies or ammunition. *Capture the machine-gun nest.* Thank you very much, General. With what? Our bare hands? Tomorrow's problem, he thought, as he put some wet sticks on the fire. Too tired to sleep, he turned towards her.

"So how come you speak German?"

At first she did not answer. Instead she inched herself round away from him facing the outer wall. In the half-light he saw her remove her top coat, uniform jacket and shirt, revealing a milk-white back strapped tightly in bandages across the middle.

She glanced over her shoulder as she unclipped the two safety pins on the front. As the bandages spiralled away from her smooth skin, she noticed him looking away, which made her smile. She shivered as she put the layers of clothing back on, then wound up the bandages into a tight ball, clipping it with the pins and slotting it in the first aid kit.

"That's better. So much for my disguise."

"Well, it had me fooled," he admitted.

"I don't know whether that's a compliment or not." The touch of warmth in her eyes again.

"Oh, I didn't mean . . ."

"Please don't be so serious, it doesn't suit you," she whispered.

Movement in the shadows; his eyes reverted to Fassbinder, twitching in a dreamless sleep. They both slid over to him. She pulled up the blanket and placed her hand on his forehead.

"What is his name?"

"Private Fassbinder."

"What would his mother call him?"

"Dieter, I think . . . yes, Dieter."

"Then I shall call him Dieter." She rubbed droplets of his sweat between her fingertips. "He's burning up. Unless he gets some treatment tonight, his mother will never speak to him again."

He held her gaze longer than he needed to. "I can't risk getting him to the field hospital, it's too dangerous. But I might get through. It's worth a try."

"And leave me here to be raped? Or you could take me with you and hand me over. That would solve your little problem."

He checked himself, looked round to make sure no one was watching, put his hands on her shoulders. "You know I'm not going to do that. You're the one thing that's made sense in this fucking war so far. You're my first sign that God is still alive.

I'm not sure what to do. I've still got time to figure this out."

He let go, sat back, looked again at Fassbinder and scratched at his scalp. The inspiration didn't come. He watched as she delved into her bag and pulled out a scrap of paper and the stub of an old pencil. She was drawing what looked like a map.

"Between the press room and the engine room there is a second, narrower corridor, about here –" she pointed "– halfway along here is a solid metal door. It is padlocked. Behind it there is a staircase down to the old boiler room."

He looked at her. Just for a moment he felt a shadow pass over him. *Was she a spy? Why was she doing this? Who is she?*

"There is a trap door in the floor underneath the coal bunker in the far corner, here . . . this is also locked." She paused, and looked up. "What? Don't you believe me?"

"No, it's just that . . ." He kept his eyes fixed on the map. "Look, how do you know all this? And you never answered my question about speaking German."

She folded up the paper and put it back in her bag. "OK. I understand, but we must hurry, for Dieter's sake."

He swigged a mouthful of water from his canteen and offered it to her. He made himself as comfortable as he could and invited her to explain.

"We used to own this factory. I grew up playing hide and seek round here with Tatiana, my older sister. I know this place better than anyone." She was looking past him into another time. "My father fought with the White Army against the Bolsheviks. They have never forgotten that."

She edged closer to him. "He always hoped one day the Tsar would return. Even when they took over this place and made him work on his hands and knees, scrubbing the floors, cleaning the toilets, he never stopped hoping."

"What did the factory make?"

"Many things over the years. Tools and equipment, tractors, components for motor cars after the last war, munitions and artillery shells in this. Over sixteen thousand people worked in here. It was quite something."

He was watching her closely. "So . . . your sister, Tatiana . . . your mother . . . your father? Where are they now?"

"My sister is much cleverer and far more beautiful than me. She has tresses of flame-red hair; she used to frighten all the boys at school." Lana ran a hand over her stubbled scalp. "Like you her eyes are full of compassion. She trained as a nurse. The last I heard she was trapped in St Petersburg. My father never let us call it Leningrad – it was a filthy Bolshevik name. Her letters stopped coming in the springtime. I worry about her every day."

"And your parents?"

She stood up, gathered her things, avoiding his eyes. "We must get moving."

"We're not going anywhere until I get the full story. I need to trust you. And what's so important about the boiler room anyway?" He realised he had grabbed her ankle, restraining her, holding her, touching her. With an electric shock of realisation, he let go.

She sat even closer, whispered voices, secret words between them. "They made my father a captain in the Red Army. There was no one left. He didn't want to fight for the Bolsheviks. They had no choice when you, the Germans, threatened our city. He is out there now trying to kill you. I haven't seen him in months."

"And you say you owned this factory?"

"My family owned this factory, other factories, farmland to the north and west of the city, an oil refinery, a shipping company, need I go on? We were one of the wealthiest families in Russia. That is why the Bolsheviks hate my father. And I am his daughter. *The spoilt little rich girl*. I've tried to make myself useful. Believe me, there is more than one Red Army fighting you."

He looked across at Fassbinder, restless in his sleep again. He needed to make a decision. But he needed to know more. "And your mother?"

"My mother is from the old Russia. She was born in St Petersburg and fled with Grandma and Grandpapa after the Revolution. She was twelve years old when she went to live with my aunt in Leipzig. They always spoke Russian at home but German became her preference. I learned it from her. She would read to us. It is such a romantic language."

He didn't need to ask.

"I don't know where she is. Still at home, running the farm I would think. Nowhere is safe until this is over. At least she will have some food." The mention of the word seemed to bring her back. "I helped my father stockpile tinned food and medical supplies in the boiler room. *Just in case*. He would smile at me through his cigar smoke and say those words, over and over. *Just in case*."

"And the padlock?"

She smiled and patted her bag. "We're wasting time."

• CHAPTER 35 •

"How much Russian do you speak?" she whispered, the words freezing into ice crystals. She bolted the door from the inside, blocking out the faint puddles of moonlight coming from the corridor. She put the padlock and keys into her bag.

"Not a word." He shone the pencil-thin beam of his torch onto the concrete steps leading down into nothingness.

Silence. Total silence. There must be hundreds of soldiers in this factory, he thought, yet they now existed somewhere beyond this impenetrable metal door. For now, they were alone.

"Then I will teach you. Repeat after me – *Ya tebya lyublyu.*"

He shook his head and took the first tentative steps down, no handrail, the stairwell too narrow to walk side by side. She was following in the darkness behind him. *Keep talking. I need to trust you.* He checked his watch. They'd only been gone fifteen minutes. He'd left clear instructions. They hadn't seen anyone in the corridor. German or Russian. Even the artillery fire had ceased. It truly was the dead of night.

"What does it mean?"

She did not answer. Cold footsteps in his shadow.

"And why do I need to learn Russian? You'll soon be speaking German." He stopped at the first landing, checked round the corner, all clear, carried on, one hovering step at a time.

"Do you believe that?"

"I used to . . . no, I suppose not, not anymore, not after this fiasco."

244

"Speaking Russian may save your life one day . . . and I won't tell you what it means. You can find out. For now, just repeat it."

At the bottom of the stairs an open doorway led into a cathedral of echoing space. Even before the torchlight had picked out their neglected features, six massive cylinders filled the darkness in brooding silence like trolls sleeping in a rock cave. Above and around them were miles of thick-clad pipes running in all directions, into and along the roof space, down into the concrete floor, through a labyrinth of low-bricked walls.

At full capacity the temperature in the boiler room must have been unbearable, he decided. Six bellies hungry for coal, pumping out steam pressure at maximum, the lifeblood of the factory.

As the diagram had predicted, empty bunkers lined the far wall. Angular wooden chutes hanging above them ready to disgorge coal from ground level, their throats long since cut by a line of heavy wooden doors. Although disused for many months, the freezing air still sparkled with motes of coal dust dancing like tiny fireflies in the torchlight.

They headed for the furthest bunker. With each step came an unpleasant yet familiar smell, getting stronger. They put handkerchiefs to their faces. He shone the area under the chute partitioned off by a low slatted wall. Sure enough, another padlock, binding two metal clasps either side of a trap door set into a metal floor.

The smell was clawing at them, wretched air caustic to breathe. It was coming from a pile of dirty rags, part covering the hinge side of the door near the wall. The torch picked out shiny cleaved surfaces on scattered lumps of coal. Amongst them was a long, thin, metal object. He noticed indentations on the metal door near the padlock.

"Give me a hand. Looks like your secret stash is not so secret." He kicked away the coal and dragged the decaying body into the next bunker. "He must have starved to death."

Despite the twisted metal, the padlock gave at the first turn of the key. They pulled out boxes of bandages, wound dressings, ampoules of morphine, a bottle of disinfectant and other medical supplies.

Amongst the tinned food was a carton of powdered milk, some bars of chocolate, salt fish, a box of safety matches, a jar of black olives, a hip flask of pure Russian vodka, a bottle of vintage French champagne and a small box of Cuban cigars.

"Cigars? *Just in case?*"

"You've never met my father."

"I look forward to that." He was surprised when she reached over and took a cigar. He saved the torch battery while they enjoyed the darkness amid the heady aroma of fine hand-rolled *figurados*. He convinced himself he was purifying the air.

They emptied and repacked their kit bags, piling in as much as they could take. He saw her place a book on the floor as she repacked for a third time.

"May I?"

"Oh . . . that's just my . . ." she protested, and put it away.

"Please?" he pressed. Was this to be another hidden depth?

She relented and passed it over. He untied a ribbon and held it close to the torch beam. Inside the soft, black leather binding appeared page after page of rich creamy papyrus, a perfect frame for her collection of sketches. Some in charcoal; most in pencil. The first two pages were in watercolours showing a farm building near an orchard.

Her detailing was exquisite, especially the portraits. Faces, hands, a whole page of eyes and mouths; there were several full-torso nudes, male and female. The interpretation, the symmetry was just stunning. He tied the ribbon, handed it back in silence.

"I've always liked to draw but I'm not very good. Tatiana is much better. She's the real artist in the family."

"Thank you for showing them to me." He stood up, tested the weight of the bags, made sure the champagne was well padded. He held his breath, dragged the body back round and lowered it into the empty space, closing the metal door. "Rest in peace, my friend. Amen."

He checked his watch again. Just over an hour. Time to get back. As they struggled up the stairs, he heard the first shots coming from the floor above. Short bursts. Intense rapid firing. Then a grenade followed by jerking sprays of machine-gun fire. They stopped at the top of the stairs. An electric light silhouetted the metal door from the outside. He could hear footsteps marching down the corridor, more and more boots in rhythmic order. German voices, couldn't hear the words, just a low murmur as the boots went past.

Then silence.

They waited. Anxious sweat in the freezing air. Pulses racing. Could feel her body heat in the darkness. Not knowing. Silence. An agony of silence. He timed it. Five minutes. Silence. Ten minutes. Flicked the torch on, scanned his watch, switched it off again. At fifteen minutes he reached for the bolt, his hand over the metal bar. Footsteps again, getting louder, ten or more he reckoned. He pulled his hand away. The door was solid. The bolt would hold.

The footsteps stopped the other side of the door. Muffled voices again, different this time. Faint smell of cigarette smoke. He wanted to sneeze. She clamped a hand over his nose. He held his breath. He wanted to kiss her soft palm.

Footsteps again, moving away, getting fainter.

Silence.

He waited a further fifteen minutes, slid back the bolt, opened the door, stepped out into a pile of cigarette stubs, every detail illuminated. Electric lights. Lights everywhere, so bright they could be seen from miles away. By the snipers in the building next door. Or from the air, no blackout curtains at the windows. *What the fuck is happening?*

They inched their way along the side of the corridor, ducking under the windows. At the third window he stopped and stood up tall. There were lights on in the building next door. He needed to get back.

No guard at the doorway. All the lights on inside the room. No guard at the window. Nobody in the room at all. Rifles and kit bags abandoned. The fire had gone out. The pile of foul-smelling tin bowls still sitting in the middle of the floor.

He heard a noise in the corner, instinctively raised his rifle, dropped down onto one knee and scanned the sights over the far end of the room. He saw the crumpled shape of Fassbinder still huddled under the blanket, slumped awkwardly against the wall. He turned and locked the door, switched off all the lights except one bulb, scuttled over avoiding the window. Force of habit.

"Fassbinder, are you all right? What happened?" He tipped some water into his mouth. Lana fished out a bar of Russian chocolate, then found a fresh wound dressing.

"Lieutenant . . . it's over. Kruger said it's over. They've all gone . . . he left me this." He coughed up the words. A frail hand snaked under the blanket, pulled out a revolver, the weapon too heavy for him to hold. It slumped onto the sodden grey wool.

She eased the gun out of his hand, checked the chamber. Two bullets. Very thoughtful.

He leaned closer, whispering again. "What's over? Where are they?"

"It's no use, he's gone again." She took his temperature, still no change, could tell from the blanket. "I'll fix him up as best I can. Poor guy, they left him for dead."

Maybe they had no choice. Maybe they left us for dead. He pulled out some tins and the matches. He struggled to re-kindle the fire, managed to get the wet sticks alight, broke up a lump of coal.

"I guess this could be our last supper; better make it a good one." He smiled as he picked up the first can. "Golden Ossetra?"

"Nothing but the best. From the Caspian. *Just in case.*" She rolled up a sleeve, found a vein, injected the morphine. "Get some sleep, Dieter; we will save you some caviar."

As she pulled back the blanket, an envelope came away with it. It was bloodied, creased and smudged but the writing was still legible. A look of pure amazement across her face. "It's addressed to you."

"For me? We've had no mail since we got here." He knew as soon as he saw it. Distinctive handwriting, his best fountain pen. It was a letter from his father.

She changed the dressing and ran a damp cloth over Dieter's forehead. She gathered up some dry blankets from around the room, stretched one out over him and used the spares to make a pillow. She laid him down, tucked him in, kissed him on the cheeks and whispered goodnight. She stayed with him until he was fast asleep and then made herself comfortable by the fire.

"*Na Zdorovie.*" She held up the hip flask, winced as she swallowed a mouthful, then offered it to him. "What does it say?"

"*Prost.*" He took a slug of the vodka. It sharpened his teeth. Took another slug. "He wrote this months ago. Where the hell's it been? He could be living there by now."

She sat quite still.

He put the letter down, looked at her. He read it a third time, then passed it over. Now *he* had to explain. She had answered his questions. He had told her nothing. She was his prisoner. He was the stoic guard. Now he needed to win her trust. Maybe the tables had turned. Maybe he would become her prisoner.

"My mother died having me. I never knew her. She was twenty-one years old. I was her first child, her only child. Her heart was weakened by sickness when she was a baby. They never knew. My father said she was the most beautiful woman who ever lived. He never remarried." He watched the flames caressing the outer edges of the coal, licking the dust off the lustred surface, prising out the black heat from within.

"Without her, my father was never ..." Hermann paused, feeling for the words ". . . complete. He never found his balance somehow.

"He joined the family firm after the war and became one of the most respected bankers in Berlin. He's always been a good father to me. He never raised his hand or abused me. It's just that ... he never seemed to be with me. He never really enjoyed anything. There was no passion, no music or laughter in our house. I watched him become a recluse. I found it more and more difficult to connect with him."

She looked up. "His name. What is his name?"

"Walther. Walther Blindt ... he is Papa. Never Daddy ... *Warmest Regards, Your Loving Papa.*"

Hermann felt the vodka warming the back of his throat. A thousand memories filled the shadows in the room: the first time he tasted schnapps; their hunting trip to Bavaria; the private lodge in the woods; his first red stag; Papa smearing blood on his cheeks.

He took another mouthful. "Things must be bad in Berlin. I never thought he would leave. He showed me where he wants to be buried. Next to her. St Matthews' Churchyard Cemetery. The corner plot near the linden tree."

She had read the letter again. "But why Switzerland? And how would he get there? The borders are closed."

Her grey eyes had come alive in the firelight. He hardly knew her. At times she appeared so mature, so experienced and so confident. What must she be? Late teens? Perhaps twenty? Same age as he was. But the very next minute she was a little girl, drawing in her book, singing in the darkness, dressing up in disguises.

He smiled. "Money has no borders, it never did. Buying into a Swiss bank, greasing some palms at the border. Clients looking to hide their prize possessions: gold; jewellery; precious stones; deeds of properties; share bonds. They will make him most welcome in Switzerland, I can assure you."

"And what did he mean 'there is a seat at the boardroom table'?" She handed the letter back.

"He wants me to join him. I never wanted to be a banker." He put the letter into his inside pocket, and buttoned up his coat. He looked around at the scene of rusting desolation, death and decay. "But right now being a banker in Switzerland would be most welcome."

She laughed; a loud, piercing, carefree, innocent sort of laugh that made the windows rattle.

"Can I come with you?"

He looked at her in disbelief.

She repeated the phrase: *Ya tebya lyublyu.*

I love you.

CHAPTER 36

It was the farmhouse from the watercolour. He recognised it as soon as they had left the snow-covered track and set off through the frozen apple trees. There was no smoke rising from the brick chimney. No signs of life at the windows. The paths had not been cleared to the outhouses and thick snow clung like a death mask to the red tiled roof. The planks prised off the front door became their only firewood.

He could see the farmhouse had been left derelict by fleeing Germans. Later he discovered it had been a hospital and then a sanatorium commandeered by the Red Army. It had been occupied twice by advancing then retreating German officers. It had been a prison for criminals, political activists and conscientious objectors. It had been a makeshift school, the village mayor's office, a storage facility for the Communist party and, for three days, it had become an overworked army kitchen. It had even been a brothel. By some miracle, it had remained largely intact.

From one of her neighbours, Lana discovered her mother Irena had suffered a bout of severe illness and depression. She had been taken to live with her housekeeper, Mrs Ivanova, in the village over the hill. Lana visited her whenever she could. Plans were made for her return home when the weather improved and she was well enough to travel.

"Please call me Sergei."

Hermann's cheeks were glowing from the vodka. A log fire had been lit more for effect than necessity. The days were getting warmer, which was just as well as finding firewood was still a challenge. Even though most of the fighting had stopped, revenge killings and the settling of old scores kept an uneasy tension across the local villages. To lift the mood, Lana had filled the farmhouse with spring flowers.

"Thank you for letting me stay . . ." Hermann ventured. "In fact, thank you for . . . well, for everything."

"Oh, there's no need to thank me. It should be me who is thanking you. From what Lana tells me, you pretty much saved her life; isn't that right, Lulu?"

"Oh Daddy, it wasn't like that. We were sort of thrown together. I think we both knew we'd have to help each other." She kissed her father on both cheeks. "It's wonderful being back home. I always knew we'd make it."

Sergei kicked off his boots and settled deeper into his favourite armchair. "You were always a resourceful little minx! I knew it would take more than the German army to stop you."

"It wasn't the Germans we feared the most." She smiled. "It was your bunch of bloodthirsty Cossacks."

"You mean the brave fighting men of our glorious Red Army!! How could you fear them? You were wearing the same uniform." He paused. "Talking of uniforms, what happened to yours, Hermann? Without it you're a spy. I can shoot you if I like."

"If you shoot me then I won't tell you what really happened," Hermann replied, feeling much more comfortable in the presence of this bear-like man than when he first appeared out of a blinding snowstorm the night before. Talking to him in German helped bridge a gap made wider by the cruelty, greed and stupidity of others. "To be honest, I still can't quite believe how we made it here."

Sergei put a large calloused hand on his shoulder. "It is a

miracle and we should be grateful for it. I have seen many terrible things in this ridiculous war. The killing; the suffering; the cruelty; all of it has to stop. You were right to come here. You are most welcome to stay in my house. You will be safe, at least while I'm here."

Herman felt some reassurance despite Sergei's final words. He had enjoyed the past few weeks living in the sanctity of the farmhouse, away from prying eyes and suspicion. Although food rations were meagre and luxuries were few, he knew the alternative would be many times worse. He had kept a low profile, never venturing far from the protection of the secluded buildings with their hidden cellars.

Lana had been like a sister to him. They had fallen into a daily routine, a platonic relationship based more on survival than tenderness. Her hair had grown out and taken on the colour of apricots captured by the morning sunshine. She would sing all the time without realising, play games around the house and had grown into a very capable teacher of the Russian language. *Ya tebya lyublyu.* He understood the literal meaning of her words but they did not ring true. A teenage crush? A passing fancy? If there was love for him, it had yet to show itself.

She continued to draw at every opportunity. He considered the freehand portrait of Private Dieter Fassbinder just before he died as possibly her finest piece in the collection so far. She had obviously cared for the young soldier and was heartbroken when the fever finally claimed his life. It was the only portrait in her book she deemed worthy of a signature.

He glanced out of the window at the nest in the apple tree opposite the back door. The fledglings were hungry again, the sound of their incessant chirruping filtering in on the breeze. He had heard them the day they arrived. He had watched their parents returning time after time with insects for their open mouths, always knowing one day they would go, live their own lives and build their own nests. That day would be soon.

"Before the fever took him," Hermann continued, "Fassbinder told us that we had been ordered to surrender. As some strange kind of proof, the messenger delivered our post. It had been stolen by the Red Army."

"We prefer to say captured. That part is true enough," Sergei conceded. "It was a condition we agreed to."

"Some of the men refused to lay down their weapons. Kruger and a few others stormed back into the factory and charged the machine-gun nest. We found their bodies the following day." He ignored the vodka, took a mouthful of water instead. "The others marched out behind a white flag."

Sergei scratched a thick, red beard sprouting from a prominent chin, the hand almost covering his mouth in apology. "I believe over ninety thousand surrendered, including your commanding officer. The conditions in the camps are horrendous. Many have been made to march to other camps. You are lucky not to be amongst them."

Hermann could imagine haunted faces filing past the window, shadows of once-real men drifting to their deaths in the snow. "With the factory deserted, we had to make a move or risk being found. Lana had the brainwave of me switching identities with the civilian in the boiler room. His clothes were a good fit and smelled so bad most of the guards we met paid us little attention. The freezing weather killed off any disease."

Sergei leaned forward. "But you don't speak any Russian? The guards must have asked for your pass at the control points?"

"I spoke to them," Lana interrupted. "He is my brother. He was wounded in the throat and could not speak. We tied a bloody bandage around a small cut we made. I explained he was mentally retarded, had run away in the shelling. His pass had been stolen. I found him hiding in the factory ruins and was taking him home."

Sergei frowned. "And what about you? You were in uniform? You couldn't just go wandering off. Why didn't they arrest you?"

She smiled. "I said I had been captured by the Germans. Before they surrendered, I escaped and was trying to find my unit when I came across my brother. They were more interested in what I was wearing under my uniform, I can assure you."

"Did any of them touch you? I'll kill them if they did," he thundered.

"No, Daddy, it was fine." She kissed him again. "With the provisions you left we could bribe some of the more persistent guards. We made it back here quicker than I thought."

"And the champagne?" Sergei brightened.

"In the wood store." Hermann moved towards the back door. "It should be nicely chilled. I'll fetch it."

While they were alone, Sergei explained that the attempt to capture Stalingrad was the wild ambition of a madman. A victory would release the oil deposits from the Urals to the Caspian Sea and fuel the German war machine. That was why they'd had to fight to the last man. Now, with the German army in full retreat, the end of the war in Russia was in sight.

This was the time, Sergei continued, to protect their families' inheritance. They may no longer own the oil deposits of the Volga basin, but they still had access to a considerable fortune. It needed to be held far away from the prying eyes of their own Soviet madmen. An end to the war with its ensuing chaos created a unique opportunity to put their financial future on a more secure footing. Switzerland would be far enough away. It was a good plan. The question, he explained to Lana, was one of trust. It was never an easy question to address.

"Chilled to perfection," Hermann announced, as he closed the door against a sudden gust of wind. He reached for a cloth and carefully rubbed the dirt off the bottle before handing it back to its rightful owner.

Sergei fished into his inside pocket and produced another letter, explaining it had been found a week after the German surrender. Hermann ripped it open, letting the first two pages slip to the floor having divulged their secrets. Lana picked them up.

After a few minutes Hermann looked up into two expectant faces. What had started as an idea somewhere in the back of his mind flushed through to his eyes, and then burst out in a huge smile. Hermann was reassured. He threw his arms around her. Sergei joined in and all three formed a family unit for the first time. A difficult decision had been made. A bond of trust had been forged in the fires of necessity.

Sergei held his glass aloft and proposed a toast. The plan was simple. It was now about timing. And, of course, how it was to be accomplished, given the bloody mayhem that had descended across Europe. Getting into Switzerland would not be easy.

Hermann proposed a toast. They chinked glasses.

Der Sangerbund.

• CHAPTER 37 •

Autumn 1903 – Bern, Switzerland

She saw his reflection in the window well before the door opened. He was tall and smart; his blue uniform was resplendent with shiny brass buttons and a peaked cap. From her family photographs, he could have been in the same regiment as her father. There was more than a passing resemblance. Hungarian? Austrian? No, Serbian, she decided; definitely Serbian.

"Tickets, please."

The mountains were far behind them now. The train had picked up speed as the landscape mellowed into rolling farmland creased with dried-up streams. The tired colours of late summer were thirsty for rain. Grey clouds filled an overcast sky, yet the promise of a downpour was just another illusion. It had become a world of illusions.

"Thank you, ma'am; you'll need to change at Zagreb and cross to the Belgrade line." He clipped her ticket, and then attended to the only other passenger in the compartment. She had not noticed him in the shadows of the far corner. He must have boarded in Salzburg, which meant she must have fallen asleep again. Sleep had been a stranger since she'd heard the terrible news.

The guard closed the door behind him. She watched him march out of sight down the corridor. Her eyes then drifted back to her travelling companion. He was wearing a dog collar under his jacket. Roman Catholic, she surmised, but she was no expert, much to her father's annoyance. Christian, she could live with, but Orthodox was too tiresome. As things were unfolding, she could not describe much about her young life as Orthodox.

"I hope you don't mind me asking –" he folded up his newspaper and placed it on the empty seat beside him "– but are you all right?"

He had turned towards her. A look of genuine concern had spread across his beatific face. He was quite tanned, which made the whites of his deep blue eyes seem even clearer. An unruly tangle of black hair had defied combing and needed to see the barber's scissors. His features were perfectly symmetrical around a broad nose, which took her gaze away from a slightly feminine mouth. There was a gap between his front teeth, which bore the stains of too many cigarettes. She thought he must only be a few years older than her, perhaps in his early thirties, but he had the worried countenance of a man well beyond his years.

"I beg your pardon?" she retorted, softening the outrage into a question. *How could he tell?*

"Please don't think me rude." He shuffled in his seat, obviously having surprised himself with his own directness. "But you look so very pale."

"Well, not all of us have had the time to enjoy the summer's heat," she snapped, and immediately felt disappointed at her own defensiveness. He was an innocent stranger on a train, concerned for her welfare. Maybe he could help her make sense of it all.

He moved seats so that he was sitting directly opposite, their knees brushing as the train lurched across the points. She felt herself stiffen momentarily, then push back deeper into the upholstered seat, arms folded across her lap.

"And you were coughing quite loudly." He fumbled in his bag. "I just wondered if you'd like a sip of water from my flask. Or perhaps we could share a sandwich? I think they are egg and cress today. My housekeeper always makes too many. You would be helping me out."

The water was a good idea but the sandwich was a step too far. Overfamiliar, her mother would advise. She took a mouthful of cool water and returned the flask. He held out the sandwiches carefully wrapped in greaseproof paper. They did smell good and it had been a long time since breakfast. She smiled and took one. He left the packet open on the little shelf under the window.

"I've had a bit of a summer cold. I'm sorry if I disturbed you." She managed a half smile. "I shall see the doctor when I get to my parents' house if it is no better. Thank you for asking."

"Did the guard say you were travelling to Belgrade?" He leaned back as he unbuttoned his jacket.

"Novi Sad." She wondered how long she'd been asleep.

"Oh, that's a beautiful little town. I attended a seminary there many years ago. It overlooked the Danube as I recall." He paused. "So how often do you see them? Your parents, I mean."

Not often enough, she wanted to say. They had been so good to her, especially her father. He had used his influence to get her into the boys' grammar school. He was so pleased when she came top in mathematics. Finishing school in Zurich would have cost him dearly. Then it was medicine at the university, one of the few that tolerated female undergraduates. He even continued with her allowance when she changed to physics at the polytechnic. So why was she treating him this way?

The train slowed as it went through a station. She noticed a young woman on the platform holding the hand of a little girl in a pretty dress. She had a dress just like it, soft, red cotton with a white collar and lace hem. *Bought for her first birthday party in January*. It seemed a lifetime ago. Was this really happening?

"Every few months if I can. Since I got married there has been so little time." She found herself twisting the thin band of gold. It was little more than a curtain ring. Why was she telling him this? Could it only have been a few months ago? It had all made sense then. The wedding. Respectability. Build a new life together. Start a family. A chance to establish ourselves. Bring her home. And now this had to happen? How cruel life can be. No wonder he is so upset. But still he has left the decision with me.

"Have another sandwich," he enthused, thrusting the packet towards her. She could sense there was something else he wanted to say.

"Thank you, I will. Your housekeeper must look after you well." She went to take a bite, hesitated, then looked up into his forgiving eyes. "Can I ask, was I talking in my sleep?"

He chewed on a crust, found the words. "I'm sorry, I shouldn't have been eavesdropping. Please forgive me."

"What did I say?" She had unfolded her arms. The decision was made. At least the easier of the two decisions.

He squirmed, a touch of colour deepening the tan on his cheeks. "You mentioned someone called Lieserl. You cried out her name several times. As if she was in danger. You sounded so upset. That's why I had to ask if you were all right."

All right? No, I'm not all right! She's my little girl, my beautiful little girl. I'm her mother yet I hardly know her. Her father has never even seen her. Society has decreed that she must grow up in disgrace, brought up by her grandparents, the same grandparents who refused to come to my wedding.

My little girl's condemned to a life of shame to punish the sins of her parents. It is so unfair.

"Lieserl is my daughter. She is . . . staying with my parents." She was unprepared for this conversation. But was that really it? Unprepared? Unrehearsed? Or was it the aura emanating from this man, diluting thoughts into words. She had never been a religious person. The scientific explanation of the universe made no allowance for a Supreme Being. But such was the turmoil in her head, any reassurance, divine or otherwise, was to be welcomed.

"May I ask your name? It will make it easier to talk. Just your Christian name is fine." He smiled and extended his right hand, having wiped the butter on a napkin. "I am Wolfgang. Father Wolfgang Karpfen. It is a pleasure to make your acquaintance."

"Mileva . . . please call me Mileva."

"I sense we do not share the same beliefs but you can trust me to keep your words in complete confidence. From the way you cried out I fear for your soul. Please share the burden with me." He smiled with his eyes, opening the palms of his hands, welcoming her into his church.

She turned to look out of the window. Open pastures sliding by, cattle lying in the shade of a tree, sunlight playing with a field of golden wheat. It was all so calm, so normal. She heard her own words as if spoken by someone else. "My daughter is just over eighteen months old. She is walking on her own now and can say her own name. I love her, we both do."

She could see her face reflected in the window as the train entered a tunnel, the miracle of electric lights filling the carriage, pushing away the uncertainty of darkness.

"Lieserl has scarlet fever. She has a nasty rash over her back and arms. Her temperature is sky-high and the glands in her neck are badly swollen. She refuses to eat and has been sick repeatedly. I must get to her as quickly as I can."

"I don't wish to pry but when did you last see your daughter? I take it she does not live with you." His words were no more than a whisper escaping from lips that hardly moved. The air pressure inside the compartment changed as the train left the tunnel and returned to the daylight.

"Father, my daughter was born out of wedlock. I love my husband so much. Albert has a brilliant mind yet he could not find a job. We married at the first opportunity, to make things right. When he completes his probationary period, his salary will increase. We had planned to bring our daughter home. But now, I don't even know if she will live. I don't know what to do . . ."

Tears flooded down her face, uncontrollable tears that burned into her cheeks yet could not permeate the toughened veneer of shame that had encrusted itself around her.

Zagreb. Next Station. Zagreb. All change. The guard's voice echoed down the corridor as the train began to slow. It was just a few more minutes away. Father Wolfgang was being met at the station and apologised for not having any more time to spend with her.

He reached his hat and bag down from the luggage rack and helped Mileva with her bags.

"The gift of life should never be taken for granted. You have been blessed with a daughter and you must do what is right for her. Whatever the consequences or whatever people in society may think."

She felt a little light-headed as she stood up, steadied herself on the window ledge. "Thank you, Father, you've been so kind."

The train pulled to a halt and a small crowd appeared on the platform as the passengers alighted. A man in a hat and dog collar was peering in. He began waving and pointing to the nearest door.

"Father Otto is a good friend, I must go." His blue eyes sparkled. "I hope your daughter makes a full and speedy recovery. And may your next child be born into a simpler world without any such complications. Are you hoping for a boy or a girl?"

"I'm sorry?" The dizziness had not gone away. She could taste the egg sandwich returning.

"Your next child?" he repeated. "The one you are carrying. Surely you must know? It is the greatest of gifts, one to be cherished. Good day to you, Mileva, and God Bless."

• CHAPTER 38 •

Autumn 1903 – Novi Sad, Serbia

"She is sleeping. Her cheeks are cooler. She even managed some of my chicken broth." Her mother kept a tight hold on the door handle. "I'll sit with her for a while. Why don't you two get some air? She'll be fine. I'll call you if she wakes."

Mileva went to kiss her mother on the cheek but the bedroom door had already closed. She looked into the other woman's eyes and smiled. Helene had been her best friend since she was three years old. In many respects she was her only friend. She was never jealous of her or even cared that Mileva was the brightest student in their class. She was happy for her friend to be awarded scholarships and win prizes. She did not envy her as others had; other so-called friends who drifted away into humdrum married lives in the small provincial town. Helene was a true friend.

As children they played together, slept together, climbed trees, caught butterflies and ladybirds together, pressed summer flowers, wrote endless letters to each other and confided their innermost secrets. Mileva often wondered if she would ever love her husband as much as she did Helene. It was a different kind of love but one just as powerful. Perhaps it was more so.

She took Helene by the hand and they skipped down the wide staircase, across the hallway and out into the warm, evening air. She opened the wrought-iron gate and led her into the gardens, floodlit by the lights from the house. They strolled past the roses where the flowers had turned to seed in the summer heat, the last few petals strewn across the dry earth and gravel pathway. The sticky-sweet air still carried their fragrance.

"My mother should've been a nurse." Mileva steered them into the safety of an old wooden gazebo that sheltered under an overhanging beech tree by the edge of a manicured lawn. A distant fork of lightening lit up the night sky. "She's looked after Lieserl so well."

They huddled together on a bench inside the structure, staring out into the gloom.

Helene squeezed her hand. "You mustn't blame yourself for what's happened. It'll all work out for the best. Lieserl's strong; she'll come through this."

A rumble of thunder. Still no rain. It was aching for rain. The night had become a dark cloak wrapping itself around them.

"Helene, I need your help, more so now than ever before." She turned to her in the darkness. "I wouldn't ask if I had any choice. If you say no, I'll respect your decision and hope always to remain your friend."

A single raindrop splashed onto the smooth surface of the sundial just a few feet away. It was followed by a second, then a third. The sky lit up again. The breeze freshened slightly, loosening the branches above them, carrying with it dank smells of moss and leaf mould.

"I want you to be Lieserl's mother. I want you to adopt her." She threw her arms around her friend and hugged her as hard as she could. She wanted them to become one, sharing their love for the innocent little girl.

"Mileva, I don't understand. You're her mother. I can never replace you in her life nor would I want to. Besides . . ."

The rain was steadier now. Big fat droplets danced in their own puddles, turning the ground to mud around the gazebo. Lightning flashed over the rooftops. A growling peal of thunder shook the tree, showering beechnuts onto the roof and the path beyond. There was no choice but to ride out this storm.

Mileva completed the sentence for her. "Besides ... yes, I know what you're thinking. You can rest assured she will survive the fever. She will grow up to be healthy and strong, the daughter both of us always dreamt of. Say you'll do this for me. I'll sign the papers and make it all legal, if you wish. I need you. We need you. Help me, please."

Mileva had decided after only one term. Medicine was not her true calling. The other students had been sympathetic. She had grown quite fond of a serious boy now working at a research hospital in Vienna. The laboratory had developed a serum from the blood of horses that had proved most effective against scarlet fever. It was still in its trial phase but Mileva's pleading had managed to secure a single dosage. While her mother was downstairs, she had administered it herself. The improvement in Lieserl's condition was all the proof she needed. Her daughter may not otherwise have survived. She felt the risk had been worthwhile.

"In your last letter, you said things were going well with your research and Albert's new job. Why not wait until Lieserl is better, and then take her home with you? I'm sure your parents wouldn't mind."

It was true; her research was at a critical stage. The results were promising. She knew Albert was undoubtedly a clever man but his ideas were fanciful. The academic community considered him to be a worthless dreamer. He had little grasp of mathematical theory and no application to learn. If they were to be successful then she must bring the structure and consistency they needed to present their arguments coherently. She must complete her research.

They had agreed to publish under joint names. The universities would come begging at their feet. She knew she could harness him, channel his thinking and change him into a dutiful husband and father. But it would take time. She had neither time nor money. It was no place to bring up a little girl.

"Helene, I am expecting another child in the spring." She fell into her embrace again, the words lost in another clap of thunder as it roared overhead. Mileva had to raise her voice above the rain hammering on the roof. "Lieserl needs a mother. She needs to grow up in a loving family. You and Toma are the perfect couple. One day I hope Albert and I can love each other as much. But we cannot fulfil our destiny in science and afford to bring up a family, especially one with an illegitimate daughter. It would make us the laughing stock of the academic world."

The rain had found its way through a crack in the roof. Water was dripping down over them and had formed a puddle on the floor. The two girls looked at each other and burst out laughing as they took off their shoes and ran in stockinged feet through curtains of water back towards the house.

Helene slipped on the path near the gate and slid into a small lake that now stretched over half the lawn. Mileva helped her up, brushing off the worst of the mud. They held hands as they rushed into the house. A few minutes later they were upstairs, wrapped in warm, fleecy dressing gowns, their clothes in a big soggy pile on the bathroom floor. Clouds of steam billowed from a hot bath. Mileva's mother had brought them a fresh pot of camomile tea and had then left them alone. The storm was fading and, at least for now, Mileva felt a sense of calmness she hadn't felt in days. Even her churning stomach had found some peace with itself.

She sat in the window seat towelling her dark hair and watched her friend slide into the water, as she had done so many times before. She was nine years old again. They had just come home from swimming in the river. Another endless sunny day. They had caught the biggest collection of sticklebacks, frogs and newts. They were too excited to eat and had been unceremoniously dunked into a hot bath together, faces glowing.

"I will do as you ask." Helene reached for the soap. "But I have one condition."

"Anything."

"If Lieserl wants to know who her real parents are, then I must tell her. It's only fair."

Mileva had anticipated the request. She was prepared this time. "On her eighteenth birthday. Then she will be old enough to understand."

She wanted to complete the sentence: *And perhaps old enough to forgive me.*

CHAPTER 39

Spring 1905 – Bern, Switzerland

"Clearly that is wrong."

Mileva cleared away the dirty glasses and plates. She wrapped up the leftover boiled eggs and salami, which would be her lunch tomorrow. And possibly the day after. She thought about doing the dishes but didn't want to risk waking him. Hans Albert was a light sleeper and thankfully had been quiet all evening.

"Can you prove it's wrong? Can you prove nothing in the universe can travel faster than the speed of light?" she retorted, trying to keep the emotion out of her voice.

The last of their regular Tuesday night guests had just staggered off into a cold Bernese evening. The town had been dusted in late-afternoon snow, which was freezing hard on the windowsill outside. The room temperature was dropping. It was time for bed, yet Mileva knew she would not sleep.

He moved to her side and squeezed her shoulder. "What's wrong, my little pumpkin? You seem most unhappy tonight. Have I upset you?"

She pulled away from him, sitting up straight in the high-backed armchair. "Why do you do it?"

"Do what?"

"Pretend so." She was trying to find order in her thoughts. "You act like you are a learned professor holding court with your disciples. You entertain these hangers-on at our expense, just so you can feel important. You don't even drink, yet you spend a small fortune on wine for them. We can't afford this any longer."

"We can't afford this any longer *on my measly wage*, you were going to say." He coloured up, turned away from her and gazed forlornly into the empty log basket.

"Albert, I love you so much . . . but this must stop."

He opened a desk drawer and pulled out a letter. "But it's going to stop, *liebchen*. Our luck has changed. This came earlier today. I was going to surprise you over breakfast. Look, they've promised to publish our paper. At last, we will be rewarded for all our hard work."

She wanted to smile but she knew him too well. He was reluctant to pass it over and went to put it back in the drawer. She insisted. The letter seemed genuine but something wasn't right. She read it again. "Your paper on the Nature of Light? YOUR paper?"

The silence was broken by the muffled cry of a baby coming from the next room. The bedroom. The only other room. Mileva was on her feet, standing her ground before him; enough was enough. The cries grew louder. She stormed out.

When she returned, the room had gone even colder. Albert had put on his hat and gloves. He offered a smile as he always did. It worked in their early days but Mileva was not in the mood. It was time to put things straight. Yet she knew a full-out assault would only antagonise him. His petulant temper was always tinder dry. They needed to work together. Another argument would only wake the baby.

"We both failed our final exams." She held up her hand to stop him interrupting. "But they rounded you up to a pass. It is a man's world and I suspect always will be in science. I can see that now."

271

She wrapped herself in a blanket and tried to settle. She could see he was listening, truly listening, which created one of the rare opportunities to register a practical idea in his overactive and highly complicated brain.

"I understand why you did it. The paper has more chance of being published now that you have your PhD. If it can get the attention of the scientific community then maybe, one day, you will become a professor. We could afford to invite round more successful guests and feed them better quality sausages and boiled eggs." She found a smile.

They both knew that the paper was more than a joint effort. The letter from the respected scientific journal was the first positive sign. Colourful dreams, fantasy ideas and expansive notions about riding beams of light across the universe had their place, but science was the realm of cold, hard empirical facts, logical theories and mathematical formulae. Arguments were proven by eloquent equations and indisputable evidence. She knew success would require both inspiration and perspiration.

"Mileva, you light up my world, you must know that. I'm doing this for us."

She had played with these thoughts over and over. To hear them out loud was both a surprise and a reassurance. "Albert, if we are to succeed you must become part of the scientific community, accepted as an equal. You must be revered and respected, not just in Europe, but throughout the world."

"I agree . . . and this is the start of . . ."

"Please let me finish." She softened the tone. "And to achieve that you must make a bigger impact than if you were already a club member. You must make them listen. You must challenge them in an area of physics that is accepted as being at the heart of their beliefs and understanding."

He stood up, paced the room, discounted the idea of playing the violin and opted instead for a pipe full of tobacco. "And what do you have in mind, my little witch?"

"Not what, but who." She moved to his side and wrapped the blanket round both of them. Coils of thick pungent smoke filled the air. It was his favourite, a Virginia/ Perique blend that he saved for special occasions and their precious few moments of triumph.

She pressed on. "Who would they recognise as the greatest ever scientist? Someone whose work is almost beyond question yet has obvious flaws within it?"

"You mean?" He blew a smoke-ring into her face, which made her cough and laugh at the same time. "You naughty girl! You are my little vixen after all."

She nestled into the warmth of his jacket, rubbing her head into his shoulder. She felt his hand exploring.

"Of course," he whispered, "we would have to prove it beyond any doubt. But together I know we can do it. Our other work on Brownian motion and the photoelectric effect should continue. But that will not win us the Nobel Prize. To do that, we must question Sir Isaac Newton. We must challenge his ideas on gravity."

The following evening, after Mileva had read Hans Albert off to sleep, she joined her husband as he pored over pages at the dining room table, many of which were written in her own hand.

"So where are the flaws in Newton's argument?" She knew this was a leading question, having discussed it with him over many years. But this time, she sensed they were closer than ever before.

He drained the last of the sherry into her glass. "Newton tells us that gravity exists but not how it works. It is some kind of force field that operates throughout the universe, holding the planets in orbit around the sun . . . and pulling objects on earth towards the centre."

"And which is the naughty planet, the one with the orbit that doesn't fit his theory?" She reached for a clean piece of paper.

"Mercury."

"So what we need is an explanation of how gravity actually works, and a formula that can accurately predict the path of Mercury's orbit using that explanation." She made a note.

"Is that all? For a minute, I thought this was going to be difficult." He kissed her but not before finishing her sherry, for which he received a playful slap on the face and a reminder that he was supposed to be teetotal.

"So Newton wrote his theory nearly two hundred and fifty years ago?" she queried.

"Indeed he did."

"Then it's time we updated it."

She pulled out their file on special relativity. They talked through the movement of objects in linear motion at constant speed; they discussed objects moving in the three dimensions of space; and the relationship between space and time, the fourth dimension. They checked their figures on light particles colliding, which reconfirmed the theory that time must warp towards the point of impact then stand still at the speed of light.

"If time can warp then why not space?" he suggested, then immediately apologised. "No, I'm sorry, that could not work."

"Why not?" She raised an eyebrow.

"Because there is nothing there, it is a vacuum, there is no mass on which gravity could exert a force." He was playing with his hair, twisting little tufts into bigger tufts.

"But suppose there was something there yet we couldn't see it?" She clapped her hands. "Just suppose space is made up of another field like gravity that imparts mass onto particles and is, itself, affected by gravity. We could not see it, but gravity would cause the very fabric of space itself to curve."

His eyes were on fire, the ideas burning for his attention. "Not only that but smaller objects would be held in their orbit not by gravity but by the curvature of space. But what kind of field could exist that we don't know about? What could it be made of?"

She skipped over to the bookcase, pulled out a thick leather-bound volume, fingered through to the right page, the page she had been reading earlier that day. "In the Hindu religion, they talk of a cosmic ocean out of which the world arose. The Bible has a similar story about Noah and the Ark. Maybe, just maybe, space is not an empty vacuum but consists of an ocean of force fields we do not understand, made up of particles yet to be discovered. After all, nobody has ever been to space.

"We know that less than half of the sun's radiation is visible. If particles emitted by the sun have mass – or pick up their mass from an unknown force field as they travel across space – then gravity would act on those particles and bend space around large objects like planets . . . or the sun."

"My little witch! I like the idea but how would we prove it? As you said, if we are going to challenge Sir Isaac Newton, then we must prove it beyond any doubt. How on earth are we going to do that?"

Mileva produced a full bottle of sherry from the back of a kitchen cupboard. She had been saving it for a special occasion. This seemed to qualify. They chinked glasses and toasted the birth of a more general approach to their combined theory of relativity.

"The answer, my dearest Albert, lies not on earth but in space." She took a mouthful, then topped up their glasses. "We know light must travel in a straight line. But if space itself is curved then a beam of light will curve as it passes through. We can't see the gravitational effect that causes space to curve, but we can see light. So if the beam of light curves, then the object emitting the light would appear to move as the light passes through the gravitational field of large enough objects."

Albert reached for a piece of last night's leftover salami and received a sharp smack on his hand. "So stars beyond the sun would appear to move through space as their light curves past its surface?"

"Exactly."

"But to prove it we would need to photograph those stars where they normally are, then calculate where they would appear to move to as the sun passes between them and the earth."

"Correct."

"And if we get the calculations right AND produce a photograph that shows the stars have moved to where we predicted, then that would prove that space-time does in fact curve . . . which would challenge Sir Isaac Newton's theories on gravity."

She gave him a kiss and popped the last piece of salami into his waiting mouth. "And make us the most famous scientists in history . . . well, the most famous for two hundred and fifty years." He chewed thoughtfully and washed it down with a mouthful of sherry. "I like it, but there is one major snag. How do you take a photograph of the sun? No camera could cope with the light exposure."

"You take a photograph when there is little or no sunlight." Mileva was ready for the question.

Albert burst out laughing, which was rewarded with another slap and a warning about waking the baby. He explained he was going to suggest photographing the sun at night but that was not the best idea he'd ever had and certainly not one befitting a potential Nobel Prize winner or the greatest scientist since Sir Isaac Newton.

"In a sense you were right." She patted his hand. "We take a photograph during a solar eclipse."

• CHAPTER 40 •

Summer 1914 – Berlin, Germany

"You lying, cheating bastard!!"

Mileva slumped into the chair. The bundle of clothes she had been ironing fell into a heap on the threadbare carpet. She prayed for tears but could find only anger. It was anger and a nagging sense of being the object of a cruel deception. Of course, she had suspected the affair. Deep in her heart she knew. How could he? After all these years? After all he had promised.

"I want a divorce. I don't love you anymore, nor do you love me. We can't go on living together. I want to remarry as soon as possible. This is how it must be. For my sake, for your sake and for the sake of our children." He perched on the edge of an armchair. He hadn't even taken off his hat or jacket, like a messenger relaying someone else's bad news.

They had only lived in Berlin for a few months. Mileva was used to the upheavals of relocation since returning to Zurich from Prague. She had kept all the packing cases and organised the family move to Berlin with military precision. It was just one of the many sacrifices she had come to accept in her role as housekeeper, mother of two young boys, devoted wife and inspirational character behind one of Europe's rising stars of the scientific community.

"Marry your cousin? That's absurd! It's incest!" she snapped, before burying her head in her hands.

"It is perfectly legal and Elsa has agreed to the arrangement as soon as our divorce is finalised," he reported. He took off his hat and mopped the sweat from his brow. A gentle breeze had crept silently through their upper floor windows yet failed to breathe any life into their drab surroundings.

"Then she will be disappointed." Mileva looked at him through splayed fingers. "And I don't mean disappointed at living with a philanderer like you. She has that pleasure to come."

He was on his feet. He tore off his jacket and threw it onto the chair, knocking his hat to the floor. He paced round the unpacked boxes near the fireplace, scratching at his scalp. "What more do you want from me? You've made my life a living hell. You ignore all my household rules; you deny me any kind of love or affection. You twist things with my sons and turn them against me. What devious scheme have you dreamt up now, for God's sake?"

"I will not grant you a divorce. I will take the boys with me and return to Zurich. You can fight me for custody if you wish. But God knows, you've shown no interest in them since the day they were born. They hardly know who you are." She spat the words. The dam wall had finally burst. She could hold back the flood no longer. "And you can pay for the privilege."

"What do you mean?" He sat down again, regained some composure, tried to make himself smaller in the chair. He folded the jacket over his knee and picked up his hat, having obviously realised he would not be getting a new one for quite some time.

"I mean, you will pay me half your salary each month."

"And the divorce?" He prepared himself for this new flanking manoeuvre.

Now she was on her feet, pacing the floor, bouncing off the

walls like a rubber ball, eventually coming to rest by an open window. It was daylight outside. The sky was overcast and thick with sticky grey cloud. The smells of another busy lunchtime drifted up from the tables outside the cafe across the narrow street. She noticed the noise levels from the animated diners were higher than usual. The imminent threat of war across Europe was occupying most people's minds. But not Mileva's. Not today.

She looked closely and struggled to recognise him. He resembled the man she had fallen in love with nearly fifteen years ago when they were students together. The man her father knew would be a bad influence. Her father was right. And he was not alone. The lecturer in Heidelberg, where she had escaped his clutches for a year, had warned her. Even her professor in Zurich thought him a waster and not worth a light.

She always knew he would be a distraction in her life, yet he amused her and seemed worth the effort in their early days. Increasingly he had drained her of all ambition. He had robbed her of any chance for her own career. Worst of all, he had bled dry any self-confidence she had ever possessed, to the point where she doubted who she really was. Or what she was capable of.

As his confidence and standing had grown, as his influence and stature amongst the leading scientific minds of the day had blossomed, she could see that hers had slowly diminished. She had been cast into a secondary role as the little wife. But now, as the fire raged between them, an inferno fuelled by endless arguments over recent weeks and ignited by his dramatic confession, another more worrying realisation became clear to her.

In his eyes, she was being painted not as the victim of their tragedy but as the guilty party. It was her inflexibility, sourness and scheming suspicion that had driven him to this decision. It was all her fault. She had forced him into the arms of another, more appreciative, woman.

As she looked at him, a sudden ray of pale sunlight reflected off a photograph on the mantelpiece. It showed a happy family of four sat around a sofa: a smartly dressed father, a loving mother and two bright, young boys. Yet it was a lie. And it had been a lie right from the very start.

And there was someone missing. Where was Lieserl? The child she had abandoned so that he would not be embarrassed in the righteous and suspicious eyes of the scientific world. She had made a mother's ultimate sacrifice for him, only to be presented with his cynical *fait accompli*.

"I will give you a divorce on one condition," she hissed.

He did not move, did not reply. He awaited his fate in silence.

"You will pay me all the money you ever receive for the Nobel Prize." Her voice was merely a whisper. She saw flashes of anger and resistance shoot across his face, soon to be followed by a cowering downward glance of resignation. Resignation or guilty conscience? It didn't matter now which was true. This was the price he had to pay, not just for all the hurt he had caused, but for failing to recognise her true value. It would be her Nobel Prize just as much as his. History would be the judge of that.

"Of course there is still one problem," she continued, lifting her chin in defiance. Again her words fell into stony silence. "You may never win the Nobel Prize. Unless I'm very much mistaken, your new sleeping partner has very little understanding of Maxwell's Electromagnetic Theory or Black-Body Radiation. The late-night conversations over supper may be somewhat less stimulating from now on, my dearest Albert. And until the theory – our theory – of general relativity is proven beyond all doubt, then you will never be accepted into the club nor win the Prize."

He picked up his hat and coat. "I will win the Nobel Prize and you can have the money."

"I will not agree to sign any divorce papers until I am confident that the theory is proven. You'd better go now and sharpen your pencil." She turned away.

Two weeks later Mileva, Hans Albert and youngest son Eduard said their goodbyes on the smoky platform of Anhalt Railway Station in Berlin and boarded the sleeper to Zurich. A thirty-five-year-old scientist watched the train depart and openly wept, telling his academic colleague that he felt like a criminal having murdered his marriage and the relationship with his sons. He repeated the thoughts to his new partner in bed later that night.

As the train thundered through a rain-swept evening, Mileva did her best to create an air of normality for the boys, knowing full well that nothing would ever be the same again. The man opposite was reading a newspaper. *Germany Declares War on Serbia* was a headline of little interest to her now.

There were more pressing concerns nearer to home.

• CHAPTER 41 •

Autumn 1948 – Zurich, Switzerland

The offices of Vogel & Lenz AG had occupied a five-storey building on Augustinergasse in the old town of Zurich since well before the turn of the century. From the windows of the partners' offices on the top floor, it was just possible to see the Limmat River as it flowed out of the lake. The post-war years were proving to be a boon for the thriving law firm, which offered a full range of client services including matrimonial, family law and probate.

"Maria, are you going down to the incinerator?"

"Yes, why?" Maria replied as she pushed the heavy trolley along the corridor towards the lift.

"Room for one more?" Herr Schmidt enquired. The small cardboard box in his hands was labelled *Incinerator*. He found a space and placed it on the trolley before she had time to refuse. "And please stay to watch it all burn before signing the docket. Frau Linder will need it for the file."

Maria Braun had taken up her articles some years previously and was enjoying her work. The firm had been good to her and was paying to put her through the professional examinations. Like the other articled clerks, she took her turn in taking confidential documents down to the basement. It was heavy work but had its advantages, especially in the winter months. An hour alone in the warmest room in the building was a good way to catch up with her studies.

Today she knew it would take longer. The commercial law team were having a clear-out before the move to the second floor. The incinerator was old but reliable. It cranked out waves of heat when it got going but its capacity was still quite limited. The partners were reviewing the investment for a new one.

She started to load up the first few boxes. While waiting for the kettle to boil, she noticed the box from Herr Schmidt had not been sealed properly. It would be last into the flames anyway. Curiosity tempted her to prise open the lid.

The box contained several files that belonged to an old lady who had died during the summer months. She was almost penniless, having looked after one of her sons for many years who suffered from severe mental illness. The lady had obviously been quite wealthy at one time but the cost of his healthcare had devoured all her savings. Her son was to be institutionalised after her death, so the file confirmed, partly paid for with the remainder of her meagre estate. The box also contained some old sepia photographs, a tangled collection of papers and receipts and even some letters, with postmarks stretching back before the First World War.

At the bottom of the box, she found an unaddressed envelope containing some pages written in a shaky but legible hand. It was dated just a few days before she had died. Maria loaded up a couple more boxes from the trolley for cremation, and then opened the letter.

Dearest Albert,

Even saying those two words is still painful for me. I don't know why I'm writing this. I shall probably never send it to you. Maybe it is more for my sake than yours. It is my way of saying I have not forgiven you. I suppose I never will.

I've been admitted to hospital again after another difficult time with Eduard. His illness is slowly consuming him. It is so sad because, on his good days, he can be lucid and quite charming. Sometimes I can see you in his eyes. The same look of mischief you used to have before it all became so serious. Eduard will often write poems for me and sing to me when we walk by the lake. Then, the next day, he is a stranger to me. He cannot control his rage, as if the anger is being released as his mind is torn apart.

I know he will kill me one day but I am his mother and the only person alive who will care for him properly. I worry about what will happen when I'm gone. It is my duty to look after him. Maybe things will be different for me in my next life. Is there a next life? I don't know. My scientific training still has no room for an Almighty Being yet there are times when I look up at the night sky over the lake and wonder about just how many stars there are. Were they all created by a random mixing of gases in a vacuum?

To some extent I suppose I am envious of your career. You achieved what you set out to achieve. You had the ambition and determination to make your mark in the world. And the scientific community did finally embrace you. Now they love your eccentricity, yet not so long ago they laughed at you. I remember the time after we made love when I scribbled down those equations. How ridiculous you thought $E = mc^2$ was. You argued that if c represented the speed of light then it could not possibly be squared as the value would be meaningless. Then we made love again, by which *time you thought it the most eloquent of equations.*

I'm not angry, just disappointed, I suppose. Anger is like a poison that leaches away over time. I just regret the things that we've both missed out on. I watched you struggle to prove general relativity. I know you have searched in vain for a unified theory that would make sense of everything. For a man so untidy, it is ironic that you have always tried to find an underlying order to things. Perhaps if we'd stayed together we would have gone on to make even greater discoveries. But it was not to be.

I get the occasional letter from Hans Albert. He is happy and settled in his new life in California. It is a great shame you were never able to repair your relationship with him. I was not surprised when he excelled in engineering. He inherited his understanding for mathematics from me, I suppose. I shouldn't think he ever contacts you. Like forces repel, it says in the textbook. He wisely chose America to escape the Nazis and seemingly then opted to live as far away from you as possible.

Finally I should tell you about Lieserl. We never really talked about her. How quickly you forgot she ever existed. She was an inconvenient truth that you filed away somewhere. In a funny sort of way, I always envied you the ability to forget things – and people, even so-called loved ones. Your conscience must be a happy place that is full of holes.

As I always knew, Helene became the best mother she could ever have wished for. We both thought she had made a full recovery from the scarlet fever. I saw the photographs of her in her school days. She was such a pretty girl and so full of life. I used to wait for news about her from Helene. Apparently Lieserl asked all the time to know more about her real parents. But she kept my promise and only told her when she was eighteen.

Helene gave her my mother's name so she grew up as Marija Savic. We agreed not to go through the formality of adoption as it may have caused problems for you later in your career. When Lieserl was eighteen she moved to Berlin to train as a primary school teacher. She used to attend your lectures in her free time, sitting in the back row. Helene told me she even said good morning to you once in the library at the university but, of course, you didn't know who she was. And she didn't want you to know.

After a whirlwind romance she married into one of the wealthiest banking families in Berlin. I was invited to the wedding but I could not bring myself to go. I will carry the shame of abandoning her to my grave. Sadly she died in childbirth at the age of twenty-one. The doctors said her heart must have been weakened by the scarlet fever. I wept for three days when I heard the news.

Thankfully the baby survived, so Helene told me. You would be pleased to know she named him after your father. Hermann Blindt was born at 8lbs 3ozs, a bouncing baby boy. I don't suppose you would be interested to know. Parenthood never did appeal to you.

They are coming round now with the lunchtime trolley. The nurse said I was to see the doctor this afternoon and they might let me go home if the wound has healed enough. But I'm not sure which is worse – being in here or being at home with Eduard.

I don't know how I should finish this letter. Your loving wife may not be true anymore yet somewhere in my heart that's still how I feel. At least in this life, I will remain your little witch.

Sincerely Yours,

Mileva

Maria folded up the letter and put it back in the box. The flames had died down and her coffee had gone cold. She thought about the letter. Albert? Mileva? The names meant nothing to her. Getting old was very sad, she thought, especially when life had not been so kind. Still, the woman had lived into her seventies, survived two world wars and given birth to three children. Others in Europe had not been so fortunate. And the file recorded that she had died peacefully.

Her thoughts were broken by the sound of the lift descending. Maria heard angry footsteps pounding along the corridor outside. The door flew open to reveal an austere-looking woman dressed all in black. She recognised the unsmiling face immediately.

"Herr Schmidt tells me to expect a docket from you. I'm going out to lunch in ten minutes and I need to file this before I go. Where is it?" Frau Linder scowled.

Maria threw the box into the incinerator, closed the door on the hungry flames, signed the docket and handed it to her. She switched out the light and closed the door behind them.

They marched together in frosty silence back down the basement corridor towards the lift.

CHAPTER 42

Spring 1965 – Geneva, Switzerland

Luc Fournier, the new headmaster of Villa St Bertrand International School, was either a breath of fresh air or a philistine modernist driving the school into ruin, depending on which member of the Board was being consulted. In his first two years, he had moved the school up the international league table a couple of notches and attracted more high-profile boarders as well as budding local child prodigies. The new engineering campus was proving popular, especially with American students.

"Mr and Mrs Blindt, so good to see you, please sit down."

But by far the biggest change was the introduction of female students in both the primary and secondary schools. Founded in 1544, it had remained an all-boys school for over four hundred years until the first three girls attended an historic geography lesson in the new wing. The local paper carried photographs that sent shockwaves through Geneva society as well as the school's illustrious alumni. Luc Fournier still received letters from disgruntled parents of boys taken out of the school before the floodgates opened.

"I have the papers here somewhere . . . ah yes, here we are. Dieter Blindt." He sat back, drew a deep breath and composed himself. Furtive brown eyes the colour of milk chocolate quickly scanned the collection of papers in the file, then fixed on their prey across the table.

"In many respects, Dieter is a remarkable boy. He's certainly made an impression at the school."

Hermann and Lana Blindt sat in silence. They had been accepted into the tight-knit community with open arms. Their wedding, some years ago, had attracted much interest and the arrival of their first-born child was duly reported on the society pages. Pressure of work had precluded attendance at previous parents' evenings but the opportunity to meet the new headmaster, combined with the importance of the decision they now faced regarding Dieter's future, had drawn them in like moths to the academic flame.

"In what way could you describe him as remarkable?" Hermann replied, catching the worried expression on his wife's face. He expected a conciliatory approach from the school.

Luc Fournier cast his eyes back into the file for an answer. But there was no answer. The grades were average at best. The mid-term exam results were disappointing and the reports on his general behaviour during games and other extra-curricular activities gave cause for serious concern.

"I mean remarkable in the sense that he ... does possess the potential to do better. All his teachers, including his form master, believe he has it in him, especially in the arts and language subjects. Overall, though, we feel he is ... underperforming," he concluded and closed the file.

"Headmaster," Lana interjected, "it's been a long and – quite honestly – frustrating evening. His form master described him as distant; his science teacher difficult; his maths teacher impossible to engage; his French teacher sloppy: and his games teacher just said he was weird. We're his parents and we love him but we had hoped a school like this would have helped to ... straighten him out, I suppose."

A crescendo of noise was building in the Great Hall with the arrival of more and more people. The teacher appointments roster had stretched into chaos. Some teachers were sat doing crossword puzzles while others, mostly the younger members of staff, were drowning in a sea of anxious parents. The headmaster suggested they carry on their conversation in his private study, which Hermann interpreted as a good sign.

"That's better. Would you care for some water?" Luc reached for the tray on his expansive leather-inlaid desk.

"No, thank you." Hermann was quick to respond. "Headmaster, we know Dieter can be quite awkward sometimes but we'd hoped he would learn more social skills at the school. He needs to mix in better. Do you think it will get easier for him in the big school?"

Luc poured himself a glass and took a slow mouthful. "That's what I wanted to talk to you about."

"So you do think he will come on when he moves up next year?" Lana provided reinforcement.

"Mr and Mrs Blindt, I'm afraid we're not able to offer your son a place in our secondary school." Luc held up his hands against the impending onslaught. "Please, this is not my decision alone. The Board was unanimous. I'm really sorry."

Lana was on her feet in protest. Hermann managed to grab hold of his wife's arm just in time. He persuaded her to calm down. But there was something in her eyes he didn't quite understand. A faraway look he hadn't seen before. The anger quickly passed, as it normally did. She seemed reassured when he spoke to her in Russian and said they should discuss their options for Dieter when they got home.

"You said it was not your decision alone. Did you recommend this to the Board?" Hermann had learned much about the dark arts of Board governance in his client dealings at the bank. The scars had cut deep into his psyche. He expected a school board to be no less political or devious. And this was one of the more powerful school boards in Switzerland.

"Yes."

"Then can you tell me what you based this decision on? You said yourself, Dieter has the potential to do better." Hermann lowered his voice as a gesture to show he was listening intently.

"Mr Blindt, some years ago I attended a lecture by Dr Hans Asperger, a leading paediatrician who has researched learning difficulties in young children. He described many of the symptoms that Dieter is now exhibiting: appearing distant, physical clumsiness, difficulties in communicating and social interaction, sudden bouts of anger or violence, misunderstanding of non-verbal communication, repetitive patterns of behaviour. Also he has a tendency towards submissiveness. He is often teased about his unfortunate birthmark."

"He's in the school orchestra, for God's sake. How can he lack communication skills?" Lana was pacing round the study like a caged animal, seeming to take an interest in the portraits of previous headmasters.

"Mrs Blindt, he plays the triangle. He's in the school orchestra because we couldn't include him in anything else. His only friend plays the kettledrum. Your son drifts around between lessons in his own world. He spends endless hours in the library on his own, doodling mostly. Sadly, his friend also shows signs of autism. We won't be offering him a place next year either."

"Autism?" Lana thundered. "How dare you! Are you saying my son is autistic?"

"Mrs Blindt, I am saying your son would be better off in a school that can cater for his learning difficulties and his particular social needs. I strongly recommend you contact Dr Asperger and try to understand his work. Autistic children can excel in languages or arts subjects, for example. I can provide you with the doctor's address, if you wish."

The journey home passed in silence. Hermann considered putting on the radio to break the tension. As he turned off the main road, the headlights of the BMW lit up the long driveway as it twisted from the ornate stone gateposts down through the woodland and on towards the lake. An owl swooped silently across the main beam and disappeared into a thicket of fir trees.

Eventually the tyres crunched to a halt in the gravel by the fountain opposite the front doors. The water nymphs playing in the rock pools were oblivious to the slamming of the car door as Lana stormed off towards the house.

"Please keep your voice down. I don't want him to hear us." Hermann fixed two large gin and tonics before settling into the security of his armchair by a cold fireplace. He watched her circling the room, taking mouthfuls of courage, preparing for the onslaught he sensed was about to come.

"Of course, you know there's nothing wrong with him." She'd finished her drink and refilled it before the ice had melted. "It's this fucking awful place. It would drive anyone mad."

They had lived with his father when they first arrived in Geneva after the war. Walther Blindt had made them as comfortable as he could but conditions were cramped until they found a house Lana actually liked. Their plan to have a brood of children all changed when she decided the pain of childbirth was too much to bear again. The apparent medical complications when the baby was born worked in her favour. She chose the name Dieter, a reminder of strangely happier times.

"Oh, not this again," he snapped. "You chose this fucking house."

"I don't mean the house."

"Well, what then?" He took a clean glass. This called for heavy-duty relief. Glenfiddich.

"Hermann, you said you never wanted to be a banker but I've watched you turn into one. You have become your father. The same polite expression; the same coldness; Christ, the same bloody arrogance. You're the perfect man to take over from him because you have become him. The bank will be in safe hands because your clients won't even think he's retired." She paused. "And as for Der Sangerbund? Jesus, the bloody Cantata will carry you shoulder high around the fucking lake. All hail our new Choirmaster. Rejoice and sing his fucking praises. Hallelujah!"

Hermann was caught between trying to make sense of where this was coming from and, more importantly, where it was going. Lana had shown signs of restlessness in the early days. She'd visited her parents and sister a couple of times back in what was now Volgograd. But since she'd opened her studio and art gallery in Zurich's old town, her social life seemed to have given her a new energy and a much wider circle of friends. Clearly he was mistaken. Something was eating away at her.

"Leave my father out of it. What the fucking hell are you talking about? We're supposed to be discussing our son's future." The whisky sharpened the edge.

Her cheeks had turned crimson and were framed by long, thin strands of auburn hair. She went to put her glass down on the mantelpiece but immediately changed her mind.

Hermann couldn't remember her ever being this agitated.

"Switzerland. It's like an open prison. Everything is so perfect all the time. No litter, no crime, no passion except for fucking chocolate and cuckoo clocks. The people are so dull, so boring. I feel like the mountains are closing in on me. Since I've lived here, I haven't painted one fucking thing worth keeping. Now they're telling me my son is autistic. *They* are autistic, the whole fucking lot of them!! I've got to get us out of here before they say *I'm* going mad."

He was rooted to the chair. Autism; maybe she was in shock. He wanted to move to her side, to comfort her, to tell her it would be all right. Dieter was a loner, a solitary ten-year-old boy who skulked around the house and showed little interest in most things. But Hermann knew he had been no different as a child. Growing up in Berlin without a mother to look after him and rattling around a huge empty house with only his father for company had made his childhood equally miserable. Dieter would grow out of it, as he had done. They just needed to send him to the right school. He took another mouthful, plucked up his courage. He had to know.

"Lana, is this something to do with the gallery?" He drained the glass, savouring the peat on the back of his throat. He stifled a yawn. It had been a long day. But he could not leave things as they were. He didn't want to spend another night in the spare room.

"The gallery?" She fixed him with a glare.

"It's just that ... you mentioned painting. How's the exhibition by your new artist going? You know, the Chinese girl you were telling me about. She sounds like fun. Was it Mei Mei?" he probed.

Lana had been introduced to her work through an American friend whose son was at the school. Apparently the artist had trained at the Arts Student League of New York and was making her name in lyrical abstraction and op art. Larry Poons himself had bought one of her canvasses and given her a glowing write-up in *Blow Job* magazine.

"Mee Mee. She's not Chinese; she's Malaysian. Big difference, not that you'd care." She fussed around with the gin bottle. Her face had turned the colour of beetroot.

"Sold many?" He decided against another whisky. He opened a small side window, which rewarded him with a cooling breeze off the lake.

"Not yet. It takes the Swiss a while to warm up to new ideas."

"Maybe we should invite her over for dinner. It would be good to meet her. Or I could drop by the gallery tomorrow; take a look at her work. We could do with a new piece for this room. Brighten the place up a bit. What was it you called it – lyrical abstraction?" He felt uneasy, like he was descending into a mineshaft, each step revealing more and more of its unfamiliar depths.

Lana went very quiet. She lowered herself into the other chair, put her empty glass on the coffee table and stared at the curtain now billowing in the breeze. She had the faraway look in her eyes again. Her cheeks were cooling as she leaned back, turning her face towards him.

"I don't think it's a good idea for you to meet her." Her voice was calm and measured, like a radio announcer preparing the listeners for bad news. "She's going back to Kuala Lumpur, next week, I think."

"Oh, that's a shame. Anyway, do you think this room would work for one of her pieces?" He was now on high alert. This whole evening had felt wrong somehow. She was acting out of character. The conversation in the headmaster's study seemed a long time ago.

Of course, the headmaster's study. It had slipped his mind. There would be implications if Dieter did not get into the big school. What would his father think? His board colleagues?

His clients? Influential people at the golf club? Questions would be asked.

And there could be other implications. Der Sangerbund? He had been a Voice since their arrival in Geneva. It was understood within the Cantata that he would become the next Choirmaster upon his father's retirement. But a disgrace within the family might change all that. Rumours about his son's mental health could be very damaging.

Maybe he needed a fallback position. Damage limitation. Perhaps consulting this doctor in Vienna would be a good idea after all. They could make a long weekend out of it. When did they last have some time away together? He couldn't remember. When did they last make love?

Lana was on her feet again, gesticulating at the featureless Alpine landscape over the fireplace. "One of her paintings in here? Mee Mee's work is too lively for a morgue like this ... look, I'm very tired. Could you sleep in the spare room tonight?" It was clearly not meant as a question.

"Lana, you need to tell me what the hell's going on. What are we going to do about Dieter? Should we ignore the headmaster and appeal directly to the Board? Or should we take his advice and go to Vienna?"

"I'm not going to Vienna." She was emphatic, her eyes in lockdown. "He doesn't need a doctor. He needs to see the world, make new friends. Stimulation, for God's sake. Meeting real people with blood in their veins, not Swiss cheese. He's bored, not autistic."

The silence was palpable. In the far distance, Hermann picked out the sound of the lake being whisked up by a freshening breeze. From the trees behind the house, he heard the owl calling to its mate in the darkness, ever hopeful, despite its forlorn cry.

"And are you bored, Lana?"

No reply.

"It's not Dieter who needs stimulation, is it?"

She shifted awkwardly, twisting the ring on her third finger. Round and round.

"You're going to leave me."

Silence. She looked away, suddenly inspecting the Toblerone imagery of the Matterhorn.

"You want to take him with you."

She kept looking up at the painting. The tears refused to flow. Her cheeks were glowing again.

"You've never loved me. This has all been pretence. I suspected from the start. We never touched, even in the old factory in Stalingrad. You liked the idea of a man; a loving husband; a family; respectability; a place in society. But there's no warmth between us. Switzerland was your father's idea. You only came with me to secure your family's future through the bank. All the time I bloody well knew but didn't want to see." He slumped forward in the chair. There was a large glassful left in the bottle. But he knew there was another bottle in the cellar.

At last her tears escaped. She made no move to dry them. They dripped over hot cheeks and down her front. She turned towards him. He could see remorse but was it real? Suddenly nothing was real.

Still she remained silent.

"I love you, Lana. Even now, I want it to work. Is there anything I can do to make you change your mind?"

His words hung in unfamiliar air. He felt out of place, as if his own lounge had become a hotel suite or a stage set for a play. She'd played the part so well. The beautiful girl, trophy wife, proud mother, the darling of society who spiced up their lives with stories from Mother Russia. She was an artist who painted her soul on canvas.

As he looked deeper into her actress eyes, he sensed that he had joined the play in the second act. He had missed out on earlier scenes that would have helped explain the plot. Other characters had been and gone, leaving their mark on the storyline. There had been twists he was blissfully unaware of. Twists and consequences and allegations he needed to understand. How could he have been so foolish, so trusting, so vulnerable? He could stand her silence no longer

"Is there someone else?"

"Yes."

One word. Just one simple word, three letters long. With it, she thrust a dagger into him. He felt the blade slicing through the skin; the very tip penetrating deep into the walls of his chest and puncturing his heart.

For years he had played this bloody game. He had been the model of correctness and diplomacy. His family had brought proper Teutonic values from an old German aristocracy to this corner of a forgotten little country. He had always done what he thought was the right thing. Now this was to be his reward.

"Who is he?"

She opened her mouth but no words came. She stared at him; calculating, plotting, weighing up her next move like a wrestler looking to find a hold, a weakness in the opponent's defence. Eventually she brushed the tangle of apricot hair off her face.

"It's not a he."

The knife twisted. It ripped apart whatever shred of hope he had left. His muscles relaxed as he swallowed the last drops of the whisky, hungry for more.

"I'm sorry it had to end like this. I'd planned to tell you but

... I don't suppose there's ever a good time." She offered a smile of consolation.

"You didn't answer my question." He had already guessed.

"You know who it is. Let's not make this any more difficult than it is. I don't expect you to understand." The tears had dried. Her actress face was set once again for her audience.

"Do you love her?"

"I said leave it . . . you know I do. I don't want to hurt you, I just want to go."

"And take my son with you. Whatever makes you think I'll let you do that? He needs a father more than most boys. How on earth do you think he will survive living with two . . ." He checked himself. He saw his open flank for the first time. It was a gaping hole in his defences, reflected in her eyes.

"Two dykes. Go on say it, two lesbians, two queers . . . and me old enough to be her mother. I know what you're thinking, what they'll all be thinking. And she's got slitty eyes, go on, shout it out . . . and she'll dump you for someone younger when she's bled you dry . . . and where will that leave you . . . and my precious son . . . well, don't expect to come back here with your tail between your legs . . . you disgust me." She hurled the empty glass into the fireplace, smashing it into a thousand shards of lead crystal.

Hermann didn't move. A young Malaysian artist. The same age as Lana had been when he met her. He couldn't get the images out of his head. He could see the two of them giggling as they worked late into the night to get the exhibition ready. Her weekend away in Paris. The two of them meeting up by chance at an exhibition.

He was watching them embracing and kissing and loving each other as they rolled around on the gallery floor. They were laughing together: laughing at him. Meanwhile he was sitting in his starched white collar and tie in the executive suite at the bank, sweating over an investment portfolio to earn the money to pay for it all. He shook his head in disbelief.

"They're your words, not mine. Please show me some respect." He wanted the other bottle. "I want you to leave him with me. It's all I ask. Then I'll let you go, give you a divorce, if that's what you really want. But he is my son and he needs me . . . and I need him."

He saw the flash of anger sweep across her face, then vanish just as quickly. He knew she would get her own way, as she always did. It was time to complete his humiliation.

"You know I can't do that. Dieter's my son too. Mee Mee and I will look after him, give him a chance in life." She paused. "If he wants to come back when he's older, it will be his choice."

"And what if I say no?" He had to hear her say it. His resignation would follow at the mention of her name. It was the one client they couldn't afford to lose. He called it blackmail; the Russians called it negotiation.

"Then I would talk to Tatiana."

CHAPTER 43

Spring 1997 – Geneva, Switzerland

"Hannibal?"

The American accent sounded familiar. Dieter Blindt lowered his newspaper to reveal a tall, slim man in a strange collection of clothing. A worn-out Sticky Fingers T-shirt hung loosely over equally faded Levi's. Draped around his wide shoulders was a tailored three-quarter length Crombie in pure cashmere. The camel colour was offset by a rust silk lining that perfectly matched his Doc Marten boots. The coat was straight from the display window of Pierre Grimaud on Sixth Avenue.

"I haven't been called that in years." He stood up and offered his hand. "Curtis Opperman, what the hell're you doing here?"

The last time Dieter had seen him, he was crawling around the floor of a London wine bar looking for his glasses, after the prize-giving ceremony. It had been some party.

"Same as you, I guess, waiting for a goddam plane." He smiled and put down his leather weekend bag. "How are ya?"

Dieter was on his way to a client meeting in Paris, he explained, then back on the red-eye tonight. He gestured towards the empty seat. The executive lounge was always quiet at this hour. He preferred an early start.

He remembered the course had been intensive. To this day, Dieter was not convinced he deserved a Masters in Finance. Curtis and the others had slaved so hard. For Dieter, it was a chance to get out of Geneva for a while. He had made some useful contacts through the Central London Business School. For him, the alumni network had proved more valuable than the qualification.

Curtis tossed his coat over the next chair and looked around for a waiter. Dieter guessed he knew it was self-service but remembered that convention wasn't the way this guy worked.

"And you?"

"Yep, still making a groove in Wall Street. I gotta connection to JFK out of Heathrow tonight. I'll be riding a desk bright and early." He ordered a pot of fresh coffee and some double toasted bagels with smoked salmon and cream cheese.

"So business or pleasure?" Dieter noticed his handsome rugged features were just as engaging. The black-rimmed glasses were straight from a sixties spy movie yet, like most things, suited him perfectly.

"Purely business, though I wish I'd brought my skis. I hear they got a fresh six inches in Gstadt overnight." Curtis winced at the coffee and reached for a sachet of brown sugar.

Dieter checked the gate number on the screen. "What kind of business?"

"You always did go straight to the point, didn't you? Well, OK. Job interview." He smiled. "We could end up neighbours. I could help you liven up the fondue parties."

Dieter thought he knew everything that moved in the banking community. It must be a significant role to attract the likes of Curtis Opperman. "And did you get it?"

"I don't know yet. They had some other guy to torture. I think it went well though. Interesting times here. You guys've certainly gotten Washington's attention." He tossed a piece of soggy bagel onto his plate.

"Curtis, it's been great to see you but I got to go." Dieter pulled out a business card. "Who is the job with?"

"Sorry, Hannibal, they made me sign a non-disclosure agreement. This really is the land of secrets . . . but I guess you know that already." The cards were exchanged. "Oh, in case I don't see you for another ten years, I just gotta tell ya. I was the only guy in the movie theatre laughing all the way through *Silence of the Lambs*. Remember we all read the book on the course? Well, when I saw Anthony Hopkins on the big screen, I thought – jeeze – it really is you! What a piece of casting."

"He must be six inches taller than me . . . and twenty pounds lighter," Dieter corrected. "I never did get it."

"No, you never did."

CHAPTER 44

Spring 1997 – Geneva, Switzerland

Dieter got the message from his father's secretary. He'd be there soon enough.

The drive round the lake had passed in a blur. He had noticed the spring flowers outside the park. He did see the bunting for the annual music festival. But the images soon faded. There were too many things on his mind. The chance meeting yesterday with Curtis Opperman had left him feeling uneasy.

Paris had gone well. He was confident at least one of the accounts could be saved. But it had become a recurring theme. Without a more aggressive investment strategy, CBG would continue to lose more clients.

He spent a few minutes in his own office pulling together the papers he would need. He took the stairs up one flight to the executive suite. When he knocked and entered the oak-panelled room, he saw a vacant figure slumped on the sill of the double window overlooking the lake.

"What's up, Father? Come and sit down." Dieter ordered a tray of hot coffee. "Have you taken your tablets this morning?"

"I don't feel so good, son." The reply was weak, much weaker than it had been just a couple of months ago. Although he was now well into his seventies, Hermann Blindt had always tried to stand tall and stay strong. The CEO was the head of the family, after all, and, as such, he should set the example.

"Is it LaSalle?" Dieter opened his diary. The board meeting was scheduled for next Tuesday.

"I've known this guy for thirty years. I'm godfather to his two girls, for fuck's sake. Now he's doing this to me?" Hermann took three bottles of pills out of his top drawer and swallowed a couple from each. Dieter couldn't help noticing the half-empty bottle of vodka amongst the stationery. The alcoholic's poison of choice; a few minutes of escape that leaves no trace. Or so they think.

"What does he want?" Dieter could see his father had not been sleeping again. New shadows under his eyes, deep creases across his upper cheeks. His grey skin was sallow. It was a tired face that hadn't seen a razor for several days.

"He wants me out. He wants to be the next CEO. If he gets his way, you can kiss goodbye to your inheritance. And now the odds are stacked in his favour." He stared so hard that his eyes began to water.

Dieter had been here before. It had taken several years for the split in the board to reach the surface. More of a gradual slip in the tectonic plates than an earthquake. He knew this was only to be expected in a Swiss bank with nearly two hundred years of incest, family politics, indecision and personal vendettas behind it. In many respects, even after thirty years, the Blindts were still newcomers. And German newcomers at that.

There had been increasing tension between the vested interests of local families with largely a French heritage and the Teutonic rigidity and financial dominance of the invaders from Berlin. He could see why they had liked the wealth and security his family had brought them but they just didn't like them. The animosity was deepening, as Hermann Blindt's health deteriorated. The sharks could smell blood in the water.

"Father, you're becoming paranoid. If Claude LaSalle

wanted to challenge you, he could have done so years ago. Why is he raking this up now?" Dieter knew the answer. It was all part of the game to make his father feel better.

"Because the world is tilting on its axis. East is becoming west. LaSalle thinks by appeasing the Chinese, they will leave him alone to run the bank post-acquisition. But that'll never happen." Hermann let out a deep sigh as he threw his head back and stared at the ornate plasterwork on the ceiling. His trembling hand stopped short of opening the drawer.

"You must resist this takeover. The Chinese are not to be trusted. There was enough Mandarin blood in Mee Mee bloody Wong. We're all foreign devils to them and always will be. She didn't even weep when she ditched my mother. She must have ice water in her veins."

Hermann pulled a file from the clutter on his desk and fished out a single page. "I received this yesterday."

Dieter saw the words but they did not register. He read it again. "But that's nearly twice the current value. No wonder the board is faltering. What's the split?"

"I reckon fifty-fifty. If it stays like that then it'll come down to my casting vote. But it would only need a couple of the others to join him and they would have a majority. The deal would go through and CBG would be swallowed up into the Kowloon & Southern China Banking Corporation."

"So is this purely about money?" Dieter returned the letter.

"Yes and no."

Hermann explained that the bank was facing two potential crises. Increasingly wealth generation and corporate banking needed a broader range of securities, investment products and much greater international exposure. CBG was losing out to international banking groups that boasted offices in the world's financial centres. Being part of the Kowloon &

Southern China Banking Corporation would give them access to those investors.

More worrying, he continued, was the question of risk and liability. The allegations that some Swiss banks had acted irresponsibly regarding Jewish investors who had perished during the Second World War were being addressed by the Swiss Government, no doubt under pressure from Washington, Dieter surmised.

An independent commission had been set up with far-reaching powers and very sharp teeth. The talk in the Swiss banking community was that at least two of the leading players were being forced into negotiating settlements well into the US$'s billions.

Hermann had undertaken an internal review of dormant accounts and other investments in CBG with a potential connection to the Nazi regime. If they were forced into a settlement, the payout could lead to bankruptcy.

"But if we became part of the Kowloon & Southern China Banking Corporation, then we'd have the muscle to compete globally and deep enough pockets to withstand any Holocaust Reparation settlements," Hermann concluded, the look of resignation in his down-cast eyes deepening.

"Yes, but any such decisions would be made in Hong Kong." Dieter paused. "Or more likely, Beijing, after the British hand it back. If the Kowloon & Southern China Banking Corporation runs true to form, they would shut down CBG and run our client accounts from a regional hub in Frankfurt or London. They'd close the Geneva office, get rid of all the staff and use the savings to pay off the cost of the acquisition and any Jewish reparation liabilities."

"Which is why my supporters are worried about taking the Chinese offer. Sure it would give them a good payout and protect them against any future legal liabilities or bankruptcy threats. But they wouldn't be able to walk the streets of Geneva again or give out jobs to their children."

Dieter produced a document marked "Confidential".

"Father, I've been working on a few ideas that could help both of us. I've crunched some numbers, which I'll leave with you. I just need fifteen minutes to present this at your next board meeting. Can you table it as an agenda item?"

Hermann blew out his cheeks. "Yes, I can, but I don't want to get your hopes up. CBG is going under. I've failed you, failed all of us. There'll be nothing left once the Commission get their teeth into us."

The paper was pushed across the desk and given a cursory glance before being locked in a bottom drawer. Dieter probed further. "When're you meeting them?"

"I have the pleasure of Jean-Francois Bergier and his attack dogs tomorrow morning. He declined my offer of lunch and insisted on seeing me in my office . . . alone."

The old man stood up slowly and took the few steps over to the window. The white sails of a sleek wooden yacht were filling with the early morning breeze. The boat leaned over as it cut through the clear, blue water, enjoying its freedom, running away down the lake.

"Have you heard from your mother recently?" he said quietly to the window.

Dieter was eighteen years old again. At the airport in Kuala Lumpur, the stifling heat making him feel sick, the clothes stuck to his back. Lana was crying as he unloaded his cases from the taxi. He knew her as Lana, not Mother their relationship never having recovered. If his father couldn't stop her, then a ten-year-old boy had no chance. He just had to endure the pain and wait for his opportunity.

After the split from Mee Mee, they had moved to an apartment above a studio Lana was renting in Pudu. Dieter hated it but he knew it was all they could afford. She insisted on sending him to an International School, where he was bullied relentlessly. They were painful years. Lana had tried to make things work but she was never accepted. Dieter recalled how she'd even considered converting to Islam.

While he was excited to be leaving Malaysia, he was nervous about returning to Switzerland, living alone with his father in the empty house by the lake. University held little interest for him. Economics at Geneva was the simplest way forward. Joining the bank would give him some independence. Anything would be an improvement on the endless arguments and emotional turmoil of two women fuelled up on high-octane oestrogen.

As the headmaster at his Swiss school had predicted, his autistic tendencies at least gave him the advantage of being able to learn languages. Malay and Mandarin had been added to his German, English and French. He could see that, from a commercial point of view, being able to understand the Asian mentality would be advantageous for his future role in the bank. He may understand it but he would never accept it . . . or give in to it.

"No, not recently," Dieter replied. "The last I heard, she was living with her sister in Volgograd. I guess Tatiana took over from Sergei as the head of the family. I see they're still clients."

"Only just. They've blackmailed us for years with the threat of taking their investments elsewhere. The oil and gas industries have been good to them. Tatiana turned out to be a bigger bastard than Sergei." He turned back to face him. "Between the Russians, the Chinese and the Jews, it's no wonder I'm going mad."

* * *

"This is your last chance, Blindt."

Torrents of freezing rain were sweeping in from the lake and hosing against the double windows. The view of the mountains had been consumed by swirling mist that clung to the old buildings and sucked all the colours out of the town. The downpour had been relentless since early morning.

"Get out, LaSalle! I will never agree." Hermann screwed up the paper and threw it at the silver-haired man leaning over his desk.

"I now have the majority. We'll vote on Tuesday. As the new CEO, I will take great pleasure in throwing you out, you drunken old sot!"

LaSalle ripped open the door and saw Dieter Blindt heading towards him down the corridor. He turned back, face flushed, fire wreathing in his eyes. "And another thing, I will not allow this fucked-up, cold-hearted bastard of yours to speak. He is not a board member and has no voting rights. You and your wretched family have held us back long enough. I'll get rid of all of you."

Hermann was on his feet, yelling at the empty doorway. "My son will address the board. While I'm in charge, we will follow the constitution. You're too late, LaSalle."

He staggered back, fell into his chair and reached into his desk drawer. Dieter took the nearly full bottle of vodka out of his trembling hands and screwed the top back on. His father showed no sign of resistance.

Dieter didn't need to read the latest ultimatum. Instead he sat watching his father struggling to breathe. "I'll take you home. You need to get some rest."

"He's persuaded two more to cross over. It will be a formality now."

"He's lying, Father. I spoke to Schwegler this morning. He said the offer is going to include Kowloon & Southern China Banking Corporation shares. The payout in cash will only be half what they expect."

Hermann looked up. "I couldn't understand how Bergier knew how many dormant accounts we have . . . or about the two Hildebrand investment trusts. That lying bastard LaSalle must've tipped them off."

"Hildebrand?"

"They came with me from Berlin. The investment was in gold and fine arts. We purchased properties in Buenos Aires and Montevideo, which were sold on to German ex-pats. The funds are now in derivatives, equities, securities. They still sit in the trust accounts. I am one of the trustees."

Dieter's face was fixed. "Money laundering for Nazi sympathisers?"

"I prefer confidential commercial transactions and exemplary client service." Hermann managed a weak smile. "Either way, there could only be one source. LaSalle is trying to increase our liability with the Commission to panic the board into taking the Chinese offer. Then he will pull the rug from under them, sell us off for a song and accept some overpaid regional job in Frankfurt."

"So what about the Commission?"

Dieter saw the change in his father's complexion. Hermann was sweating heavily and holding his left arm. He went to stand but his legs gave way and he crashed to the floor. Dieter leapt to his side, loosened his tie, flipped him into the recovery position and tried to bring him back into consciousness. He pressed the intercom.

"Call an ambulance."

• CHAPTER 45 •

Spring 1997 – Geneva, Switzerland

Schwegler slammed his fist on the boardroom table. "Gentlemen, I call for order."

He had been the Secretary for as long as anyone could remember. His role was to ensure board meetings were conducted in an orderly fashion and in accordance with the bank's constitution. His other duty was to diffuse tension in the room. Today, this was proving to be a real challenge.

Schwegler continued. "Dieter Blindt is entitled to present his paper. The rules clearly state that the proposer does not have to be present in the room. Claude, I ask you to be seated and remain silent. Herr Blindt, please proceed."

Dieter had visited his father in hospital early that morning. He seemed to have aged. The doctor was satisfied that his condition had at least stabilised but he remained in intensive care, purely as a precaution.

"Gentlemen, what I am about to propose has been discussed and agreed with my father, your CEO." Dieter accepted the best wishes for a speedy recovery from nine of the ten faces sat expectantly round the oval-shaped table. LaSalle continued to look out at the lake.

"May I start by saying I actually concur with Monsieur LaSalle in many respects." Dieter saw his head turn. He had his attention at last. "My main point of contention is how we should manage our affairs in the future."

Dieter presented the case that the bank should expand to become an independent banking group controlled from Geneva. It should develop its operations to include corporate finance, asset management, wealth generation, transactional trading, hedge fund management and acquisition & mergers, amongst other services. He urged that the bank must work more closely with the leading international accountancy firms to stimulate work referrals and joint client initiatives. He proposed to appoint PYKD as the bank's new auditors and advisers.

In addition, they would grow through a more aggressive client acquisition strategy targeting high net-worth individuals and their corporate enterprises. They would acquire other banks across Switzerland, then consolidate back-room operations to reduce support costs and streamline client service delivery. He identified key acquisition targets, singling out one in particular.

"Gentlemen, Banque Populaire Geneve is in a similar situation to us. The Bergier Commission is breathing down their necks. They have holes in their investment strategy and are haemorrhaging clients. What they don't have is a board with the will to fight on." He fixed his eyes on LaSalle. "The Kowloon & Southern China Banking Corporation made them a lucrative offer in exchange for certain information. The offer was subsequently withdrawn. The Chinese then proceeded to target their most vulnerable clients."

Dieter saw LaSalle squirm in his seat. "And, just like in our case, the Chinese found an informant within the bank to feed confidential information on dormant accounts through to the Bergier Commission, thus forcing their hand and bringing the price down."

There was uproar in the room. LaSalle was on his feet, shouting over the pandemonium. Schwegler again had to call for order.

"Monsieur LaSalle." Dieter's eyes narrowed. "Do you deny having passed confidential information to the Bergier Commission without approval from this board?"

The silver-haired man in the grey pinstripe suit went silent. He flicked his eyes around his supporters in the room then back at Dieter. His neck was flushed. "I . . . I have done no such thing. It is outrageous. This is defamation. I'll sue you!!"

"Then perhaps you can explain this." Dieter handed out copies and passed the original signed copy to Schwegler for the minutes. It was an internal memorandum between two senior members of the Bergier Commission recommending that Bergier himself write to Claude LaSalle and thank him for providing the details of client accounts at CBG with possible connections to the Nazi regime and the Holocaust.

"Where did you get this?! This is a pack of lies! I know both these commissioners; they're honourable men. They would never be complicit in a scandalous fabrication like this. I will see you in court, Blindt."

LaSalle went to storm out of the room but was grabbed by Schwegler, who advised him that they would be taking a vote very shortly and it was in his interests to stay. Reluctantly, LaSalle resumed his seat.

"Gentlemen, I stand by my accusation. My source is reliable and this document is absolutely genuine. But now to conclude my presentation . . ." Dieter's eyes remained ice-cold. "I propose to commence takeover talks with the President of BPG. In the document before you, I have explained how the acquisition would be funded. At the price I'm recommending, the President has given me his personal assurance that our offer would be accepted by their board.

"BPG would be the first of four acquisitions and help us to create the Canton Banking Services Group, for our long-term security and future prosperity. They already have offices in New York and London. We will establish a presence in the other main financial centres over the next three years. The numbers are all in here."

In view of the unusual circumstances, Schwegler recommended that the board allowed Dieter Blindt to remain in the room while the vote took place, pointing out that he himself could not vote. This was agreed by all but one member present and duly minuted.

Schwegler explained that they would follow board protocol and have an initial show of hands. If the decision was not unanimous then they would move to a formal vote. He clarified the proposal tabled by Claude LaSalle and seconded by board colleague Michele Pappan: that the board accept the Kowloon & Southern China Banking Corporation memorandum of understanding that would take them through the formal acquisition and due diligence processes to accept an offer for CBG.

The room fell silent. Schwegler asked for those in favour.

Immediately LaSalle, Pappan and three other members held up their hands. Dieter was not surprised and made a mental note.

The Secretary then asked for those against. The short delay reflected more of a synaptic gap, Dieter decided, between the bullied participants desperately trying to decide which way the tide was now running. In a few moments, the remaining five hands were duly raised.

Dieter watched a smile creep across LaSalle's glowing face. As the deputy CEO, and in the absence of the CEO, he would have the casting vote if the board remained split after the next round. Dieter wondered if the Commission allegation had backfired. It was too late now.

Schwegler ensured that the formal vote was conducted properly and that each member returned his voting paper. After a few moments, he announced that the split was exactly the same.

As Schwegler explained the process for resolving split decisions by the board, Dieter was listening to raised voices coming from the office outside. Suddenly the double doors burst open.

In the doorway stood the diminutive figure of a well-dressed old lady with tidy, silver-white hair. She was wearing a dark woollen coat with matching handbag and highly polished court shoes. A thin leather attaché case was wedged under her arm.

It was her accent that Dieter immediately recognised. He stared at the woman in total disbelief. Despite her formal business dress, he could see that the years had not been kind to her. But why should they have been? Kindness was a quality she neither valued nor practised. Her whole life had revolved around herself and her own desires. People either fulfilled her dreams or got in her way. He knew this from personal and bitter experience. So why was she here?

"Gentlemen, please accept my apologies for this interruption," she announced in a whispered yet confident voice. After a nod from Schwegler, the yelling and commotion ceased and the double doors were closed quietly behind her. She unbuttoned her coat and sat down in the empty chair at the head of the table.

"For those of you who don't know me, my name is Svetlana Maria Blindt. My maiden name is Zaytseva and I have been legally married to Hermann Blindt for the last thirty-five years. I am sorry to have to advise the board that my husband suffered another major heart attack this morning and passed away in the intensive care unit less than one hour ago."

Lana explained that she had been contacted by her estranged husband. She had travelled from Volgograd and had brought with her their marriage certificate, passport, birth certificate and other documentation as proof of her identity. She also had a copy of her husband's certificates proving ownership of his shares in the bank. She passed the file over to Schwegler, whom she recognised.

"Our marriage has been unusual, to say the least. Although we have not lived together for many years, we have both tried, in our own unique ways, to show our son Dieter that we love him and want to support him. He has worked hard and sees his future here in Geneva. Herman showed me a copy of Dieter's presentation, the same one I believe you have seen this morning. I know Dieter will make an excellent successor for Hermann as your new CEO and I want you to give him that chance."

She put her hand on Dieter's shoulder and whispered in his ear. The time for grieving will come, she explained, but for now they must remain strong.

LaSalle was on his feet. "This is preposterous. She is not eligible to attend this meeting. How do we know they are not divorced? I don't believe a word she says. Hermann has put her up to this."

"That's enough!!" Schwegler demanded.

Dieter sat stony faced as the constitution was again consulted. It was confirmed that only votes made in the room by board members eligible to vote would count. If an eligible person did not attend for reasons of death or serious illness as authorised by a registered medical practitioner, then a vote could be cast on their behalf by a legally approved representative or spouse providing the probate was in order and their estate was uncontested.

"Herr Schwegler, you will need a copy of this for your files." She handed him the death certificate. He checked the details and arranged for a copy to be taken.

"On behalf of my late husband," she continued, "I cast his vote in favour of rejecting the proposal from Monsieur LaSalle. If I may, Herr Schwegler, I now propose that Dieter Blindt is appointed as the new CEO with immediate effect and that he receives the full support of the board to implement his plans for your future success."

*   *   *

"You always were a devious bastard, Dieter."

The private dining rooms above Galileo's Restaurant were divided into smoking and non-smoking, as well as with view and without view. Each room was named after a famous character in Swiss history. Tonight called for a special celebration. Dieter had booked his favourite room, which occupied the corner of the building, between Carl Jung and Henri Nestle. The Ursula Andress Suite was both smoking and with view. *Lonely Planet* had listed champagne cocktails on the balcony at sunset amongst the top ten things to do before you die.

"The memo cost me five hundred thousand Swiss francs. Every man has a price. All very Swiss." Dieter wiped a glutinous swab of crayfish and mayonnaise off his chin. "I've made an arrangement with the Commission regarding a mutually agreeable settlement. I think we all understand each other now."

"You mean it cost the bank half a mil, don't you?" Curtis signalled to the waiter for a third bottle of the Petrus 1982. He showed his disappointment at being told they only had the '89 left. He insisted on clean glasses.

"Same thing." Dieter tried the new wine, which proved to be acceptable. "Anyway, LaSalle had passed on our files to the Commission, which, of course, he denied. We both knew the memo was fraudulent but he couldn't take action for fear the truth would come out. And, after I fired him, he couldn't afford the legal fees, especially as I've withheld his severance package while PYKD are digging into his expense account."

"As I said, devious bastard." Curtis smiled. "So how does this play out?"

Dieter declined the cheese board and opted instead for cigars and brandies. He explained that the BPG deal would be completed by the end of the month and a rejuvenated board for the re-branded group would be announced. The new name of the Canton Banking Services Group would be shortened to the acronym CBSG. Once that was complete, they would commence due diligence for the acquisition of the other banks. By this time next year, CBSG would be beating the Chinese at their own game.

"Curtis, I want you on the new board."

"As what?" He approved of the cigar.

"Director of Investment Strategy."

"That's quite a promotion, I suppose I should say thank you."

"Is that a yes then?"

"Absolutely, count me in buddy." He swirled the cognac in the oversized balloon glass, gazing into its depths. "Dieter, I've known you a long time. There's one question I want to ask you. I guess now is a good time. What makes you tick?"

Dieter's expression didn't change. He didn't understand the question. It must be an Americanism, he decided, and shrugged his shoulders.

"OK, let me try it this way." Curtis finished the brandy. "You play the lone wolf yet I know that's not you. For such a private guy you have one of the most influential contact networks of anyone I know. You're now the head of that . . . what do you call it? The Choir Boys?"

"Der Sangerbund. It's an organisation I'd like to talk to you about. But only if you say yes."

"Exactly. You act the hungry CEO looking for world domination but you shun the limelight. You say it's about money but you never show it off. Then you pretend you love the power and control it gives you. But your eyes never changed when you told me about shafting LaSalle. So the question is – who the fuck are you, Dieter?"

Dieter could see his father being laid to rest in the Cimetière des Rois amid a small crowd of well wishers and family friends. His mother threw the first handful of soil before the coffin was lowered into the rich alluvial earth. They held hands as they strolled towards the waiting cars. Her hand was so cold. She was returning to Volgograd. He knew he would never see her again. He tried to find tears. Maybe he had no tears.

Dieter heard his own voice but they were not his words. *I am your boss.* He was ashamed of how it sounded. But the words were correct. It was time to establish a new set of ground rules. He knew this would take all his strength. Curtis was the one person in the world he wanted to share this evening with. But did *he* feel the same way?

Curtis topped up their glasses and drew on his cigar. A broad smile swept across his face. "The fuck you are. We're either in this together or not at all. Partners in crime."

"You're not in New York now. I control the bank that employs you. You will be well rewarded." Dieter softened. "We will get very rich together. What's the problem?"

"You're the problem. I'm not sure how you'll handle it. I've seen what you do to people who know too much or get in your way." Curtis signalled for the bill. The waiter explained there was no bill. It had all been taken care of.

"Curtis, I respect you. When I heard it was you BPG were bringing in, I could finally see how this could work. We need a sharp mind driving our investment strategy. Together we can do it, don't you think?"

"Yes, I do . . . but you still haven't answered my question."

The waiter brought their overcoats. They took the stairs down to the ground floor. An icy blast hit them as they stepped through the doorway, bringing Alpine air straight off the peaks.

Dieter's car appeared at the door. "Can I offer you a lift?"

"I'm at the Loderen; it's only a couple of blocks. The walk will do me good." Curtis turned up the velvet collar and put his hands deep into his pockets.

Dieter watched the solitary figure drifting away. He fastened his seat belt and pulled the heavy door closed, blocking everything out. For a moment he was back in London. George Michael was singing. They were in the bar across the road from the Business School. The last lecture on Financial Modelling had dragged on all afternoon. Curtis was playing pinball and dancing in time to the music. Skintight jeans stretched over firm buttocks. Gripping the flipper handles. Singing out loud, his American drawl in perfect harmony. Oblivious. Innocent. Or was he? Deep down, did he really know?

Dieter turned up the heat in the Mercedes, flicked on the headlights and set the navigation for home. The engine was purring as the familiar sequence of warning lights blinked out. He drove slowly, his eyes still swimming in brandy. A few flakes of snow smeared the windscreen and proved no match for the heavy wipers.

He tried to clear his mind. Now he was in Kuala Lumpur. His mother was explaining how his grandfather Walther Blindt had died. The thermometer had hit forty in the shade. She had come out of the bedroom wearing Mee Mee's robe and was fixing them both a cold drink. He had heard them together like naughty schoolgirls. He could smell their musk on the flimsy silk garment, the bittersweet perfume of their animal lovemaking.

He'd died peacefully in his sleep, she was explaining. He had lived in Geneva since the war but his heart was always in Berlin. Dieter could barely remember his grandfather. Another sad old man living in a lonely Swiss town. They flew his body home so he could be buried next to her. St Matthew's Churchyard Cemetery. Near the linden tree.

The afternoon heat was too much. The robe kept slipping off her shoulder. Pale flesh, beads of sweat. He couldn't look. His own mother. He felt ashamed. She was talking again. Your grandmother died when your father was born. She was twenty-one. It's a secret, her life was a secret and you must never tell anyone.

They called her Marija but she was christened Lieserl. Her real name was Lieserl Einstein. Your grandmother was Albert Einstein's only daughter. Whatever people say or do to you in your life, always remember, you are an Einstein. You must live up to his legacy. You must uphold the tradition. She made him swear to keep the secret.

The Mercedes was accelerating out along the Route de Thonon, following the signs for Veigy-Foncenex and Thonon-les-Bains. The road was quiet, the car had warmed up and he should be safely home in forty minutes. But another thought would not leave him alone. He could feel the sensation. He could not fight it. *To touch his perfect body, touch him now.*

Dieter was the most senior man in the bank. He was an Einstein. He was one of the wealthiest men in the canton. He was the Choirmaster. Head of Der Sangerbund. Established after the First World War to uphold and protect true German values. *Honour, Trustworthiness, Fraternity.* He'd pledged the oath. There was no going back. People respected him.

But they didn't know who the fuck he really was. What was the truth? One thing he knew. Not everybody had a body like Curtis Opperman.

Dieter saw his hand reach out and press cruise control. He wanted the Mercedes to take him straight home. But it refused. The ache was too strong. He found himself stepping into the lobby of the Loderen Hotel. Instead of cruise control, he was pressing a different button.

The lift doors opened. A yawning space presented itself. He hesitated, took one step inside, then quickly withdrew before the doors hushed back into place. He turned and left the building.

Why did he say where he was staying? Does he know? Has he always known? Does he want me? Was I being invited upstairs? This was torture. He couldn't take the risk.

And Curtis Opperman was the biggest risk of all.

• CHAPTER 46 •

Autumn 2008 – Geneva, Switzerland

"Dr Satapathy, good afternoon." Curtis adjusted the laptop setting for full screen.

"And good morning to you, Mr Opperman; it is lovely to meet you at last." She smiled as she sang her greeting in perfect Indian-English. "If I can call this a meeting."

Curtis Opperman loved intruding into people's lives. The webcam could show him what was happening without his victim being aware. It was like peeping through a keyhole. Within seconds he had adjusted his mental picture of Dr Sushma Satapathy by her clothes, her mannerisms, eye contact and by the pictures on the wall behind her.

"Well, it's a bit more personal than a phone call, I guess." He found the file. "I've no idea how it works. Anyway, I've got some good news for you. Your application has been approved."

He watched as her eyes shot wide open, tears filling up the corners. Her hands clamped around her mouth in shock, her reply lost in the fingers. He knew how much it meant for the school.

"The board were most impressed by the way you presented your case. I've been authorised to move the money into your account this afternoon, our time. It should be accessible for you by tomorrow morning."

"Oh, thank you; thank you so much, this is wonderful news," she gushed. "Wait till I tell the team, they'll be thrilled.

We'll start the building work right away. The children will be so happy; I must go and tell them."

Curtis had taken over Dieter's position on the board as a Director of BANK-ED. He had been in email correspondence with the school principal and had championed their case with the other board members. Dieter had explained the chairmanship of the charity rotated annually but CBSG continued to control and invest the finances as they had been one of the founding partners. He was pleased that Curtis would represent CBSG and become chairman next year.

"Don't go, Dr Satapathy. I've got more good news for you." He smiled at the screen. "Next term we will be sending you two interns through the BANK-ED regional office in Dubai. They will act as volunteers. We will pick up their costs. Our regional manager will contact you to make the arrangements. I understand they're both training as teachers and need some real-world experience. I'm sure you can keep them busy."

The good news kept coming. Curtis advised her that the regional manager was authorised to take nine more of her students for placements in the UAE and Saudi Arabia. He would make the travel arrangements with her and provide visas, local accommodation and some expenses. The placements had yet to be clarified but would most likely be in domestic service, factory employment and in the booming hospitality industry.

The email asking him to go through to Dieter's office flashed up on his screen. He cut the call, wished her well and promised to come and see the school next time he was in Rajasthan.

A few minutes later he was taking a seat outside Dieter's office. He wouldn't be long, his secretary explained. Curtis had never noticed the array of certificates that had blossomed on the side wall. In many respects, they answered some of his questions but the enigma still remained. As he checked them out, the heavy wooden door opened and two men appeared.

"So welcome on board, Klaus, I'm looking forward to working with you." Dieter seemed to be pumping blood into the pale man's hand. "Frau Schelling will sort out your expenses and show you out. Goodbye."

The man was whisked away as Curtis followed Dieter into his office, unable to hold back the smile. "Jeeze, where did you find that guy? He looked like a regular SS Commandant from central casting."

"I should have introduced you . . . no, second thoughts, you might have put him off." Dieter was sat on his throne, hands braced on his desk, his diminutive portrait framed majestically against the distant mountains. "Herr Doktor Klaus Buchwald will be our new Director of Security and Compliance. He comes highly recommended. He starts next month."

"And do we need one of those? Could be dangerous surely?"

Dieter analysed the question, dissecting every word. "We need to look whiter than white, especially with what's happening in the financial markets. He will be my white blood cell. He will remove any impurities and silence my critics. As you are my eyes and ears outside, he will be my watchdog inside."

"Nice to know you really appreciate me." Curtis shook his head.

"So what is happening? I've heard the term GFC. It looks like the markets have gone into turmoil since Lehman Brothers filed for Chapter 11." Dieter tossed the morning paper across the desk. The headlines made grim reading.

"Makes me proud to be an American. Only we could screw over the world's financial markets then name it after deep-fried chicken." Curtis knew the sarcasm was wasted. "Well, it's not my fault, boss, I'm not on Wall Street now. I guess we're all going down the crapper. Greed, arrogance; a sub-prime meltdown. It's happened before and it will happen again. It's just the wheel turning but for now it's trouble."

"I'm calling an emergency board meeting for tomorrow morning. I want an update with recommendations for our short-term investment strategy. And less of the wisecracks." Dieter fixed him with a glare. "Some of my clients might top themselves if the equity markets keep plummeting. And I know other banks that will go under. Thank God we acquired and consolidated when we did. It will give us a fighting chance of getting through this."

Curtis explained that the major banks had stopped lending to each other and there was a rush to switch into gold. "Nobody trusts nobody and we're all passing the buck. We need to be cautious out there. I'll be ready for the board meeting. Meantime, we need to hang on to what we've got, move quickly when the phone rings and set up new income streams."

"What kind of income streams?"

"You'd call them counter-cyclical; I'd call them untraceable." Curtis still wasn't sure about him. He found the lack of emotion on Dieter's face unnerving. "I'm guessing that's what BANK-ED is all about. A seemingly whiter-than-white, untraceable income generator."

Curtis was not surprised that, as one of the BANK-ED founders, Dieter Blindt had been recognised last year by the international community with the Lorenzo Bartolini Memorial Foundation Award for the promotion of Gender Equality.

The file said BANK-ED had been set up in 2001 as a global charity by a group of independent Swiss banks. To be politically correct, Curtis applauded the idea to promote the empowerment of women in developing countries through education and employment opportunities. An investment of US$5000 for an underprivileged, independent school in India fitted perfectly into its charter.

He could see that Dr Sushma Satapathy would now be able to build the new orphanage at the Laneshaya School for Girls near Jaisalmer and extend the boarding facilities for most of her 284 students. He knew five thousand US dollars went a long way in the Indian sub-continent.

The website explained that the girls were from the poorest villages across India. They were aged between six and twenty-one and ranged from the academically gifted to the mentally or physically handicapped. Some went on to higher education, some returned to their villages and others went overseas to find work. Curtis could see that many just remained at the school because they had no family, no home and nowhere else to go.

"BANK-ED is a good charity. It operates in forty-three countries around the world. I think we should take our global citizenship responsibility seriously." Dieter was impassive as he delivered his sermon.

Curtis was going to react but held it back. There would be a better time. Clearly his boss had other things on his mind "Your email mentioned DRIPFEED. Is this another of your charitable ventures?"

Dieter produced a file. "Yes, it is. I give my time for free. They also get invited to bank networking events. It was a start-up in the technology incubator at Geneva University. We put up the money; interest-free for two years. They targeted Africa originally and have expanded into India and South America."

"I'm guessing seed-corn funding in exchange for an equity stake and a seat on the board?" Curtis was trying to be diplomatic but he couldn't let it pass.

"And what's wrong with that?"

"Nothing . . . so what does DRIPFEED actually do?"

"They've developed specialist software that monitors water usage for irrigation systems in agri-projects, food production and farming. It automatically channels water to where it's needed, monitors wastage and pollutants, improves return on capital investment in pipelines, water pumps, storage tanks and sprinkler systems. It can even predict future demand cycles," Dieter explained.

"At least it sounds kosher. Where do I fit in?"

"I want you to take my seat on that board as well. Keep an eye on them. See if there are other investment opportunities they are missing out on. And if they've topped out, ditch them and sell our stake." He passed over the file.

"So if DRIPFEED helps the starving children of Africa, would I be in the running for the UN Medal for Third World Regeneration Initiatives?"

"Yes, if they think you're worth it. It was quite an honour. It's only awarded every three years." His face remained fixed.

"Then I noticed the Al-Kardai International Prize for Human Rights and the UNESCO Life Long Learning Award. I didn't realise you'd been so busy schmoozing it around the traps. And didn't you come third to be Global Ambassador in the World Bank Freedom from Poverty Campaign last year?"

"Not third, second runner-up."

"I stand corrected. Many congratulations."

* * *

"I'll send you our proposal. We'd love to have you on board. Thanks again for coming." The tall, well-dressed man shook hands and showed them out into the lobby.

Dieter Blindt had been impressed by Dr Stefan Lenz. When

Niklas had invited him to the meeting, Dieter was unsure what to expect. He'd heard mixed accounts about CERN. It smacked of a publically funded ego trip for a bunch of unwashed scientists who mistook the concept of funding for actually earning a living.

Accordingly, he'd imagined the head of the commercial partnership arm, CERN-CONNECT, to be a sixties drop-out full of scientific gobbledegook. Instead, Dr Lenz had showed a genuine understanding of money. He could see the business opportunities created by the European Nuclear Research Centre as well as the scientific importance, being a doctor of theoretical physics himself. By partnering with real-world organisations, it would be possible to achieve *win-win outcomes*, as he put it. Outcomes that were quicker to find than the origins of the universe.

"OK, Niklas, let's cut the crap. How does this work?" Dieter had taken a corner table in the cafe off the lobby. It was still early morning and few of the other tables were occupied. The latte tasted good.

"CERN-CONNECT was really set up as a PR exercise to show there was commercial value in what they were doing. Some countries have been paying into CERN for over fifty years, without much to show for it. The Americans gave up on their hadron collider twenty years ago. CERN needed someone to be singing their praises outside scientific and government circles."

As Niklas was talking, suddenly dozens of young scientists filled the lobby, spilling out of a lecture theatre nearby, all seemingly shouting to each other at once. The buzz was electric. Dieter could see that Dr Lenz was right – if they were getting this excited about First Beam, then they would need sawdust on the floor when they actually got First Collision.

"But now CERN-CONNECT has truly become a money-spinner," Niklas continued. "Two of my US clients are making good profits out of it. They use CERN data storage and communications networks that are faster and more secure than the Internet. One of them sends their people over on CERN scholarships."

Dieter was listening. He liked the scholarship idea. And could Dr Lenz be a useful member within Der Sangerbund? "OK, keep going."

Niklas pulled out a file. "You asked me to look at the tax implications for a takeover of one of your banking clients. I wanted to put it in the context of a partnership arrangement. As you know, they are bleeding money, your money. They owe you millions. Their debt ratios are ugly so there's no realistic chance of ever paying it off. In effect, they're bankrupt."

"You'd never think so to look at the director's car park." Dieter drained the last of his coffee.

"Quite. So you acquire them, load it up with other debts and create an entity for tax relief. You could offset future tax liabilities against this debt."

"I get that but what's the CERN connection?"

Niklas proposed that, after acquisition, the company become a research partner patenting new technologies coming out of CERN. It would sell off the IP rights to the telecom industry worldwide. With the right tax entity in place and using the bank's offshore accounts in Jersey and the Cayman Islands, it would make the whole venture waterproof.

"You would pay less tax as a bank; get ownership for one Swiss franc; partner with CERN at a cost that will come out of savings elsewhere, then siphon off any profits into tax-free accounts offshore. Easy when you know how." Niklas smiled.

"So what's the catch? PYKD tax partners aren't known for

their generosity towards banking clients." Dieter could see wider angles. Handled properly, they could bury more than just losses into this company. The political association with CERN could be very advantageous, if they ever got their hadron collider working.

"Well, of course, we'd get some fees out of it, and the audit teams would have another client to terrorise." He paused. "But you'd need to clear out the current directors and appoint the right CEO."

Dieter offered a rare smile. "Someone like Dr Lenz, for example?"

*　*　*

He did not recognise the face in the mirror. The man looked tired and confused. He was out of place, lost in a strange world.

The sign on the bathroom wall asked guests not to smoke or spit on the floor. The washbasin, barely supporting his weight, was cracked and deeply stained in yellow with ugly, brown smears. One tap didn't work. The other leaked cold water that tasted like it was being piped from the park lake opposite.

It had said Auvergne Residence in broken, neon lights above the front entrance. A three-storey, square, concrete building in a dishevelled part of Lancy he didn't know, not far from the railway lines. Tourists in Geneva rarely visited this part of town. They offered rooms by the hour or the day. There was no need to sign in. Cash was the only form of identity required. He'd paid for the privilege. This room was on the second floor. The lift smelled of cold urine and body odour. It was not working. He didn't remember climbing the stairs.

His bald head was oiled in a thin film of sweat. The lips looked pinkish, sore and swollen. Darting bloodshot eyes picked out the lines on his chubby face. There were more lines than the last time he looked. Only the strawberry birthmark over the right temple seemed familiar.

He was naked. Grey, flabby folds were flecked in shadow from the solitary bare light bulb. Chest hairs that used to be black were silver-grey and matted to the skin with sweat. On his shoulders and arms smooth patches of marbled skin were studded with pimples and moles. Across his belly and abdomen there were long, thin welts and reddening marks from the leather belt. He knew his buttocks would be worse.

His cock was slimy and limp, a small, flailing eel too long out of the water, gasping for life but not wanting to live. He peeled back the foreskin, revealing sores and teeth marks on the cap underneath. It was resting on a dried-up sack of what looked like lychees and walnut husks. The pain behind his eyes was throbbing deep into his skull. The pain in his backside was a thousand times worse.

He heard a knock on a distant door. A shadow skipped across the mirror. A commotion in the darkness, whispered voices, the pfizz of a ring-pull, rasping sounds of zips and discarded nylon clothing. A stranger appeared in the doorway, filling the reflection. He was much younger than the man in the mirror. This man was tall, muscular build, his body a graffiti of tattoos and piercings. A baseball cap turned backwards on his head. He wore a thick, gold chain strung like a horse collar around his neck. He was naked apart from a red leather pouch that was much too small to contain his bulging excitement.

"Hey Joe, my mate's come to see you." The man in the red pouch reached out an arm and dragged the other man into the mirror. Shorter, swarthy olive complexion, strange lopsided hair, he had plain features, not as slim. A cigarette was hanging from his lips; strands of greasy smoke drifted up into the darkness. He stubbed it out on the threadbare carpet.

Suddenly the second man became an acrobat struggling to get out of his socks. He had a tattoo of a scorpion crawling up his left thigh. He had a bigger cock. He was hard and ready. They kissed, stray hands finding each other, the red leather pouch pulled aside amid pumping, giggling, crouching.

Why is he calling me Joe? He was calling me Joe when we met at the railway station. I was never Joe. Whoever I am, I'm not Joe. He watched his own lips mouth the word Joe into the mirror. He spotted what looked like a smear of blood on his front teeth, managed to wipe it off, licked it clean. It didn't taste like blood.

"He's called Joe as well. We're all called Joe tonight." The red pouch slurped from a can and belched. The other Joe was on his knees, the tattoo of a dragon flying across his pimply back. "C'mon Joe, let's party."

But he didn't want to party anymore. He wanted to go home. But he had no home. He didn't know what he wanted. He looked down and saw the eel twitching back into life. But it was not his life. Joe the party man had seen to that.

He noticed the man on his knees now had his arms wrapped around the top of Joe's legs. He had spread his knees wider, revealing a dark cleft between his firm buttocks. He was making noises like dirty water swilling down a blocked drain.

Suddenly a beer can whistled past his ear. It crashed into the mirror and bounced off onto the linoleum flooring where it died, regurgitating a pool of brown spawn all over the cheap floral patterns. The mirror had cracked down the middle, one half now hanging slightly off the wall.

The man in the mirror saw that he had also cracked. The half with the birthmark was out of alignment. He had become a grotesque parody, split down the middle. One Joe was watching the others fucking each other against the doorjamb.

The other Joe was pretending not to be there. He wanted to be somewhere else. A curtain of beer drew down over the broken glass, drowning the face in foul-smelling liquid.

The man in the mirror turned towards the door. He was walking slowly, awkwardly. He was numb from the waist down. He saw the creature break apart and stand at its full height, facing him. He could smell its sweat; feel the sticky hot breath burning into his face. It took him with its four hands and forced him down into a filthy mire of pleasure and degradation; into a world without honour, without duty and without expectation.

This was his home. He knew now. He had always known.

This is who the fuck he really was.

PART THREE

"Darkness cannot drive out darkness; only light can do that. Hate cannot drive out hate; only love can do that"

–Martin Luther King, Jr.

CHAPTER 47

Present Day – Delhi, India

"South African?" Lonsdale repeated.

Detective Sergeant Steven Mole felt himself beaming down the phone. He had something worthwhile to report and had even caught up with his emails between regular trips to the bathroom.

Lonsdale must be impressed, he decided. It was good old-fashioned police work. The interviews at the field centre had proved most revealing, as Dr Bhattacharya had predicted. He found the centre manager himself to be a fascinating man and full of great insight when it came to the SINAC volunteers.

"Yes, sir," he replied. "Tracey Fenwick. She's a Brit but her mother's from Durban. The twins wouldn't have known that."

"So what did she actually hear?" Lonsdale prompted.

Steve could imagine him sitting with his back to a rain-streaked window. A buff folder would be open on his desk. He'd be scribbling notes on his pad and doodling balloon questions in the margin. One balloon meant interesting. A double-ringed balloon meant the question must be asked.

"Tracey was in her room directly opposite where the twins were staying. It was hot so she'd had the window open and could hear them talking on the way back from the dining hall. It was the evening before Okki Stanton was murdered. She clearly heard them say they couldn't take the risk any longer. They were going to talk to the *koorleider*."

"Who?"

"The Choirmaster. It's a similar word in Afrikaans, apparently," Steve explained.

"And you think the Choirmaster hired them?"

"Yes, sir."

"So why hasn't this Tracey girl spoken up until now?"

Steve could see the terrified look on the girl's face, the fear behind her eyes. "She thought they'd come back for her. When I told her they'd gone for good, she made a full statement. It's pretty conclusive. I'll send you the transcript for the file."

"Good work, Detective Sergeant," Lonsdale acknowledged. "Does Chaudray have proof of their real identity yet?"

"Not concrete proof, sir, but he has some leads. They've travelled to India many times before on different passports. They weren't blonde last time. He's still checking with their Home Affairs people."

"Then I can save him some time, Detective Sergeant. I ran the photos past Francois and he recognised them immediately. Twin sisters but one is a few inches taller than the other?"

"Seven centimetres, sir, according to the SINAC records."

"Well, Interpol know all about them. It's quite a sad story really."

Lonsdale paraphrased, skipping to the relevant bits. Lieke and Lotte de Jong were born into a poor Dutch family, and are now aged mid-twenties. The father was a butcher who would take out his business failure on their mother. She found solace in a bottle and died when they were in their teens. He then turned his attention to the girls who suffered terrifying abuse, multiple rapes and regular beatings. They fell through a crack in the justice system and were repeatedly ignored by the school and Amsterdam social services.

"The father was arrested for selling off sub-standard meat. That's when the full story came out. The girls were shipped off to Aruba to stay with their only living relative, a maternal uncle. But things just got worse for them in the Caribbean. Interpol have hard evidence of sexual abuse by the uncle and the girls even being sold into prostitution to willing Dutch and American cruise ship passengers. The uncle got seven years, no probation."

Steve could imagine Lonsdale shaking his head down the phone but he sensed his boss hadn't studied the photos of Okki Stanton in the morgue. He was fresh out of sympathy.

"So what happened?" Steve prompted.

"They both enrolled at the Xavier University School of Medicine in the capital Oranjestad, funded by money we think they'd siphoned off from the uncle's bank account."

"No doubt money they felt they'd earned for him."

"Quite. They only completed three years of the course but it was long enough for them to learn their trade . . . and their nickname."

Steve was making notes. He knew time was short before having to make another emergency dash to the bathroom. "Nickname?"

"The Bella Donnas. Quite creative for Interpol, I thought."

"Sorry, sir, I'm not following. Bella Donna? Learned their trade?" He had to get off this call. The human bowel waits for no man, his father once told him.

"Yes, Detective Sergeant, they're renowned for their skills with anaesthetics, sedatives and poisons. They specialise in kidnapping, extortion and sensitive assassination work."

Time had run out. He had to go now.

"Interpol have open cases in Russia, South America and Asia that bear their fingerprints," Lonsdale continued. "They've made it onto the most-wanted list, albeit near the bottom."

"Sir, talking of which, I've got a touch of the Delhi belly, I'll have to go." Steve wasn't sure why he was apologising. "Can I call you back in a—"

"I've got a meeting with the Super in five that could take the rest of the day," Lonsdale snapped.

Steve could feel his stomach churning. "Sir, I reckon by tomorrow I'll have enough evidence to convict them. I believe they were hired to infiltrate SINAC and dig into Project Amrita. They discovered Okki Stanton knew enough to blow the whistle so they drugged her, strung her up and made it look like suicide. It was a botched job but that didn't matter because they knew the kidnapping was going ahead and they'd be long gone when the police arrived . . . if the police ever arrived."

"So where are they now?" Lonsdale insisted.

"Sir, I really must—"

"Are you on a mobile, Detective Sergeant?" Lonsdale's voice was thick with irritation. "If so, get on with it. I haven't got time for this. I take it you can talk and crap at the same time?"

Steve added another bizarre experience to his growing collection. He never suspected that his promotion from beat bobby to Guildford CID would result in a conversation with his boss from the toilet of a hotel room in Delhi. At that moment, relief was the only emotion he was truly feeling.

"We don't know where they are, sir." He tucked the phone under his chin, washed his hands and flushed, having given up trying to be polite. At least he wasn't on Skype. "We know they were holding her in a lock-up in the town centre. The problem they've got is trying to keep a secret in India – you're just never alone. There are eyes watching everywhere. They must've moved her to a secure location. But they could be anywhere. Chaudray has notified the ports, border crossings and airfields but they could be in Timbuktu by now."

There was a pause on the line, for which Steve was grateful. He was back sitting at the table next door. He hadn't worked with Lonsdale very long but he was getting to know the man's approach. Ask questions, play devil's advocate, squeeze out the good stuff, ruminate, and then make a decision. He'd obviously done it that way for long enough. As they would say at the Detective School, it was a tried and tested methodology.

"The Bella Donnas are less important to this inquiry, Detective Sergeant. I know what you're thinking. I've been there; don't forget. They may have tied the knot but the real killer gave them the cord. You have more chance of getting this Choirmaster from here. I want you back at your desk on Monday."

Steve felt a surge of disappointment. He tried to argue a case to stay on and see it through but he was met with firm resistance. Lonsdale did make one concession.

"Unless there are other arrangements, you should accompany the girl's body back to her mother in Amsterdam. I take it her father will want to stay on and find the killers. The Indian police can take care of that."

"So I'm still on the case, sir?"

"Absolutely. I've given my word to Francois. Incidentally, he's passing through Schiphol Airport this weekend so perhaps you could arrange to meet up. I know he'd appreciate an update on the Bella Donnas."

"It would be good to talk to him, sir."

"Now I must go." Lonsdale was about to hang up.

Steve recalled the conversation in Dr Bhattacharya's office. They were discussing the interviews, in particular his meeting with Tracey Fenwick. The Brahmin sat transfixed while

Steve thought out loud, hypothesising about the shadowy figure behind this tragedy. Steve found the old man's words comforting yet provoking.

"Sir, one more thing, I asked the field centre manager about finding the real killer."

"Hurry up, Detective Sergeant."

"Well, he sort of looked straight through me. He said if I wanted the truth I should try looking the other way. It sounded a bit odd. What do you think he meant?"

"Detective Sergeant, it could mean he's been at the whacky backy for all I know. I don't want you coming back here in flowing robes with burning incense. I don't think Guildford is ready for that yet."

"No, I think he was trying to be helpful. I don't think he's involved in any way, you know, trying to throw me off the scent. It was just a funny thing to say."

"I'll be right there, sir," Lonsdale called out. "All I can suggest is that he thinks the killer is connected to the two girls in other ways. You may need to look somewhere else to find the link. Let's talk on Monday."

Steve disconnected. He was replaying the conversation with Lonsdale in his head. *Move her to a secure location.* Where would two blonde girls find a secure location in a country of 1.3 billion Indians? Are they even still here – private plane, over the border into Pakistan? Or a container ship out of Kandla, pick up an Emirates flight from Dubai? There were too many permutations.

Look the other way. Extortion, kidnapping, assassination. *Bella Donnas.* Choirmaster.

His chain of thought was broken by a sharp knock on the bedroom door.

344

• CHAPTER 48 •

Jock was rolling a small, gold object between his fingers. Lal had picked it up off the floor of the deserted warehouse. The tiny clasp had been ripped open. Jock recognised it immediately but had never realised what it was supposed to represent.

"The Goddess Lakshmi. She's the consort of Lord Vishnu," Lal explained. "Our goddess of Wealth and Good Fortune."

"It's the same goddess that Nisha has in her temple at home. She says prayers to her every morning and every evening. It was on a bracelet I bought for her birthday last year. She said she'd never take it off. Her good luck charm, she called it. I understand now. I just hope and pray this goddess can keep her safe." Jock slipped the amulet into his pocket.

It had been a long day. They had regrouped back at the hotel. Lawrence was feeling his age. The situation was difficult enough without having to play referee all the time between the varied hand of characters he'd been dealt. Add to the mix the emotional charges running through Toby and Jock, the rigid bureaucracy of Chaudray and the uncertainty of what would happen if Nisha was never found. Or worse, if she was found floating in the Ganges.

But despite the tiredness, Lawrence felt strangely alive. It wasn't that long ago he was sitting in a soulless bachelor pad in Watford, rejected by his wife and children, no friends apart from a loving golden retriever and seemingly too old to find a job. His life had felt like a burden too great to bear. Meeting Hannah, the move to New York, the confidence people now had in him and his immersion in the convoluted world of diabetes research over the last twelve months had been so uplifting. It was such a great pity that they'd all been dragged into this senseless tragedy. But in a funny, bizarre sort of way, he felt they could be at a turning point.

"So Nisha was definitely here?" Toby's eyes were shining.

Maybe he has taken my words to heart, maybe he can see a way forward, Lawrence reflected. *I need to channel his energy. Whoever is behind Nisha's disappearance has had the upper hand so far. We must force them into an error.*

"We know Mukka drives a truck up to Delhi from the south," Lawrence added. "Thinking about it, a truck is the best way to move around in this country. There are millions of them. There are virtually no roadblocks or toll gates or even speed cameras. Unlike in a car or on a train or even at an airport, two blonde women and a hostage in the back of a truck could move around unseen and unchallenged . . . but only for so long."

"How do you mean?" Lal's phone pinged with yet another text.

"Well, I guess they couldn't live in a truck for a week. Someone would poke their noses in if it was parked up or spot one of the girls squatting by the roadside. So they must be using the truck to get to somewhere they think will be out of sight and out of mind."

"And yet still be in touch in case they have to be in Delhi. And they'd need Internet access, phone signals, medicines, groceries and drinking water, whatever," Toby concluded. "So they can't drop off the grid completely."

Suddenly Lal grabbed a piece of paper and a pen, scribbled down a phone number off his screen and made the connection. He became quite animated, gesticulating with his free hand, pacing the floor. He wrote an address on the same piece of paper and sat down, beaming triumphantly to his waiting audience.

"I'd asked the man who owns the lock-up how he knew Mukka. Apparently, he just turned up one day, said he'd take the place on a weekly basis and paid cash in advance. He's been one of his most reliable customers," Lal continued. "Anyway I'd left him my card and asked him if anything . . ."

"For fuck's sake, get on with it! Who did you just call?" Toby's face had turned scarlet. Lawrence would normally intervene but this time he was in agreement. The clock was ticking.

"The man got a call from one of Mukka's customers, someone expecting a delivery. The customer couldn't reach him on his mobile so he rang the Delhi number he had on file. They want to bring the delivery forward to tomorrow," Lal spluttered as he tore the note from the pad, "so I rang him to find out what he knew. He's given me his name and company address but he was reluctant to tell me any more over the phone."

"Well, where is he?"

"Agra."

This time Lawrence had to intervene before a fight broke out. And given that Lal was six inches taller than, twenty years younger than and twice as fit as his Geordie friend, there would only have been one outcome. Toby would have murdered him. All about attitude, he smiled to himself.

"How long by car?" Lawrence took the lead.

"We have a new expressway. I'd say about three hours." Lal started checking his app.

"I'll drive. We'll be there in two." Toby was on his feet, hand open for the car keys.

"Toby, wait." Lawrence grabbed his arm. "Let's think about this."

"Fuck thinking! I've been sitting here for days bloody well thinking. Meanwhile lives are at stake. Let's go." He moved to the door.

"OK," Lawrence conceded. "Toby; you, me and Lal will hit the road. Jock, you stay here. You're in no state to travel and you must keep Project Amrita moving. Besides, we need to know who's behind the drop box."

"Sorry, forgot to say, still no joy with that," Toby apologised. "The boys in London said the drop box people are being awkward."

". . . and you must get things ready for Uppsala." Lawrence squeezed the back of Jock's neck. There was little resistance.

He nodded in agreement.

"I'm still not sure Uppsala can go ahead without Nisha." Jock choked on the words. "She knows so much—"

Before Lawrence could react, Toby grabbed the young man by the shoulders, noses almost touching. "Jock, I've got news for you. Remember you told us about your dream, about your father's dream? About eradicating poverty from the world? About humanity living in everyone? Well, it's now become my dream as well . . . and I don't give up on my dreams. We're going to do this . . . and we'll do it together. Do you understand me?"

Lawrence saw a glimmer of a smile creeping across Jock's bruised face. The smile led to an embrace as the two hugged each other, tears of determination welling in their eyes. *Moksha?*

"There's just one condition." Toby re-emerged.

Jock stared at him, perhaps for the first time realising that Toby was old enough, even wise enough, to be his father.

"I want you to join Rotary. Singapore, New Delhi, Amstelveen, Weybridge East, I couldn't care less which club. Ranjit is right. With a million members behind us, we'll get this done quicker within Rotary. Do I have your agreement?"

"Yes."

They embraced again. Toby reached into his jacket pocket, pulled out his Paul Harris badge and pinned it onto Jock's T-shirt. Lawrence watched as, in a strangely Rotarian sort of way, they sealed it with a handshake.

"Toby, we'll grab the passports and some stuff from upstairs. Jock, could you take a cab over to the Windsor Connaught Hotel? Detective Sergeant Steven Mole is in room one-two-four-seven. He'll need Okki's passport and the rest of the paperwork. I'll bring it all down. Tell him we'll arrange for Wanda to meet him at Schiphol." He paused. "Lal, bring the car round and fix up a meeting with this guy in Agra."

Within twenty minutes they were driving through the suburbs of South Delhi, following signs to Noida and the Yamuna Expressway. Lal was driving. Lawrence was trying to find his phone, which was purring away in a pocket. Toby was sprawled out across the back seat, fast asleep.

The traffic was thickening into yet another rush hour as the light began to fade. Dull shadows poured out from the surreal high-rise apartment blocks. They were a startling contrast, Lawrence thought, to the low-rise city centre with its incongruous mix of tree-lined colonial elegance and ugly urban squalor.

"Hannah!" he shouted, as Lal pointed to the snoring figure behind them. "Where are you?"

"Heathrow. I'm boarding in ten minutes," she replied. "How about you?"

"On our way to Agra. We've got a lead. It's flaky but it's all we've got." He lowered his voice. "I'm missing you, gorgeous."

"Me too, lover boy," she smooched. "How's Nisha? Is she OK? Poor Jock must be worried sick," Hannah shouted over a boarding announcement.

"As far as we know she's still alive but we're playing catch-up. These bastards know what they're doing. We're running out of time."

"Did you say Agra? You're not taking a floozy to the Taj Mahal, I hope?"

"Not quite. I'm taking two blokes to a fruit and veg wholesaler on an industrial estate." He grabbed hold of the handle above the passenger door as Lal screeched out onto the other side of the road, swerving to avoid a motorcycle, two rickshaws and a stray dog.

"I heard from Kitty last night. The diabetes project is going off the rails. I need you back. Gene's away with stress. The presentation they produced is goddam awful. I'm going to kick some ass when I get back."

Lawrence closed his eyes as Lal overtook a tour bus, which was itself overtaking a slow-moving truck. They crossed into the path of an oncoming petrol tanker. A cow in the middle of the road looked on apathetically. "I could live without Gene so feel free to boot him out. The presentation has got to be right. We need to make a splash at this conference if we're going to keep the funds rolling in."

"They're calling my flight." She paused. "So I'll be back in Brooklyn for a few days, tidy up my speech, then I'll meet you in Sweden, if it's still going ahead?"

"You bet. Jock reckons we'll have nearly three thousand people in the great hall and a television audience of several million around the world. SVT will be streaming it live and Jock has tied in the BBC, CNN and Al-Jazeera. He's working on a couple of others but according to him we won't need TV coverage."

"Why's that?"

"Because he reckons everyone on earth will get the message."

"What message?"

"You'll find out," he teased.

"Gee, thanks. Do you want me to sort out your conference presentation or not?"

"I know you love me." He opened his eyes and then wished he hadn't. The sign saying Expressway 5 kilometres was the only good news. An elephant was walking calmly towards them with ten or so minders. Yet another emergency stop roused the sleeping passenger in the back.

"We're boarding, I'll have to go. You guys take care. I'll call you when I land. Now go get Nisha back. Love you."

Lawrence could see Toby edging into the corner of his eye, yawning and scratching at the stubble on his chin. He hoped the sleep had done him good. He was still insisting on taking the wheel as they pulled over before hitting the expressway.

"No animals or pedestrians on this road, right?" Toby clipped himself in and adjusted the mirrors. Lawrence assumed he was talking to Lal, who was now in the back seat, but it could have been rhetorical. He'd been in India long enough to know that road signs were mostly ignored and the animals couldn't read.

"I've arranged to meet Mr Kapoor at his warehouse at eight p.m. We need to keep moving. The expressway should be clear but the roads around Agra are not the best," Lal advised, the master of understatement as ever.

A monochrome disc was floating on a flat-calm horizon, all colour bleached away by dull, grey smog. For a land so colourful, Lawrence realised, he couldn't recall seeing a blue sky or a pink sunset. Silhouettes of brickwork chimneys punctured the half-light, and clusters of ramshackle dwellings huddled together around dirty clumps of trees beyond the steel-wire fence.

Lawrence could see spirals of dust as families walked

together across barren fields. Mothers' faces were caught in the firelight as they prepared the evening meal. Excited children played cricket in the gathering darkness with bits of wood and a tatty old ball. He realised bad light never stopped play in an Indian village.

Ahead, the ribbon of grey-black stretched away into nothingness beyond the main beam. For Lawrence, it felt surreal to be sitting in an air-conditioned luxury car hurtling down an empty motorway while all around an oblivious India continued its daily struggle for survival.

They refuelled and picked up some supplies at a newly built service station. Lawrence was relieved when Toby tossed the keys back to Lal. There had been fewer animals on the road than he'd expected but it was by no means a clearway. They had only avoided certain death on four or five occasions. Even so, Toby had done well. Agra forty-two. They should make it in time.

As Toby settled into the back seat, his mobile chirped into life. "Max?"

Lawrence tried to give him some privacy by asking Lal how well he knew Agra. Despite it being perhaps India's most famous tourist destination with world-class hotels on offer, he revealed it was not the place he was most proud of. He explained that Agra had been chosen by the Mughal emperors five hundred years ago as their capital city. The Taj Mahal and the old fort nowadays were like a magnet for unofficial tour guides, ticket touts, street vendors and rickshaw-wallahs who flooded in from the poor villagers to eke out a living.

It had become a regional centre for chemicals, engineering and manufacturing, amongst other heavy industries that had created one of the worst air pollution problems in India. The once-beautiful Yamuna River had not escaped the ravages of industrialisation, for which Lawrence could see he was most apologetic.

Perhaps when Jock and Toby had achieved their dream, Lawrence mused, and the sightseeing attractions were left in peace again for the tourists to enjoy, then maybe the Taj Mahal would return to being the *teardrop on the cheek of eternity.*

The expressway ended as abruptly as it began, as if they had run out of blacktop. Lawrence could only smile as once again they returned to the pandemonium of Indian roads.

Toby sounded pleased with his call. "Max had dinner last night with that banking client I mentioned in Geneva." Toby was leaning forward, hot breath on Lawrence's neck. "Herr Doktor Buchwald was charming, apparently, and very knowledgeable about British military history. I bet they rattled on for hours about the RAF and Switzerland's role in Second World War."

"Was that your CRM project?" Lawrence interjected, showing an interest. He was happy to keep Toby preoccupied until they found where they were going.

"Yes, it was fine until the top brass got involved," Toby replied. "Anyway, they're reviewing things and will keep the project on hold until they can give us a clearer brief. Max did a good job."

"How come?" Lawrence was bemused. "It doesn't sound very encouraging."

"Max twisted his arm, ever so nicely. They've agreed to pay all our invoices plus a late-payment fee. They've even given us a project manager within the bank as a point of contact. Max thinks they'll be ready to go again soon."

Lawrence was holding open a street map for Lal, who braked hard to avoid a donkey. If he did have satellite navigation coverage for Agra, he'd decided not to trust it. They were following a truck laden with boxes of what looked to Lawrence like tomatoes and cucumbers. The truck lumbered to a halt in the middle of a crowded street before turning right into an industrial zone.

Most of the surrounding office buildings were in darkness. The warehouses and manufacturing plants were still busy. Lal tried to overtake but the road was too narrow even for him and there was a stream of trucks coming the other way.

"I think he's going where we're going," Lal announced. The truck swung onto an ocean of pitted concrete at the back of a squat two-storey building. A sign on the gate announced Kapoor Fruit & Vegetable Wholesalers Ltd. The truck did a pirouette and then reversed into one of the numbered loading bays. Two men jumped out from the cab and two more appeared from under the canvas round the back.

Lawrence watched as a small army appeared through a heavy plastic curtain and spilled out onto the loading bay. They started pulling out boxes, helped by the labourers from the truck. Boxes were being carried two or three at a time into the flat-roofed building. Even before Lal had found a safe place to park, the vehicle had been emptied, dockets exchanged and it was on its way back out of the gate.

They made their way round to the main door but it was locked. The lobby area and the front offices were in darkness. Lawrence found a side door, which opened out into a large packing area. Hundreds of crates were being filled by hand. Men, women and children were unpacking fruit and vegetables, inspecting them for quality and then re-packing them into delivery crates. At first no one looked up. Then a tall, thickset supervisor in a dirty brown coat blocked their way.

"You can't come in here, this is private. Are you police?" the man snapped.

Lal replied in Hindi. Immediately the man's face softened. He wobbled his head and pointed to a blue door in the far wall. As they made their way through a maze of trestle tables, conveyors, stacks of crates and piles of produce, Lawrence had to keep smiling and nodding to the shift workers beaming at him. The speed and accuracy at which they worked left him truly amazed. In all his life he had never seen or smelled so many varieties of fruit and vegetable.

The blue door opened towards them and revealed a narrow flight of steps leading up into darkness. The breeze-block walls were whitewashed and seemed to be closing in on plain, concrete steps. Toby pressed the time switch, which flooded the stairwell in humming white light. They made their way cautiously up two flights to another door that opened into a corridor. The bustling activity and smells of the packing area melted away. The interior corridor had no natural light and was also whitewashed breeze-block lined on both sides with the blank faces of closed office doors.

At the far end facing them was another closed door. Lawrence guessed this was Mr Kapoor's office. It was the only one occupied. Lawrence was trying to get his bearings. The office they were heading towards must be above the entrance lobby. But there had been no lights on upstairs or downstairs when they had tried the main door.

He touched Lal on the arm and pointed towards the gun nestling under his jacket. Lal understood and released the strap over the holster in readiness.

They were halfway down the corridor when Lawrence heard a ping. The timer disengaged. All the lights went out. It was total darkness apart from the thin light edging the doorframe.

They stood in silence and watched helplessly as the door began to open.

• CHAPTER 49 •

Hannah now understood why there was a dog run in Brooklyn Bridge Park. A designated area made good sense, given the number of dogs to be exercised and the selfishness of some dog owners who refused to clean up after them. The compound contained the obvious pollution problem. But Trigger was a big dog full of limitless energy and needed more space than the "exercise yard", as she referred to it, could ever provide.

Also the proximity to the water was another torture. She knew from the look in his eyes that he longed to launch himself into the East River, especially on days like today when the mercury was already nudging twenty-five degrees at seven in the morning.

Up until this year, Hannah had always thought of herself as a cat person. But her Siamese kittens had long since grown up and discovered a world of adventure beyond the cat-flap. She still loved their unique brand of self-promotion and attention seeking but they had drifted away from her over recent months. Or had she changed? Maybe she was now looking for a different kind of affection?

Trigger, on the other hand, had only one thing on his mind. Well, maybe two things, she decided, as he eyed up the piece of toast she was buttering. Although he was Lawrence's dog, he was happy to share his affection equally, which she liked.

Trigger wanted to be your best friend and be there for you, whatever you did or didn't do to promote that friendship. Normally, after their morning walk, he would curl up in the corner, having emptied his water bowl. But today it was different. He seemed to recognise her restless determination.

She took her breakfast over to the laptop and swallowed a mouthful of coffee before flicking on the screen. *Curtis Opperman*. She needed to do some digging. She wasn't meeting Kitty in the office until 10.30 a.m. That gave her time to find some answers, to fill in the blanks. Twenty years of blanks.

Her initial search proved unsuccessful. There were dozens of online profiles for Curtis Opperman but none were the guy she knew, the guy she lived with, the guy whose reappearance had kept her awake these last few nights.

She would expect an investment banker to fly below the radar, especially given the high-profile nature of some of the deals he used to be involved in. But these days, surely, there would be links to what he was doing, who he worked for, where he lived?

Hannah smiled to herself when a blond head came to rest on her lap. Had she been hitting the keys too hard? Had she been mumbling expletives to herself with each dead end? More likely, Trigger could sense her frustration and had come to offer his full support. And a stinky, wet, chewed-up tennis ball.

She finished the coffee and tossed the ball across the room, much to Trigger's obvious delight as he scurried off after it. She was going to try a new angle through his banking connections when the mobile rang. She checked the caller's name on the screen.

"Good morning, Hannah, how are you? Hope it's not too early?"

"Good afternoon, Max, not too early at all, I've been up for hours," Hannah replied, making the assumption he was back in London.

The banking connections also came up short. She tapped

in Google Images in desperation. Hundreds of men called Curtis Opperman – and one or two strange-looking people of indeterminate sex – flashed across the screen. She didn't recognise any of them.

"I'm just replying to your email," he continued. "I've checked Toby's diary. We're both free for the American Diabetes Society fundraiser in November; thanks for the invitation."

She knew him well enough by now to know there was something else on his mind. He could have confirmed this by email. Maybe he wasn't sleeping either.

"That's great, Max, I'll get the office to book your hotel rooms and send you the details. We normally meet for drinks beforehand. If it's as good as last year, you're in for a wonderful evening." Hannah paused, wanted to test her reasoning. "Have you heard from Toby?"

The line went quiet. Hannah thought they'd been cut off.

Eventually Max came back, his voice uncertain. "Well, I suppose . . . the short answer is yes, but we've only had brief conversations as I know he couldn't really talk."

Hannah knew the feeling. Lawrence couldn't talk openly either, which often caused more confusion than if he hadn't called at all. She guessed Max wanted to swap notes.

"This trip to Agra sounds like a waste of time," Hannah ventured, taking the initiative. The tennis ball had returned. She threw it further this time. It went under a sideboard, which kept Trigger wildly amused. "Has Toby forced them into it, do you think?"

"That's his usual style," Max said, almost apologetically. "They could be going in the wrong direction. Or Nisha could still be in Delhi, for all they know."

"I agree. But I suppose we're not there, we don't know how difficult it must be," Hannah conceded. "Still, having your guy

Lal protecting them gives me some comfort. Thanks for doing that. I know Lawrence is finding him a useful ally."

'It was the least I could do. Actually it was your friend Viren that gave me his name. He'd worked with Lal previously, said he was trustworthy. I'd like to say Viren sends his regards . . ."

". . . but you'd be lying, I guess." Hannah smiled to herself as she remembered the conversation in the Saints Lounge. She asked how his trip to Switzerland had gone.

"I suppose you'd call it a success, but you never really know with a Swiss bank. They always keep the cards close to their chest. At least they've agreed to keep us on board, for now."

Hannah was trying to concentrate on what Max was saying when suddenly an old photograph of Curtis Opperman appeared on the screen. She recognised it immediately. It was the day he'd been made head of department. There he was, posing with the CEO and his new boss, the Vice President of Investment Services. Champagne all round, smiles and congratulations, Wall Street and the Charging Bull in the background. He had been so excited. She'd booked a table at Le Querce, his favourite restaurant on Seventh Avenue. He'd shown up late and drunk. She should have known then.

"I wish Toby'd been with me," Max continued. "It's never easy when you're outnumbered. Still, the American guy they've given us seemed genuine enough. We need someone arguing our corner on the inside. I just hope he lives up to his promises."

Hannah clicked off the screen. What did he say? An American guy? *Concentrate, Hannah.* "What kind of promises?"

"They've made him our go-to man. We need someone to open doors, tell us what's really going on and fight our corner with the boys on the sixth floor. He promised to do his best. I believed him. He's been with the bank a few years, reckons he knows his way around. He said he was a graduate from the school of hard knocks on Wall Street."

"Your client, Max, what did you say their name was again?" Hannah couldn't think straight, the words coming out in a rush. Had he told her this before? She didn't want to raise any suspicion. But it was too much of a coincidence. An American banker in Geneva? Worked in New York?

She could tell Max was hesitating. Was she putting him under pressure, asking him to overstep the line on client confidentiality? *Why does she want to know?* she could almost hear him thinking down the line. But she wanted an answer.

"CBSG. The Canton Banking Services Group of Geneva. Why do you ask?" His tone had changed. More formal, inquisitive, curious.

"I used to know a guy ... an investment banker ... he moved to Europe about twenty years ago. He joked all the time. Just wondered if it's the same guy, that's all. My natural Brooklyn curiosity, I guess." Hannah was trying to be calm while inside her stomach was churning. She could taste the toast coming back. "If it is, I might be able to help you. Run a name past me, Max."

Hannah had typed CBSG into the search box. Her fingers hovered over the keyboard expectantly. Max was slow to respond.

Curtis Opperman.

• CHAPTER 50 •

Dieter Blindt clicked off the secure screen, ripped the mouse from its socket and threw it across the office. It smashed into a wooden cabinet and curled up on the floor to die, its wire tail twitching.

How dare they accuse me! This is political horseshit. They've known all along. Where else do they think the money comes from? Oh, they're more than happy to bury their greedy snouts in the trough when there's plenty of swill. Happy to let me rinse it through our laundering schemes and then splash it out on villas or sports cars and stash it away in trust accounts or sweaty little tax havens.

The special meeting of the Cantata had been called by one of the Voices in Paris. It followed a dawn raid by the French authorities looking for tax avoidance scams and possible links between their legitimate fundraising activities and the criminal underworld. The Voice was a director of a global charity supported by CBSG, a long-standing member of the Cantata and an increasingly vocal opponent of the moral direction now being set within Der Sangerbund.

The warrant had been issued after an insider reported an unusually large financial transaction passing through the regional office in Dubai. It was allegedly recorded as an anonymous donation by a respected Saudi patron in return for voluntary services provided by Nepalese refugees. After a thorough search, the investigators left empty-handed. But the damage had been done.

I told them to keep the tax authorities on board, but oh no, they knew better. We've always had one senior inspector or a French minister within our ranks. But once Maurice retired they let it slip. They want the rewards without putting the effort in. It was sloppy and unacceptable. I must stiffen their backbones or kick them out.

Dieter tried to ignore the light flashing on his phone. He kept seeing the worried faces on the screen, listening to the threats and allegations, the spineless chatter of petty-minded, corporate men who'd had it too easy for too long. Their world, his world, was under attack, yet they could neither see it nor understand where it was coming from. Everything Der Sangerbund had created would be washed away in a tsunami from the East. He alone would have to resist, to save western civilisation. With or without Der Sangerbund.

The light kept flashing.

"Yes?"

"I've got Rick Graziani on the line, Herr Blindt," Frau Schelling announced.

"I've told him I'm not interested."

"He's very insistent; it's the fourth call he's made today."

Rick Graziani. Dieter could see his odious, smiling face leering at him across the dinner table. Northern Hemisphere Director of Pegglers Executive Search, based in Chicago, flown all the way over to little old Geneva just to make this proposition. *His client would be honoured; non-executive chairman, only six days per month. You're the man they want, the man they need if they're ever gonna hit their funding targets.* Dieter wondered when it had all changed. There was a time he'd have jumped at the chance. The Global Humanity Fighting Disease Fund invests over US$6bn every year into research projects for Alzheimer's, Zika and Motor Neurone.

Established in 1997 and based in Switzerland, the fund had impressive partnership programmes and heavy backing from the USA. As chairman, he would be invited to all the right dinners, which would enable him to cherry-pick new members for Der Sangerbund. The Latin American connections could be lucrative, he'd once decided.

But today it looked like a second-tier fund, struggling to attract the talent, lacking the kudos and light years from finding a cure for anything. *Why the fuck should I do this? Will I be rewarded by the Cantata for all my devotion and hard work? Will Der Sangerbund acknowledge how I have strengthened their networks and granted access to new trade deals?*

"I pay you well to deal with these people, Frau Schelling. Now get on with it."

"Herr Blindt, I have Curtis Opperman waiting to see you. He said you requested the meeting. He's been here for . . ."

Dieter hung up before she'd finished. He didn't want to think about Curtis fucking Opperman. He wanted to fire him. He wanted him out of his life forever. There were plenty of investment specialists on the market who could replace him. His client following was only as loyal as the returns he made for them. And there was still the unanswered question of what he was doing in New York. The decision was easy. So what was stopping him?

He knew what it was. The same reason it had always been. And that only made things worse.

CHAPTER 51

The knock on the door had more than disturbed his train of thought. Steve needed to take precautions. He had never felt comfortable with weapons. The bare pass level attained after extensive firearms training had proved an accurate assessment of his proficiency. It was with some reluctance that he was issued with a weapon before making this trip. Given the circumstances, it seemed right to be cautious. Normally he would just have opened the door.

"Who is it?"

On reflection, not much about his short time in India had proved normal. A murder made to look like suicide; a violent kidnapping; possible industrial espionage; ransom demands made through drop box accounts. That was before he got to Indian police bureaucracy and the Hindu teachings of Dr Bhattacharya. He checked the weapon, removed the safety catch and stood to the side of the door.

"My name is Jock Lim," a thin voice replied. "Lawrence McGlynn sent me."

Steve checked the peephole. The man was alone. He recognised him from photos on the SINAC website. He put the gun away, opened the door and made his guest feel as welcome as he could in the pastel banality of his hotel bedroom.

"Lawrence said you would need this." Jock passed over a large Manila envelope.

Steve laid out the various documents, checking them off against the list the funeral director had given him in Chaudray's office. Okki's UK passport, the export and death certificates, coffin-sealing certificate, customs declaration . . . the list went on. He wasn't sure if the formalities at this end would be more or less frustrating than when he got to Schiphol. He was quite relieved to hear that Okki's mother and their funeral director would meet him when he landed. "Okki was a great friend. We both loved her so much. She didn't deserve this. If only I'd . . ."

"Jock, you can't blame yourself. There was nothing else you could have done," Steve consoled as he poured some water. Even allowing for the bruising on his face, Jock was carrying too many scars for a man only a few years younger than himself. At their respective ages, they could be brothers, ripping into all that life had to offer. Yet before him sat a pained warrior unsure from which direction the next blow would come.

"She'd still be alive if I'd just kept her out of it." Jock sipped some water.

"Jock, we'll do everything we can." Steve risked another emotional tangent. He could see Jock was fragile, his feelings like a swarm of bees buzzing behind his eyes; distracting, threatening, stinging.

"I just feel so lost without Nisha. She means everything to me. I must get her back." Jock pushed tired fingers through his spiky hair. "Whatever it takes."

"Lawrence told me about the drop box address and this Swiss company. I think it would be a mistake for you to transfer the IP rights but we need to know more about the connections here." Steve grabbed a file from the coffee table. Even from his short time in CID he knew very often in fraud cases people stole things to stop other people having them. It was less about ownership and more about denial. "Have you had any contact with this company, Josef Graaf AG?"

"I've never heard of them."

"Interpol have spoken to the chairman, Ulrich Graaf. He is fifth generation, been with them all his life. There are three other family members on the board. They all stringently deny any knowledge of you, SINAC or Project Amrita." Steve was scanning the file.

"So how could they be involved?"

"I don't think they are," Steve replied, "but I feel there's a connection here we aren't seeing. They're based in Bern and have been manufacturing luxury watches, clocks, jewellery and components for over one hundred and fifty years. It all seems very legit."

"What kind of components?"

"Clockwork mechanisms, digital chronometers . . . I'm not sure; the report doesn't say much." Steve could see Jock had brightened, seemed more engaged. *The bees are quieter, I have to keep pushing.*

"It's just that they could be working with one of our SINAC partners," Jock suggested.

"We need a list of all your suppliers as quickly as possible." Steve closed the file. Just for a moment he felt he'd been cast in the role of Lonsdale; the wiser head, prising out reluctant nuggets of information, asking the sharp questions. The list of suppliers was an obvious angle. Hindsight always tasted sour, yet was full of nutrition.

He pressed on. "Maybe the connection is someone who works for them. An employee or a contractor; someone in marketing or advertising, even a journalist or a lawyer, I suppose."

Steve could feel the pain as Jock's eyes searched back through names and faces, relatives and employees, advisers and friends he knew. It was a genuine line of enquiry but unlikely to work while there were still so many combinations and permutations. He needed to improve the odds. He needed a fresh approach.

"Jock, have you had much involvement with intellectual property rights or patents, licences, copyrights, that sort of thing?" Steve enquired.

"Not directly. I'm using the law firm in Singapore that my parents always used. They handle all my personal affairs and SINAC work." Jock paused. "They have the rights for Project Amrita pretty much watertight. Why do you ask?"

"Well, I'm no expert on this but it strikes me there could be two possible outcomes. You must carry on communicating through the drop box. We need to find out who their advisers are. Maybe Interpol will have more luck loosening some legal tongues." Steve managed a smile.

"Two possible outcomes?"

"Someone wants the IP rights to make money. They could sell off your technology under licence or use it themselves in a new product they bring to market. Maybe they could embed the technology in a new component," Steve suggested.

"But we've got proof of what we've developed. There are patents listed, research files on record at CERN, witness evidence from Nisha's team in India. No court in the world would uphold their title claim, surely?"

Steve could think of several countries where the legal system would not be so sympathetic or ethical. The scales of justice would be loaded from the start. Apart from which, the legal transfer of IP rights would be formally documented and trying to prove coercion could be difficult.

"More likely this is about the denial." Steve was thinking out loud again. "They want the IP rights to stop anyone else having them. They could enforce injunctions against you to stop Project Amrita ever getting off the ground."

"But that would lead back into the courtroom," Jock surmised. "And we would then know who owns what."

"I'm not so sure we would. Someone like Josef Graaf AG would be the front for a corporation with registered offices in the Cayman Islands or a brass plate company in Panama or Macao." Steve heard his own words as if spoken by Lonsdale. Why hadn't he thought about this before? He would need to get hold of the Surrey police legal team.

"In that scenario," Jock reasoned, "Josef Graaf AG would be owned by someone else. Didn't you say they've been a family business for more than 150 years? Surely they're not planning to sell out?"

"They may not have to."

CHAPTER 52

A large-framed man was holding the door open, allowing sticky yellow light to flood into the corridor. Lawrence spotted the other light switch on the breeze-block wall nearby. Too late as ever.

The man invited them to join him around a large boardroom table, directly underneath a whirling steel fan. The downdraught was welcome after the cloying humidity in the corridor. The temperature outside must still be in the mid-twenties, Lawrence surmised.

The man lumbered over to an untidy desk in front of blackened windows and armed himself with a pen and paper. Lawrence reckoned he could only have been a few years older than himself, more like mid to late fifties, he guessed. He was wearing a three-quarter-length brown kurta over unremarkable, cream, linen trousers. Worn leather sandals padded dusty feet across a fake marble floor. His uneven brown skin was mottled, giving the impression he'd suffered some kind of eczema as a child. Or he'd been mixing with the wrong company.

"My name is Harjeet Kapoor, I am the owner. I don't have much time." He spoke quickly, the words clear but without warmth. He checked an oversized, gold-plated wrist-watch, as if to prove the point.

Lal took the initiative. "We spoke on the phone. You're expecting a delivery from a man called Mukka. You called his number in Delhi."

"And you are . . .?"

"Lal. Chakrapani Lal."

"Mr Lal, I make a great many calls every day. I'm not sure who you're referring to." His eyes were darting between them. Until now, Lawrence had given him the benefit of the doubt. But now the doubt had gone. He was sure. He didn't trust him. A glance across at Lal was acknowledged.

"I arranged for us to meet you here at eight p.m. You must recall that conversation?" Lal pointed to his phone, the animation returning.

"No I'm sorry. I don't know what you're talking about. I think I must ask you to leave." Kapoor stood up, agitated, the mottled skin on his bald head gleaming despite the waves of cool air wafting down from the low ceiling.

"Then why are you here? This office was in darkness only a few minutes ago. You must have been expecting us?" Lawrence could see Toby was ready to explode. Maybe it was time to use a more direct approach. Or perhaps he could try a softer line first and then release the attack dogs if Kapoor continued with his memory loss.

"I came in to pick up some files and heard a noise. Who the hell do you think you are, questioning me in my own office?" Kapoor hesitated. "Are you from the police?"

"You're the second person to ask me that," Toby whispered, the anger brewing just under the surface, "and what if we said we were?"

Kapoor glared at him, taking his measure. He sat down, fidgeting uncomfortably.

Lawrence intervened. "Mr Kapoor, we just want some information and then we'll be gone. We want to know about this supplier of yours, Mukka. He must deliver to you on a regular basis as you have his numbers on file. You called him to bring an order forward to tomorrow? Ring any bells?"

On the walls behind him, Lawrence could see photographs of what must be generations of Kapoors, given the family resemblance. A father or uncle was cutting a ribbon with a local dignitary or perhaps a politician. A sepia photo of a grandfather with a tiger sprawled at his feet. There were lavish weddings and family get-togethers.

Lawrence was starting to understand the haggling process that Indians seemed to enjoy so much. It was a power game; who had to concede, who had the upper hand; who could save face and who must acquiesce. He saw a flicker of respect cross Kapoor's shining face. The eyes were moving slower now like he was weighing up how much it would cost to get through this encounter; or deciding how much they knew.

"Mukka, did you say?" Kapoor consulted his phone with an elaborate pressing of glass keys. "Ah yes; I think I know who you are referring to."

He pressed the top button, returning the screen to darkness. It was a glimpse of the merchandise. Lawrence knew something would have to be offered in return. Or would it? He was British after all, and decided he should act accordingly. He was getting tired of playing other people's games. There was still the option of the attack dogs. But he sensed this approach was getting through so he needed to keep trying just a bit longer.

"We just need a name and a number," Lawrence continued.

"And why should I co-operate? I don't know who you are or what you will do with this . . . information." Kapoor looked determined.

Lawrence restrained Toby with raised eyebrows. But to his surprise, it was Lal who leapt to his feet.

"Lawrence, I've just remembered something." Lal apologised as he turned towards Kapoor. "Where do you supply?"

"I'm sorry, what did you . . .?"

"You're a wholesaler." He gestured with his hands. "Which areas do you supply with fruit and veg? Shops, restaurants . . . how far do you deliver?"

Kapoor seemed wrong-footed. "All around Agra; in fact, most of Uttar Pradesh as far as Lucknow. And since last year, we cover Jaipur and other parts of Rajasthan. Why do you ask?"

Lal turned back and moved towards the door. "Excuse me, I must make some calls . . . in private."

Lawrence pierced the silence after the door closed. "Mukka? A mobile number?"

"The man you are referring to only visits when we have a special order," Kapoor parried.

"What type of special order?" Toby had found a pencil and was twisting it into submission.

"He supplies us with okra and chillies," Kapoor conceded. "He asks a fair price. He buys from local growers. They are always good quality. I need him to deliver before noon tomorrow."

"Local growers where? Where does he live?" Toby snapped the pencil, flicked the two broken parts across the table.

"I don't know where he lives. Down south somewhere. The weather is better for the chillies. I call, he appears. We pay cash. It's that simple." Kapoor checked his watch again. "I really must be going."

Lawrence figured one last attempt at voluntary co-operation was needed. Time was against them now. "A serious crime has been committed and we believe this man is caught up in it somehow. We think he is innocent but we must speak to him and clear his name before the police find him. We will keep this conversation between us and not tell him how we got the number."

"I'm not able to divulge the confidential details of our suppliers. Now you must leave." Kapoor was scrolling through a list, no doubt intending to text someone.

The muffled voice in the corridor ceased. The door opened without a knock and Lal was back. "Lawrence, I have a cousin who owns a couple of restaurants. He tells me that Kapoor Wholesale has a poor reputation. They will not buy from them anymore."

Despite an indignant look from Kapoor, Lal went on to explain that the fruit sold was often underweight and never washed. The vegetables were generally poor quality and turned up late. The last deliveryman they had was rude and insulted one of their customers. And another was offering back-handers to restaurant managers for increased order values.

"But that's not all." The same triumphant look had returned to Lal's beaming face. "Mr Kapoor has been done for illegals. It is a most serious matter."

"What? This is nonsense; I don't know what he's talking about." Kapoor had sent a text as he retreated across the room, taking up a defensive position behind his desk. In the window's reflection, an unseen hand reached for the top drawer.

Lal drew his revolver. "I don't think that's wise. Unlike you, I have a licence to own this. That was another call I had to make."

Kapoor withdrew his hand. His shoulders sagged as he collapsed into a high-backed swivel chair. From down the corridor came the crescendo of running feet. The door burst open and three men in brown coats muscled breathless into the room. The supervisor called out but was silenced by Kapoor's raised hand. The situation was under control, he was assured; they could return to the packing area downstairs. They were thanked profusely as they departed. The returning footsteps were slower and much softer.

"Illegals?" Toby asked.

"Over forty thousand children are abducted in India each year. Many end up in places like this as slave labour. Their families will be threatened if they refuse to work. The owners like Kapoor pay them a pittance or nothing at all. Also India is the destination for human trafficking from the poorest of countries," Lal explained.

"There are poorer countries than India?" Toby looked confused.

"Bangladesh, Nepal, Bhutan, Myanmar, Afghanistan, Pakistan, there are many more." Lal kept the gun trained at Kapoor. "And of course we have the constant misery of war zones. There was a big influx from Sri Lanka during their civil war. Now we've got people fleeing from the Taliban, Al Qaeda and the Islamic Front. Refugees are easy picking for the traffickers."

"So that explains about the police questions," Toby concluded. "There must be illegals working downstairs?"

"I would not be at all surprised," Lal confirmed, as he indicated for Kapoor to move away from the desk. "The chances are he failed to give the local police a big enough bribe and got done for a minor offence as a warning. But the Delhi police would be a different story."

"Gentlemen, I underestimated you." Kapoor had slowly resumed his place at the head of the table. "If I give you this information, what assurances do I get that you will not . . ."

Toby grabbed him by the throat. Lal went to restrain him but Lawrence caught his arm. He thought of the children downstairs being forced into slavery. A tsunami of human misery went crashing before his eyes, all brought about by the heartless greed and cold-blooded profiteering of the likes of Harjeet Kapoor. Lawrence was happy for Toby to let off some steam.

After a few moments Kapoor coughed and rubbed the bruised skin on his neck. He read out Mukka's mobile number, which Lal wrote down.

Whether the number was bogus or not, Lawrence had already decided he was going to notify Chaudray about Kapoor, whatever the outcome.

"One more thing," Lawrence added. "When we arrived, we watched a truck reverse into one of your loading bays. Clearly your people were expecting it. So given how many trucks are going in and out, you must have a supply chain system of some kind?"

Kapoor nodded.

"And that means you must record the vehicle registration numbers?"

He nodded again.

Without being asked, Kapoor moved back to the side of his desk, indicating to Lal that he was staying well away from the drawers.

Kapoor pulled out a cardboard file, scanned through page after page of printed sheets and scribbled down a registration number on a scrap of paper, which he handed to Lawrence.

Before anyone could move, Toby swung a perfect right hook that sent Kapoor flying across the office. He hit his head on the desk and plummeted to the floor, one of his front teeth cupped in the palm of his hand, blood spattering onto the fake marble.

"That's for failing the Four-Way Test."

CHAPTER 53

Nisha's back ached from sitting in the truck for hours. In fact, she was aching all over, some places worse than others. She didn't want to think about what had happened while she was unconscious. The stabbing pain inside told her enough. She was alive and that was all that mattered for now. She knew her chance would come.

When the blindfold was removed, she could see her hands were still tied but the chain had been replaced. The new one binding her feet was longer. It would, at least, allow her to walk. That is, when they untied her from the chair.

"Our client is not happy. And if our client's unhappy, then we're unhappy," Lieke snapped. She was dressed all in black. Running shoes, knee-length denim shorts and a thin V-neck T-shirt all perfectly matching the NYC baseball cap. A blonde ponytail was allowed to swish out of the back as she strutted around the poorly lit room.

The air was foul. Nisha looked down. They had wrapped her in a dirty, torn cheesecloth dress that smelled like sour goat's milk. The floating material itched where it brushed against her smooth skin. The faded pink and orange colours clashed like a prison uniform. She was no longer wearing any knickers or bra. She needed a shower but knew full well that no amount of soap and water could wash away the dirt eating away like battery acid inside her.

"Where am I?" She pushed against the ropes lashed across her chest and laced through the chair-back. No give, too tight.

"Your new home." Lieke opened her hands like a real estate agent introducing a potential buy-to-let. "I won't say welcome, because it may be your last."

Nisha could see the room had been derelict for many years. She recognised some of the technology from old photographs in the University Science block. The heavy metal cabinets and clockwork machinery were from an industrial era before she was born. Instead of computer terminals and digital screens, there were simple switches, panels of buttons and lights, rotating knobs that could have been from a Bakelite museum.

On the walls, redundant display panels yawned like half-open mouths, never again to light up. The few internal windows in the airless room were mostly frosted glass, although some panels were clear, revealing glimpses of a dark building beyond that echoed in eerie silence. It could have been day or night. The room itself was stinking hot and reeked of diesel oil, rust and stale vomit.

The solitary door in the far wall briefly opened as Lotte came in carrying a small bag. Nisha gladly accepted some fruit and a mouthful of mineral water. Her stomach protested at the influx of food, a sudden knot of cramp twisting her insides, adding to her general discomfort.

"So why is your client unhappy?" Her words filtered out through bits of chewed apple. *Keep playing their games; keep playing for time.*

The sisters weren't listening. Instead they were huddled in the corner below a sign that read WARNING in Hindi with an arrow pointing to a large red switch now covered in cobwebs.

After a few whispered minutes, two high fives, a kiss and a smack on the bottom, Lotte moved to a blackboard on a side wall that was covered in smudged writing. She found an old rag and wiped it clean. From a desk drawer she pulled out a plastic box of multi-coloured chalk stubs, which she positioned next to another chair underneath the board.

Meanwhile Lieke had been checking the battery life on what looked to Nisha like an expensive SLR camera. She attached a microphone boost and anchored it to a tripod she fished out of a pile of bags that had been disgorged from the truck. Having checked the alignment to the chair and blackboard, Lieke untied her and pushed her over to the hot seat.

"Our client wants to know everything you've been working on, this EPT," Lieke continued. "What it is, how it works and the science behind it."

"Your fiancé is not helping us," Lotte added. "He's refusing to co-operate. He's putting your life at risk. We figure we can bypass him. You help us; we'll help you. It's that simple."

"I very much doubt you'd understand," Nisha stalled. "There seems little point in doing this."

"We will record you," Lieke countered. "They have people who can work it out."

"Jock owns the EPT, not me." She spat the words. "If you want to know how it works, better ask him."

"So is this your idea of co-operation? We're trying to save your fucking life here!" Lieke yelled, her voice echoing off distant walls beyond the glass.

"You release me and tell me where I am. Then I might reconsider." Nisha could sense a shift in their position. Was it the client who was driving this idea or were the girls going beyond their brief? Clearly Jock was playing for time so she must do the same. But he was not facing two assassins in a derelict building.

Suddenly hands were back on her shoulders holding her down. Nisha didn't see the needle this time; it was barely a scratch on the side of her neck. Cool fluid was swimming into her veins. One of the girls was counting down. She never got to five.

Nisha was floating through space, gently drifting down onto the soft ground. After an eternity she opened her eyes. The sight was almost overwhelming. Thousands upon thousands of stars studded the cloudless night sky. Astral fireflies were dancing in the ether of a warm summer evening. A shooting star flashed low across the horizon only to be swallowed up in the milky reflection of moonlight hanging like mist over snow-capped peaks. The moon itself was a perfect crescent torn in the sky, high overhead, the glowing entrance to a heavenly cave.

She was lying on her back, savouring the sweet aroma of dry meadow grasses mingled with the familiar fragrance of Alpine flowers as they bathed in perfume after another long, hot day. The sound of church bells filtered up from the doll's house village in the valley below. She felt happy; happier than she could ever remember.

The tiredness in her hips and legs was slipping away into the warm earth. The memory of a stunning sunset as they walked up the hill was still fresh; a spectrum of watercolours painted onto a blue-black canvas; the changing light metering out the last few strides to the grassy summit.

"I just want to capture this moment forever," a man's voice whispered in her ear. She could feel his body heat now as he leaned over. He kissed her lightly on the cheek. She smiled, reassured he was lying there beside her; he would always be beside her. She reached out and took his hand, squeezed it almost to make sure it was real. She wanted the stars to be real. She wanted to live like this forever.

The tinkling of cowbells in the field across the narrow track made them both sit up. A tall, slim girl was threading her way confidently between the snorting shapes of motionless animals, a wicker basket hooked over her arm. She was wearing a full-length taffeta dress in navy-blue or black. As she climbed a wooden stile, her white petticoat flicked up, caught like breaking waves in the same moonlight that played with her silvery hair.

"I've brought you some supper and a flask of hot coffee," the girl announced, laying out a thin woollen blanket on the soft grass.

"You're an angel, Lieserl, our little angel," the man replied, accepting a plate and diving into the boiled eggs, salami and pickles.

Nisha poured the coffee into three mugs and added the cream and sugar. This is how it was meant to be. She had been blessed with a loving husband and a beautiful daughter. She had always somehow known they were a gifted family that could bring love and joy and great learning to the world. They were bonded together with the unity and strength of particles in an atom; unbreakable, unstoppable, eternal.

"So what do you see, Mama?" Lieserl found a space between them and huddled down into the warm grass, their eyes once again fixed on the silence of the night sky.

"I see a vast, blue ocean connecting a great many worlds we have yet to reach. And, like the ocean, there are tides and currents that will carry our knowledge to those distant worlds, reaching out to people like ourselves; people we must love and embrace if they are to help us in our understanding."

"But Mama," the young girl continued, "how do you know this?"

"Because they have been here before." Nisha turned her gaze towards the constellation of Orion. In her mind, she traced the line of the three-star belt away from the Dog Star Sirius towards a pinprick of light just above the clear Alpine horizon. "If we reach out, they will come to us again. They are waiting to see if we're capable of understanding what they can teach us."

"You mean if we can find the single theory that explains the laws and principles of Nature?" The man's voice was merely a whisper in the darkness "The theory I never found."

"Yes and no, Albert," Nisha replied. "They want to know that we can understand it and use it for the benefit of all our people. We've already made the breakthrough. The EPT is all the proof we need. We can see the ocean now; we can harness its great strength; we can ride the cosmic waves and swim in its fathomless depths."

"Then what's holding us back?" Lieserl turned to her mother, kissed her on the cheek, placed an arm around her and squeezed her tightly.

Nisha paused. She could hear the calming voice of Dr Bhattacharya reading from the Rig Veda. *Neither not-being nor being existed at that time; there was no air-filled space nor was there the sky which is beyond it. What enveloped all? And where? What was this unfathomable ocean out of which rose up, in the beginning, desire, which was the mind's first seed?*

The Vedic teachings must be observed if humanity is ever to achieve moksha, the good doctor had explained, and break free from samsara – the eternal cycle of birth, death and rebirth. We must go beyond the constant hunger of human desire to attain and consume for oneself at the expense of others. *No man must live for himself alone but must look to serve all mankind. Only in this way can he see the truth behind the fog of ignorance.*

She imagined sitting once again with Jock on the ground under a spreading Bodhi tree in the courtyard of the university. The branches diffused the sweltering heat of the afternoon sun and swayed gently in a welcome breeze. The Brahmin had slipped into a trance-like state, his voice soft and rich with wisdom.

Our desires make us look foolish in the eyes of those who truly see. If we are to understand our world, the universe and what lies beyond, we must start by serving all humanity. We must embrace the examples set by Lord Vishnu and his consort, the Goddess Lakshmi. We must protect and preserve the world and all the creatures within it; we must drive out ignorance and create knowledge for the benefit of every human being; above all, we must resist evil in the world; we must resist the destructive powers of Lord Shiva.

"That is our challenge now, Lieserl." Nisha kissed her, squeezing Albert's hand at the same time. "We will not fulfil our destiny and achieve moksha until we apply the learning for the benefit of all. Only then will they return to help us."

"Explain this science Mama, so that we may understand." Lieserl offered her a notepad and a pen with which to draw. "How can you be so sure about the EPT?"

Nisha could see her own hand recreating the mathematics behind the theory. In the margin of the page she noted some explanations and assumptions that brought meaning to the symbols. When she had finished she handed it back to her daughter.

Before the notepad was put away, a man's hand reached across and gently took it. He studied the formulae, tilting the page to catch the best of the moonlight. After a few minutes he burst out laughing, the notepad falling into the soft grass, his legs and feet drumming with joy on the ground. "My little witch; my clever little witch! You always said we needed eloquent equations and indisputable evidence. I can't believe you've done it!"

"A problem shared, my love," Nisha replied, "you were so close but you denied yourself access to the vast wealth of human knowledge held in the teachings of others. Your ego would not allow me or anyone else to share the glory. It's taken me two lifetimes to realise this. Now reborn, I must fulfil my destiny."

Lieserl retrieved the notepad and put it in the basket. She kissed her parents and wished them goodnight, striding back towards the wooden stile, and then she disappeared into the darkness.

Nisha slid over to fill the space between them.

"I missed you, you know. But I suspect not as much as you missed me. We were so good together. Sadly ours is a story of a destiny destroyed by the failings of human desire."

As she spoke, they entwined their fingers. She felt no emotion ripple through him. He was as preoccupied and calculating as ever. Was it autism? Was it bloody-mindedness? It didn't matter now. Her incarnation was to be Nisha and the path ahead with Jock lay before her.

He cleared his throat. "You talked about others who have been here before; the ones who hold knowledge that we must prove worthy of sharing."

"Yes, it is true."

He waved his arms across the majesty of the night sky. "Then where are they?"

"Albert, you know where they are," she said softly.

"You mean?" He pointed towards a light just above the distant mountains.

She squeezed his hand "Yes, my husband ... my eternal husband."

*　*　*

"Leave her now, we have enough." Lieke switched off the camera and unclipped it from the tripod.

"Do you think they'll be pleased?" Lotte untied the rope and secured the leg-chain to the metal chair with a padlock. The board was swathed in writing and mathematical formulae. She wiped it all clean.

"I couldn't give a fuck. Nothing much ever pleases them. For all we know, Jock has signed the forms and we're done. I hope he has anyway. It would be a great shame, she's such a pretty little thing." She stroked Nisha's hair and kissed her cheek as she slept.

"I'll let them know," Lieke continued. "Let's get something to eat. Then I'll take the first watch."

"Stop worrying, we're safe enough in here." Lotte turned towards a scurrying noise in the darkness beyond a broken window. "There's only the rats for company."

"And a few hundred ghosts."

CHAPTER 54

Steve had said his goodbyes to a tearful Wanda Stanton in a security building near the main terminal at Schiphol Airport. To his surprise, the formalities had been handled at both ends with sensitivity and a great deal of warmth, in particular by the Dutch authorities.

Steve had always been impressed by their ruthless efficiency. Today the officers he met had showed genuine sympathy. Even the funeral director had conducted himself with calmness and compassion. And they all spoke perfect English purely for his benefit, he realised afterwards, as he waited at passport control in the main terminal building.

"Did you say satellite imagery, Detective Sergeant?"

He had been checking the monitor when Lonsdale answered. The Gatwick flight was boarding. He had just enough time to cover the thirteen minutes to the gate.

"Yes, sir. I was reading the in-flight magazine about the ASTER project. It's a joint venture between the USA and Japan, taking high-resolution thermal images. The article said they've recently spent millions upgrading the software."

"I thought you said our missing girl was still in India? What's Japan got to do with it?"

He jogged past a couple pushing a trolley that contained more hand luggage than he'd ever owned. *Why do they need so much stuff?* He jumped onto a travellator and shimmied between clumps of flight crew dressed in brightly coloured uniforms. They were chatting away, oblivious to everyone and everything around them. He heard a soft, female voice prompting him to mind his step. The sign advised the gate was closing in eight minutes.

"I think she's still in India, sir. It's just a hunch but I reckon there aren't that many places they could be hiding her." Steve had found the right route at last. His shoulder bag was getting heavier.

Although the software was more widely used for collecting data on volcanic activity, land surface climatology and earthquake damage, the thermal imagery could give them a lead, Steve explained. Or, at the very least, save them time.

"I've never been to the sub-continent, Detective Sergeant, but I would think there were thousands of places they could be hiding."

"Sir, Nisha's picture has gone viral across the main social media platforms. It's a big story; all over the newspapers and TV stations. Local girl; beautiful, young scientist, high-speed car chases, kidnapping, murder; they've even had the Chancellor of the university and the Chief of New Delhi police appealing for witnesses. A substantial reward has been offered by an anonymous businessman."

"So why do we need all this satellite technology if a billion people are already looking for her? What did you call it – thermal emissions? What are you trying to say, Detective Sergeant?"

The digital clock blinked away another minute. He could see the gate now in the distance. A trickle of sweat ran into his left eye. He tried to wipe it away, only to lose his balance in the process. The bag slipped off his shoulder and collided with an elderly passenger. Steve apologised as he ran past. The tirade of expletives made him grateful he didn't understand Dutch.

"Sir, can I give you my best pick? There are three locations in Northern and Central India I think they may be using." Steve could see the back of the queue below a flashing sign. He managed to drop his passport and boarding pass as he pulled them out of his jacket. He stopped and went back, clamping the phone under his chin.

He gave the locations to Lonsdale before he came within earshot of the other passengers. As he presented his documents to a young lady, the Gate Closed sign lit up. She pointed to it, shrugged her shoulders and turned back to the computer screen.

"And what do you want us to do, Detective Sergeant? Reposition a satellite?" Lonsdale paused. "Detective Sergeant . . . are you there?"

"Yes sir, just a moment." The noise of a jet engine roared into the room. Steve could see the gate doors opening as passengers filed out towards the plane. He added his warrant card to the pile of documentation and tried to explain the urgency. After much pressing of keys, sighing and checking of documents, she finally accepted his boarding pass, ripped it in half and wished him a pleasant flight.

"Sorry, sir, I'm back." He had joined the back of the queue. Would there ever be a convenient time to talk to his boss? "I was thinking, if we had thermal images of those locations taken at night, it might help to narrow the search."

"Why at night?"

"The temperature really drops away at night, especially in Northern India. Warm bodies will be easier to spot."

"I'm not sure our budget will run to that but I'll make some enquiries," Lonsdale promised. "Good work, Detective Sergeant. Keep reading the in-flight magazines."

While he'd been waiting at Indira Gandhi International Airport, Steve had visited a number of top-end jewellery stores. He had developed a sudden interest in men's watches. Only one still stocked the Josef Graaf range. The store manager did his very best to encourage his potential young customer to look instead at the Omega and Rolex models in the same price bracket.

As well as the quality and design of the timepiece, Steve was advised to consider after-sales service guarantees, chronometry, brand signature and functionality. Such questions had never been necessary while his Timex continued to be his loyal servant. The words of advice from the jeweller and his subsequent Internet search had given him even greater insight into the fickleness of branding in luxury goods.

Steve was nearly at the door. *Why couldn't they allow the use of mobile phones on regional flights?* One of the ground crew was pointing at his phone and waving a hand across his throat.

"There's something else, sir. It's about the IP rights and this Swiss company, Josef Graaf AG." His time was up. The last passengers were climbing the steps. Agitated cabin crew were leaning out of the front door of the plane. The whine of the engines intensified.

"I think I can see how it all fits together."

• CHAPTER 55 •

Lal insisted Toby should keep left. The car was speeding towards a junction. Despite the late hour, the traffic was still busy and most of the roadside shops were doing brisk business. The signs gave implicit directions to places they didn't know, for not the first time since leaving Agra.

"But the satnav says right." Toby pointed to the screen.

Lawrence had just woken up. He could tell that Lal was trying to remain diplomatic. It was the voice he would have used to explain to a superior officer why they were hopelessly wrong. The commotion over the satnav must have nudged him out of a thin sleep. He dreamt he was at a firing range surrounded by men dressed as spies. He couldn't trust anyone. When he came to shoot at the target his gun jammed. He could feel the panic rising in his throat. Suddenly a cold hand gripped his shoulder. He spun round and no one was there. Then he woke up.

When he'd nodded off they had been discussing the various merits of the .32 calibre Ashani semi-automatic compared to the Belgium-made Browning 1910 blow-back pistol, on which the Indian version was based. Lal believed their model was far superior for accuracy and reliability, which was no great surprise. That was all Lawrence could remember about the gun they had removed from the desk in Kapoor's office.

"It may be more direct but the roads in Rajasthan are inferior. We must head towards Gwalior and stay within Madhya Pradesh," Lal reasoned.

Toby went left at the junction. Lawrence could see that his Indian driving skills had improved. He had learned not to wait for a gap in the traffic but to point and go. Smaller-sized vehicles simply moved out of the way. It was a game of Russian roulette with the bigger ones; a question of who blinked first.

"Do you want me to take over?" Lawrence offered, guessing it would be another two or three hours yet.

"Please." Toby yawned. "These roads are exhausting. I'll pull over when we're outside the town."

Lawrence wanted to believe they were getting somewhere. But then again, he had spent half his life living with the illusion of progress. They would know soon enough if they were chasing shadows. As Toby had said, sitting around thinking about what to do wasn't going to find Nisha or help Jock fulfil his dream.

What Lawrence found most interesting was how things started to happen when they pushed. It was like a hydraulic pressure in the system. Some people stepped up; others disappeared. He had been surprised by Senior Constable Chaudray. From a slow start, the man had shown a true dedication to his duty. They would be more than lost without him.

The truck was registered to Muktendra Dhaliwal at an address outside Jhansi, so Chaudray had told them. The owner had an All India Permit to drive a heavy goods vehicle with trailer. There were no convictions on file, nor had he been in any trouble with the police. The vehicle was fourteen years old, bought with cash from a reputable dealer and licensed to carry food products. Mukka, as he was known, ran a tidy operation, paid his taxes and kept his nose clean. At least, Chaudray warned, that was what the computer said.

"I don't believe what Chaudray said about the phone

records." Toby pulled over, the wheels kicking up clouds of dust into the darkness.

They got out into a blast of hot, dry air and stretched their legs. Lawrence passed round a bottle of mineral water. Lal relieved himself behind a dusty ashoka tree set back from the road. The haze above them had cleared, revealing a clear starlit sky. There was no sign yet of the moon. A few cicadas chirruped in the trees nearby.

Lawrence reckoned they'd been travelling over six hours from Delhi. And for all the madness of the crowded roads, the potholes, the litter and the stray animals, India was growing on him. This was a journey he'd like to do again with Hannah, in daylight, with a knowledgeable guide and no life or death pressure. It was the real India, for better or worse. It had warmth, beauty and genuineness. It was a curious mixture of honesty and naivety. It was India off the tourist track. He knew they would return.

Lal climbed into the back. Lawrence buckled up and adjusted the mirrors. Toby checked his watch, picked up his phone, started dialling Max's number, then stopped. It would keep. A truck went past at speed, the first they'd seen for a while. The road was much quieter since they'd left the town. Lawrence indicated – force of habit – and pulled out.

A little further on the road surface had been upgraded into a smooth blacktop, which reduced the noise level from the tyres. He picked up speed. Jhansi two hundred and eight kilometres, the sign said. Nearer three hours than two, he reckoned. He was learning.

"They can pin-point where a mobile phone is located these days." Toby addressed the windscreen, his voice carrying over the snores coming from the back seat. "So why did Chaudray say he couldn't help us?"

"He said the most recent records didn't help us," Lawrence corrected. He swerved to avoid something asleep or dead on the road, most likely a dog. "No calls have been made for nearly two weeks and the phone itself is not emitting any signal, suggesting the SIM card and the battery have been removed. I suspect the Bella Donnas have seen to that. Also Chaudray checked out the girls' numbers Dr Bhattacharya had on file. They've become inactive as well."

"So you think they're using other SIM cards?"

"And Skype, which is not so easily traceable," Lawrence added. "Chaudray did say Mukka's phone records before he disappeared were quite revealing. He expected to see a pattern of usage up and down the corridor from Jhansi to Delhi. Most of the numbers called or received were in that area, mainly from suppliers or customers like Kapoor."

"But?" Toby interrupted expectantly.

"But clearly this man has been travelling all over India. Down to Kochin, over to Chennai, even going east as far as Kolkata." Lawrence glanced across. "So I guess he wasn't delivering vegetables."

"Then what else is he up to?" Toby took another swig of water, then offered Lawrence the bottle.

The bigger question on Lawrence's mind was how they knew each other. From the professional way the kidnapping had been staged, he suspected that the girls never left anything to chance. They must have known – or been recommended to – Mukka and his assistant long before hiring them. The destination, the route they were to take, Internet access and communications with their client, the need for provisions wherever they were holed up. All this required trust and careful planning.

"Chaudray is going to check out Mukka's tax and financial records. Maybe he's been using a credit card to buy fuel. He said he'd call me tomorrow if he found anything," Lawrence remarked, "but I'm not hopeful. We could find ourselves in Jhansi with no next move."

Toby brightened. "C'mon Lawrence, that's not like you. You're a glass-half-full, positive-thinking sort of guy. You're the one that's kept us all going … well, kept me going at least. I'll never be able to thank you enough. You've given me hope."

"And a dream; don't forget the dream." Lawrence smiled. "Think how many Paul Harris awards they'll give you for eradicating world poverty."

"I'd be invited to speak at the Rotary International Convention." Toby laughed. "Now that would be something. Have you been to one of those?"

"Never. Somehow I guess Leeds didn't capture the imagination quite like Sydney or Sao Paulo."

The road opened out into a dual carriageway, the shiny blacktop reflecting their headlights, just the occasional truck passing the other way. They shared a sandwich and the rest of the water.

"Anyway, Nisha might be in Jhansi. I'm really looking forward to meeting the Bella Donnas," Toby threatened.

"Toby, our friend Chaudray can only protect us to a point. You mustn't do anything stupid when we find them," Lawrence warned. "He can turn a blind eye to you reducing that crook Kapoor to a bleeding, snivelling wreck, but premeditated murder is another thing."

"Double murder," Toby corrected.

It was nearly dawn when they crossed a long road bridge over blackened waters on the outskirts of Jhansi. Oatmeal light seeped through walls of threatening cloud away to the east. Low timpani rolls announced thunder as it enveloped the far plains. Dream-like slashes of lightning forewarned early monsoon rains.

Birdsong drifted on heavy air when Lawrence opened the passenger window. Lal had been driving since they crossed back into Uttar Pradesh. He disengaged the satnav when they stopped at a roadside stall. Toby turned away to make his insulin injection. They refuelled with enticing samosas, warm roti breads and a fresh batch of idli with dipping bowls of chole. Mugs of thick, sweet chai were gulped down. Lemon-scented towels fished out of a steaming vat helped to wake them up.

Lal reset the satnav and turned off the volume. They soon found the industrial zone just a few kilometres past what looked to Lawrence like the ramparts of an old fort perched high on a granite outcrop. A few stalls and shops close to the road were open but the rest of the town was quiet.

The industrial zone itself was deserted and much smaller than the one in Agra. Occasional streetlights marked the grid pattern and picked out the crumbling facades of old warehouses and factory complexes. Lawrence noticed plenty of For Sale signs dotted about amid piles of rubbish and roaming packs of stray dogs. Things were tough in Jhansi, he decided.

Lal turned off the headlights and held a finger to his lips. They opened all the car windows and breathed in a heady mixture of industrial chemicals and muddy ooze from the banks of the river. Thunder was getting closer and the first heavy droplets of rain bounced off the windscreen.

Lal pointed as he drew up to the kerb. A side street stretched away over to their right, beyond the protection of the lights. The single-storey building on the corner was surrounded by a high barbed-wire fence. Lawrence could make out a sign that looked like M&D Transport but the lettering was faded.

Nothing moved. No headlights, no traffic. Lal killed the engine, just a faint glow from the dashboard. Nearly 5 a.m. Lightning forked high overhead, quickly followed by more growls of thunder. The rain continued to fall, smearing their view and dancing in the puddles, filling the potholes.

Lal checked his revolver and grabbed a torch. He led the way, climbing through a gaping hole in the perimeter fence, skipping between piles of rubble and running over to the side of the building.

The rain had become torrential with the old gutters and downspouts unable to cope. The security lighting no longer worked. There were no lights to be seen anywhere. They could hear the sound of water beating on a metal roof. Most of the windows were intact but the concrete shell was pockmarked and the window frames looked rotten in places.

They hugged a moss-covered wall, creeping slowly towards the rear. Lal stopped as they reached a bolted double door. He fumbled in his pocket.

Lawrence assumed he would fish out a spike or something to pick the lock. He needn't have bothered.

With an almighty crash one of the doors burst open, flying back on its hinges, the padlock still gripping the latch, the other end no longer attached to anything wooden. Toby's boot had gone clean through. So much for stealth, Lawrence thought to himself, smiling.

Once inside, Lal clicked on the torch. He threw the powerful beam around the echoing vault of a large room. Very quickly Lawrence realised it was a storage area with four sealed loading bays like giant air locks dotted along the side wall. That would be the rear wall of the complex; the access road must be on the other side of the building.

Water was dripping from skylights and cracks in the roof

tiles, making greasy puddles on the floor. Stacks and stacks of boxes were piled up everywhere. Lawrence didn't need a translation. He could smell cabbage, turnips and overripe tomatoes. One stack must have contained onions and garlic. Lawrence looked around, drew breath, stood quite still. His heart sank.

It all looked like a normal wholesale distribution operation – a little grubby in places and would never meet UK health and safety standards, but it didn't look like the home of an international crime syndicate.

"I'm guessing Mukka sublets this part of the building," he whispered. "We need to take a proper look around."

Lal adopted Toby's more direct approach with an interior door. His shoulder was enough to splinter the doorframe, allowing them to squeeze through. The torch picked out another vast room with corridors leading off into darkness. Huge industrial pipes criss-crossed the ceiling and mushroomed out of the floor.

Most of the room was empty, with marks on the walls and floor where machinery used to be, no doubt sold off when the business went under. The bulky iron machines that remained looked like they'd been there forever. The cost of moving them would be more than the scrap value, Lawrence reckoned.

The silence was disturbed by a rustling noise coming from the pipes above them. They stopped. Lawrence held his breath and followed the torch beam as it strafed across the ceiling. Another noise, louder this time, like a scratching sound, bone on metal. Lal flicked the torch, running it over the outer casing.

Another sound, this time heavier. Coming from the darkness above and behind them. They spun round. The torch found a hole in the plasterboard roofing behind the pipes. A pair of eyes reflected the light, and then disappeared. Lawrence felt something shoot past him, no more than a presence, a disturbance of the air. He took a step back, his feet crunching onto something, throwing him off-balance.

"Bats," Lal advised. "Let's go this way."

Lawrence had never seen bats that size before. They came pouring out of the roof space, flitting across the torch beam, like puppet shadows in their own silent movie. He had read about vampire bats and rabies in India. It was too late to worry now. He wiped the droppings off his shoe and jogged to keep up.

They made their way between two large presses, the floor still marked out in striped yellow and black tape. The route took them to a corridor running between two rows of internal offices. It had once been carpeted but only the underlay remained in places amid dark stains and rat droppings.

The walls were half plasterboard and half glass, both clear and frosted. A suspended ceiling deadened any sound. But there was no sound, the silence pressing on their ears. Lal kept the torch fixed on a dark-coloured door facing them at the end of the corridor. As they got closer, Lawrence could see that, in fact, another corridor ran across it, stretching away into nothingness.

They reached the corner. Lal tapped his ear and pointed in both directions. He flicked off the torch. Lawrence listened hard, straining for any sound.

Voices, low whispered voices, drifted through the darkness. Lawrence grabbed Toby's arm as they groped for the side wall. They edged along slowly, the voices getting louder.

They stopped, crouching outside one of the offices. Above them, a flickering light sparkled behind frosted glass.

CHAPTER 56

His headache was getting worse. He'd tried tablets, strong coffee and even a shot of single malt. *Did he suffer from migraine?* Dieter considered it a leading question. There must be a link on his file between Asperger's and other mental disorders. He'd lied but was beginning to wonder. Once again, the lights in his office were too bright. Even the one blinking on his phone.

"I have Herr Muller for you," Frau Schelling announced.

"Put him through."

The morning had been sunny and hot. The last of the winter snows had retreated up the north-facing Alpine slopes. The forecast said showers but since lunchtime the rain had been intense. A deepening area of low pressure was thick with heavy, grey cloud.

"Herr Blindt?"

"Frank." Dieter was not in the mood. It had better be good.

"We've been in touch with their lawyers in Singapore," Muller replied in a monotone, non-committal voice. "The client has instructed them to proceed."

"And?" Dieter sensed trouble.

"They want written proof that we are acting for Josef Graaf AG."

"Well, of course you are." Dieter tried to restrain himself. "Do you doubt my word, Frank?"

"No, of course not, Herr Blindt, but you understand my predicament—"

"I understand perfectly," he interrupted. "I pay you to handle predicaments. Now get on with it. I want the IP rights transferred now, today. And make sure you leave us out of it. Clear?"

"Clear." The line went dead.

There is a big difference between accountancy firms and law firms; one is business, the other is personal, his father had once told him. One screws up and you get fined. The other screws up and you go to prison.

Dieter understood the advantages of using a global accountancy firm like PYKD to act for the bank. They could open doors, frighten off the regulatory authorities and make sure that financial firewalls were in place to keep out the marauding hordes. Their fees were effectively a club membership.

Despite all the new rules over compliance and security standards, Dieter knew that money talked. And always would. The penalties for fraud, insider trading, rate fixing and other financial scandals were meted out in fines and fiscal punishments that the clients ended up paying. Accountants and bankers could always avoid prison.

With legal advisers, the opposite was true. Small was beautiful. Frank Muller's grandfather Bruno had been adviser to the board, long before Dieter was born. The relationship was absolute; the membrane of trust always remained intact and was never questioned.

Dieter was not especially interested in this IP transaction. In fact the whole thing was becoming tiresome. For the appearance of a kidnapping to ring true then a ransom demand of some kind had to be made. The twins offered a more direct route to getting what he wanted. They just needed a little more time. And if you need to buy time, get the lawyers involved. Time was their currency and they were past masters at justifying their use of it. But with the headache deepening, Dieter had other things to do.

The Client Activity Report from Buchwald was marked urgent, for his attention only. He ignored the arse-covering preamble and fixed on the numbers in red. Another six Russian clients had closed their accounts; that made twenty-eight this financial year.

It was the wheel turning, an inevitable result of the falling oil and gas prices. The Russian oligarchs no longer had the buying power they once had. The banking club membership fees were obviously starting to hurt. No doubt the super yacht market would be awash with tasteless floating vodka palaces.

But these were long-standing clients who could not easily be replaced. The withdrawal of their investment portfolios would weaken the bank's buying power and damage their global reputation. The connections through his mother's family in Volgograd had been a useful source of new money. And new money opened doors. Some ventures were above the line; most were far below.

But what did it matter? It was only about money. The pain behind his eyes seemed worse. He took two more tablets and turned to look out of the window. A sharp knock on the door brought him round.

"You wanted to talk about IT?" Curtis bounced into the room. He quickly sensed the mood and closed the door quietly behind him. "Are you OK?"

"Keep it short," Dieter snapped, turning back to the window where the light was kinder.

"I think this software company we've hired is kosher." Curtis helped himself to a large Scotch. "The guy they sent over from London knew his stuff. I'm told around town their CRM systems are good. Bottoms up."

"I don't want it." Dieter watched as a car careered through a flooded side street, sending a sheet of water spraying onto a row of shop windows.

"Probably not the best time to do this," Curtis replied. "Maybe tomorrow, if you're feeling better."

"My mind won't change by tomorrow. I don't want the staff seeing our dirty laundry." Dieter rubbed the birthmark over his right temple, and tried to draw out the pain.

"One man's dirty laundry is another man's erotic underwear." Curtis smiled, regretting the words as soon as he'd said them.

Dieter closed his eyes. He still considered the role of a private banker to be nearer the trusted adviser of a lawyer than the commercial hunter of an accountant. Look after your clients and the money will follow. The trouble was that not enough money was following from legitimate ventures. The bank was heading for trouble. The corporate wolves were at the door and baying for blood.

Curtis went for a refill. "Dieter, we're leaving money on the table. Only last week we lost a Dutch client because he wanted help with his offshore portfolio. But our compliance guy didn't tell the broker in my team."

Curtis held up his hands "Don't start! We're doing the best we can but our systems are inadequate. We can't keep track of our bigger clients. *Gotta speculate to accumulate.* This British firm is a lot cheaper than ASP."

"Who?"

"Exactly." Curtis risked another smile. "Only the biggest global software supplier and you've never heard of them. No offence by the way. I won't ask you what CRM stands for."

Dieter winced as he turned away from the window. The light had become unbearable. "Certain files must be kept under lock and key. I want no trace on any computer system. Clear?"

"You mean like BANK-ED?" Curtis whispered.

At the mention of the word, Dieter could see a room full of young Indian girls, their faces hidden in shadow. Did they look grateful and excited? Through his own generosity their school had improved classroom and boarding facilities, much greater access to learning and education, overseas scholarships and work placements. The UN ambassador himself had praised Dieter's personal contribution and hard work in this area when he presented the certificate. *Congratulations, you are a true philanthropist, a shining example to other business leaders.*

"We had a problem with the latest consignment." Curtis was reading from a file.

Dieter knew already. He tried to focus. Expectations had to be met, duties fulfilled. There was no loyalty these days. It was a global business like any other; local resources supplying a global demand. Commodity pricing was becoming more competitive. It was survival of the leanest and most secure. He had spent years constructing layers of protection. His status had to be maintained.

"We're under pressure to respond." Curtis closed the file, fixed his eyes across the desk.

"Dr Satapathy?"

"She's asking too many questions," Curtis replied. "We need a sweetener, one of your spontaneous acts of human kindness."

The light was crushing him. A twelve-year-old Indian schoolgirl smiled as she slowly turned the handle of a vice, the imaginary metal plates biting deeper into his skull.

"Do we still have an internship at CERN?" This was the best Dieter could come up with. He needed stability. But there was no stability. There was only the way things had always been. And, like the computer systems, it couldn't continue like this. The crack in the mirror was widening.

"Yep," Curtis replied. "After their expensive two-year refurbishment, CERN has come under even more pressure to do something useful. What are you thinking?"

"Put one of her students into CERN," Dieter explained. "Media coverage, high-profile internship, research at the frontiers of science ... even fly the good doctor herself over and show her around."

"I'm liking it." Curtis smiled. "We're involved in a project to improve refraction indices to maximise fibre-optic cable performance. Fuck knows, don't ask. It's the sort of thing a bright young female scientist would get their rocks off for. Leave it with me."

A few minutes later Dieter was pulling out of the car park. His peripheral vision was fluttering as objects blurred in and out of focus. His mind was drifting, the effort to concentrate proving just too hard. When the phone rang, he considered not answering it. Was it habit, curiosity or concern? Whatever made him do it, he pressed the button.

"Blindt."

The female voice sounded excited but distant, the line echoing. He didn't catch everything. Their location was secure. The scientist woman had refused to co-operate. They had to use other means. He lost the connection for a few seconds. When she came back the voice was talking about fascinating results.

"Sanskrit?" Dieter queried.

"Yes, some of her notes are in English, some in Hindi and some in Sanskrit," Lieke repeated. "And you'll need an astrophysicist with advanced mathematics. I've emailed you a recording."

Dieter was not ready for this conversation. This was not the time. He seemed to be surrounded by people who were not listening or were pursuing their own agenda. Try as he might to keep things under control, the situation kept slipping beyond his grip. Why couldn't they just kidnap the fucking girl and get her to talk sense?

"Recording?" he snapped.

"Nisha was talking to another scientist while she was under."

"What?" He had heard enough.

"They were discussing everything from general relativity to extra-terrestrial life forms."

Dieter swung into the kerb, screeched to a halt and grabbed the phone out of its cradle. "You expect me to watch a video of a woman doped up to the eyeballs explaining scientific formulae in Sanskrit and talking about fucking Martians!"

"It's not like that; you don't understand."

"Give me one good reason why I shouldn't finish this." Dieter was drumming fingers on the steering wheel.

"You mean . . . terminate her?"

"What else do you think I mean?!" He was yelling down the phone.

"You need to know who she was talking to," Lieke replied. "It was her husband, the man she claims to have been married to in a previous life."

Dieter went to press the button. He didn't want to hear any more. The pain had to stop. He held the phone away from his ear but could still hear the two words that changed everything.

Albert Einstein.

CHAPTER 57

They had taken up crouching positions either side of the door.

Lawrence could see just enough of Lal's expression. He would go through with both of them following, Toby first. Lal was to throw himself at whoever was inside; Toby and Lawrence were to check behind the door and any blind spots. Lawrence didn't know what he would do if he saw a gunman. Thankfully he didn't have time to worry about it.

Lal levelled his weapon and kicked hard at the door. It burst open on impact. They charged into the room. Lal shouted for nobody to move. Before Lawrence was through the doorway he heard the first shots ring out. Lal screamed and fell to his knees clutching his shoulder. The gun went spinning out of his hand. Toby dived after it and rolled for cover behind a row of old filing cabinets.

Lawrence managed to drag Lal out of the firing line. He propped him up against a side wall and flicked on the torch. He inspected the damage. Blood was pouring over his hand and shirt front. Lal assured him it was a flesh wound and the bullet had passed straight through. Blood was also oozing from the exit wound. Lawrence pushed his handkerchief onto it and wedged him against the wall to keep it in place.

Deep breaths; stay calm; find some composure. Toby was still groping for the gun. The torchlight found it in a corner. At least they had some means of protection.

Lawrence gathered himself. What had he seen in the room? Blurred images melted into each other. He listened hard.

Silence. Pure, clean silence. No movement. Just flickering shadows on the wall behind him.

Lawrence was breathing heavily. The blood pumping in his ears muffled a sound. It could have been footsteps on the concrete floor. The sound grew louder; definitely footsteps and low whispered voices. They seemed to be getting closer. In the half-light every noise was amplified. There was nothing he could do. He looked around for a better place to hide but the office was almost empty. Only twisted and broken old furniture left to rot.

When they'd been crouching outside, Lawrence noticed his hands were shaking. He felt exposed and useless. He had considered taking Kapoor's gun from the glove box. Although now he wished he had, he had never fired a gun in his life. He would be more of a threat to Lal and Toby in this situation than any assailants. As he scanned the torch round looking for escape options, the beam was steady. Adrenalin must have kicked in. Now he needed to make some good decisions.

He peered round the broken leg of a desk. At the far end of the room there were two shapes cloaked in shadows. Probably both male, he thought, although one of the Dutch girls was quite tall. As he watched, one of them seemed to grab something off a low table.

He flicked a glance towards Toby and held up two fingers. The room was bigger than it looked from the outside. Other people could be taking cover. He was trying to work out a plan of the building but the maze of rooms and internal corridors made it too confusing. Was there another exit? He hadn't seen one.

Suddenly a burst of gunfire drilled the air. It shattered the windows behind them and shredded what was left of the office door. Sparks flew off the filing cabinets above Toby's head. An empty beer bottle exploded, sending up a starburst of emerald crystals.

In the silence that followed, Lawrence heard the voices again. Male voices, agitated and louder this time. He hoped for a translation but Lal was slipping away. He had stained the wall crimson. The shoulder was a mess. He was losing too much blood. They had to get help.

When Lawrence looked round he saw Toby on his feet, resting his arm on the filing cabinet. He took aim and fired a volley of shots. There was no return fire. Toby yelled out and started to run, firing indiscriminately. Lawrence ran after him, trying to keep the torch covering the shadows. Two of the candles ahead of them had gone out, leaving the room in almost total darkness.

"Come on, through here!" Toby shouted out, pointing the gun towards an open doorway.

"Wait!" Lawrence had caught up. "Lal will die if we don't get help."

"Then you stay here." Toby turned, but Lawrence grabbed him by the arm.

Lawrence sensed a trap. All his life he'd tried to make rational decisions but maybe it was time to let go, let his instinct take over. "We need two minutes to check out this room. Nisha could be in that cupboard for all we know. I'll use Lal's phone to get an ambulance and ask Chaudray for help. You take the torch and have a look around. Then we go after them. But we go together. We nail these bastards together. Agreed?"

Toby hesitated. "Agreed."

It took less than two minutes. Lawrence called Chaudray first and got straight through. Help was on its way. Toby had found sleeping bags, half eaten food and other stuff left behind. It must only be the two drivers. So where were the girls? Another part of the building? The answer lay in the darkness.

Within a few strides they were back in the main room. They stopped and listened. Nothing. No scurrying noises. The bats had gone. Even the rain had stopped hammering on the roof.

They walked slowly towards other silent offices. They found a new corridor running away to what looked to Lawrence like the other side of the building. He wasn't sure it was the way to go. They could be waiting in a side office. There would be no way out, no cover. Sitting targets. Rats in a barrel.

Bang. A loud noise up ahead echoed down the corridor. A heavier door. An exterior door being kicked open. People running, footsteps on concrete. Then Lawrence was at full stretch, the torchlight bouncing off the walls and ceiling. Toby was panting to keep up. They turned a corner. The corridor ended at a fire door now swinging on its hinges. Moonlight was dappling the roadway outside.

Lawrence was trying to focus. Which way? Left or right? Run through the doorway, two shots and goodnight. Fifty-three years old. All that life lived. All that life yet to live. Over in two seconds. *Hannah, I love you. Did I ever tell you? I want to tell you. Right now.*

They had nearly reached the doorway. He had decided. They burst through, turned to the right, back towards the street. They'd only taken a few strides when suddenly, behind them, a diesel engine growled into life. Lawrence turned. Headlights came on, blinding them. Main beam in their eyes. Nowhere to hide.

The engine roared, crunching through the gears, the lights brighter as it accelerated towards them. A wall on the opposite side blocked their escape. They had to go back. It was charging now, an angry elephant, spray billowing out from the front tyres. Only a few more seconds.

Lawrence went to grab Toby who sidestepped him, pushed him hard. Lawrence tripped over the step, fell back into the corridor. Toby was bathed in white light, down on one knee in the middle of the road, a victim awaiting his execution.

Toby took aim and fired three shots. Breaking glass. The light dimmed. The second shot must have hit a tyre. A squeal of brakes. Shadows swinging violently behind him as he kept his position, the weapon lowered to his side. The third shot? Lawrence didn't know.

A sickening impact. Metal on brickwork; more breaking glass; a muffled scream. The whole building shook, plaster tiles drifting down from the false ceiling, a shower of glass hitting the corridor behind him.

Lawrence got to his feet, ran outside. Toby had disappeared. The truck was angled onto its side, half embedded in the factory wall. Toby was trying to wrench the door open. The acrid smell of burnt rubber mixed with diesel oil. The fuel tank must have ruptured, a huge lava flow of oil spilling out across the access road. *Tank must have been full? Planning a long journey?*

Toby managed to drag a body out of the wreckage, laid it out on the ground near the cab, jumped back in. When Lawrence reached the man he knew it was too late. That explained the third shot. There was a burning hole where the man's right eye would have been. Death must have been instantaneous. Brain tissue curdling in a pool of diesel oil. He went to retch. His throat was too dry.

Lawrence decided against dragging the body away from the truck. It would be no use; there wasn't time. One spark and the fuel would ignite. Instead he grabbed an old blanket from behind the passenger seat and laid it over him. The only decent thing he could do. A mark of respect. With the blanket fluttered out some papers and what looked like a business card. He stuffed them into his pocket.

Whispered voices were coming from inside the cab. Lawrence climbed in to see if he could help. The frame of the truck lurched as the weight shifted. It slipped further into the wall, sending another shower of debris onto the road.

Toby was trying to get the driver out. The man looked in a bad way. His body was twisted under the steering wheel and wedged half into the wall itself, his legs tangled under metal and wires from the dashboard.

Then the voices went quiet. Toby was backing out. Lawrence made room. He eased himself over the passenger seat. Shone the torch. Lawrence could see the driver was not moving. A piece of metal was embedded in his skull, protruding through his right temple. Unblinking eyes were fixed on a crescent moon dancing in and out of scudding clouds overhead.

Lawrence needed to warn Toby about the fuel spillage. Before he could speak a distant siren pierced the night air. It was quickly joined by another echoing off the factory walls. Police? Ambulance? They didn't wait to find out. They ran down the access road then out onto the side street. Lawrence turned off the torch, felt for Lal's keys in his pocket.

Before they reached the car, the sirens had been joined by the deep, deep thudding of a police helicopter, its twinkling red, green and tail lights racing towards them out of low cloud. A searchlight was crawling over the buildings further down the road.

Lawrence fired up the engine and set off. He kept the headlights off and drove slowly until his eyes had adjusted. He couldn't risk braking as the tail lights would show. An incoming tide of grey was flooding from the east, washing the shadows from the streets, bringing monochrome definition to the road signs.

Toby spotted it first. Gwalior and All Other Routes, off to the right. Another exit from the industrial zone. It smelled like they were close to the river. The sirens were far enough behind them. Lawrence turned right, rejoined the main road and flicked the headlights on just in time as a police car shot over a low bridge in front of them. It passed at full speed in a blur of flashing lights.

They crossed the river going back the way they'd come. Lawrence remembered seeing a pull-in set back amongst some trees. The traffic was thin but the first rays of daylight had roused some pedestrians from their beds. They pulled off the road and Lawrence killed the engine.

Toby was the first to say what they were both thinking. Indian police bureaucracy would have detain them for days had they waited. Or worse, they could have been arrested. Unlicensed use of firearms; at least two men dead and possibly a third. At this distance they wouldn't know if the truck had exploded. Extensive damage to a derelict property; breaking and entering. Lawrence was sure there would be other charges.

"Will Lal be OK?" Toby ventured.

"I told Chaudray where to find him."

"He's a good man. We'll miss him."

"So now what?" Lawrence swigged some water, and passed Toby the bottle. "Should we go back? Turn ourselves in?"

"How would that help find Nisha or the assassins?"

"Well, what do you suggest? Where next? We've run out of clues. Jhansi was our only lead. And remember, if we go on, we don't have a translator." Lawrence shrugged.

"He told me where they are." Toby managed a dry smile. His

face was covered in dust and grime, tiny cuts on his cheeks and chin, but the tiredness in his eyes had gone. Toby was alert, alive and hungry to keep moving.

"Who told you?"

"The driver. Mukka. I think it was a confession. He knew he was dying. He wanted to set the record straight. Karma; isn't that what Dr Batty called it? Give himself a head start in his next life maybe? Do you remember what Chaudray said? No previous convictions, clean record. I think our friend Mukka was dragged into all this. He needed the money; he was given no choice, who knows. He was happy being a driver, delivering and collecting things for Mr Big, our Choirmaster. He was paid to go all over India."

"Collecting what, delivering what?" Lawrence thought he heard a noise in the bushes. The sunlight was thickening now, low rays like honey pouring over patches of mud. A thin mist was rising from the drying earth. He could hear more traffic on the road. The location wasn't safe. They must keep moving.

"I don't know. Maybe he thought the kidnapping would just be another job. Drop them off, carry on with his day job. Deliver some provisions when they needed them. Keep out of the way. He hadn't reckoned on us or the police looking for them. He may not have known about Okki being murdered." Toby swallowed hard, took another mouthful, rinsed and spat it out through the open window.

"So you think they'd come back to load up with fresh supplies? They kipped down out of the way and then we showed up. It makes sense, I suppose, but what about the guns?" Lawrence started the engine.

"I don't think they'd ever used guns before. The Bella Donnas must have armed them as a precaution. I'm no expert but they couldn't hit a barn door, which is why they legged it. Lal was just unlucky."

Lawrence smiled. "Spoken like a true marksman."

"I was aiming at the tyres. It must have hit the bonnet and ricocheted into the cab. That poor guy wouldn't have known what hit him." Toby looked genuinely shaken.

Lawrence waited for a gap and swung out between two trucks, heading away from Jhansi and back towards Gwalior. "So where are we going, by the way?"

Toby was scrolling through the satnav. "Well, his English wasn't that clear and I'm not sure how it's spelt. He said it was south for about three hours."

"South, as in back over the bridge?" Lawrence glanced across. "As in back to where the police will have roadblocks; searching for two armed white men on the run in Lal's car?"

"Yes, that's a point." Toby scratched his head, spiking up greasy grey hair into little peaks. "Do we tell Chaudray what we're doing and run the risk of him pulling us in?"

"Or worse, getting the police involved in a rescue attempt. They go in heavy handed and Nisha gets caught in the crossfire," Lawrence reasoned.

They drove in silence for a few minutes. The road ahead was clear. But they may be going the wrong way. If he speeds he will be attracting the wrong sort of attention. Their circumstances had changed.

His thoughts were too confused. Lawrence needed to think out loud. He slowed down. "We need to become invisible. Take the SIM cards and batteries out of our phones. Use only cash at petrol stations; try to keep away from built-up areas; put some dirt on the number plates in case of cameras"

Go left at the next junction in three hundred metres, the woman in the satnav instructed. Toby looked up. "We're locked in; a good, strong signal. It says two hours and thirty-two minutes. We should be there late morning."

Lawrence confirmed they had plenty of fuel. He passed Lal's phone over and pointed to his own in the glove box.

"Then we keep going and do a reccy when we get there," Toby added. "We can call Chaudray when we know what we're dealing with."

After they turned at the junction, Lawrence found he couldn't get comfortable. He fiddled with the seat and the mirrors. Then he felt a damp patch on his trousers. He remembered the papers he'd shoved into his pocket. He handed over the soggy bundle.

Toby could see the papers were all in Hindi. Receipts, purchase-order dockets, other stuff, nothing much of interest. Then he saw the business card.

"Muhammad Akthar."

"Who's he?" Lawrence swerved to avoid a drifting pedestrian.

"Regional Manager – Middle East & India."

"Middle East? Where's he based?" Lawrence overtook a cart being pulled by two oxen.

"Dubai."

"Dubai? Why would two fruit and veg deliverymen be connected to someone in Dubai? Who does he work for?"

They slowed into a series of bends through a wooded section of road. A helicopter thwooped overhead at speed. They re-emerged just in time to see it disappear into a bank of low cloud.

Toby sat pensively as he tapped the card on his index finger.

"A charity outfit called BANK-ED."

CHAPTER 58

Summer had arrived in Guildford and, to celebrate, Detective Inspector David Lonsdale was wearing a short-sleeve shirt. Not only that but he had opened the unwashed windows of his second-floor office, allowing warm air to carry a mixture of honeysuckle and petrol fumes into the room.

"Bankruptcy, Detective Sergeant?"

Steve was fumbling through a thick pile of documents. Explanations always seemed to flow better at his desk in the basement.

"Yes, sir. Apparently Josef Graaf AG is on the verge of going under. They're heavily in debt to the bank, which, according to Max Hartley, may itself be on the slippery slope. He reckons the market's looking for greater consolidation. His client CBSG is on the acquisition trail."

"Get to the point." Lonsdale peered over the top of his bifocals. "I need an informed guess."

Steve took a deep breath. He knew that if he hit the right note, the senior officer would press the button there and then. He was hoping his grunt detective work would pay off.

"CBSG buys in, then bankrupts Josef Graaf AG. The transaction will stay below the radar during the turmoil of the acquisition. It then adds the watchmaker to the long list of other businesses it controls and puts another brass plate up near the entrance."

"I'm back with you, Detective Sergeant; keep going."

"Someone within the bank then siphons off the IP rights for

this Project Amrita and puts it into a separate legal entity, also owned by the bank, but under his or her direct control."

"An insider?"

"Yes, or someone close to the deal, an accountant or lawyer, maybe. Once extracted, it would be very difficult to trace the ownership, especially within a private Swiss bank. Then finally, Josef Graaf AG is sold off at a knockdown price."

"Or folds completely, just another casualty of globalisation and Swiss arrogance." Lonsdale seemed pleased with the hypothesis. "But it gives us a bigger problem. There must be dozens of people who could set this up. Also the IP rights would have been transferred legally."

Steve was ready for this. "Sir, you said to me once there is no smoke without fire."

"I like to think pearls of wisdom rather than tired cliché. Go on, Detective Sergeant."

"I just wondered if Francois had any books running on this Choirmaster or CBSG. I managed to grab a quick coffee with him at Schiphol. Genuine guy, very straight I thought . . ."

"Very straight you thought . . . for a Frenchman." Lonsdale smiled. "I am allowed to say such things; rank has its privilege."

Lonsdale concurred with Steve's logic and had nearly completed an email to his Interpol connection when a heavy knock on the door shredded his concentration.

"Wait."

Steve was pleased with Lonsdale's reaction. He'd already tipped off Francois but wanted his superior officer to make the first official move. Lonsdale read it through on the screen again and pressed Send.

"Come."

Steve turned to see a tall Chinese woman stride confidently into the room carrying a plain, brown file. She was wearing an elegant, white, silk blouse, tucked neatly into a tight pencil skirt. Short, black hair was cut in a bob and a long pearl necklace was intertwined with the cord of her office pass. Steve guessed mid-forties, but he'd been wrong before.

As she pulled up a chair, he caught the hint of pomegranate and citrus fruits, gently overpowering the honeysuckle. Her gold-framed rimless glasses gave her an air of authority. He'd never seen her before but Lonsdale was clearly expecting her.

"That was quick. What've you got for us, Maria?"

"I think we may have something." She spread photographs across Lonsdale's desk, pulling out two, which she presented in a steady, clear voice, no trace of an accent. "The first site we looked at was clear. But this was a satellite image taken a year ago over the second site near Nagpur, the Tadoba Tiger Reserve. It was taken at the end of June when the park closes for the summer. It was late evening, mid-week."

"Sorry, Maria, this is Detective Sergeant Steven Mole," Lonsdale interrupted. "It's his hunch you've been chasing. Maria is the brains behind our new Forensic Technology team."

Maria nodded and continued. "You can see a cluster of unoccupied buildings here, away from the main centres, here and here. Now this shot was taken over the same buildings just two days ago. There are heat traces here and here, but nowhere else for miles."

"Could they be tigers?"

Lonsdale was marvelling at the clarity, while no doubt hoping Maria's handiwork could be buried in the set-up costs of their latest forensic toy, Steve decided.

"They could be, the heat signature is different to ours but that wouldn't really show at this range," Maria replied, deadpan, shuffling the pack, pulling out another. "I did a Google Earth search in the same area but that was pretty inconclusive."

Steve explained his logic for the kidnappers using a tiger reserve. End of season, too hot for the tourists, no prying villagers nearby, yet still within reach of an urban centre and with an Internet signal. It was worth a try, he argued.

"This is the third one we looked at. Again this was taken at the end of last year . . . I've seen others of this particular site that show just how derelict it is."

Steve saw Lonsdale's attention flick back to his screen. He apologised and clicked open the email reply from Francois Chabert. Interpol were not usually so prompt. The words "strictly confidential" had been added to the subject box.

"This was taken last night. In the corner of that building, there are heat traces, but I couldn't get it any clearer, sorry." Maria talked Steve through other pictures of the site, which showed up as a big dark hole from every angle, yet the surrounding urban area was teeming with life.

Steve had done some background research. It would have been a bold decision by the kidnappers. As Lonsdale was apt to say, if you want to hide something, put it where everyone could see it.

"What is this shading? Is that just the satellite range?" Steve looked hard at the clearest photo. It felt more and more like a long shot, but this technology was fascinating.

"I'm not entirely sure but we had a case like this where I used to work. The blurring looks very similar," Maria explained.

"And what caused it, in that instance?"

"Radioactive contamination. The camera can see what the eye can't." The reply was matter-of-fact. Steve could see it was just another job to her. *But people's lives could be at stake here. Innocent people may die if we get this wrong.*

"So are you saying this location could be radioactive?" Steve flicked through the rest of them. The same blurring occurred on all the heat-sensitive photos.

"Not necessarily. It could be another form of radiation. Electromagnetic waves, chemical pollutants in the soil, even something in the bedrock like monazite or thorium. India is rich in rare earth deposits," Maria added.

"Thorium?" Steve could see Lonsdale had finished reading and wanted to talk; in private. Was thorium a piece of the jigsaw? Even if it was, Steve needed to cut this short.

"Yes, it's what we could be using to generate electricity instead of oil. I believe India already has a thorium reactor. Of course, thorium is only one explanation," Maria concluded.

"OK, last question. Probability. What are the odds that the heat images in this shot are human?" Steve had picked out the best angle.

Maria hesitated, flicked a glance at Lonsdale and was given the nod to proceed. "We talk more standard deviations than probabilities, but the bottom line I would say was around eighty-five per cent but—"

"Thanks Maria," Lonsdale interrupted, "I appreciate your help. Can you leave these with us and we'll take another look."

Clouds had drifted in from the west, taking the sun's glare off the side wall. Lonsdale closed the windows after Maria had gone. He lingered, staring out at the trees, lost in thought. Steve could sense the email had touched a nerve. He was pleased now about his connection with Francois. He was trying to peer over and read it off the screen. He didn't need to. Lonsdale read it out for him.

". . . there are between forty thousand and sixty thousand children kidnapped in India each year; that's one every seven minutes. Official statistics show at least eleven thousand will never be found. Human trafficking is an international business and India is the hub for Asia. There is a close connection with narcotics. Children are often injected with addictive drugs and become dependent. Once sedated and controlled they will be sold through Internet auctions to the highest bidders for prostitution, slave labour, exploitation . . . even for medical experimentation and body parts."

Steve sat in silence. He saw Lonsdale wipe a speck of dirt out of his eye. He had known about trafficking for many years but hadn't fully understood the implications. Having now witnessed first-hand the slum conditions around New Delhi, somehow it had become real to him. So was this connected to the murder of an innocent girl?

". . . Interpol has been monitoring activities across India for several years. Undercover research has proved unreliable. We believe that trafficking operations are funded globally through banking syndicates on behalf of their clients or possibly for their own interests. As yet we have no concrete evidence. Hearsay allegations have been made by people in the industry who are too frightened to testify.

"CBSG is one of the Swiss banks that has been identified. The bank supports charities with considerable access to underprivileged children, including BANK-ED, which funds projects for schools in India, and GEN-UP, a newly created charity promoting gender equality in developing nations. They recently sold their interest in DRIPFEED, which subsequently folded despite impressive results in improving irrigation usage in agri-production within developing nations.

"Switzerland is the home of the World Health Organisation, the Red Cross, Médecins Sans Frontières and a number of global charities. As such it is widely recognised as having a unique role in supporting those most vulnerable in society, especially in developing nations.

"He finishes off by saying we need to proceed with caution ... and we can count on their full support." Lonsdale clicked off the screen.

No smoke, Steve reflected. He could see the faces of women washing their clothes in putrid, filthy water; children playing cricket in piles of rubbish and human excrement. He could smell the despair of parents forced into selling their daughters to feed their sons. And behind the images, he could see men in dark suits profiteering from human misery; people collecting awards for their compassion and generosity while arranging the next consignment of children on container ships or in refugee convoys or in the back of a truck; frightened, defenceless children drugged up and spirited out of an orphanage in the dead of night.

"I think we are on the same page here, Detective Sergeant." Lonsdale had steepled his fingers, which Steve knew was a sure sign they had been joined by the devil's advocate. "So I will let you hypothesise."

"Our Choirmaster is a big name in the Swiss banking community. I'll say *he* but they may have let a woman slip through, I suppose."

"Unlikely, but carry on." The steeple changed shape, then re-formed. The devil's advocate was listening.

"He likes the idea of putting something back into society, to help those less fortunate than himself . . . but actually it's about ego, power, control and status."

"And about keeping in with influential people and organisations who can tip him off to what is happening," Lonsdale added. "You scratch my back . . ."

"On the surface it's all very respectable but behind the scenes he is laundering money, organising crime syndicates and creaming off the top. If legitimate clients are proving a bit stodgy then he can top up the numbers with slush funds through Mexico or India or wherever."

"So what's changed?" Lonsdale prompted.

"One day he gets wind of a scientific breakthrough that can potentially eradicate world poverty. The charity behind it is out of his sphere of influence; an Asian outfit that is trialling a new technology in the poorest villages in India."

"A country that provides him with a lucrative supply of human capital." Lonsdale nodded his agreement with the hypothesis so far.

"The last thing our Choirmaster needs is an end to world poverty," Steve added, "not just from a financial point of view, but then he would have no control over the people who could testify against him."

"So what to do?" The devilment playing in Lonsdale's eyes. "Why not kidnap the scientist behind the breakthrough, find out her secrets or steal the IP rights, then bury the whole thing. Make sure that no one ever uses it. Poverty generates cash, a tiny proportion of which he pays back as charity funding. The poor people of India keep leaving the villages and filling the urban slums looking for work while he continues picking up awards at UNICEF dinners."

"But the assassins he uses for the kidnapping make a mistake. They try to cover it up as a suicide, and then the police get involved."

Lonsdale checked his watch. "I have a meeting. I want you to keep digging in Switzerland. This Choirmaster; I want to know who he is."

"Yes, sir." Steve was gathering his papers.

"Use Chaudray, Francois or whoever, and keep me informed. We will need watertight evidence if we are to tackle a Swiss bank. Meanwhile, try and rescue this scientist. Do you know where she is? Sorry, I wasn't paying attention."

"Well, it's not certain – only eighty-five per cent according to Maria – but my hunch is they've taken her to the one place no one would think to look . . . or indeed want to go anywhere near."

"You can tell me the story later, Detective Sergeant. I just need a name."

"Bhopal."

• CHAPTER 59 •

Lawrence had found what he euphemistically called an Internet cafe somewhere in the crowded back streets of Bhopal.

He'd used up most of the loose change in the slot and had sent Toby out to get more. The free time would help him clear his head. His mouth felt like the floor of a reptile house and he would kill for a good night's sleep in a comfortable bed.

Like Toby, he wanted to get on with the search but they needed to be ready. Toby's evangelical transformation from lost executive to pumped-up man of action was truly a blessing. It was just an exhausting type of blessing. Lawrence knew he had to encourage his friend, who was still riding the rapids of emotional turmoil and had yet to grieve properly for the loss of his daughter. Encouraging was one thing but running unnecessarily into a bullet was another.

In contrast he'd not felt so excited about his own prospects in years. He didn't want this new life to vanish in reckless stupidity, having waited so long to find the right person to share it with. They had to tread carefully now. There was so much at stake. He didn't want to tell Jock they'd screwed up and Nisha was dead.

The men in the cafe couldn't speak a word of English. It was all men, he quickly realised, apart from a solitary woman in a full-length blue burka who appeared after Toby had gone. She sat down at a terminal but didn't stay long. Maybe because the place was as ripe as a boxing gym, the ambience made worse by columns of ants, brittle skeletons of dead insects and piles of rat droppings.

He checked his emails and decided not to risk replying to any. He didn't know if his location could be traced but he didn't want to find out the hard way. With his last ten rupees he printed off an old magazine article. Toby came back too soon, carrying a bag of loose change, some batteries, bottles of cold water, a local map and a mixture of dodgy-looking pakuras and onion bhajis, which were drowning in warm grease.

Lawrence noticed Toby was puffing, and sweat had pooled into the sleep lines across his stubbly face. He was going to explain that they were at fifteen hundred feet above sea level and the average daytime temperature would be nudging forty degrees. But he reckoned Toby had worked that out without the help of Google. They agreed not to speak until they were back in Lal's car. It was tucked away in the shade of a side street that resembled a war zone, opposite where a building had collapsed.

Toby found a vein, made his injection then put the needle away before biting into the bhaji. He spluttered out the words as bits of deep-fried onion pebbledashed the windscreen. "For some reason I've got Bhopal mixed up with Chernobyl. What's the story here?"

"They were accidents that happened within a couple of years of each other, back in the eighties. The death toll here was much higher," Lawrence explained. "People are still dying thirty years on. It's the worst ever industrial disaster."

Toby carried on eating until Lawrence started to read out the article. He put the bhaji back in the bag and wiped his hands.

"The American-owned Union Carbide Corporation opened a factory in nineteen sixty-nine, near the remote rural town of Bhopal in central India. The plant produced a pesticide called Sevin, which contained methyl isocyanate or MIC. In seventy-nine, the site expanded to allow MIC to be manufactured and stored on site, together with phosgene, a highly toxic substance used in the MIC manufacturing process. Phosgene gas had been a chemical weapon in First World War."

Lawrence continued reading. "People from the villages flocked to Bhopal looking for work, despite the fact that the plant had a poor safety record. On the night of the second of December nineteen eighty-four, an exothermic reaction forced the emergency venting of pressure from the MIC holding tank. The company claimed this was sabotage. Others have claimed it was corporate negligence. The outcome was a cloud of poisonous gas that descended on Bhopal, killing nearly four thousand innocent people.

"It goes on to cover the various legal battles and civil unrest that have taken place over the years. Bhopal is still an emotive issue. The article says stillbirth and neonatal mortality rates continue to be horrendous. The site remains contaminated and has pretty much been abandoned. As the saying goes, Union Carbide never really left." Lawrence folded the papers.

"It sounds like an accident that was waiting to happen," Toby added.

"And when it did happen, it was the poorest people who suffered," Lawrence explained. "The gases were blown over a town that only existed because of the poverty in the surrounding villages. The materials in the gas cloud were denser than air so the poison hugged ground level. Children and shorter people inhaled more toxins, as did the people who ran. There was no escape."

They sat in silence. Lawrence kept getting the feeling that he had been brought here, like it was some kind of destiny. He'd never found God or felt the slightest bit religious in his whole life. But the conversations with Dr Bhattacharya, the spirituality of the country, the pervading optimism of its people despite all the odds and the continuing triumph of hope over the worst forms of adversity, all combined to make him believe that he needed to be here and that India was steeped in a divine influence.

If ever proof was needed for human beings to pull together and eradicate poverty, the story of Bhopal must be the best example, he decided. He would never have come here voluntarily. Now he was proud to be here, despite the circumstances and the imminent threat of danger.

"So why have they come here?" Toby pulled out the map, together with a bunch of keys Lawrence didn't recognise.

"I'm guessing they would most likely have an antidote for the toxic waste or poison gas," Lawrence said, "so a derelict site that most people avoided could be an ideal place to hole up for a few days."

Lawrence pointed to their current location on the map and calculated it was walking distance to the site. "I got an email from Jock. He's in Uppsala getting ready for the launch. Nothing's signed over and the clock's ticking."

"Mukka gave me these. He said she was safely under lock and key, which suggests a hidden room or somewhere in a secure building. It's a sprawling complex." Toby picked out a key edged in purple tape. "It'll be dark soon. Why don't we go have a look round? Then we can decide if we want to call in the cavalry."

"Do you think we still have that option?" Lawrence looked surprised.

"I'm not sure."

"I had an email from Steve Mole asking us to contact him urgently. It was sent a few minutes after one from Chaudray demanding we call him, or present ourselves at the nearest police station."

"When were they sent?"

"Hours ago," Lawrence confirmed.

"Which suggests they don't know where we are. So they're blind until we reappear." Toby managed a half smile.

"The element of surprise. It may be our only advantage. Let's go."

CHAPTER 60

"Did you say something?" the young man whispered to the ceiling.

He was naked, spent, lying back in a glacial moraine of sweaty pillows and stained cotton sheets. A slimy, limp cock was retracting into a dark matting of undergrowth, like an exhausted snail.

"'Cos if you did, I didn't hear you." The man straightened himself, pulling back the foreskin, letting it breathe.

Dieter Blindt was also naked, standing next to him by the bed. He wanted the man to go. In fact, he hadn't wanted this to happen in the first place. It had started out in all innocence. He just happened to have clicked on the website. The man was a student, visiting friends in Geneva, and wanted to know where the action was.

Dieter had allowed things to go too far. He poured himself another drink, didn't offer one, needed to take the taste away. *A little brandy clears us of this deed.* But it doesn't. It only makes the guilt taste worse. If he kept his back to him he might get the hint. *Fuck off, leave me alone.* It wasn't hard to think. Why was it so hard to say? He perched on the end of the bed, staring out into the vastness of another starlit sky.

The man slipped off the bed and padded over to the dresser. Without asking, he fixed himself a quadruple brandy in a tumbler. *Philistine, lout, no breeding.* But still Dieter had to watch every movement; the bend of his back to get the ice, the inviting cleft.

Whoever he was, he thought, the beard suited him. It accentuated his lips. Dieter tried to look away, too late, saw it twitch, his own snail awakening. The curtains were still open. What if someone was watching them from the building opposite? Or taking photos? Putting clips on Facebook or You Tube? What kind of behaviour was this for the chairman of a respectable bank?

He saw his own hand reaching out, involuntary, touching himself, holding, feeling the blood like an incoming tide, filling the veins, stiffening the desire.

"You want more? You're a randy little bastard, aren't you?" The man turned round fully, presented himself, hands on hips, laughter playing in the corners of his eyes.

It was no good. Dieter had no answer. He reached forward, grabbed him, pulled him closer and took him, the tongue working its magic once more until the man's words subsided into a deep purring sound. Dieter immersed himself in a world without obligation; a world where he could slip the leash and indulge his fantasies without having to account for his behaviour to the stone faces carved around the boardroom table.

Sometime later he found himself in the shower. More precisely, Dieter was in the shower. Blindt, on the other hand, was watching him, sitting in a dark suit and tie on the edge of an oversized bath. Dieter was pummelling and scratching at his scalp in a torrent of steaming water, trying to get it right, trying to make it whole again. If he stayed in the shower he knew they couldn't continue the conversation. The man in the suit would have to remain silent.

Dieter was drying himself, towelling his body as hard as he could. There was no crack in this mirror. But there were two faces. The other face in the background belonged to a man who was composed, calm, clear-headed, just what you'd expect. Of a chairman. Of an Einstein. And he was wearing a tie. *How can you even contemplate doing this?*

Dieter closed his eyes, rubbed the moisture off his clean pink face. He looked again at Blindt. "She is getting in the way. I don't need her now. The twins can finish this."

Nisha is our great-grandmother. She is Mileva, Albert's wife, our father's grandmother. She is the genius behind the Einstein legend. We would be nothing without her. Don't pretend you don't know. You must stop this nonsense. You must get over there; you must meet her, cherish her and love her. This is not acceptable, no way for a man in your position to behave. Why are you doing this?

"She is just another slut, an Indian slut, pretending to be a scientist, that's all. How can she be related to us? Her mind is drugged. She is playing tricks on us."

Dieter stumbled through to the kitchen, throat itchy dry, head throbbing. He thought about more headache tablets, reached for mineral water from the fridge. Blindt handed him the bottle. He was sitting in the fridge, on the bottom shelf, his jacket collar pulled up against the cold, ice crystals on his tie.

She is a young Indian girl now because her spirit has lived on. She had to fight the injustice of her ideas being plagiarised. Einstein would have been nothing without her. We'd have been nothing without her. She had to fight male chauvinism. Now she has to fight racism in a country where women are sold into slavery and prostitution. And you profit by it; you create this human misery. You're a monster, you make me sick.

Dieter slammed the fridge door shut. Was there anywhere he could go? He went to the cupboard; headache tablets in the first aid box. Blindt was waiting for him. *The people of India must get to share in our scientific progress. The white man has raped and plundered, stolen and exploited them and their*

431

country since the Middle Ages. What gives you the right to lord it over them? Why should they kowtow to you?

"They are people of the gutter," Dieter snapped. "I will not listen to this in my own home! We created this civilisation with our bare hands. We built the bridges and the roads and the railways. We dug the tunnels. We created the corporations and the banks that keep the world moving. Now these lazy bastards want to take it all from us. I won't just sit here and watch it happen. I won't allow CERN to be a science laboratory for some girl from the slums."

He swallowed three tablets, or was it four? He made himself a coffee and walked through to his study. Blindt spun round in his chair to face him. *I'm ashamed of you. What would our father think if he could see you like this? He had faith in you and how have you repaid him? You bring disgrace on our good family name. Now you want to destroy an innocent girl trying to use science to eradicate poverty from our world. How can you live with yourself?*

Dieter threw the coffee at him, the cup crashing into the back of the empty chair, a shower of hot liquid drenching the keyboard on his desk. "You evil, sick bastard, how dare you accuse me! You're the one who shakes hands with the UN Peace Ambassador an hour after you've shagged the bellhop against the toilet door. I watched you fix your tie afterwards. Don't come round here accusing me."

Blindt was circling the desk.

I've heard enough. If you want to be respected as a decent human being, then, for God's sake, start acting like one. But if you want to steal children from a school while presenting a cheque for the sort of money you'd spend getting your pathetic little cock sucked, then you carry on. But don't expect me to come with you. I disown you.

Dieter was incandescent. He could feel the words burning into him. "Get out!! I'm not you, not my father or Albert fucking Einstein. I'll be who I want to be and to hell with you. I will not go on living this lie. You're the one to be despised."

He collapsed into the chair, the momentum spinning it round, his head reeling, pain shooting behind his eyes. He tried to make the voices stop, the madness tearing him apart.

"Hey, who are you talking to?" A small voice filtered through from the bedroom next door.

The words came to him from another world. Who was it this time? Hermann Blindt? Albert Einstein? Sergei? Or Mee Mee fucking Wong, calling from the bedroom; bring me cold water, let me play with your sweet little cock.

A man wrapped in a bath towel was standing in the doorway. He was scratching his beard and laughing out loud. He had a sparkle in his eyes that suggested to Dieter that they knew each other.

"You are one screwed-up fuck. I've been lying there listening to this crap. Who've you been talking to?"

"Who are you?" Dieter tried to focus. Why was a stranger wandering naked around his apartment in the dead of night? What was going on?

"You serious?" The man cocked his head on one side. "You don't know who I am?"

"No. I want you to leave. I will call the police. What would people think?"

"That's not what you said in the taxi coming over here, for Christ's sake!"

Dieter motioned towards the door. His feet were floating slightly above the carpet. The pain in his head had softened into a dull ache; his mouth was dry. He had to sleep now. Or did he have to wake up now? He wasn't sure. Something wasn't right. Maybe he should take a shower, try to wash some sense back into his head. But hadn't he just been in the shower?

The young man dressed in silence and let himself out. Dieter stood by the window and looked down onto the deserted street. He didn't recognise the street. He didn't recognise anything.

Did he live here?

CHAPTER 61

Click.

Lawrence could tell the padlock had been oiled recently. It was the only thing that had as far as he could see. They'd combed through the old Union Carbide site earlier in the afternoon. Twisted metal everywhere, piles of rubble, stanchions and scaffolding hanging precariously, pipelines fractured and corroded. There were old flare towers and storage tanks toppled and strewn around the site amongst strangled weeds and mutant brown grasses.

It was a place where hundreds of people had worked; a place where hundreds more wanted to work, dreaming about a better life. The photos in the magazine article had shown how they wore the uniform with pride; their names on badges lovingly sewn onto the boiler suit.

Lawrence felt like he'd been inspecting an abandoned graveyard, all hope gone. Another country would have levelled the place and built a proper memorial to the thousands who died, he decided. Maybe that will come in time. After all, India was the epitome of hope. An amazing transformation was taking place. Two countries sharing the same land mass. But surely thirty years must be long enough?

Before they'd set off, Lawrence had insisted on moving the car closer for a quick getaway. He knew they couldn't walk far in this heat. Even keeping to the back streets in the dark they still looked conspicuous. He was in no doubt the police would be on their tail. Two strapping English blokes trying to stay hidden was not going to be easy.

He'd tried to plan ahead but there were too many variables. Given the high media profile, there didn't seem to be a way they could spirit Nisha out of the country, let alone get her to Sweden in time for the launch. Passport issues, police involvement and the logistics of booking flights and transfers were all stacked against them. He decided to take one thing at a time. The first step was a ten-minute instruction by Toby on using a gun. It didn't feel comfortable. But it might save a life, he reasoned.

He'd checked the times of flights. Raja Bhoj Airport was fifteen miles northwest of the city with good motorway links. The main runway had been extended to handle international flights. Most of the destinations were to the Middle East and Asia. *One step at a time.*

"Stay three paces behind me," Toby whispered. It was the only part of the plan he'd come up with. Covering his back, watching the shadows, giving him room to fire. Lawrence had suggested sneakers. They would make less noise on the metal treads beyond the padlocked gate.

The stairway led up to a suite of offices, which had once overlooked the site. Was it the general manager's office or the control room? The external windows were boarded up. Lawrence had tried to find a plan of the site online. No luck. They were blind. That may prove to be an advantage, he thought.

As they moved through the gate, he did think about locking it behind them. In the end, he decided to keep the exit route clear. He pulled the gate too, hanging the padlock on the latch to deter any beggars looking for a quiet place to sleep.

They crept slowly up the stairs. Lawrence's trembling hands gripped the revolver. He released the safety catch and kept it pointing into the barbed wire tunnel that arched up and over their heads. He didn't trust himself. Each step was carefully measured. They were moving so slowly Lawrence felt he might overbalance and fall. He was concentrating too hard on where he was putting his feet.

As they climbed, darkness swallowed the stairs. The streetlights could not reach this unholy corner of a forgotten world. The air was hot and carried a pungent chemical smell. It was poisoned air for the lungs of the dead.

Toby stopped on the landing. Dark patches on his shirt, sweat pooling on the back of his neck. The gun held out nervously in front of him. The street noise was just a distant drone. A pencil torch was throwing a narrow beam onto a closed door directly in front of them. Lawrence thought he saw a flicker coming from inside the room. It could have been a reflection. It could have been his imagination.

"Try the handle," Lawrence whispered as Toby was about to kick the door in. "Element of surprise, remember?"

Toby twisted the knob and the catch released. No creaks or groans. Mukka must have oiled this as well. He won't be oiling anything else. They'd come this far. People were dead; others could soon be dead. He could be dead. Everything was on the line now. Keep calm, concentrate. And Lawrence, he told himself; remember this is India. *Expect the unexpected.*

Toby stepped into the room, a laser light from his torch catching the sharp angles, the unfamiliar equipment, broken chairs, panels of long-dead lights, levers, switches and buttons. A heady acrid smell seeped out of the walls. Lawrence's eyes were watering, itchy and sore. He heard his own rasping breaths, each one shorter than the last, almost panting for clean air. He shook his head. *Where are they?*

Toby had taken three paces, then stopped. Lawrence

followed the beam to a point near the boarded-up windows, only a few feet in front of them. The room seemed to be L-shaped. He could sense an open space away to their right.

He focused back on the light that was dancing over something dark and smooth. The texture looked different to the hard, metal cabinets around it. Softer somehow, more of a delicate, waxed surface.

The room was silent. Lawrence sensed nightmare creatures hiding in the shadows, ready to devour them. But, for now, nothing moved. Without taking his eyes off the object, he reached behind him. His hand was swimming through thick, oily waves. A finger touched something. Smooth, round metal, familiar shape . . . the door knob. Pushed it closed, heard the click.

Toby twisted the torch into another setting. The beam became wider, more of the object coming into view. A mottled sheen on a wax surface, dark patterns absorbing the light. Lawrence must have realised at the same time. A final twist of the beam revealed every detail.

"Hi Pops." The voice was slow, deliberate, almost seductive in its delivery. Each word echoed softly. "I just had to see you again . . . and tell you how much I love you."

The object rose up and moved gracefully towards them. In the torchlight, the woman looked like a ballerina, all poise and control, both hands behind her back, her hips swaying with the movement.

"Stay where you are," Lawrence called out, surprised Toby hadn't reacted. He braced himself. The gun felt heavy like a rock, his hand wavering. He moved to Toby's side. His friend was staring at the bewildering creature.

"Remember when I had my face painted like this, Pops?" the voice continued. "At the school open day. You said I looked very scary, like a real man-eater."

Lawrence pulled Toby back, giving them more room, more options. He thought about rushing the woman, but didn't know what to do. He couldn't see what she was holding.

"Okki, is that really you?" Toby ventured the words, wavering, unsure, wanting to believe, knowing it couldn't be. *But the school open day? The tiger face paint?*

It was such a close match to the colour of her hair. She won the first prize; the headmistress laughed. She was nine years old. She didn't want to wash her face for days afterwards. Lawrence knew the story.

The torch had become a spotlight. Lawrence could see the gold and black stripes extended over her whole body. He was drawn in by the intricacy of the patterns, the delicate curves, the perfection of her muscles as she padded slowly towards them.

Her slim, naked body was enticingly close. Firm breasts coated in layers of body paint, nipples etched in black; her shaven femininity daubed in gold paint, seemingly so natural and so powerful. On her head, a mop of auburn hair, tousled and combed to look just like her. The illusion was so clever.

To his horror, Lawrence saw Toby moving towards her, opening his hands to hold his daughter once more, wanting this nightmare to be over. The woman, likewise, brought her arms out from behind her back. Reaching for him; *Daddy, hold me, kiss me; tell me we can go home.*

"Toby, watch out!" he yelled, trying to close the gap. He saw the gun too late. Both her hands clasped in a firm grip. It was a mime in super-slow motion. *Why doesn't Toby shoot her? Why don't I?* Lawrence threw himself at her, pushing out with all his strength, dropping his weapon.

A first shot pierced the air, followed by a second and a third. Lawrence felt the impact with her shoulder. Warm skin stretched over firm muscle and bone. The body paint smudged as he knocked her out of the light. He heard her fall, expected another shot straight at him. But the tiger had vanished into the forest. Padded footsteps running at speed, down the L shape. He heard a door open, then close. A fluent movement, probably rehearsed, the trap set. He heard the click of another oiled lock.

A rush of blood, anger coursing through him; he was ready to give chase but the groans made him stop. Toby was heaped on the floor, the torch bathing him in a monochrome filter, turning the blood from red to black. One bullet had grazed his temple, searing the skin, a steady trickle of blood seeping out onto the concrete. But there was too much blood from that single wound. One of the other shots must have hit him. It was point-blank range.

He knelt down, tried to lift him but he was too heavy. Wanted to pull him upright, find the other wound, staunch the bleeding, vision blurred, *for fuck's sake, help me someone.* He was pulling at his shoulders, easing him round, hoping he'd regain consciousness. *Come on, Toby, help me, it's me, Lawrence, don't give up, we're so close now.*

But he knew it was no use. Lawrence felt the change, the body letting go, sliding down into the abyss. Toby's eyes fluttered, then closed. Lawrence tried to find a pulse, slippery fingers pushing and probing, not really sure where. He listened to his chest, no heartbeat, no air, no movement. All he could do was lay him down gently, move his head slightly to avoid the dark pool flowering out from under his neck and shoulder.

A thousand images rushed towards him. Toby in his office, at the Rotary meetings in Weybridge, laughing after Dr Bhattacharya had left the hotel room. Toby couldn't die. Not like this. He fumbled again with his wrist for a pulse, still nothing, no vital signs.

Lawrence looked up. A familiar figure was standing over him. He recognised the face immediately. His father looked the way he always did; a black woolly hat perched on his balding head. He was broader than he was tall; a working-class Yorkshireman and proud of it. No frills, a man of few words. In all the years since his death, Lawrence hadn't really appreciated the gentle wisdom of this man. He needed some of it right now.

You can't help him, lad, you did your best. His father remonstrated. The figure turned towards the darkness. *You came here to save the girl. Better get going before they do something you'll regret for the rest of your days. You're a McGlynn. You don't need anyone else. Stay strong and you won't fail.*

Lawrence remembered some of the things he'd wanted to say but never got the chance to. The heart attack had been so massive, so sudden. As the figure melted away, he knew he could make amends one day. But not today.

He prised the gun from Toby's hand and picked out the other door in the torchlight. *For Toby. For Nisha. For the poor bastards in Bhopal. For the children begging in the slums. For the orphans in the villages who never had a chance. For the believers trapped in the netherworld of poverty where life has no meaning, no value.* His father was right. He could do this.

The hand holding the torch was rock steady. He slid through the door and closed it behind him. He moved into a room bigger than the last and panned the walls, sweeping over more panels and dark screens. A dusty notice, this time in English. *Safety Is Everyone's Responsibility.* The irony was suffocated long ago in a cloud of poison gas.

The torch found a recess in the far wall partly covered by a makeshift curtain. It looked out of place, a recent addition, a screen of some kind. He took the first stride, leaning on the outside of the rubber sole, trying not to squeak on the concrete. He kept the gun pointing at the shadow beyond the curtain. The barrel remained steady but doubt was riddled into his fingers. He knew it but they didn't. *Concentrate. Keep moving.*

The curtain rippled in an imaginary breeze. He stopped, listened, a low growling noise coming from the recess. He tried to swallow, his throat and lips parched, nostrils bleached and sore. A painted hand with accentuated claws strummed the edge of the material, then slowly pulled it back. A tiger appeared out of the shadows, standing tall and defiant, the patterns on the shoulder blurred and uneven. As he watched, the face of another tiger appeared at its hip, the markings almost identical, a menacing expression sunken into a mask of black, white and gold. The mouth opened into a growl, taut skin pulled back over a row of proud, white teeth.

The second tiger rose to its feet and moved out into the light. It was taller – much taller – and somehow more frightening because it seemed more in control. An economy of movement so measured that Lawrence almost failed to notice her nakedness under the paint. A more muscular frame with powerful legs, a shaven V that showed no sign of weakness, the eyes calculating and unblinking, fixed on his, drinking in his fear.

The tigers held hands briefly before parting, stepping away from each other, symmetry in motion and a perfect reflection from an invisible mirror. They performed accentuated sidesteps, from tiptoes down onto padded feet. As the gap between them increased, Lawrence had to flick the torch wider and wider across the room. That was when he spotted the third tiger, curled up on the floor at the back of the recess.

It was not moving. Instead the head was turned away from

the light, a long back curved towards him. The colouration was different, the richness of the gold paint much deeper, less of a contrast with the swirling black stripes.

When he looked back, the other tigers had vanished. A pincer movement; they would circle and pounce from the shadows. He could feel them prowling, eyes burning into him. He was too far from the back wall to retreat. He had to go forward, get to her quickly and check she was OK.

He heard a noise, turned his head, the torch picking out a flash of gold and black as it disappeared behind a cabinet. Suddenly a dull thud behind him; he felt a searing pain in his right buttock, shooting up his spine. He twisted and fell awkwardly into some old boxes, breaking the fall but tangling his arms, trying to keep hold of the torch, the gun skidding away. He knew he wouldn't have fired it anyway.

He tried to move, the pain stabbing deeper, couldn't reach the spot, his arm punching through cardboard. Finally he was able to sit up, stretched round and pulled something out of his rump, the pain easing.

Feathers, a sharp point, the tip of the dart smeared in his own blood.

CHAPTER 62

"You must be crazy!" she replied, putting the empty cup and saucer back on the tray.

Max wasn't impressed with Jerusalem Shores. He'd only ever been to one other old people's home. He smiled as he corrected himself – retirement village. That one also smelled of over-cooked broccoli and unfulfilled dreams.

At first he'd resisted the family pressure to lock away his ailing mother in one of these places. He knew how angry his father would have been, but in the end there was simply no other choice. The old man was not around to look after her. And none of the other family members volunteered to help out. It was a practical solution, no matter how painful. Mercifully, it hadn't been for long. She died peacefully in her sleep. He was comforted to know they would be swilling chilled Chardonnay and picking hot chicken drumsticks together again somewhere in the clouds.

"I've always been crazy, you know that, Sylvia." He smiled as he offered her another chocolate digestive from the packet he'd smuggled in. Her resistance crumbled, as it always did. He poured more coffee and added a drop of cognac to soften the sugar. The hip flask quickly vanished before an angry care attendant stormed through the empty lounge.

"Well, it may have escaped your notice, Mr Hartley, but we're not as young as we used to be." She took a sip. "Quite honestly, I'm past it. I doubt I'd even get up the steps these days."

"You're in luck, they don't have steps these days," he chirped, "and besides, I'm only talking about three or four people, tops. It'll be a breeze."

"Listen to you, always the charmer." She reached for the packet. "And when're you planning this little escapade?"

Max had been putting his old friend Sir Freddie Pickles through his paces at one of their regular real tennis matches in Hampton Court. The idea emerged over a noggin of brown ale in the bar afterwards. Max was surprised by the enthusiasm and unconditional support he received. By the third pint, the arrangement was settled.

But that was logistics and hardware. The people issues were trickier. It called for more than just tact and diplomacy. It would need very attentive personal care from a seasoned professional. There was only one person who could pull this off. And the good news was that she had always had a soft spot for good-quality cognac and dark-chocolate digestives.

"It must be this week, maybe tomorrow. I want this done right." He pulled some papers out of his bag. "And it's only for a couple of days. I'll have you tucked up with your cocoa before lights out on Saturday, that's a promise."

"I haven't done this in years, I might've forgotten how to?" She ran liver-spotted hands over her ample bosom, just pausing long enough to get his attention. "I won't fit into the uniform anymore. No, I'm sorry, it's very flattering and it's so good to see you after all this time but I can't do it, you need someone younger. What about Nadia, you always had an eye for her?"

Max wasn't sure how much he needed to tell her. It wasn't a question of trust. He would trust her with his life, and may well have done over the years. He needed to untangle this first in his own mind. Whichever way he cut and diced it, it always

445

seemed to end up complicated and somehow ridiculous. And it could all be for nothing.

Worse, he might not get past first base. Sir Freddie may change his mind. On the other hand, it might be a lifesaver. A dream fulfilled. There was only one way to find out. Keep planning, keep pushing and keep talking.

Let alone explaining it, he felt a strange sensation even talking to her again. They had been so close and, to some extent, always would be. Was it possible to deceive a former lover? She no longer looked like the woman he used to fantasise about. But then he had to accept that he was no longer a pin-up from a men's health magazine.

He was swimming in memories. On balance, it hadn't been fantasising; it was pure animal lust. Dress it up as much as you like; the mutual desire between consenting adults for pure sexual gratification? She was the older woman, more experienced, single and unrestrained with a reputation for no-holds-barred fulfilment, yet always very selective in her choice of wrestling partner. And, best of all, she was forbidden fruit. *Thou shalt not covert the cabin crew.*

"Sylvia, listen to me, I wouldn't ask if it wasn't important. You're the very best and always were. I need you; it's as simple as that. This'll not be without some risk for reasons I'll explain when you stop being a pain in the arse and say yes." He lowered his voice as the female attendant returned, moving slower this time. Max could feel her eyes scanning his intentions with wary suspicion. She carried on walking towards the staff room, flat shoes squeaking over disinfected linoleum.

"What risk?" Her brown eyes were as sharp as ever.

"Was that a yes?"

Her hand paused over the third biscuit before withdrawing.

It moved instead to straighten her knitted cardigan then fluttered back to her lap. She dropped her nose and smiled at him over her bifocals. "Of course that's a yes. But there's one condition, lover boy."

"I think I can guess."

"Absolutely right. And it doesn't involve cocoa." The look in her eyes; the same look when she blocked the doorway that sleepless night at The Oberoi in Cairo. The largest swimming pool in Africa, it said in the brochure. Just as well, as it turned out. "But I might let you off with dinner."

"You drive a hard bargain." He regretted the words almost before saying them.

The smile evaporated as she looked straight past him, her face the picture of innocence once more. Max could hear a tinkling sound. He turned to see an orderly in a green uniform carrying a small plastic box.

The young black guy had two white leads hanging down from a green, yellow and red woolly hat that resembled a tea cosy. He was nodding in time to a distant rhythm only he could hear. His expression changed when Max made eye contact. A huge smile revealed a keyboard of fluorescent white teeth, interspersed with rich gold fillings.

"Ya medication, child," he shouted, thrusting the box forward, liquid shoulders rolling with the beat.

Sylvia smiled, swallowed the handful of brightly coloured pills with some water and returned the empty box. The young man went off happy, always to wonder who *did* shoot the deputy.

"So who else are you dragging along?" She accepted a swig from the hip flask.

"I've got Tim and Brian with me. You'll have Tina to help out."

She paused. "I thought you said only three or four passengers. Why would I need Tina?"

He'd forgotten she was the mistress of understatement. Always calm, always attentive to even the most ungrateful and belligerent individuals, a cool head in a crisis, not that he could ever remember anything worse than running out of vintage Bollinger. He smiled as he recalled how she'd coped with the sleeping member of the Saudi Royal House with excessive flatulence. The fly spray excuse was a stroke of genius.

"We'll have very important guests in need of some serious TLC. I know you'll make them feel comfortable."

"So what's the risk?"

"There are some people who'd prefer us to fail. It could be a bit bumpy."

"Max, if it wasn't bumpy, I wouldn't be interested." She leaned over and kissed him on the cheek. "Now get me out of this fucking place."

CHAPTER 63

Lawrence stumbled to his feet, steadied himself and flicked the beam over the boxes. He spotted the gun, bent down to pick it up, lost his balance and found himself tumbling towards a bed of concrete. He tried to reach out but his arms weren't his anymore. The floor had turned into a bowl full of dough that was rising up to meet him; soft, springy, uncooked pastry cushioned him and drew him gently into its folds.

He thought he heard a dog barking. Not a serious bark, more like a puppy playing on a beach, rolling in white sand, juggling with a tennis ball. Trigger came bounding over to him, dropped the ball at his feet, licked his face, a puppy once more, all pudgy features and paws too big for his legs. Lawrence threw the ball into the dunes. Trigger bounded off after it, ragged prints in the sand, an excited tail flicking in the sea breeze.

Suddenly he heard a yelp, saw the puppy scuttling back down the dune slope, hiding between his legs. They watched as, over the crest, a magnificent tiger appeared. The yellow ball was in its mouth. It padded slowly towards them, making rivers of sand from each enormous paw print.

The puppy made himself so small he finally disappeared. The creature stopped in front of him, dropped the ball. It spoke to him, the words soft and low. Saliva was dripping from an armoury of cruel teeth.

"Put these on." The tiger indicated for a pair of yellow swim goggles to go over his eyes. "We want you to watch us. It will be the last thing you ever do. My sister likes being watched when we make love, don't you, princess?"

Lawrence's head was pounding as he came to. He tried to move his arm. It was handcuffed and chained. He was sitting on the ground in the recess. A hurricane lamp on the wall lit up most of the room. A warm body sat next to him. The third tiger, now uncoiled, body paint smearing on his bare arm.

He looked down. Bare arm, bare chest, bare thighs; he stared in disbelief at his own pubic hair and shrivelled cock. To complete the humiliation, rolls of flab billowed out from his waistline. And round his feet, manacles were interlaced with the chains being used to restrain the third tiger, which were then padlocked to a thick metal pipe running up the wall.

"They used a stun dart," the third tiger whispered, putting on her goggles, her voice calm, resigned. "I've had to live with this tiger fantasy for days. Okki must've told them about something in her childhood. They've been giddy about it ever since. I'm Nisha, by the way, and I'm very pleased to see you, whoever you are."

"Lawrence. Lawrence McGlynn. I'm a friend of Okki's dad. I'm so relieved you're still in one piece." His goggles were too tight and quite uncomfortable.

Through little round windows he watched the other tigers setting up what looked like incense burners. No doubt, in their drug-fuelled madness, they would conduct some kind of bizarre religious service before the assassination. "Sorry I'm naked. It's not usually the way I greet people."

"Well, you're not completely naked. They stripped you and painted your face but gave up with the rest." Nisha half-smiled. "They didn't have enough body paint."

"That's a polite way of putting it, thank you." Lawrence

tested the handcuffs; no give. "So are you strong enough to make a run for it?"

"I'm not going anywhere until I see them roast in hell." Nisha went quite still. She shuffled round to face him. "They must not get out of this room alive."

"Well, after we've unchained ourselves, killed them with our bare hands, got dressed and found a way out of here, avoiding the police, do you think you'll make it to the airport OK?" He smiled. "Sorry, it's my British sense of humour."

Nisha started to explain about her ordeal but was cut short when the tallest tiger struck a match. She padded round the room, bringing the tea light candles to life under the three burners. Meanwhile Lotte had pulled a sealed jar from a backpack and handed it over. Lieke held it up to the light, inspecting what looked to Lawrence like pink-white sugar crystals.

"We tried to make these as pure as possible," Lieke explained. "It took several days. We were lucky to get good quality charcoal with excellent absorption rates, a most effective catalyst. It's very simple, very quick and very deadly. Basically it's an exothermic reaction of carbon monoxide and chlorine gases, nicely chilled, then crystallised. Anyone can make it, if you know how."

"Make what?" Lawrence remembered the magazine article. *They aren't serious?*

"Phosgene oxime crystals," she replied, shaking the jar. "We wanted you to know what it must have been like for the good people of Bhopal. An authentic local experience. We thought it quite fitting in a way; a neat ending to our little kidnapping adventure. We're so glad you could join us, Lawrence. Always good to have a man around."

"How do you know my name?" This was no religious

451

ceremony. He'd underestimated them once again.

"We've been expecting you for days," Lotte replied. "Our client told us what happened to Mukka. To be honest, he wasn't our first choice of driver. He had a loose tongue. We'd worked with him before. Still, he got us here OK. And I suppose it's made it more exciting knowing you would find us. But I suspect the police want to speak to you more than we do at the moment."

"She was following you round town, dressed in that." Nisha pointed to the blue burka hanging up on a nail in the recess.

"So with your friend dead in the next room, the police as clueless as ever and nobody else apart from our client knowing we're here . . . I think we can safely assume that help is not on its way." Lieke squeezed open the seal on the jar. "We'd like to stay and watch. More for research purposes, I suppose, or perhaps for future reference. We haven't used phosgene before. It could be quite exciting."

Lotte fished out two thin, white bio-suits, gloves and black, rubber gas masks. She zipped her own up, climbed into industrial boots, slipped on the mask and tested the respirator. Lieke carefully tipped an exact number of crystals onto the top of each of the burners. Almost immediately slim tendrils of white smoke reached up into the silent air. They interlaced to form a thin layer of mist across the low ceiling before starting to clear and dissipate.

Before suiting up, Lieke had explained that death would only take a few minutes; the swim goggles would save them from eye irritation, an unpleasant side effect. And they needed clear vision to watch, for one last time, how lovers should be with each other: soft and tender, yet stimulated and frantic in their quest for the perfect orgasm.

She continued with the chilling explanation of the torture

that awaited them both. Once the crystals had heated sufficiently – which wouldn't take long given it was already well over thirty degrees in the room – they would experience coughing fits, a sore throat and chest pains until the water in their lungs had reacted with the gas, leading to choking, circulatory collapse and pulmonary oedema. The shortage of breath would become acute but the pain would not last, she concluded, as if trying to comfort them.

Nisha started coughing almost immediately and scratching at her arm. Lawrence jumped to his feet and tried to reach the nearest burner but the chains were too short. He pulled over two chairs and made Nisha jump up. All the time he was watching the tendrils turn to plumes as the crystals melted and the air became more acrid. He found two dirty rags, held one over his nose and mouth, passed the other to the coughing tiger stood on the chair next to him.

His mind was racing. They'd got to keep as high off the ground as possible. Must slow down the breathing, make the clean air last longer, get into the catatonic state of a Hindu yogi like Dr Bhattacharya had described, slow the heart rate and bring on a trance.

But why, a quiet voice was asking. No one was coming. What was the point in hanging on? He was just adding to their sadistic pleasure, living with a false hope they could be rescued. These were professional killers with no compassion. Their client must have ordered them to finish this off. The kidnapping was over. There was no way out.

He was standing tall on the chair but his mind was slipping away. Each breath was agony, like a fire burning in his chest, his lungs incinerated by molten lava. He was drowning quickly in his own hot fluid.

As he looked across the room, he could see his assassins

touching each other through their suits, their masks casting weird shadows, a grotesque mating ritual, a parody of creatures from a science-fiction movie. The rubber masks, the clinical white bio-suits, the pain and suffering they were causing, all seemed to heighten their sexual pleasure. Lieke was straddled across a table while Lotte was stroking her with gloved fingers from behind. She began to moan, the muffled sounds building with her climax.

Lawrence tried to catch Nisha as her legs buckled. She fell heavily off the chair. They both ended up on the floor. There was no air now, just suffocating fumes. He pulled her up, managed to get them both sat on the chairs, best he could do. Maybe he should stop struggling, just let it go. He'd done all he could. There were no more options.

The goggles were biting into his face, which felt hot and itchy. He wanted to scratch all the skin off and plunge his head in a bucket of ice-cold water. He held his breath, the pain like a knife in his throat. He looked at the two white tigers now so engrossed with each other they had become oblivious to their surroundings. Lawrence could tell they hadn't noticed what was happening behind them.

At the far end of the room, the well-oiled door was slowly opening.

• CHAPTER 64 •

She extended a sweaty palm. "Jock, good to see you again. How are you?"

Uppsala was bathed in mid-summer sunshine, which seared the granite crystals on the outside walls of the Great Hall, and beamed rainbows through the stained-glass windows. Hannah marvelled at the centuries of dust motes, which danced, like columns of gnats, from light to shade and back again across the vast room.

It all seemed so familiar to her. Was it from the last time she was here, several years ago, making her presentation in that very room or was it from the dream she'd had in Lonsdale's office?

Jock ignored her hand and went for the hug. "Hannah, thanks so much for coming. It means everything to me. How was your flight?"

"Shocking. The boys in Seattle reckon this Dreamliner is turbulence-free? Give me a break." She covered a yawn. "I'm so glad I got in early. A good night's sleep and I'll be fine by tomorrow. Am I still on at eleven a.m.?"

"Yes, right after the coffee break. Are you good to go?"

"The Cesspool of Human Misery: Fighting the Diseases Linked to Poor Sanitation." Hannah laughed. "They won't want lunch after I've finished with them."

"I think they'll have forgotten about lunch when they see what's lined up." Jock smiled.

"So you pick it up from me at eleven forty-five, right?"

"Yes. I wanted Nisha to lead that session, it's her baby, after all." He panned his open hands around the Great Hall. "Noon on the Summer Solstice. It seemed only right."

"I've never seen so many media trucks. Half the world must be watching." She fingered her pass. "And thank God you sent me this. I'd never have gotten through security."

Hannah could see Jock had drifted off. Just the mention of her name was enough. She could see the hounds running behind his eyes. Wild excitement, closing in on a dream, so close now yet the success would be hollow without her. She had to ask even though she knew the answer. She'd had no word from Lawrence for days. The signs were not good. It sounded like a wild goose chase. Delhi, Agra, Jhansi, Bhopal. If she was still alive, Nisha could be anywhere.

Jock shook his head in silent defeat. He could only pray she was still alive, he whispered. Had Hannah heard from Lawrence?

"Not directly. I got a call from Steve Mole, the British detective? He's been trying to reach them. The Indian police are up in arms about a hit-and-run accident. It all sounds very messy. I hope they're OK."

Hannah saw the door open at the far end of the hall near the front entrance. Another group of TV producers and journalists was being shown round by the university media-relations team. They huddled under a bronze statue of Gustavus Adolphus, the Swedish benefactor who founded the building in the seventeenth century.

A learned professor in flowing robes had joined the tour group and was pointing out features of the statue and the large cupola arching high over the centre of the room. Hannah watched as the colourful entourage filed out into a side room.

In other parts of the hall, sound engineers and camera

operators were vying for the best vantage points. Miles of cabling like errant snakes were writhing across the floor and towers of arc lights were being erected into the darkest corners. Technicians were trying to subdue the cables with screeching rolls of gaffer tape.

Hannah was amazed by the sheer amount of equipment they seemed to need and their nonchalance at the disruption they were causing. Last time she presented, the microphone system had packed up. Today there was so much equipment she was starting to worry that their conversation could be overheard by a stray microphone. She decided it was wise not to continue.

She left Jock fiddling with the EPT machine settings. She needed to send some emails, check in with Kitty and run through her speech one last time. Her mind was toying with a swim in the hotel pool, trying Lawrence again, picking something vaguely nutritious from room service and getting an early night. She was glad now she'd rejected his dinner invitation. Knowing Curtis, there was bound to be a catch. He'd probably changed his mind and decided not to come after all.

She crossed the auditorium past two engineers who had decided to conduct their argument in English, having previously been yelling at each other in Norwegian and Russian. She dodged round a tour group and pulled aside one of the great doors that led back out into the lobby.

"Hello, Hannah."

Curtis was standing alone in the middle of the elegant marble floor, a media pass nestled comfortably over a burnt-orange silk tie. He must have detached himself from the tour group. His tall frame was etched into the stained-glass window, the light casting a halo around his smooth handsome features.

He was wearing a dark-blue blazer with pale-grey slacks.

His dark hair was distinctively styled, as ever. The pale tan shoes set just the right note, a gentle kick in the guts of conformity.

She stood quite still. Clearly he hadn't changed his mind. In fact, if anything, he looked more determined than during the Skype call, determined to get his own way. How many times did she have to say no?

He held out an open hand, nodding towards the door. "Ragnar Lodbrok Hotel?"

"You were always a smart ass, too smart for your own good."

"I was going to impress you with my impeccable logic, you know, your preference for smaller boutique hotels, personal service, more intimate and homely yet offering the privileges of understated luxury for the discerning traveller." He took a single step towards her. "But I cheated and checked you out on their register."

"Smart and deceitful."

"I know what you said but I'm hoping to change your mind. I booked a table for dinner. The restaurant was highly recommended. I had to twist some arms just to get in. The town's buzzing. I thought eight-thirty should give you time for a swim and freshen-up. The receptionist said they have an excellent sauna at your hotel."

Hannah took his hand as if it was the natural thing to do. They slid out through the main door and threaded between an armada of media trucks littering the square in front of an old church. They strolled along ancient cobbled streets down towards the river. Hannah found her sunglasses in time to defeat the glare from the pastel and white stone buildings. The air smelled fresh; green leaves tinged with marigold and geranium from overflowing baskets, which were hanging precariously off the old stonework.

"Smart, deceitful and very presumptuous," she added.

"You mean about dinner?" He wasn't for letting go.

"You know what I mean." She slipped her hand away.

"Too late for old time's sake? As I said, I've got something important to tell you. I just need a chance to explain. Is that too much to ask?" He stopped next to a small fountain. "I've got to be more interesting than room service?"

Hannah could see again, in her mind's eye, the restaurant underneath Seventh Avenue. Le Querce, his favourite. The entrance was narrow; a spiral staircase, the bizarre salt-water fish tank in the lobby. Interesting was not the word that came to mind. She'd never thrown a glass of wine over anyone before. But my God he'd deserved it that night. So fucking arrogant! He was lucky she didn't let go of the glass.

So why would she consider even talking to this slimy toad again, let alone having dinner with him? At the back of her mind there was a niggle. The conversation with Max? BANK-ED? CBSG? The Choirmaster? She needed to know the truth, to understand the connection.

"OK, I'll let you buy me dinner . . . for old time's sake. Then that's it. *Kapisch*?"

"*Kapisch*." He kissed her on the cheek. "Meet you in the lobby at eight. It's about a ten-minute walk."

Hannah watched him cross the footbridge. He waved before disappearing into one of the myriad of cobbled streets that ran like veins through the old town.

Can people really change after twenty years? He was so handsome then, she almost couldn't bear to look at him. And he was so attentive, more attentive than Mike had ever been. There were always fresh flowers in their apartment. Attentive and understanding, making allowances when she had to work late. Unlike Mike. So was she caught on the rebound? They split the rent, bought some things together. The cream sofa she never liked. What had gone wrong?

Hannah had reached the front of the hotel. She fished in her bag for the room key and waited for the slowest lift in Christendom. She pulled aside the metal grille. Wood panelled; claustrophobic. Capacity of six, it said. It must be a lift for dwarfs. She tried to smile. *Curtis Opperman. Where do you fit in?*

She found herself fiddling with the room key. It was coming back to her. *Something to do with a key.* The lift began to rise. *A key fitting into a Yale lock. Round, metal lock in a pale-blue door.* She waited for the third floor to appear. *The apartment was in a dingy little alleyway just off Wall Street. His apartment, not theirs. She'd found the address by accident, a utility bill he left on the dresser.*

Blue door opening into a dark room, vertical blinds across the window, sepia light filtering in from the street. The grille was tightly closed. She was trapped in the moment. *There was a poinsettia on the hall table. Smells of cold pizza and body odour. Of course.* Alone, no escape, no air, high wooden walls.

Hannah held her breath. *She was staring across the room. Figures moving in the shadows. Had to get out, had to breathe. Couldn't move. Nowhere to run.* The lift reached her floor. It shuddered to a stop. She remained still. The light flashing impatiently. Silence.

She forced herself along the deserted hotel corridor. Standing outside the door, the key weighing heavy in her hand, listening. She found the slot, hesitated.

A low drumming sound. Her instinct was quick to react.

There was someone in her room.

CHAPTER 65

There was just enough light for Lawrence to see the figure slip through the door, closing it softly behind them.

One person, armed but alone, danced behind a cabinet. They were dressed from head to toe in black. What seemed like night vision glasses over a mask covering the whole face, a breathing apparatus protruding to one side; gloved hands held a weapon, shouldered and ready to fire.

Lawrence wasn't sure if Lieke's morbid chemistry lesson had been overheard. Whoever it was would need time to get into position. He forced himself into a violent coughing fit, pointing at the nearest burner. He didn't have to overact as the pains in his chest were now almost unbearable. Nisha had passed out, a rag doll in his arms. He struggled to hold her as the sweat-smeared body paint turned to ghee. He just managed to catch her chin and push her face up higher.

Suddenly Lotte looked round, sensing danger, grabbed her weapon and was on her feet, staring into the half-light at the far end of the room. Lawrence could see her mask had steamed up. She tried to call out to her sister but the words were cushioned in rubber. It wouldn't have mattered. Lieke had drifted away on a warm tide of orgasmic ecstasy.

A short burst of gunfire, a lightning flash, piercing the air, there and gone in an instant. Lotte was pushed back on impact, careering towards them across the concrete floor, clutching her chest. A red rose blooming, blood in the snow, the bio-suit shredded. She struggled to move, collapsed back onto the floor, desperate for clean air but daren't remove the mask.

Lawrence was caught off-guard by a sudden movement. Nisha's eyes snapped wide open. She was on her feet, judging the distance, legs coiled underneath her. The tiger pounced, going straight for the throat, painted claws pinning the semi-conscious figure to the ground.

Nisha ripped off the mask, discarded her own yellow swim goggles and slid the black rubber gear over her head. Lawrence saw her inhale. The long deep breaths were followed by wild swings with tightly clenched fists. A right then a left, her rage burning, each blow landing heavy, the frenzy relentless.

Out of the corner of his eye, Lawrence saw the other white tiger leap into darkness. A ghostly figure that melted into the night. He coughed, a trickle of blood in the spittle, had to get fresh air. The crystals in the nearest burner had almost gone.

He threw his arms around Nisha, pulling her back from the lifeless corpse. Lotte's eyes were seared and bloodshot. Blood congealed in long streaks from her nose and mouth. Her face bruised and swollen, a patchwork of strap marks, red blotches and virgin skin. Across her chest a deep pool of crimson flecked with shards of the white material.

Nisha slowly began to calm, her heartbeat grinding down, pale knuckles emerging from her fists. When he released her, she collapsed into a heap on the floor, curling up into a foetal position. Low sobbing sounds gurgled inside the protective mask.

Lawrence tried to remain standing but his legs had turned to jelly. He slid down onto his knees, hanging on as long as he could to his last breath. The next lungful would burn him to hell. Time had run out.

He heard a new sound, struggled to look up. The figure in

black was running towards him. Lawrence reached out but the figure rushed straight past him towards the recess. It tore down the makeshift curtain, grabbing at some clothes lying strewn across the floor. Amongst them Lawrence could make out his own blue shirt and trousers.

The curtain was flung over the first burner, extinguishing the candle, smothering the vapour. The other two quickly followed, his shirt momentarily catching fire before stamping feet brought it under control.

The room was spinning. Lawrence's head was too heavy. He let it slump down into an envelope of thickening air. It was a cruel irony. *Expect the unexpected.* He could never have anticipated a brave rescue attempt. Now one assassin lay dead. Poisoned or beaten to death? He preferred poisoned by her own hand. Perhaps Nisha got the mask in time. She might make it but, for Lawrence, he knew it was over. There would be too much toxin in his bloodstream by now, surely? Without fresh air he only had seconds remaining.

He tried to call out but his vocal cords felt like charred remains. No sounds, just hot gravel searing his words. He managed to raise his arms, shaking the chains, a final toll of the bells.

Despite the swim goggles his forward vision was blurred. He saw the figure in black grab a bunch of keys off a hook, shake Nisha by the shoulder, help her up, point to her wrists and extend a long black arm in Lawrence's direction.

Then it moved towards the boarded-up windows, picked out a chair and lifted it up off the floor. Suddenly it dropped with a crash. The figure doubled up in pain, clutching at a shoulder.

Lawrence knew it was too far for him to get out of the room and he was too heavy to carry. The figure in black didn't seem to have the strength to kick the windows out. They had run out of options.

His eyes closed. In the misty light his father stood waiting for him. *You did your best, son. Let them sort it out now. The girl will be fine. There's plenty of fresh air over here. Leave them to it. Anyway, we've got a lot of catching up to do. What was it you wanted to say?*

Gloved hands were round his head, yanking him back. He opened his eyes in time to see the swim goggles disappear. Stinging air was scratching at his eyes, a thousand needles pricking into his retinas. The room had become a kaleidoscope with electric fish schooling then darting away.

The same gloved hands were back, covering his head in foul-smelling rubber. For a moment the fish stopped and everything went black. He tried to move his hands but they were being held in a tight grip. Panic rising then melting in the heat, his muscles exhausted, all the fight leached away.

Hands adjusted the mask. He could see again, clearer this time. He let go of the air in his lungs, his last breath. He'd hung on as long as he could. He sucked in the next breath, fearing the worst. To his surprise, a low whistling sound accompanied a lungful of air less sharp, less painful. It was still acrid, still burning but bearable. He gulped for more. The next was slightly sweeter, flowing more readily.

A man's voice was coughing. Lawrence turned his head. The figure in black was silhouetted against the hurricane lamp, rays of light fanning out from its head and shoulders. It was a deep-sea diver without its helmet, rubbing its eyes with heavy black gloves, lumbering to find the discarded yellow swimming goggles.

Chakrapani Lal.

How on earth? What's he doing here? How did he know?

464

It didn't matter how. He was here and they had a chance. But Lawrence could see Lal was weakening fast without the respirator. The weight of his protective suit, the oppressive heat in the room, the injuries he'd sustained, the poison gas filling his lungs. Lal mouthed something to him, the words failing to penetrate the mask.

Lawrence felt a release of pressure around his ankles. He looked down to see Nisha had found the right key. She quickly stripped him of his handcuffs and chains. Lawrence made it to Lal's side just in time to catch him as he slid towards the floor. He managed to get his arms under his shoulders, forgetting in the rush, a sharp wince of pain, panicked brown eyes glaring up through the yellow goggles.

Nisha passed Lawrence his clothes. He propped Lal up on the chair and slipped them on, doing up his shoe laces, the shirt still smouldering. He tried to think. Smash the windows; carry Lal out into cleaner air, alternate the mask between them. A combination of all three? The burners were out but the air was still poisonous.

Lawrence reached for the other chair, took careful aim and hurled it with all his strength. The chair bounced off the board yet a muffled sound suggested the glass breaking behind it. The board had splintered and a hairline crack had appeared down the right-hand side. He thought about trying to smash it out. But he could go straight through. Stand on the chair and kick from there? He decided to give throwing the chair another go first.

As he picked it up, he noticed Nisha had slipped on the burka and was refitting her mask. Only her flashing brown eyes were evident through the finest of slits, buried deep again within the rubber. He watched in horror as a shadow passed across the hurricane lamp. He yelled through aching lungs but

465

the mask swallowed his words. He pointed but Nisha could not turn round in time.

Like a praying mantis, the shape extended a long, white, synthetic arm around Nisha's throat, the gloved hand gripping hold of her shoulder, the arm itself forcing its way under her mask. The stricture on her windpipe caused her to kick out. There was enough light for Lawrence to see the barrel of a gun being pressed firmly into the side of Nisha's head. The kicking legs stopped.

Lawrence froze in mid-throw. He put the chair down, slipped off his mask and handed it to Lal, who didn't refuse, quickly slipping it on and securing the lower edge to his protective suit. Lawrence could hear him coughing inside the respirator. He reached for the goggles, loosened the strap this time, adjusted them so he could see as clearly as his stinging eyes would allow. He tried to convince himself clean air was filtering in through the crack in the window. He held his breath.

"Drop it, slowly." Lieke had removed her mask and indicated for the others to do the same. Lal slowly released the weapon from round his back, placed it on the floor and kicked it away.

Nisha was pushed forward into Lawrence's arms, the three now standing together, just too far away from the white tiger to make a move. Lieke kept the weapon trained across them. Lawrence saw her flick a glance at her sister's body, a twisted white mannequin lying motionless, deep-blue fish eyes glazed into red-rims, streaks of black smeared across the tiger's face.

There was no emotion. No tears. No anger. The look on Lieke's face was one of composure, restraint, another day at the office. She stifled a cough.

"We came here to do a job, nothing more, nothing less," she explained, the words clear, the intensity focused. "My sister knew the risk. It's unfortunate. Now it's come to this."

Before Lawrence could move, Lieke raised the gun, took careful aim and squeezed the trigger.

A single shot exploded from the muzzle. The aim was deadly accurate. The sickening crack of metal on bone, no time for screams, matter-of-fact, a duty discharged.

The wall was hosed in blood and brain tissue.

CHAPTER 66

Lawrence retched, turned away, hands on his knees, coughing up phlegm laced with blood, hawking thick glutinous strands from his mouth, the bitter aftertaste remaining. The lower he slumped the stronger the poisoned air. He forced himself to stand up straight.

"Put this on." Lal flung across a mask as he stepped over what remained of Lieke's tortured body, the gun still in her hand, the roof of her mouth and most of her skull blown away. "We've got to go."

Nisha had pulled down her veil and was struggling to get the other mask back on. Streaks of amber and gold smeared across her face, her whole body shaking. Lawrence could see she was in shock. *What must she be feeling? This wouldn't have been the revenge she wanted, not this way. From terror to revulsion to relief in two seconds. Another emotional tourniquet of twisting relentless pressure. No wonder Nisha was fixed to the spot.*

But this wasn't the time or the place to make sense of it all. Lal was right. They had to get out. Fast. Lawrence grabbed the hurricane lamp and put his arm around her, leading the way. Lal was already at the door and had taken off his mask, panting down lungfuls of cleaner air. He slipped the automatic back over his shoulder.

"We can talk later, hurry. They'll be here in ten. This way."

Lawrence didn't ask who would be here. The police? The ambulance? If he was being truthful, he didn't really care.

Nisha was alive. He was alive. And now he knew Lal had survived. That just left one unaccounted for. But the answer to that question was more painful. Denial was not going to help.

They struggled to keep up with Lal who was talking Hindi into his lapel as he jinked through the outer room. A thin, powerful, torch beam was criss-crossing between obstacles from a mounting above his wounded shoulder.

Nisha spotted it first. Caught by the torch, then flooded by the hurricane lamp Lawrence was carrying. It was a solitary figure propped up between a wall and a metal cabinet. Nisha stopped short but quickly realised the figure wasn't armed, wasn't moving.

"Toby, is that you? My God, you're alive!" Lawrence felt ridiculous as the words spilled out.

Simultaneously the wail of two sirens pierced the silence. Lawrence was tipping water from Lal's canteen onto Toby's motionless lips, most of it cascading down his shirt front and pooling into his lap. The wrist pulse was very faint. There was barely a flicker behind his closed eyelids. But it was a flicker. Toby's blood was seeping from Lal's makeshift dressing. He never thought he'd be so relieved to see dark stains on the wall. Dead men don't bleed.

"He'll be OK." Lal screwed the top back on the canteen. "The ambulance will take good care of him. We don't want to be here when they arrive."

"I can't leave him like this." Lawrence stayed on his knees, inspecting the wound. "You go if you want to, I'm staying. I never thought I'd see him again . . . you can't imagine . . ."

"With the ambulance will be the police," Lal explained. "They will arrest you both. Chaudray was furious. We'll all be thrown in jail. It will ruin everything. We must go. Now."

"Ruin what?" Lawrence replied but Lal was already in motion.

Above the sirens came the screeching of tyres. Doors opening and slamming, excited voices from the ground floor – Lawrence couldn't tell what they were saying – echoes coming from the front of the building. Next came the sound of running feet, suddenly drowned out by the whoop whoop of a helicopter making a low pass overhead. A police SWAT team? Twitchy fingers on automatic weapons? A simple misunderstanding; the wrong words in the wrong language; British High Commission involved; a belated apology from the Indian police.

On reflection, Lawrence decided, Lal was right. It was time to go. He couldn't help his friend even if he stayed.

He looked at Nisha, the tiger's face exhausted and drained. He was about to ask her the same question he'd asked what seemed like hours ago. He didn't need to. Suddenly she was on her feet. She managed a smile, her whole face brightening up for the first time, creases in the grease paint. "Yes, I'm strong enough. Your friend here is right. Let's go," she whispered, the words hoarse from the gas.

Lawrence squeezed Toby's shoulder, wished him luck and placed the lamp next to him. He ran off after them, stumbling into unseen furniture, keeping his eyes fixed on the narrow beam of light dancing ahead.

When he caught up with Nisha, he tried to explain who Lal was. He saw her nodding but the pace was quickening. There would be time for introductions later.

They skittered down the metal staircase, their footsteps smothered by the noise level rising outside. Through the gate, Lawrence tossed aside the padlock, leaving the way clear for the ambulance crew.

"Lal, this way." He pointed to a passageway dead ahead. "We left the car over there."

"We're not taking the car." Lal's response was swift and concise.

"But how do we get out of here?" Lawrence was wheezing, sweat stinging his eyes. "We're miles from the airport."

"We're not going to the airport, just keep running." Lal extinguished his torch as they fell through a rusted old doorway and out into the complex.

A cardboard moon was pinned onto blue-black velvet. Pinpricks of starlight were just visible through the urban haze. Looming silhouettes of trees rose above twisted metal fixtures. Clumps of dark tangled scrub now covered the abandoned ground. The air was still and hot. Lawrence was just grateful he could breathe it again.

Streetlights sparkled in the distance around the perimeter fencing. An arc light had been set up behind them near the main entrance, capping a building in a shock of halogen.

He could hear heavy boots clattering on metal stairs. Echoing commands were being shouted. Clearly stealth was not to be their opening gambit. It sounded like people were moving into position. Lawrence wondered if Chaudray was amongst them. He will be livid when he discovers the carnage upstairs. *For the love of God, please take care of Toby. You know it wasn't his fault. I can't bear the thought of losing him again.*

Lal ducked through a bush that had grown up around an old storage tank. Lawrence followed Nisha, getting increasingly concerned. Were they being led into a trap? He had covered this area with Toby earlier in the afternoon. Just weeds, metal pipes, old machinery, baked patches of mud. He knew they were getting further away from the perimeter roads. They could easily be surrounded sitting out here in the open.

They pushed on through more scrub and bushes. Lawrence could feel a sudden breeze on his face, the branches around them

471

swaying, a low rumbling noise coming from up ahead. He could just make out a shape, something squatting on the open ground.

Lal called out for them to mind their heads, the words barely audible over a pulsing heartbeat of engine noise. The shape was in complete darkness, no lights inside or out. Lawrence could sense movement but see nothing. Suddenly a voice called out from behind a door sliding open, a new torch beam picking out a metal step below a high sill.

They piled into the helicopter and were helped on with seat belts and headphones by a short stocky figure dressed in night fatigues, his brown skin smudged with oily black paint. Before the door was pulled shut, the pilot told them to hang on tight, his voice singing in the headphones.

The machine lifted and accelerated away in one graceful movement, sweeping over the treetops, which disappeared into a jewel-encrusted sea of fluorescence, the lights of Bhopal quickly shrinking below them.

Lawrence had never travelled by helicopter before. The exhilaration, a sudden rush of vertigo, the majestic view, his heart pumping as they rose effortlessly over a tangle of electricity pylons. He wanted to be excited but it all just added to the rising panic. He was out of his own control and had no idea what was happening. But at least he was alive, he reflected, despite the searing pains in his throat and chest.

The Dhruv banked sharply over the city centre and turned to the west, a distant sunset still smouldering on the horizon. Dark patches appeared between the sparkling lights of the built-up areas. Lawrence had read that Bhopal was a city of lakes, surrounded by rolling hills and one of the greenest urban areas in India.

The blight of the Union Carbide disaster was truly a legacy from a greedy world, a poisonous stain on a beautiful landscape. But right now, just for this moment, it was one of the most magnificent sights he'd ever witnessed.

Low-level cabin lights came on and Lawrence could see they had more room to spread out than he'd first realised. Behind them was an empty row of seats with ample room for stretchers and medical equipment. When the dashboard lights flicked into life, he could see more of the military signage. See it, but not read it.

Lawrence braved another look out of the side window. Above them, he could make out the wingtip and tail lights of a commercial airliner descending into Bhopal Airport. As he looked, the landing lights came on, dazzling the space around them. In response the Dhruv climbed and turned to the south and east, circling away from the city. *Where the hell are we going?*

"These are good friends of mine." Lal's voice sounded strangely distant considering he was sat next to them. "I will not introduce you, it is better that way. We should be on the ground in less than an hour. Please make yourselves comfortable."

Lawrence and Nisha gratefully accepted bottles of cold water and a picnic box of sandwiches, fresh fruit and vegetarian samosas. They dabbed on some eye lotion from a first aid kit. The cold water stung their throats, Nisha coughing her first mouthful back up into a towel.

Lawrence remembered the warnings and left the fruit. Funny how the mind works, he reflected, smiling to himself. Food poisoning had been the least of his worries an hour earlier.

As they settled into a cruise, he introduced Lal and explained what had been happening with Jock and Toby while Nisha had been held hostage. He sensed she was hesitant yet to talk about her ordeal, the wounds clearly too fresh.

"Why did she kill herself?" Lal posed the question Lawrence wanted to ask.

Nisha found her voice. "They'd made a pact. Lotte told me one night when we were on the road. All they had was each other. If one goes, they both go. Love, family, duty bound them together. They were sisters, lovers, best friends, workmates and, I suppose, almost parents for each other. Lieke had nothing left to live for, no one to share it with."

She paused. "I will never forgive them for Okki or the terrible things they did to me. But I can understand how they became so evil. Raped and abused, sold into prostitution. When they lived in Aruba, their uncle would take a room near the docks. Male cruise liner passengers lined up to take turns with them. Drugged and handcuffed to the bed. Sometimes two or three men at a time. She told me he used a cocktail of local rum, morphine and amphetamines. Voodoo Hoodoo, they called it. They became addicts. They only had each other."

"So what were they doing here?" Lawrence asked, then apologised for interrupting.

"The Choirmaster was one of their biggest clients. He would send them all over the world to do his dirty work. Assassinating people; taking out competitors; kidnapping and extortion; sending messages to underworld bosses. Of course, being young and pretty meant they could infiltrate almost anywhere. And the authorities rarely suspected them as they looked so innocent, so normal.

"Posing as student volunteers for charities provided excellent cover. They'd visited India many times. Most of their work here was in human trafficking and child kidnappings. Mukka was their regular driver but they had others."

"Did they say anything about this Choirmaster?" Lawrence prompted.

474

"They never met him," she explained, hands folded softly now on her lap, the burka smoothed out and more comfortable. "He engaged them through an intermediary. They'd established themselves as experts in poisoning. It gave them an identity, a place in a world that had abused them."

"So how did this all start?" Lawrence was intrigued.

"It's sad in a way," Nisha replied. "Lieke said they'd taken out a drug trafficker in Panama for an American client. It was an induced cardiac arrest using a compound of digitalis. They mixed it themselves. Lotte posed as a prostitute. Neat job, pinprick in his scrotum. The guy sounded despicable. They didn't know but the mark did freelance work for one of the Choirmaster's children's charities. When he died so suddenly, that got his attention."

She paused, fidgeting in the seat, seemed uncomfortable and swallowed more water. "The Choirmaster must have been impressed as he hired them for his own operation. He dealt with them through one of his own people, a middle man. They never met him either. Another American guy, they called him The Gecko."

The lights below had thinned out into small clusters of electronic fireflies, connected by poorly lit threads. The centipede lights of passenger trains appeared and disappeared into low cloud.

Lawrence could only see a horizon on the instrument panel. His nerves had settled a little. He risked a bite of samosa, which tasted strange. Lawrence hoped it was the after effects of the gas. "So this Gecko works for the Choirmaster, running bogus children's charities? How can he get away with it? I can see the lizard connection."

"The Gecko arranges online auctions, donations, fundraising. He pays out field agents, manages credit card transactions and liaises with their regional offices, the boots on the ground. It's an organisation within an organisation. I think The Gecko is the moneyman. They called him Gordon once by mistake, then started laughing. I didn't get it."

But Lawrence did. The name seemed quite appropriate. The Gecko was now another character he hoped to get his hands on before this was over. He could see the strain in Nisha's eyes. Just talking about it was painful. It would take time for these wounds to heal. She needed to rest now.

He sat back, drew a slow breath and turned to face Lal. "So how did you know where we were?"

"I must have passed out after you left me." He winced as he turned, seemed to think twice about touching his shoulder. "When I came round in hospital, Chaudray was leaning over me, angry as hell. He accused me of conspiracy against the law, not keeping them informed, vigilante tactics. He refused to co-operate further. He was issuing warrants for your arrest. *Typical bloody British riding roughshod over the Indian legal system*. It was a real rant."

"He must have flown down from Delhi after the accident."

"Accident? Two men dead; one with a bullet in his brain," Lal corrected.

"Toby was aiming at the tyres. It was them or us."

"Anyway, I couldn't tell him where you were going as I didn't know," Lal continued, "He didn't believe me, of course. He really put the screws on, refused to let me sleep. There was a big argument with my doctor at one stage."

Lawrence could sense he was telling the truth. But it didn't answer his question.

""Chaudray got a call. He was angry with someone, I couldn't hear properly. He was pacing up and down.It was against hospital rules to use his mobile on the ward. The nurse dragged him off to see the doctor again. I could hear the shouting from down the corridor." Lal smiled.

"What's so funny?"

"In his rage, he'd slammed the phone down on the bedside cabinet before storming off. It nearly broke the glass."

"I think I can guess." Lawrence had learned much about the Indian culture. *Lead us not into temptation.*

"I had a quick peek at his inbox. Purely out of concern for your safety, you understand."

"Quite."

"He had received an email from the British policeman Steve Mole. It included a thermal image of the Bhopal site with clear evidence of warm bodies in a secured area. It was only a hunch but the British detective thought it worth checking out."

Lawrence was impressed. He wished he'd thought of that. If he'd joined the dots from Delhi to Agra to Jhansi it might have given him a clue. On second thoughts, maybe not.

"So how did you get to Bhopal? We had your car. And besides, you must have been under house arrest at the hospital?"

"I wanted to make sure the hunch was right." He clicked off to speak to the pilot, pointing at his watch. The helicopter swooped down into light cloud. In a few seconds he was back. "Our Air Force has the real-time equivalent of Google Earth. We bought it from the USAF. It's not as good as theirs; we're about three hours behind. But it's good enough. I called in a favour and patched through to their systems. I thought I might see you or Toby wandering about. Bhopal isn't a tourist destination."

"We realised that. And did you see us?"

"No, but I spotted my car on one of the frames. You'd parked it near the hospital building that collapsed a few years back.

I could trace my Priority parking sticker on the windscreen. Very clever technology."

"And Chaudray?"

"When he went to the restroom, I made a run for it. Then I called in another favour." He squeezed the shoulder of the stocky co-pilot, who beamed an enormous smile. "I would trust this man with my life. We go back a long way. So when I explained about Nisha and the kidnapping, he fully understood. You're a national hero; did you know that, Nisha?"

Lawrence had forgotten that the other three could hear every word. He hoped it was not being broadcast somewhere else. He told himself to be more trusting.

"Don't be ridiculous!" Nisha snapped, the trace of a smile creasing the corners of her mouth.

"By the time I got to Bhopal," Lal continued, "it had turned dark. I noticed the padlock was hanging loose. I wish now I'd reacted sooner. It might have saved Mr Toby catching a bullet."

The pilot relayed something to Lal, who explained they would be landing in ten minutes. The cabin lights went off as they started their descent. Ahead in the distance, Lawrence could see what looked like an airstrip. A long, thin line of runway lights filled the front windscreen. As they got closer, Lawrence traced the line of an aeroplane landing ahead of them, the puff of smoke clearly visible as the wheels touched down.

"I thought you said we weren't going to the airport?" he asked. Lal had picked up a signal and was checking messages on his phone.

"Not Bhopal Airport." He looked up. "The runway isn't long enough. Besides, we need some privacy."

Before Lawrence could react, the helicopter dipped sharply, spiralled down and dived for a patch of open ground that lay in darkness near a cluster of buildings some distance from the long runway. He saw the ground rising up to meet them, felt queasy, ears popping and averted his eyes to the reduced glow of the instrument panel. A buzzing noise sounded and the pilot made the necessary adjustment. A sudden gust of wind buffeted the craft, making it pitch and roll. He could taste the samosa returning, held his breath.

The landing was near perfect, both skids touching down together, the power cut to idling speed. The co-pilot opened the side door. He pointed to a plain, metal door below a single, bare bulb, in a drab-looking concrete building. Nisha pulled up the veil as a precaution.

As soon as they disembarked, the engine noise increased and the helicopter rose into the night sky. It dipped its nose almost in salute and vanished into low cloud.

Lal got to the metal door first, ushering them inside. He ran up two flights of stairs, turned left along the corridor that ran along the top floor and sprinted away.

Lawrence, struggling to keep up, quickly realised that Lal knew the building well.

Nisha pointed at a restroom door. Lal explained they had to keep moving and that there were restrooms and showers where they were going. Nisha looked across at Lawrence, who shrugged his shoulders. He trusted Lal. He had to trust Lal. *But why the urgency?*

From the signage, Lawrence could make out they were inside an Indian Air Force building that seemed to be used for combat training. Some doors had keypad access only; most were unlocked. Only a handful of staff in uniform were drifting about, not surprising given it was the early hours of the morning. The building smelled of floor polish and disinfectant with a heavy undertone of diesel oil.

They followed Lal into what looked like a staff canteen. The room was deserted apart from two individuals with their backs to them. They were deep in conversation at a table over by a row of vending machines and a poorly lit self-service unit. They seemed to be poring over charts spread over two tables. Lawrence could see they were both in uniform but the design and colouration were quite different from the ones he'd seen so far.

As they got closer, Lawrence noticed it was a man and a woman. The man was in a black jacket with silver epaulettes, a peaked cap on the table next to him. His dark, tidy hair, laced with silver-grey, was just touching a starched white collar. From his skin colour, he was obviously European. So too was the woman. She was smartly dressed in a grey jacket with dark-blue flashes. A pale-blue scarf around her neck was tied stylishly to one side. A pillbox hat was perched on a thin pile of documents in front of her.

"I think you already know each other," Lal announced. They both stood up and turned round.

Lawrence recognised the man immediately. The aftershave was distinctive.

"What the hell are you doing here?"

CHAPTER 67

It had taken forty lengths of the pool, twenty minutes in the steam, followed by a slow drenching back in the en suite for Hannah to find some equilibrium. The maid had been putting fresh towels in her room. She was most apologetic for the intrusion. Hannah was cursing herself for allowing the memories back in.

"And the sole for me please . . . same, lightly poached, no garlic." Hannah closed the menu.

Curtis poured the wine and then buried the bottle with nervy hands deep into the ice bucket. Arneis. One of her favourites. A white Barolo. His memory as sharp as the lapels on his jacket, Hannah observed. Nothing new there. Memory was one of his better qualities. When he wanted it to be. But, like most men in her experience, his memory was selective.

"I've a confession to make."

She tilted her head to one side. *This'll be a first – a Curtis Opperman confession.*

He took a slow pull from his glass. "The day I saw you coming out of the squash club, I have to admit I noticed your friend first. She looks a real handful."

"Kitty. *She* has a name. And yes, you're not the first man to notice her . . . qualities."

He continued the story about that day but his explanation for why he'd followed her from Central Park back to her office went too far. He had to retract his description of the silver-haired man she was with as being far too old for her. *His clothes didn't suit him* was a feeble attempt at a recovery.

"Be very careful, Curtis," Hannah warned. *So what was he doing in New York? What's this all about?*

Curtis went for a change of tack. "All set for tomorrow? The Reuters guy reckoned a TV audience over twenty-five mil. Advertising slots are selling at Superbowl prices. Not bad for a science lecture; my congratulations."

"You were always a cynical bastard. That was one of the reasons I left you."

"Excuse me, it was a mutual parting of the ways. The timing was wrong. We both knew it. What did ever happen to that Persian rug?"

Hannah smiled as the starters were presented. The little white vase of blue and cream flowers was moved to make way for her finger bowl. Langoustines. Clean, fresh, simple. Friendly, polite service. She wanted to relax. It was an excellent choice of restaurant, she had to admit. He had booked a table in an alcove away from the main dining area, which had quickly filled up. The restaurant was full.

"It's in my apartment." She sat back, wiped her hands. "Look, you didn't invite me here to talk about Persian rugs. What do you want, Curtis?"

He didn't reply, just carried on savouring the truffle soufflé. His know-all smile again, the outstretched arms. "You're wrong, actually. I did want to talk about Persian rugs. And about the time we spent together. The little things we enjoyed. That abstract for the lounge. Or the weekend in Boston, you remember, when the marathon was on and we couldn't get a hotel room?"

He paused, looked away, as if the next words were sticking in his throat, a grudging admittance. "And I wanted to congratulate you on what a fabulous career you've had . . . so far, I mean. I read all about the cancer thing last year. I know you won't believe this but I felt so proud, just being able to say I knew you."

She rearranged the little pile of shells. "Is this your way of saying you made the wrong call, after all these years?"

"I feel I owe you an apology. It must have been quite a shock. I never got the chance to explain."

"You don't have to explain. It was perfectly clear. In a way, you helped me. It's all about choices. I made the right choice that day." She paused. "Curtis, I don't want to go back over it."

"I just thought we could have a quiet, civilised dinner ... for old time's sake. There is no right or wrong." The big-eyed inquisitive look, head slightly angled ... she knew the drill. "Yes, I made the wrong choice, I'm sorry. Does that help?"

The starters were cleared away. The waitress lit a solitary candle. Outside was still daylight as the shortest night of the year crept in. Two streetlights flicked into life, their glowing cores hardly noticeable.

Hannah watched people and shadows and bicycles drifting past the window. Solitary people, loud groups of people, people in jackets and ties, people in shorts and T-shirts, girls in brightly coloured dresses. People were clattering over the cobblestones, coming out of doorways, chatting on the street corner. Each with their own lives to live. Each with their own choices to make.

When she looked back he had drained the bottle and ordered another. Her glass was still half full. She didn't remember him being this intense. A thin sheen of sweat had formed on his upper lip and temples. He draped his jacket over the back of the chair, causing the waitress to return and open the little side window. It didn't help, only letting warm air filter in with the laughter and shouting and cigarette smoke from the street outside.

Hannah was combing through her emotions. Anger and frustration had been joined by the irritation of this unexpected intrusion. But why had she agreed to tonight? Was it all a coincidence or was he connected in some way? Was she just curious about what he had to say? People can change. Even arrogant sons of bitches like Curtis Opperman. But did she want to hear what he had to say? What could be so important? There was only one way to find out.

"OK, I'm listening. So why are we here, Curtis?"

He spooned some cabbage and potatoes onto his plate, topped up his glass from the second bottle, offered to fill hers, an offer declined in preference for more sparkling water. Playing for time, she decided. *Surely he's not thinking?*

"Promise you won't laugh," he continued. She assumed he'd found an angle. "I've been invited to become an Ambassador for UNICEF."

She choked and nearly swallowed a fish bone. Then she laughed. She laughed so loud some of the other diners across the hallway looked over. The waitress needed convincing everything was all right. Hannah drank more sparkling water, trying to drown the words like hiccoughs.

"You? Curtis Opperman? UNICEF? Jeeze, now that's a real doozy." She snorted bubbles into her napkin. "Don't tell me, the Holy Father is thinking about St Curtis? I can see it now. Corporate Raider shapeshifts into Champion of the Poor."

"I feared you'd be like this. Take it seriously, will you?" He put down his knife and fork. "I've changed, that's what I'm trying to tell you."

"Normal people change. But not Wall Street sharks. Not you, Curtis. I'm sorry, not you." She wiped her eyes, took a slow breath. "And since when did you take anything seriously? Serious is not a word in your vocabulary. Everything is a game to you. Winners and losers. Millionaires and bankrupts. Life is a game of chance with the odds stacked in your favour."

Hannah couldn't hold it back. "What the fuck do you know about poverty; about people dying of starvation; about two point six billion people not having a toilet to crap in? How does that figure on a balance sheet?"

She looked away, realised she'd crossed the line. But he needed to know. And laughing in his face after all these years felt so good.

The darkness outside had thickened. In a doorway across the street, Hannah noticed someone talking on a mobile phone, sliding in and out of the shadows, the light clicking off when the call ended, returning him to darkness.

"I haven't worked on Wall Street for years," he retorted, "and if you must know, the bank I work for donates generously to help poor children all over the world."

"You mean, CBSG?" She watched for the reaction.

"Yes, CBSG. One of the most respected banks in Switzerland . . . how did you know?"

"Quit the sales spiel, Curtis. I made it my job to know. I don't fucking trust you, for Christ's sake. You got previous. Now can we get it over with?"

"Hannah, you've got this all wrong. CBSG supports SINAC projects in Africa, Central America and India. They do excellent work. We're excited about this scientific breakthrough they've made. It could be a game changer for world poverty."

"Curtis, you shafted your own brother over a car," she reminded him. "You never visited your mother when she was dying of cancer. You even made a turn on some tax avoidance scam for a children's hospital in the Bronx. I'm guessing that's not the profile UNICEF would shoot for."

"Hannah, it was a long time ago. I've grown up. I've seen some things, some terrible things. Now I've got a chance to make a new start. I've made my money. It's time to give something back."

Hannah looked at him. She heard the words but she didn't see them in his eyes. *He's hiding something. And he wants to involve me in it. Keep digging, girl.* "So where would you be based with UNICEF?"

"New York." He turned the empty bottle upside down in the ice bucket. The waitress was quick off the mark. He decided against a third, opting for a large glass of Amarone instead.

"Ah, right, I get it." She smiled. "Pack in banking, spirit the money away in some dirty little offshore tax haven, move back to Manhattan and play Santa Claus for the rest of your days, is that it? So that's why you were skulking round Lexington Avenue."

"They formalised the offer when I was there."

"And pick up again with kind-hearted Hannah, the love of your life, someone to nurse you in your old age, a respectable girl on your arm for all the UNICEF dinners, someone to stop them asking too many questions."

"I've changed, Hannah, you've got to believe me."

She turned towards the window. *How dare he do this? Who does he think I am? I should leave now. I must try Lawrence again.*

She could see the man was still in the doorway across the street. The phone light clicked off again. He stepped out of the shadow. He was staring at her. She thought he looked out of place, a dark business suit and tie, balding, stocky build, heavy black shoes anchored to the cobbles as if he was standing in clay.

"You were fucking another woman. You laughed at me. In your own apartment, remember? Not our apartment, *your* apartment. And that very same morning we were talking about our future together. You knew I wanted kids. You played me for a fool. You humiliated me." She paused, lowered her voice, eyes narrowed into slits. "Curtis, answer me one question. Does anything *really* matter to you? Would any girl do? Is this just another of your childish games?"

She looked again. The man had disappeared but the feeling of unease remained. Sure he could have recognised her from the publicity posters. Her picture was all around town. But this felt wrong, his gaze too intense, too deliberate.

Curtis was silent. She could sense the undercurrents running through him. What was he trying to say? He drained the red wine and went to order another. The waitress was serving a table across the hallway. She waved back to him then pointed to the main dining area. Curtis put the glass down. "Look, I thought twenty years would be long enough to ask for forgiveness. She meant nothing to me. I was curious, I guess, just had to know what she was like." He picked up his jacket, which had fallen off the chair-back, and fumbled as he tried to straighten out the lapels. "Hannah, I need you. I want this job with UNICEF to work out. Can we give it another try? It would mean so much to me . . . and to the poor kids who need our help."

"Curtis, what are you afraid of?" She fixed him with the question that wouldn't go away.

"Afraid?" he replied, turning his head, becoming aware of a commotion in the main dining room, raised voices over the background of dinner conversations and clinking glasses. "Whatever makes you think I'm afraid?"

Hannah saw the waitress backing round the corner towards them, seemingly locked in conversation with a troublesome diner. "You ran away from New York to avoid the scandals. Don't give me that headhunted crap. You fucked too many of the wrong women, simply because you could. You made enemies in high places. They fired you and told you to leave town. I guess Switzerland was far enough. We both had friends on Wall Street, remember?"

"That's ridiculous. It was a great career move, a huge promotion. The world's private banking capital. How can you possibly say—"

"Curtis, you're a joker and a coward, you always were. The Peter Pan of Wall Street, a pretty boy who never grew up. You've gotten away with murder. So I'm guessing you've crapped in your own bed once too often. Now it's time to skedaddle back to New York with your tail between your legs . . . or someone else's legs, more likely . . . but you need a cover story for your new friends at UNICEF."

The waitress turned to face them, almost in apology. Suddenly hands appeared round her shoulders. She was pushed out of the way and fell heavily across the table for four. They stood up and glared at the man now filling the space.

Hannah recognised him immediately. She thought he looked taller in the street. He planted his feet next to their table, setting himself to launch some kind of assault. She could see the perspiration on his forehead and damp patches on his shirt front.

He was glaring but not at her. Curtis had jumped to his feet, partly losing his balance, knocking the wine glass over, the dregs spilling out across the white tablecloth like a flick of red paint on a canvas.

The man completely ignored the other diners. His face was pressed up towards Curtis, who had steadied himself and was using a height advantage of several inches.

"I think I'll have a quiet dinner in the room tonight." He smouldered, the accent polished German, the pronunciation menacing. "You bastard, what the fuck are you up to now?"

Hannah saw a young man appear. She assumed he was the duty manager. He was flanked by two of the kitchen staff. Before he could open his mouth, he was silenced by a raised palm. The duty manager looked at Curtis, who gestured that he had the situation under control and that he just needed a minute.

"Hannah, please excuse this interruption," Curtis apologised. "This is a colleague of mine. Clearly there has been some misunderstanding."

"Hannah? So this is the famous Hannah, eh?" he slurred. "The one with the *pert little ass who was too stuck-up for her own good*?"

"I think my friend here has had too much to drink. I'd better take him back to his hotel."

"My hotel?" He spat the words. "Does that mean you're not coming back? So, you'll be fucking this little tart tonight, will you?"

Hannah watched as the drama seemingly unfolded in slow motion. Curtis arched his head back, then lashed forward, cracking into the top of the man's nose, bone shattering bone, both men crashing to the floor, writhing in pain, blood spattering over the reclaimed pine flooring. She wasn't sure who threw the first punch as they wrestled into the table legs, which quickly capitulated, showering them both in the detritus of what had been a delicious meal. She rescued her handbag.

As the duty manager and some of the other diners tried to separate them, Hannah could see the waitress reach into the pocket of her apron and pull out a mobile phone. Before she'd finished tapping in the numbers, Hannah explained that her dinner companion would be settling the bill. And that he could afford to pay for any damage to the restaurant. As requested, she left her name and hotel details before leaving. She declined the offer of a taxi; the walk back would do her good.

Outside a gentle breeze was pushing warm air along the back streets of Uppsala. Most of the crowds had drifted away, no doubt towards the nightclubs down by the river. Overhead the sky was still light, just one or two of the brightest stars managing to pierce the pale-blue canopy.

As she turned towards her hotel, she gave herself the credit for seeing through Curtis and his little escapade. There was a time his puppy-dog eyes would have melted her resolve. People can change but not you, you scheming bastard. Who was that other man? What was his problem? She neither knew nor cared. Curtis was no stranger to trouble, most of which was of his own making.

She double locked the hotel door and put the chain on. She pulled the curtains and got ready for bed. The light on the bedside phone was flashing. A new message. Before she played it back she checked her mobile – *you have six messages*. And emails and texts.

She played them all back with a growing sense of disbelief.

CHAPTER 68

"I could ask you the same question," Max replied, as he gathered up the charts. He positioned his cap neatly on his brow and smiled as he handed Sylvia her pillbox hat.

After the introductions, Lawrence was even more confused. Sylvia was charming and clearly knew Max from a previous life. A former colleague, she had come out of retirement to help him. He understood all that. But colleagues doing what? Their sense of urgency was making him feel uneasy.

He noticed Sylvia had warmed to Nisha who was still coughing and shaking. She'd wrapped a blanket round her and found a mug of hot, sweet tea. Not too full, she explained, as they needed to get moving.

"I'll get you another cup after you've rested and freshened up. I've got some nice things for you to change into. And get ready for some serious pampering. Come with me, pet."

Sylvia, Nisha and Max moved quickly towards a green door next to the self-service counter. Lal looked across at Lawrence, as if he was waiting for his next instruction. Lawrence took a big mouthful of tea.

"Can someone tell me what is happening?"

"Yes, Lawrence, you're coming with us and we need to leave in five minutes or we'll miss our slot," Max replied, holding the door open.

"Leave to go where? What slot?" Lawrence shook his head. "I can't go anywhere until I know Toby is safe and being looked after. Do you remember him, Max? My friend? Your boss?"

"Mr Lawrence, you get going, Mr Toby will be OK." Lal intervened. "By now he'll be in Bhopal hospital. I'll make sure he gets the very best care."

"And Chaudray? Didn't you say there were warrants out for our arrest?" Lawrence asked.

"I can straighten everything with the police, leave it with me," Lal reassured, "but I would appreciate my car keys back before you go."

Lawrence fumbled in his pockets and tossed them over "Why the rush?"

"Because this young lady has a date with destiny." Max nodded towards Nisha as he checked his watch. "She is due on stage in less than . . . five hours."

Lawrence was none the wiser about what was happening but felt he needed to go with the flow. He followed them out into a long corridor, having shaken Lal warmly by the hand. He wanted regular updates on Toby's condition and briefly explained about their luggage and belongings still locked in the boot of the car. Lal almost pushed him through the door.

Lawrence was running to keep up. Through another green door, down some steps, through a large room with pictures of fighter aircraft on the walls then back up another longer flight of stairs, their footsteps echoing off the bare walls.

Through a series of side windows he could see the silhouette of a huge building up ahead. He assumed it was some kind of aircraft hangar; the dimensions were truly enormous. The glow from behind the roof could have been from the airport he'd seen from the air.

Or could it be the dawn breaking? The dawn of the longest day of the year. Max had said five hours. There was only one place Nisha was due to appear on stage.

He was trying to untangle his thoughts as he skipped

through another doorway and started down what felt like an air bridge. Warm smells of diesel oil and aviation fuel seeped in through the membrane walls.

From India to Sweden in five hours? Impossible, he thought. But what did Toby say about Max that day in his office? Former Wing Commander in the RAF? First-rate test pilot for British Airways? *Surely not.*

As he neared the aircraft door, Lawrence could see another woman just inside the cabin holding a tray of drinks. Two champagne flutes, frosting up. She was younger than Sylvia and dressed in the same uniform. She offered Max some orange juice and put the tray down when Lawrence took the other glass. The girls took Nisha away through a heavy, blue velvet curtain into the main cabin.

"Bring your drink," Max announced as he invited Lawrence to step through the open cockpit door.

As he did so, Lawrence noticed the badge on Max's lapel. The unmistakable design.

Concorde.

• CHAPTER 69 •

Hannah didn't know where she was. She slowly emerged from a light sleep, checked the bedside clock. 5.45 a.m. Pale curtains were billowing gently in the breeze, allowing glimpses of primrose sunlight. She'd woken repeatedly during the night, the last time only three hours ago. It had never been truly dark.

"Open Up. Police."

Another sharp knock, louder this time. She pulled on her dressing gown and opened the door, keeping the chain on. Two burly policemen and a policewoman filled the space. The woman was taller than the male officers. Their faces were set in stone. An identity card was flashed. She released the chain.

"You are Dr Hannah Siekierkowski?" the policewoman announced, the tone direct, a statement not a question. Her English was perfect, her manner mildly irritated. This certainly wasn't a social call.

"Yes."

"We need to ask you some questions. Get dressed," she continued, demanding and retaining Hannah's passport.

Hannah noticed one of the male officers was looking at her laptop, which had gone into standby. He pressed a key, which brought up a security screen requiring a password. The other was poking at the hard copy of her presentation slides on the bedside table.

"What's this all about?" Hannah snapped. "Leave those alone, they're private documents."

"You are to come with us. Now," the policewoman insisted.

Hannah tried to explain about the televised event and having to be at the Gustavianum for make-up and a final rehearsal. The officers were unmoved.

She tried a different approach, seeing if they would ask whatever questions they wanted there and now, in the hotel room. It would save time and the embarrassment of being driven away in a police car, especially with half the world's press milling around town.

Again they refused.

"So am I under arrest?" She shook her head, a tangle of thoughts running through her mind. There had been some confusion at customs in Stockholm when she'd flown in, her passport refusing to scan. Could that be it?

"You are not under arrest," the policewoman confirmed. "It is important you co-operate with us. Get dressed . . . please."

"I would like to contact the American Embassy in Stockholm before I go anywhere."

The level of irritation was growing. The policewoman unclipped her handcuffs. She explained it was the end of a long nightshift. Hannah acquiesced. She swilled her face in the bathroom and slipped on some clothes. She sent Lawrence a text, knowing he wouldn't get it until they landed. At least he would know where she was.

They had parked the police car at the rear of the hotel, away from prying eyes, no flashing lights. Hannah was bundled into the back of the Volvo with the policewoman. They sped off, turning left, then right, through narrow cobbled streets before reaching the main street, Svartsbakgatan, turning south down the dual carriageway. Hannah was following their progress on her mobile.

The streets were quiet but some of the media trucks were already on the move. Hannah could see the main police station buildings were coming up across the central reservation. The Volvo accelerated past the turn-off and continued on towards Rabyvagan.

"Where are we going?" she protested.

No response. Instead, she followed the little red arrow as it stuttered across the screen on her mobile. It swung a hard right over the river onto Luthagsesplanaden. As they turned left into Kyrkogardsgatan, the policewoman reached over and grabbed Hannah's phone, flicking it off and zipping it into her uniform pocket. It would be returned later, Hannah was told.

She sat back and watched a patchwork of gardens and residential estates fly past. Early morning sunlight glinted off the twin spires of the red-brick cathedral.

Ten minutes later they swung into the side entrance of a large modern complex. Hannah recognised one of the buildings. She'd been here before, during her last time in Uppsala.

The sign said Akademiska SjukHuset. *The University Hospital.*

"Before we ask any questions, there is something you must do," the policewoman explained as the rear doors of the Volvo were unlocked. "You need to prepare yourself."

CHAPTER 70

"Who?"

"Sir Freddie Pickles."

"Never heard of him." Lawrence heard his own voice echoing in the headset, the words layered over the background hum of the engines.

"I'm not surprised. He was never much for publicity." Max unclipped himself from the pilot's seat. Lawrence followed him out. One of the co-pilots was finishing his tea and smiled as he went past, locking the cockpit door behind him.

"He must have deep pockets." The curtains had been pulled back. Lawrence was looking at row after row of empty leather seats. The interior had the aura of an upmarket saddler. He saw Nisha come out of a cubicle near the aft galley in a smart, charcoal business suit. She was eying herself in a full-length mirror. Sylvia started fiddling with her hair, which was still wet. They both burst out laughing. Was this the same bedraggled tiger he'd seen only a few hours ago?

A digital sign confirmed the cockpit instrumentation. They were cruising at Mach 2.7, altitude sixty-one thousand feet with an ETA in Stockholm of two hours seventeen minutes. The deep-blue ocean beyond the starboard windows had been slashed by a streak of amber, the only sign yet of a new dawn.

"He's pumped twenty-five million pounds into this project." Max took one of the other bar stools. "That's loose change for him. He made plenty out of the property boom. Sir Freddie believes in the constant need for progress. He was one of our best customers. I'm told he wept the day Concorde was put on the scrapheap."

Max explained that this particular aircraft had been decommissioned and left to rot at Heathrow. Sold for £1, it had had a two-year refit that had improved engine efficiency, reduced noise levels and fuel consumption, increased power output for shorter take-off distances and added numerous creature comforts like bigger seats, entertainment systems, a bar area, where they were now sat, and four flat-bed cabins with full en suite facilities. Sir Freddie was even planning a sauna and adult play area. Lawrence didn't ask.

"So did he just toss you the keys and say bring it back in one piece?" Lawrence helped himself to a beer. He wasn't sure what time it was but the effects of the gas still burned like hell and an ice-cold beer for medicinal purposes couldn't do any harm, he decided.

"Not quite but we've become good friends over the years," Max replied. "When I told him about Toby and the importance of the event in Uppsala, he volunteered to help. He's planning to be there. I'll introduce you. He's a fellow Yorkshireman and passionate about his cricket. You can bore each other to death about the batting prowess of Geoffrey Boycott."

"But is it legal for this plane to fly?" Lawrence smiled at the memory of a cold afternoon with his father at Headingley, suffering as he watched the legendary opener playing more for his batting averages than the expectant Yorkshire crowd, "not that I'm concerned, you understand. I'm already wanted by the Indian police."

"Perfectly legal. It was granted a certificate of airworthiness several months ago and has a special flight permit for air displays and private usage. We aren't allowed to carry passengers or operate as a commercial airliner, if that's what you mean. If anyone asks, you're cabin crew on a training flight." Max returned the smile.

"I think what I meant was, do we have legal access to air space? I seem to remember the problem with Concorde was the noise levels over built-up areas. And, of course, the public outcry over the Paris accident."

"It wasn't the safety record that grounded Concorde," Max lamented, "it was politics ... and, of course, jealousy. Over seventy-four aircraft had been ordered by seventeen of the world's leading airlines the day Concorde first took off. Only twenty were ever built. Neither the Americans nor the Russians could master the avionics at supersonic speed. This is one ingenious piece of engineering that changed the world. Sir Freddie is right – humanity took a big step backwards the day it was decommissioned."

"Then maybe, along with the announcements in Uppsala later on today, we could tack on a return to supersonic travel?" Lawrence narrowed his eyes to absorb the growing intensity of the amber dawn. "By the way, which way are we going? How are you going to avoid the sonic boom problem?"

"I was less concerned about waking people up on this trip. The direct routing should have taken us over the Middle East, Ukraine and Russia. I'm not sure Sir Freddie's got round to fitting counter-measures yet for surface-to-air missiles."

Max reassured him that they could outrun the missiles: it was MIG fighters that posed a bigger worry. "So we're going the scenic route, more of an air cruise really. Turn left out of Nagpur, nip across the Arabian Sea, follow the Gulf up to the Med, turn left, then zip up between Italy and Spain, over the Pyrenees, then hang a right up the Channel. We should be in good time for a pickled herring breakfast in Stockholm. Nisha will be on the helicopter transfer to Uppsala before Hannah has pulled up the first slide. Piece of cake, if you say it quickly."

Clearly the fashion parade had been a success. Lawrence could see Nisha had settled on a smart blue/green business suit with heavy gold accessories that reflected her Indian heritage. She was striding up the cabin with her entourage.

"There's another question I almost daren't ask." Lawrence stumbled for the words.

"Please don't concern yourself," Max reassured him, "the cost is being split between us and Sir Freddie. I'll square my expenses off with Toby when I see him. I've never bought aviation fuel on a company credit card before. This whole trip has been quite an adventure. We must make sure we get the right outcome."

They both looked at Nisha. Despite the strain etched into her face and obvious signs of tiredness, she flooded the cabin with colour and style and elegance. Lawrence's beam of admiration was the only comment he needed to make.

If they could get there in time, the outcome was no longer in doubt.

The issue now was time.

CHAPTER 71

The policewoman had pulled open the heavy drawer, releasing the body from its makeshift tomb. Hannah had been in countless morgues over the years but this time was different. She didn't know what to expect.

"Do you recognise this man?"

The pale-blue latex cover was turned back to shoulder level. Hannah gasped when she saw him. The leathery tan had gone. His silver-streaked dark hair was matted and plastered to his scalp, bald patches showing through that she hadn't noticed the night before. The self-assured confidence had been replaced with a tortured sadness, a resignation that something wasn't to be. His plan this time had failed. There was to be no way back to New York. His past must have finally caught up with him.

"Yes, his full name is Curtis Dwayne Opperman. He is . . . an American citizen." She realised her mistake. "At least he was when I knew him many years ago. He may have changed nationality since then."

Hannah wanted to feel the emotion running through her. Here lies the man I made love to, played with, slept with and screamed at. The man I wanted to be the father of my children, to share my life with. But here was the man who lied to me, betrayed my trust and ultimately destroyed my self-belief for so many years. The mark from the head-butt was etched onto his forehead, a futile symbol of a futile act.

The policewoman drew the cover down to waist level, revealing a naked torso with signs of bruising over the chest and lower arms. A single puncture wound over his heart had been cleaned up but Hannah knew the incision must have been a killer blow. Before the policewoman could intervene, Hannah ripped off the cover and dropped it to the floor. Was it instinct that made her do it? Had she seen something else written on his face? It didn't matter now. The wretched truth was clear for all to see. One of the policemen moved away over to the open window.

"We believe this assault was committed shortly after the time of death," the policewoman commented, her voice quieter, her gaze concentrated on the horrific injuries. "The murderer used the same weapon, judging by the serration patterns and aperture dimensions of the stab wound."

Hannah could feel herself asking how anyone in their right mind could commit such an atrocity. But the words stayed in her thoughts. She already knew the answer. This butchery was not committed by someone in their right mind. This was the work of someone out of all control.

"Where were you between midnight and three a.m.?" The policewoman had snatched up the cover, draping it over the corpse and the small white enamel bowl stained by the blood-soaked genitals.

"I was asleep in my room . . . alone," Hannah replied. "I'm sure there is CCTV coverage of the hotel lobby."

". . . which shows you entering the building at nine forty-seven p.m." The other policeman was checking his notes. "But doesn't confirm that you were alone last night?"

". . . or that you didn't slip out after midnight through the rear entrance, arrange to meet up with Mr Opperman, stab him through the heart before exacting your sexual revenge on his lifeless body, then pushing it into the Fyris," the policewoman added.

That explained the bloating in the lower abdomen and the small marks on the flesh around the wound. There must be eels in the river. Hannah tried to explain about the incident in the restaurant, only to discover that the police had already interviewed the restaurant manager. He had not wanted to press charges as the cost of the damage had been covered by a credit card payment.

"This is absurd," Hannah protested, "whatever happened to innocent until proven guilty? I hadn't set eyes on the man for twenty years. It was meant to be a quiet dinner. The person you should be talking to is his colleague, the guy who attacked him."

"Do you know his name or where we could find him?" The policewoman was too quick to respond.

That's what this is all about. They think I might be connected with that madman. She checked her watch. "Look, I'm really up against it here."

She focused on the policewoman. "I know you have a job to do. I want to co-operate fully. Curtis was a friend of mine. We had our differences. Whatever the nature of our relationship, I hate to see him like this. Underneath he was a good man but his affable nature meant he was always getting caught up in things he knew were wrong. He wasn't evil; he was just fascinated by it, flirted with it. I guess it found him out. Look, I want you to catch the person that did this."

Hannah continued. "Can I suggest we return to your police station, I make a full statement and you retain my passport until I've made this speech at the university this morning? Hopefully I can then convince you I'm not a murderer."

The police officers agreed to her request. The policewoman added that the matter would now be taken out of their hands and passed over to an officer specialising in criminal investigations. Hannah hoped this would introduce a more conciliatory approach.

"Just one more thing." The policewoman was pushing the drawer closed. "We found a note in his hotel bedroom."

Hannah froze. She heard the word but couldn't think. She made the connection. Her mind filled with a buzzing swarm of questions. Was CBSG behind all this? The drop box? Josef Graaf AG?

She couldn't breathe, needed air. Of course. The man with his feet in clay. She had to make a phone call. *Detective Sergeant Steven Mole. His number's in my phone. They've got my phone.*

The policewoman was staring at her. She had asked the question twice but Hannah didn't reply. On the third time, she got as far as taking the handcuffs out of their pouch. Hannah snapped back, apologised and asked her to repeat it.

"Do you know someone called the Choirmaster?"

• CHAPTER 72 •

Ladies and Gentlemen, may I now introduce our keynote speaker....

Hannah's face was flushed despite the make-up. Her presentation had been greeted with rapturous applause. She was used to autocue work but the size and complexity of this event was truly demanding – especially on an empty stomach. The simultaneous broadcast across terrestrial and satellite TV was combined with a confusing array of social media platforms, intranet and podcasts. She was relieved the technology gods had been in a good mood. Now it was time for the main event.

As Hannah left the stage, she saw Nisha waiting in the wings. She was being bombarded with instructions and hardwired into the broadcasting systems. She looked so delicate, so beautiful, so innocent and yet so strong. Hannah threw her arms around her and squeezed with all her strength, breaking the microphone link and earning dark looks from the sound engineers. She kissed her and wished her luck with the presentation.

Hannah swiped her card through the security access door and made her way round to the auditorium. Lawrence was waiting for her on the front row. He grabbed her in a powerful embrace. They kissed deep and hard until being pulled down into their seats by excited members of the audience around them.

"God, I've missed you," he whispered, "you were sensational."

"Shhh," rebuked the woman behind them.

Ladies and Gentlemen, please welcome on stage, Dr Nisha Patel.

A spontaneous eruption brought everyone to their feet, clapping and cheering. Over the coffee break rumours had been flying. Would she make it, was she coming, was she dead; is she still in India? Hannah decided the overwhelming applause contained a mixture of relief and anticipation.

As she watched the young scientist stride over to the podium microphone, Hannah suddenly felt very strange. The purposeful movement was the same. The backdrop was the same; bouquets of the same flowers in the same places. There were even the same three rows of Nobel Prize winners, scientists, royalty and world leaders sat behind the stage in their finest robes and colourful gowns. Just like in the dream in Lonsdale's office. The only thing different was the young lady herself. She was wearing the same robes and a bluey-green silk dress. But this time, shining blue-black hair had replaced the auburn tresses.

The stage lights dimmed, leaving a solitary figure captured in a cone of light. TV cameras eased silently into position. Nisha picked up the autocue, then looked out into the packed auditorium. She breathed deeply and smiled.

"Ladies and Gentlemen; let me start as I intend to go on; by telling you the truth."

Hannah saw the laughter in Lawrence's eyes. He also believed truth had become a scarce commodity in a world of sound bites and political agendas.

"My name is not Dr Nisha Patel. In fact, officially, I have no name as I was never given one by my parents. I became Nisha to my foster parents, my Aunty and Uncle Patel. They told me I was born in a tiny village in Uttar Pradesh that did not have any electricity or regular water supply. My parents could not afford another girl in the family. Thankfully, they had enough compassion to leave me at the gates of an orphanage school some miles away. Others like me would have been killed soon after birth. You might say I was born lucky."

An embarrassed laughter rippled around the great room.

"My second bit of luck was being good at maths. I must thank my teacher, Mrs Joyti Singh. She inspired me to think about a future in science. With her help I managed to get to the big school in Delhi and from there I graduated in Applied Electronics and received a doctorate in electromagnetism. None of which you wanted to know but it is relevant to my demonstration today."

Again the room echoed with applause and laughter.

"I said I would tell you the truth. In fact today there are two demonstrations. One to show you the technology we have developed, and a second to show you the exciting future we now have at our fingertips. It is a scientific breakthrough that will transform our world and take all of us to a brighter future, rich and poor alike."

Hannah was studying the guests on the stage. She could see the full spectrum of emotions ranging from childish excitement through mild enthusiasm into hard-nosed scepticism. She recognised some of the faces, particularly the world leaders from the USA, China and Russia. She'd read science journals about some of the Nobel Prize-Winners sat away to the right.

The Vice-Chancellor of Uppsala University, Emeritus Professor Magnus Sorensen, looked the same as he did in the dream. Next to him was a woman in a rich purple and navy blue robe with a mortarboard perched precariously on a mop of dark hair. Hannah put the woman nearer the sceptical end of the spectrum as she hadn't smiled once.

"Before I throw the switch, I need to explain the science behind what you are about to witness. Being surrounded by such a learned audience is somewhat daunting –" she turned her head and gave a nod of respect while waiting for a big screen to descend above her head "– so I will say from the outset that copies of my theories and research papers will be available to take away as you leave and will be posted online at four p.m. today local time."

Hannah could feel the sceptics in the room warm a little at the prospect of having something they could tear to shreds afterwards. Millions of eyes in the room and around the world followed Nisha as she moved across the stage.

"We call this the Electron Particle Transformer or EPT. Again, being truthful, the name is a bit of an understatement. This piece of equipment is capable of transforming particles and subatomic particles far more complex than mere electrons. But more of that later, in the second demonstration.

"For now I want to show you how we can adapt electricity into a harmless digital signal that can be transmitted by microwaves anywhere within a wireless grid, similar to the coverage of a mobile phone. To do this I'm going to need three volunteers."

Magnus Sorensen was on his feet. He offered his hand to the woman in the purple robes but she glowered at him before looking away. By then two other volunteers had appeared and clustered around the EPT. Nisha handed out what looked like three wooden table lamps with bare bulbs and small black boxes attached to the base.

"These are in fact simple lamps fitted with one-hundred-watt bulbs. Our volunteers can move around anywhere they wish. Instead of a plug connecting them to a power source they have been fitted with a receiver. Once I throw the switch, electricity will flow by wireless connection and make the bulbs light up. Can I ask the volunteers to move anywhere they like in the room?

"For the purposes of this demonstration, the EPT is plugged into mains electricity. You'll be hearing from my Uncle Ranji after lunch about how we intend to produce and distribute free electricity using the earth's limitless magma resources. It is time for science to take us away from the fossil fuels that are destroying our planet."

The screen above her head suddenly came to life and split into quarters. The TV cameras zoomed in. Each of the presenters was also holding a wooden lamp.

"I'd now like to introduce you to four of our other volunteers. The lamps they are holding are exactly the same as these. Ashwini is standing by the Gateway to India in Mumbai; Henri by the Eiffel Tower in Paris: Brad is on the footpath over the Brooklyn Bridge in New York City: and Michelle is standing on the steps outside the Sydney Opera House."

"Look, our apartment is just over there to the left." Lawrence pointed at the Brooklyn Bridge and was told off again.

"Is everyone ready? Fingers crossed."

All seven bulbs lit up the instant Nisha flicked the switch. She repeated the demonstration numerous times, with the same result. Again the room erupted with a standing ovation lasting several minutes. Hannah noticed that even some of the sceptics reluctantly joined in the applause. The room was alive with conversation. Nisha waved her arms for everyone to be seated. She thanked the volunteers and said goodbye to the four on the screen, which returned to darkness.

"Thank you. That was a simple demonstration. But before I throw the switch again, I need to tell you about my third piece of good luck. Being born in India meant I was brought up in a Hindu family. This wonderful religion has given me a unique set of values through which to understand the world, in particular the scientific world.

"We Hindus believe in the cycle of birth, life, death and rebirth or samsara. How we behave in this life will determine our destiny. During the long course of my extended lifetime, I have been fortunate to witness some amazing scientific discoveries. I suppose I've always been a scientist at heart.

"Theories about relativity were being discussed in the time of Galileo. And not just in the so-called western world. Science also has its heart in China and India and Arabic-speaking countries. The concept of gravity and gravitational waves dates back well beyond Newton. The secrets of the stars and the universe were being explored before the Moguls ruled India.

"Science is a privilege and must be studied for the benefit of everyone. It is not about intellectual property rights and ownership. This is why we are making public our discoveries today. This technology is free for everyone to use. We want this breakthrough to be a celebration for all humanity."

The applause like a peal of thunder rippled around the back of the room, then crashed into the open space, a crescendo of noise, another standing ovation.

"I do not want to live in a world where one per cent of the population owns more than the other ninety-nine per cent combined. Or where two billion people live without access to electricity or clean water, or where children die in squalor without ever having a chance to realise their true potential . . . their destiny.

"We have created poverty. It is a human disease that we can now eradicate. We will harness the power of our scientific knowledge. We don't need to spend billions of dollars on bigger and faster hadron colliders to tell us what we already know. The Higgs field exists. It has existed for millions of years, except, of course, it didn't have that name. Like gravity, it pervades everywhere. We Hindus simply see it as yet another property of the Cosmic Ocean.

"Science is not a political weapon to control people and resources. Science must return to being part of the fabric of our society. Super symmetry, dark matter, string theories, standard models, unified field theory ... each year the list gets longer, the research funding gets greater, the degree of abstraction more exaggerated yet the practical applications get more remote. The questions remain: Where did the universe come from? Is there a God? Are we alone in the galaxies?

"The breakthroughs we seek, the spark of an idea we need, may be in the hearts and minds of the people trying to survive in the slums or refugee camps. Maybe we should treat them with more respect and ask them these questions."

Muted applause. Hannah could feel people around her squirming. It was fascinating, stimulating but also very uncomfortable. Nisha was right. Hannah knew she was telling the truth. But truth was not what people wanted to hear. And it was certainly not the way to secure research grants.

"Let me show you something. We understand that the sun emits plasma clouds of magnetically charged gas particles through solar flares. The plasma, consisting of supercharged ions and electrons, is deflected around the earth's outer magnetic field. At the poles where the field strength is at its most concentrated, some of the plasma is drawn down towards the surface where it reacts with gases at the extremes of our atmosphere.

"As this regularly occurs between sixty and four hundred miles above the surface, it means the interaction of the plasma cloud with the earth's atmosphere can be visible at night. The colours will be brighter depending on the intensity of the plasma cloud or solar wind as we call it. The colours themselves are determined by the distance above the surface and the gases involved. Reddish colours reflect a greater distance above the earth's surface.

"Interaction with lower-level oxygen molecules produces greenish colours while nitrogen turns blue. At the North Pole, the phenomenon was christened the Aurora Borealis by Galileo. We call it the Northern Lights. Over Antarctica, we call it the Aurora Australis or Southern Lights."

As Hannah watched, she felt as if invisible threads had wrapped themselves around her hands and feet, tying her to the chair. Instinctively she wanted to move. On the stage Nisha had switched from the podium to her clip-mic as she moved again towards the EPT.

Behind Nisha the woman in the purple robe had stepped down from her seat and started walking in the same direction, off camera. Hannah decided she was moving towards the restroom, or perhaps her sceptical mind had heard enough and she was leaving. The timing was unfortunate but at least it wasn't being broadcast, judging by the live TV monitors scattered around the hall.

"We are not alone in enjoying the Northern Lights. Our radio telescopes have detected similar events on Jupiter, Neptune, Saturn and Uranus. Even gases in the ionosphere on Venus display peacock colours when the solar winds blow."

The woman stopped. Now she was in frame. She turned towards Nisha. The concerned face of a security guard appeared at the edge of the curtain.

"The Higgs field imparts mass to subatomic particles everywhere in the Cosmic Ocean. Some interact more than others, gaining more mass. By modifying the EPT we can create the same magnetic and electrostatic properties of the sun's plasma cloud . . . bear with me a moment . . . then use the Higgs field to spread them across the earth's atmosphere and beyond into space. This will be a small demonstration of the power we now have at our fingertips. Science working for the good of all humanity—"

As Nisha opened a top panel of the EPT, the woman suddenly leapt across the stage, grabbing her by the shoulders and pushing her off-balance. The mortarboard and wig fell to the floor, revealing a man's sweaty face under inches of make-up, captured on the big screens. A gleaming bald head crowned a face wreathed in pure anger. He flicked off the purple robe and pulled Nisha towards him, unclipping the microphone and attaching it to his own lapel. With his free hand he was pressing a long serrated knife hard against her throat.

As the cameras zoomed in, Hannah recognised him immediately. The man in the restaurant. The man with his feet in clay, the so-called colleague of Curtis Opperman. From the note the police had found in Curtis's hotel room, she surmised he must be the Chairman of CBSG, Herr Dieter Blindt. Hannah – and the rest of the world – must be staring at the face of the Choirmaster.

Armed security guards poured onto the stage surrounding them, amid loud gasps from the audience. The TV screens went blank, then switched to a test card. Technical fault, we apologise, normal service will be resumed.

"So you think you can change the world with the flick of a switch?" His voice echoed around the room, dark and menacing, guttural tones strained through a Germanic accent, a low rumble of encroaching thunder.

"We control science, not you. Our civilisation. Copernicus,

Galileo, Newton, da Vinci, Einstein, Darwin, Tesla, Faraday, Edison, Kepler, Nobel, Boyle, Hawking, the list is endless. Now you want to destroy our heritage, take away our birth right? You want science to be controlled in Asia? This is not a civilisation. It is a disgusting copy of our world. I will not let this happen."

As he finished speaking, a single shot rang out across the great silence. Hannah saw the knife slide away and drop to the floor. Nisha jumped out of his grasp as the arm that was holding her fell onto the EPT, accidentally flicking the switch. The hole in the man's temple began to ooze blood. The sniper's bullet had passed straight through and sparked off the back wall behind the stage.

The EPT hummed back into life, this time with a slightly higher-pitched note. The Choirmaster slumped into the open panel. A luminescent stream of magnetised particles was passing straight through him before being projected out into the main auditorium.

Nobody moved. Suddenly the room filled with colours; blues and greens and pinks, swirling and dancing, in an eerie silence. The big screen had come back to life. The same coloured lights were visible all around the world.

The test card disappeared as TV screens round the room came on. From the four main locations they showed people had stopped in the streets. In Mumbai, people were waving their fingers through the spectral colours, smiling and playing. The Sydney Opera House was bathed in coloured lights as a huge crowd gathered.

In Paris, a human chain had formed between the static cars down the Champs-Élysées. Traffic had also ground to a halt on Brooklyn Bridge; the drivers getting out, revelling in the moment, impromptu dancing, strolling around, sitting on the cars, shaking hands, recording the event and uploading files onto the Internet.

Before Nisha could reach the switch, gravity had taken over and pulled the broken body down onto the floor. It lay in a pool of crimson and purple. With one flick the light show ended. She leaned over and recovered the clip-mic. She took a deep breath.

"Ladies and Gentlemen . . . he was wrong."

CHAPTER 73

Niklas Blomqvist had moved offstage away from the commotion, just as the armed police moved in. The Choirmaster lay dead. The man he had looked up to and respected all these years. The man who had made the connections, opened doors, secured his career moves, arranged new clients, swelled his bank accounts.

"I can't talk now. Wait."

But it was no longer the Choirmaster. The man had become a murderer of innocent children, a monster with unlimited powers, a grotesque parody of a business professional hiding behind a mask of public respectability.

"Yes, he is dead," Niklas resumed. He could tell the other man was somewhere in the main auditorium. Even on the secure line, the announcements echoed in his earpiece.

The Voice was measured, deliberate. He advised Niklas that the police sniper was a member of Der Sangerbund. It would have been a clean shot. He had strict instructions to take out their leader if he should make an appearance. It was important that the Swedish police did not arrest him. The Choirmaster's secrets had to die with him.

The Voice continued. Niklas listened attentively. Curtis had reported the incident in the restaurant but the Cantata had already been briefed. The physical damage was minimal. It was the outburst that shocked the other diners. Too many people had heard him, recorded him and broadcast his outrageous views. The Choirmaster had managed to escape before the police arrived. It was not the first complaint. Since being admitted into Der Sangerbund, Curtis had continuously advised a minority grouping within the Cantata that the Choirmaster made repeated sexual advances towards him, to the point of infatuation. He had even threatened to fire him if he did not acquiesce.

Niklas could see Ingmar Persson coming his way through the crowd. He ducked behind a curtain, found an empty dressing room and locked the door behind him.

"Curtis was a fool," the Voice explained. "He protested his innocence and argued that he had never encouraged any sexual attention. We should not have allowed him into our ranks. He was careless, unreliable and weak. The Choirmaster forced our hand. His flirtatiousness was his undoing. We are better off without him. Without both of them."

Niklas heard the announcement that the hall was to be evacuated. He needed to cut this short but one question kept reverberating. "Der Sangerbund was established after the Great War to restore Teutonic pride and protect our western civilisation. There has always been a Blindt as the leader of the Cantata, as the Choirmaster. Dieter is the last in the line. What will happen now?"

The Voice was quick to respond. A new era was to be established following the destructive reign of the last Choirmaster. It had been agreed that Der Sangerbund needed to legitimise its various business activities and re-establish its core values within an extended membership. A new Choirmaster had provisionally been chosen. His appointment created the opportunity for an additional Voice within the Cantata.

Niklas went very still. He could hear footsteps beyond the door as people filed out of the exits. A siren continued to call for immediate evacuation. But in the cocoon of the dressing room, Niklas listened for the words he'd waited so long to hear. It was to be an honour, a privilege, the culmination of his commitment, his devotion to the duty of membership. But events over recent weeks had troubled him.

"You say *legitimise our business activities*. Will that include our involvement in children's charities in developing countries?" Niklas enunciated each word as clearly as he could. As he waited for a response, there was a sharp knock on the door. He must evacuate now, a voice called out.

"You will be contacted next week. A full meeting of the Cantata will take place at the end of this month. If you are to join us, Niklas, you must be very careful in the questions that you ask. And to whom you ask them. Do you understand?"

"I understand."

CHAPTER 74

Hannah and Lawrence both agreed it was a beautiful service. They had joined Toby on the gravel footpath outside the lychgate. It was three days after the longest day. The fierce morning sun failed to penetrate the waving green hair of an old willow tree, dappling them in welcome shade. Coots pierced the morning silence as they picked their way through the tall grasses in the shallows nearby.

"Okki loved this place." Toby's voice was unsure, still searching for safer ground. "We used to come here for picnics when she was little. We'd swim under this tree and pretend it was a pirate cave. The church was her castle and she was the beautiful princess."

He leaned heavily on the walking stick and then staggered towards an old wooden bench. Lawrence caught him in time and eased him down. Hannah sat the other side and kissed him as she adjusted the bandages strapped over his head. The bleeding had stopped, at least on the outside. Maybe this wound would never heal.

The last group of mourners nodded as they strolled past towards the car park. Wanda was the last one out, fumbling awkwardly with the latch. The others stopped and waited for her. She managed half a smile towards Toby before joining them in the sunshine.

"We were never a church-going family," Toby continued. "It just seemed the natural place to come. The minister was very helpful. I was pleased it was in English. They've done their best

519

for her. I'm sure there's nowhere else she'd rather be. It's all such a waste."

"Toby, we want you to know we love you. When you feel up to it, we want you to come and stay with us. Wanda is charming. It's a devastating thing for both of you." Hannah kissed him again. "You must take your time and stay strong."

"To be honest, I'm not sure I'll ever get over it." He looked down, making little circles in the gravel with his stick. "But the one thing I've learned in the last few weeks is that time is precious and we have so little of it."

Hannah looked behind him at Lawrence, who was gazing out across the river, deep in thought. She'd never missed anyone so much in all her life. Being apart had been agony. She vowed never to let him out of her sight again. He was a good man who wanted to do the right thing. From now on, they would both do the right thing and do it together.

"So I've come to some conclusions." Toby sat back, stretched and circled his shoulders. "Not much else you can do when an Indian police officer is shouting at you in Hindi and your translator has joined in the fray."

Toby seemed to find some inner strength. "Okki had so many dreams. To help the people in those villages, to make a real difference."

"She did make a difference, you know that." Lawrence put his arm around him.

"Lawrence, you and I have been in Rotary for years. We've paid lip service to making a difference. By tossing coins in a bucket or selling a few raffle tickets, we may have fooled other people but not our own consciences. We can do so much more. Correction, I can do so much more."

Hannah saw an open-topped sports car weave its way through the departing mourners and pull up in the car park.

A young blonde woman in a pretty peach-coloured dress climbed out. She put on a matching hat and styled it in the wing mirror. She grabbed an enormous bunch of summer flowers from the boot and was marching along the footpath towards them. As she tried to check her mobile phone, she tripped and nearly stumbled into the river. Hannah smiled at her as she got closer and wished her good morning.

"*Goedemorgen*," the woman sang out in reply, slipping through the gate and crunching on purposefully towards the side door of the church. Hannah remembered seeing a notice on the board about a wedding at lunchtime. The Circle of Life. Out of despair comes happiness. Toby was right; time is precious and we must use it while we have it.

"I've decided you were right, Lawrence." Toby nodded. "I'd run out of dreams. The things in life I thought I wanted have all been achieved. In fact, I have been drifting along, living a life full of material things that haven't brought me any joy. Seeing the excitement on Okki's face when she told me about digging toilets meant more to me than any new car or big house."

Hannah saw the look of concern sweep across Lawrence's face as he tried to reason with his friend.

"You must still be in shock," Lawrence explained, "and should give yourself more time before making any rash decisions."

The words sank slowly in the calm waters of the Vecht and meandered with the lazy current down towards the sleepy Dutch town of Weesp on the far bank.

"As Jock inherited his father's dreams, so I must take on what Okki has started," he announced. "Her dreams will become my dreams and I will see them fulfilled. For her; for Wanda; for me; for the people who dare not dream, the people living in misery."

The ensuing silence was broken by the first peal of the bells. The crisp metallic sound brought the birds to life, filling the air with chirruping music. Two butterflies danced like fairies in the cool air around the tree.

Within minutes Hannah could see the car park starting to fill, little clouds of dust announcing the arrival of the wedding party. Smartly dressed men and giggling clusters of women and children disgorged themselves from cars with ribbons and bows tied to aerials and door handles. Their voices echoing with laughter, a joyous commotion of groupings and photographs and wide-brimmed hats and yet more flowers.

Toby stood and turned his back on the pirate cave. "I've agreed with Jock that I will become his business partner. We will run SINAC together. I will help him get Project Amrita over the line. The technology may work fine but I can see now how difficult it will be to get the Indian bureaucracy moving."

They stood, hugging him. Lawrence shook his hand but as ever had to ask the practical question.

"Lawrence, I've agreed to sell most of my shares in the company," Toby explained, "that will free up my time. Max is more than capable of running it without me. The new owners want me to stay on as non-executive chairman. It's more for appearances to keep the customers happy. Also, they want to do more business in Asia and have asked me to open an office in Singapore. That will work perfectly with my involvement in SINAC."

"And how about Rotary?" Lawrence prodded, remembering a promise made somewhere in the back streets of Delhi.

"Absolutely," Toby sparked. "We're going to set up a virtual Rotary club based at Raffles Hotel. Jock will invite some of his new friends from UNICEF to join us."

"UNICEF?" Lawrence looked puzzled.

"Sorry, Lawrence, I meant to tell you." Hannah smiled. "Jock has been offered the Ambassador role with UNICEF, now that Curtis Opperman is ....er, no longer available. It's a huge honour. I guess the Uppsala event swung it."

"It was the light show that swung it," Toby added. "Apparently UNICEF were meeting in New York that morning. The room filled with green and blue light. Frightened the shit out of them. Jock said they were very impressed that one small charity could get so much global attention. His invitation to become an Ambassador was a no-brainer. There may be hope for UNICEF yet."

"Hold on, rewind." Lawrence looked even more confused. "Curtis who?"

"The guy they fished out of the river," Hannah explained. "Don't you listen to anything I tell you?"

"You mean The Gecko, your old flame, the one who wanted a piece of my action? That greasy little toad." Lawrence stuck out his substantial chest. "He was lucky I didn't get my hands on him. He'd have begged me to drown him."

"He didn't drown; he was stabbed through the heart by an unrequited lover," Hannah continued. "The guy had been so jealous he'd cut off . . . never mind, it's all over now. The police have closed the file."

"You mean Curtis the Gecko was trying to get into your knickers while he was fighting off the unwanted attentions of his boss? Christ, those guys must have been screwed up." Lawrence moved aside to let some wedding guests go past. He took the first steps towards the car park.

"I spoke to Steve Mole; he sends his regards, by the way. Apparently, Interpol have quite a file on the Choirmaster and Der Sangerbund. They've known about this organisation for years but have never been able to pin anything down. Steve said once they connected the Choirmaster to the kidnapping and the Bella Donnas, it all fell into place. Their psychologist reckoned this Choirmaster guy didn't know who or what he was," Hannah explained. "In the end, they think he committed suicide. He must have hated himself so much. Or maybe it was his guilty conscience. I guess the thought of Curtis running off back to New York finally pushed him over the edge."

"Suicide?" Lawrence sounded surprised.

"He could see there were snipers crawling all over the place. Security was so tight. He must have known he would never get out of that room alive," Hannah reasoned.

"Then how did he get a seat on the stage?" Toby strolled out into the sunshine behind them.

"The police said they found the badge owner in her hotel room." Hannah held open the gate to the car park. "His fingerprints were all over the room. It was the same knife, the one he used on Curtis, the one he held to Nisha's throat. The serration pattern matched."

"So who was she?" Toby asked.

"One of the education specialists he'd sponsored through BANK-ED. The Choirmaster paid for her. They were similar height and build. They reckon he'd planned the whole thing."

"So who really was this Choirmaster?" Toby made his way over to the car.

"Blindt," Hannah replied. "Herr Dieter Blindt. The police psychologist thinks he was torn apart by what she called the dichotomy of his public and private lives. He wanted to be seen as the chairman of the board, an upstanding member of the Swiss banking community and a leader amongst the world's charities."

"Dichotomy of what?" Lawrence found the keys to the rental car and pressed the button before going to the wrong door. He smiled and walked round to the driver's door.

"In his public image, he needed to live up to his parents' expectations and uphold the family name," Hannah continued.

"What, Blindt?"

"No, Einstein," Hannah corrected. "Nisha told me the whole story. He was Albert Einstein's great-grandson. But it was sort of a family secret. When he realised Nisha claimed to be his great-grandmother in a previous life, it must have poisoned his mind. It was already a pretty mixed-up place."

"Do you believe all this reincarnation stuff, you know, Nisha was Einstein's wife?' Lawrence looked sceptical.

"Not really, but you gotta ask how she knows so much about him. Blindt's mother had run off with a female Malaysian artist, apparently. He had a thing about Asia's role in the decline of western civilisation. Throw in some gender issues, dirty little perversions and a running battle with Asperger's. He was one fucked-up sonuvabitch."

"And this code name? Choirmaster? Doesn't sound like a Choirmaster to me," Toby added.

"He was the head of a men-only cabal called Der Sangerbund. Powerful and corrupt men in high places, opening doors, sworn to secrecy, doing deals with each other behind the scenes. Blindt used his alumni connections to play people and keep them in his circle. The accountant that tipped him off about Project Amrita was one of them. The Stockholm police are questioning him right now."

They climbed into the rental car, leaving Toby's Jaguar in the car park. It was only twenty-five minutes back to Amstelveen. Toby invited them in but Lawrence explained they had a plane to catch.

"There's one more thing." Toby was half out of the car door. He pulled an envelope out of his pocket and handed it to

Hannah. "I said we can do more to help people in need. Well, there's something I want you to do for me. I suppose it's my way of saying thank you to you both."

"We can't accept this!" Hannah was shaking her head, drew a hand across her mouth. She showed it to Lawrence. The car stalled. "Toby, you can't be serious!" Lawrence swivelled round and peered at him through the headrest. "Fifteen million euros?"

"I'm very serious." Toby swung a leg out onto the sweltering driveway. "I want you to find a cure for Diabetes. Type 1 and Type 2. I know you're close. Add this to your research funding and nail this sucker once and for all. It's one of the worst diseases we face. I know from personal experience. Millions of people are suffering needlessly. Do it for them, do it for me."

They embraced on the driveway. Hannah kept thanking him until Lawrence checked his watch and bundled her back into the car.

"Ciao, Toby, give our love to Wanda." Hannah called out of the passenger window. "See you at the wedding."

Toby waved back as he limped off towards the house. The electric window hummed back up and Lawrence turned the air conditioning on full. At the red light, he set the navigation system for Schiphol Airport.

"At the risk of being shouted at again . . . what wedding?"

"I asked the police psychologist about your condition." Hannah smiled and punched him on the shoulder. "She recognised all the symptoms. She called it SHD. Quite common in middle-aged men apparently. No known cure."

He accelerated. Schiphol Airport in twelve kilometres. "Go on, I'll buy it. SHD?"

"Selective Hearing Disorder. Apparently the patient can only hear what they want to hear."

Lawrence accelerated, overtaking a car towing a caravan. "Now that makes sense. It's also a disease common amongst golden retrievers. I bet I caught it from Trigger. How is he, by the way? I've really missed him. Obedience, companionship, unconditional love, gratitude . . . and a complete lack of sarcasm."

"Touché," Hannah replied. "Jock and Nisha's wedding. They announced it at the drinks party on Sunday night. Mid-September, in Delhi. I said we'd be there. Toby and Wanda are going. I'll need a new hat."

"I know why I didn't hear it." Lawrence took the off-ramp and slowed as they followed signs for Rental Returns and Departures. "I was getting cosy with my new best friend, Sir Freddie Pickles."

"Who?" Hannah took the Harry Nilsson CD out and slipped the case into her bag.

"I introduced you after the toast, you remember?" Lawrence smiled. "Jolly British chap, friend of Max's."

"I don't remember any toast . . . just champagne."

"Did that psychologist say anything about Selective Memory Disorder in middle-aged alcoholic females?"

She punched him again. "That reminds me, I didn't get to say goodbye to Max. I really liked that guy. He was a great help."

"Don't worry; you'll be seeing him again, very soon." Lawrence pulled into the covered parking area and started unloading cases.

"I thought he'd gone back direct, Stockholm to London?"

Lawrence put the cases on a trolley, checked the mileage and returned the keys. Hannah gathered up her things and was scanning the signs for check-in. He crept up from behind, grabbed her, spun her round and gave her the most suffocating kiss she'd ever had. Any resistance quickly melted. They were in India again, swimming together in warm water.

Get a room, was the helpful advice from a small group of teenagers wandering past.

They came up for air.

"I wanted to talk to you about India." Lawrence was pushing the trolley towards the lifts. "I'd like to take you back there. Perhaps we could extend the trip in September?"

"Sounds romantic."

"As Toby said, what are we all waiting for? Life is too precious and way too short."

"You mean ...?" Hannah stopped, looked hard into his eyes. "Was that what I think it was, Mr McGlynn?"

"And if it was, Dr Siekierkowski, how would you respond?"

"Oh no, you don't." she snapped. "Ask a straight question and I'll give you a straight answer."

They made their way towards Check-In and Departures. They turned a corner when Lawrence suddenly swung a sharp right, guiding the trolley towards a door with no signage, just a keypad. He punched in a code and the door clicked open. They went through. The door hissed back into position.

The long corridor was semi-lit, the trolley wheels squeaking on the rubber floor tiles.

"Where are we?" Hannah felt confused.

"VIP security entrance." Lawrence kissed her again.

"Is this where we're meeting up with Max?"

"Max is flying us to New York. We'll be there in three hours."

"You serious? That's not possible."

"It's a very special plane for a very special person." Lawrence smiled. "And I don't mean because she has a cheque for fifteen million euros in her purse."

"We need to talk about that."

"We do. And we will. After we're airborne and I've got a very straight answer to a very straight question."

ACKNOWLEDGEMENTS

A Litany of Good Intentions is a work of fiction. It is the second book in The Human Spirit Trilogy and features, as its main theme, the eradication of world poverty and all the miseries that poverty creates: death and disease; violence; crime and exploitation; human trafficking, kidnapping and child slavery; suicide, fear and despair, to name a few.

The idea for the story began in the auditorium of the Rotary International Convention at the Sydney Olympic Park in June 2014. A humbling yet inspiring speech to eighteen thousand people by Jack Sim, founder of the World Toilet Organisation, highlighted the implications for 40% of the world's population lacking even the most basic of human facilities. In this day and age – with all the scientific advancement, wealth generation and technological achievements of the last century – how can we stand by and watch children dying of waterborne diseases that are a direct result of poor sanitation?

As a voluntary organisation, Rotary does more than most to alleviate some of the pain and suffering. Over a million kind-hearted people working at the grass-roots level does make a difference to people in need all around the world. Visit www.rotary.org for more information. In the words of the founder Paul Harris, "Whatever Rotary may mean to us, to the world it will be known by the results it achieves."

But while 2.6bn people have no access to a toilet, we support billions of dollars being pumped into scientific research to create bigger and faster hadron colliders. China is allegedly investing over US$6bn into its Supercollider project. The research will look further into the origins of the universe, the existence of and possible uses for the Higgs field and the nature of the so-called God Particle. As an introduction I would recommend the DVD *Particle Fever* (www.particlefever. com by Ro'Co Films), which tells the story of First Impact at CERN, The European Council For Nuclear Research, based near Geneva, Switzerland.

Three other excellent – and mercifully easy to read – reference points were: *In Search of Schrodinger's Cat* by John Gribben; *QED: The Strange Theory Of Light And Matter* by Richard P. Feynman; and the funky *Black Hole Blues: And Other Songs from Outer Space* by Janna Levin.

This is not to say that scientific research should cease until everyone on the planet has access to a toilet or electricity. Or that science should only be directed towards improving the human condition. What seems apparent though is the divergence of current scientific research away from the practicalities of everyday life. Expensive and often obscure research into string theories or super symmetry, for example, should have a practical application in the real world, as Dr Nisha Patel stated. Science by the people, for the people, to paraphrase.

The Hindu concept of samsara – that another life awaits us after death – is fascinating and fits well with a story where Good will always triumph over Evil and Justice will prevail to right the wrongs. Dr Nisha Patel, being the reincarnation of Mileva Einstein, a woman so talented yet so deeply wronged, is now a bright, young scientist living in an age – albeit still with considerable difficulties to overcome – where she could bring her generations of knowledge to bear in making a scientific breakthrough that will eradicate poverty in her own country and ultimately change the world.

ACKNOWLEDGEMENTS

While several text books on Hinduism proved insightful – *The Myths and Gods of India* by Alain Danielou; *Seven Secrets of the Goddess* by Devdutt Pattanaik; and *Hinduism* by Rakesh Raina – there is no substitute for visiting India and talking to Hindus about their religion and way of life. Treat yourself to a trip to Rishikesh. Also, read *Shantaram* by Gregory David Roberts for a beautifully written introduction to Indian sub-culture.

A painting of Lord Vishnu and the Cosmic Ocean on the wall of a hill fortress in India linked well with Einstein's theories on gravity and general relativity. The idea that space appears to be a vacuum yet unseen forces are at play – forces as yet beyond our comprehension – opens the door to wider thinking and perhaps allows the people back into the protected world of scientific exploration.

Einstein: A Biography by Jurgen Neffe, and *Einstein's Miraculous Year* edited by John Stachel, proved invaluable for background research but the starting point for the story of Mileva and her influence on Einstein's early career should be the DVD *Einstein's Wife* published by PBS Video (www. pbs.org). Whatever the truth about what really happened, the fact that Einstein's theories became mainstream thinking gives hope to even the most amateur scientist.

Three further influential DVDs need to be acknowledged. *A Prayer For Rain* starring Martin Sheen (distributed by Revolver Entertainment) tells the graphic story of the Union Carbide disaster in Bhopal and is worthy of the critical acclaim it achieved when released in 2014.

In the same year, the Indian crime thriller *Mardaani* was released by Yash Films, addressing the key issues around child kidnapping, human trafficking and the abuse of women in India. *Trade* starring Kevin Kline (distributed by Lionsgate) follows the same themes but set in North and Central America. Same problem, global reach.

Ironically we define poverty in monetary terms, yet money is seemingly the root of all evil, and certainly the impetus behind human trafficking and slavery, with an estimated 46 million people enslaved today around the world (http://ragas. online/). The secure storage of and access to personal wealth inevitably leads to the story of Switzerland and its historical place in the secretive world of private banking.

The Swiss and the Nazis by Stephen P. Halbrook, *Why Switzerland* by Jonathan Steinberg and *Imperfect Justice* by Stuart E. Eizenstat provided an illuminating introduction to that history and important background material for the Holocaust Reparation themes within the book.

There were too many people supporting me in this project to mention here but two in particular need to be recognised. A big thank you goes to Dave Taylor for his continuing encouragement and support of this project. And without the blind devotion and untiring belief of my wife Jacqui, this book would not exist. The debt I owe her can never fully be repaid.

A Litany of Good Intentions is a work of fiction. As a crime thriller, it was created to be provocative – informative – entertaining. The story ends with Lawrence about to ask his beloved Hannah a fictional question. That question will be answered in the third book of the trilogy.

I hope you enjoy finding out.

Andrew Harris